BEST SERVED COLD

A SPICY ROMANTIC COMEDY

BABES OF BREWING

ANGELA CASELLA

ALSO BY ANGELA CASELLA

Babes of Brewing

Best Served Cold

Worst Nanny Ever (September 2025)

Beauty and the Brewer (January 2026)

Unlucky in Love

The Love Fixers

The Love Bandits

The Love Losers

The Love Destroyers

Spin-off Standalone

The Thief Who Saved Christmas

Finding You

You're so Extra

You're so Bad

You're so Basic

You're so Vain

You're so Phony (coming soon!)

Fairy Godmother Agency

A Borrowed Boyfriend

A Stolen Suit

A Brooding Bodyguard

A Reluctant Roommate

Bringing Down the House (Nicole and Damien's story)

Highland Hills

(co-written with Denise Grover Swank)

Matchmaking a Billionaire

Matchmaking a Single Dad

Matchmaking a Grump

Matchmaking a Roommate

Matchmaking a Player (novella) by Angela Casella (May)

Bad Luck Club

(co-written with Denise Grover Swank)

Love at First Hate

Jingle Bell Hell

Fraudulently Ever After

Matchmaking Mischief

Asheville Brewing

(co-written with Denise Grover Swank)

Any Luck at All

Better Luck Next Time

Getting Lucky

Bad Luck Club

Luck of the Draw (novella)

All the Luck You Need (prequel novella) by Angela Casella

This is for those of you who've been wronged in love.

They may not have treated you the way you deserved, but screw them—a second chance is waiting.

Maybe it'll even be with their brother.

CHAPTER ONE

SOPHIE

"Uh, Otis?" I ask, waving the phone screen at my twenty-one-year-old cousin. My hand is jittering, causing my two-carat diamond ring to sparkle in the light streaking in through the kitchen window. "Can you come take a look at this? I need a second opinion."

Otis sighs as he sets down the toast he was preparing, spilling a glop of jam onto his grandmother's granite counter. If I don't clean it up, it will probably remain there until we both die. He once found—and ate—a chocolate bar that had been wedged between the couch cushions for an uncertain amount of time. My cousin is sweet, mostly, but cohabitating with him has not been the highlight of my time in Asheville. Now, though...

I've never been a lucky woman. Bad luck follows me around the way other people are trailed by loving pets. I know better than to tell anyone this, but in my lowest moments I worry I'm cursed. Still, I'm hoping against hope Otis will be able to explain away the text message that just ruined my life.

My pulse thunders as he takes the phone in his sticky hand and peers at the screen.

"What the...?"

He glances at me in disbelief.

I feel my hope shriveling like a raisin. So, the text says what I thought it did...

> BigCatchBabe: I can't wait to see you this afternoon. I've been thinking about it all week. After I suck your cock, you can bend me over that barrel again. ;-)

"Uh, Soph." Otis returns the phone, which I nearly drop, clumsy from nerves. "Doesn't this person realize you don't have a cock?"

"It's not my phone," I snap, slapping it down on the counter with a resonant crack. Hopefully, it broke.

Don't freak out. Don't freak out.

But panic has already cracked me down my middle, heartache seeping out. This is bad. So bad I have to borrow a phrase from Jane Austen to describe it: it's a *ruinous affair*.

"You stole someone else's phone?" Otis asks, his forehead furrowing. "But why?"

Without looking at him, I respond in a gush of words. "It's Jonah's. He just bought me a new one, and he set the wallpaper so it's the same as his. They're basically identical, and he took mine by mistake this morning. When I realized what happened, I thought it would be funny to text him from his own phone—he *always* uses his birthday as his password—but then this text popped up, and..." I swallow the rest of the run-on sentence. "You think someone's playing a joke on him? Like one of his buddies?"

His mouth falls open, closes, and then opens again. I'm hoping some brilliant explanation will spill out. Instead, he rubs his chin and says, "Yeah, guys don't joke around like that, Soph. Not unless they're secretly blowing each other."

"So you think...?"

He looks like he does every time I ask him to do something around the house—panicky. I can see sweat beading above his upper lip as he shifts his weight. Avoiding my eyes, he stammers, "You know what? I gotta go. I forgot, but I have this thing. It's pretty important, and yeah...I'll see you later. Sorry."

"For what?" I ask numbly as he edges away, abandoning his toast.

He lifts a shoulder, shamefaced. "For...you know...being a guy."

"You don't have anywhere to be," I accuse, the words sharper than they should be. He *is* lying, obviously, but he's not the one who did this to me.

Jonah is.

Jonah Price is my fiancé of four months.

He told me he wanted to marry me after our first date and bought me an iPad three weeks later, loaded with my "favorite songs." Truthfully, it was his favorite music, but it was still an attempt at thoughtfulness. So was the way he proposed, with a bouquet of handpicked flowers.

My great-aunt Penny would point out that he'd woven poison ivy into the arrangement, but he's not a florist. How was he supposed to know?

Jonah has been my silver lining for months, my proof that my life isn't as hollow as it sometimes feels. But if this text means what I think it does...

My knees go weak.

It's like twelve years have been rewound and I'm sixteen again, stuck in the worst moment of my life. Rinse, repeat.

"Can I leave?" Otis asks as he scratches his head violently. "I think that might be better for both of us. I mean...Jonah hates me anyway. He's definitely going to find some way to blame this on me."

"How could it possibly be your fault that he's running

around town getting blow jobs?" The thought is distressing enough to reduce me to a puddle, and I grab the phone and sink down to the floor. It's sticky, suggesting the toast isn't the first snack Otis made today. I mopped it last night, and I'm going to have to mop it again later. Only this time, I probably won't be able to tell myself, *Only four months left before the rest of your life begins.*

I was supposed to move in with Jonah after the wedding. We'd picked out new curtains together, and he'd surprised me with his very particular opinions about those *and* the bed linens. Why would someone with very particular opinions about such things cheat on his fiancée?

He and his mother had also controlled every stage of the wedding planning. I'd wanted to DIY the invitations and favors, but his mother had thought I was joking—and then responded with genuine horror when she realized I wasn't. *She'd* chosen the invitations. Jonah had selected the venue, after rejecting my idea of holding it at Buchanan Brewery, where I work as a taproom server and part-time manager. I couldn't contribute financially after blowing most of my personal savings on my wedding dress, so I hadn't felt like I was in a position to argue. My parents weren't helping either, given we weren't on good terms, and I wouldn't accept a dime from my great-aunt.

"What am I going to do?" I ask. "What am I going to *do?*"

Otis makes a worried sound, then opens the fridge and removes a beer. He pops the top with the bottle opener fridge magnet and hands it down to me. It's from the six-pack of Hair of the Dog IPAs I brought home from work last night. I'd gotten the beer for Jonah, but he'd turned up his nose and insisted Big Catch's IPAs were superior.

Now, that seems doubly insulting.

"It's 9 a.m.," I say numbly.

My cousin pops open a second beer for himself. "Yeah, but I

don't know how to make a mimosa. The proportions always get messed up."

"You're staying?"

He sighs and settles onto the sticky floor beside me. "Yeah. Sorry I tried to leave. I know you don't have any other friends. Grandma would have been disappointed in me if I'd left."

One of the pieces of my shattered heart digs into my chest, in danger of metaphorically puncturing a lung. He's right. I don't have any friends here. I moved to Asheville less than a year ago, after Otis's grandmother, my great-aunt Penny, was diagnosed with breast cancer.

At the time, she was living alone, and she'd refused to move in with Otis's parents, who'd vacationed in Florida five years ago and stayed. Otis had moved in with her, but he frequently forgets to feed his goldfish, so the family had insisted she needed someone else to take care of her—and everyone knew I was the most in debt when it came to Ginnis family karma points. So I'd ditched my plans, left Greensboro, and moved into this house.

For the first time in my life, I'd felt necessary to someone. But Aunt Penny had pushed me to get out of the house, insisting I needed to meet other young people or I'd "wither on the vine." It was true that she hadn't needed help around the clock, so I'd gotten the job at Buchanan Brewery.

To be clear, I don't have a huge interest in beer, but our next-door neighbor's family runs the brewery. She'd agreed with my great-aunt that it would be unthinkable if "a sweet young thing" were left to wither, and the next thing I knew, I was working in the taproom.

I met Jonah that very first week, after accidentally spilling a beer on him. (Don't ask.) He'd been wearing an expensive suit, because he'd been there in an official capacity. He was a distributor who helped breweries get wider distribution for their beer, and guided stores and bars in choosing the local, or local-ish, beers that would sell well for them. Basically, he made a profession of being charming. He joked that he was the best middleman money could buy.

Instead of flipping out about his ruined suit, he'd asked me out.

I'd never had a charmed life until that moment. In my experience, bad luck usually led to more bad luck, not a date with a man in an expensive suit. So obviously I'd said yes.

Meeting him had felt like a turning point.

Right around then, my aunt, who'd been reacting badly to the chemo, had started drinking a tea blend our next-door neighbor, Dottie, had made for her, which helped her tolerate the treatments. My first date with Jonah had gone shockingly well, and he'd asked me out again, and again.

I'd felt useful *and* wanted.

True, Aunt Penny had never really taken to Jonah, whom she'd called a huckster, but she thought every salesperson was a huckster.

My aunt's cancer had officially gone into remission last month, thank goodness, and she'd left on a three-month long European vacation with her best friend to celebrate "kicking death in the balls."

For all intents and purposes, my role in Asheville is over. I could quit my job at the brewery and start working toward my dream again, but the thought makes me strangely anxious, as if it's a balloon lost to the wind.

And now this...

I take a sip of the beer, then a glug of it.

That's the spirit," Otis says as I start coughing. "So...I can't think of a chill way to say this, but we both know what's going on here. If you tell Jonah, he's going to make up some excuse. Maybe he's already on his way over here to switch the phones back. He's got to be panicking."

I take another glug of beer, trying to dampen my own panic. "He...he's got a meeting this morning, at one of the breweries he distributes for. He won't be able to leave without offending the owner."

"Is it at the blow job place?" he asks.

I flinch. "No. Big Catch is owned by one of those mega-corps. They do their own distribution. His meeting's at Silver Star. The owner is really touchy about technology. He doesn't let any of the employees use their phones while they're working."

"Well, Jonah's going to panic when he realizes he messed up, and he'll have some explanation, and..."

"You're worried I'm going to believe him," I say flatly.

"Yeah. I mean, he's persuaded you to go along with his BS before."

Just then, the phone buzzes again. I drop it like it's a hot potato and the music just stopped.

Otis meets my gaze, sighs, and grabs it.

He checks the screen and flinches. "Uh. I don't know how to tell you this, but it's another one."

"What?" I squawk.

He hands it over, and I take it with a shaking hand. It's a conversation with "SilverStarBabe."

> Do you have time to get breakfast after your meeting? I know you've been busy, but I've barely seen you for weeks.
>
> My therapist says we need to find ways to reconnect.

I glance at Otis in disbelief. "How is this happening? Is this a bad dream? Jonah told me just this morning that he can't wait to wife me."

He grimaces.

"He was being sweet," I say automatically, because defending Jonah to Otis and my aunt has become a reflex. Shaking my head, I say, "No, it was stupid. But...seriously. Is this a dream? I don't understand..."

He reaches out, and I'm about to hand the phone to him so he can take a second look when he pinches my arm instead.

"Ow," I cry out. "What was that for?"

"Sorry," he says, nearly fumbling his beer. "Just wanted to make sure. You know, I'm surprised too. I never would have thought Jonah had this much game. He owns five pairs of Crocs, and he thinks Africa's a country."

"So did you," I point out. I was the one who'd filled them both in. Otis had taken it with his customary easy acceptance, but Jonah had given me the cold shoulder all day.

You don't need to correct people, Sophie. You're not a teacher. It was a barb he'd known would hurt, since the dream I'd abandoned was opening a crafting business with classes for young children.

Jonah's like that sometimes. He can be sweet and so adoring, but he can also be a bit of...

Well, a jerk.

I've told myself he's just not good at reading other people's emotions. Some people are naturally empathetic, and others need to be reminded, constantly, that other people have feelings. I'm a type one, and he's a type two. No big deal. But maybe I was making excuses for him because I was desperate to hold onto the only silver lining I had.

I swallow, trying to regain control of my emotions. "So, we think Jonah has been cheating on me, right? Like...possibly with more than one person. There's no other explanation?"

That would mean the man I'd fallen in love with didn't exist. That he was a fantasy created to fool me.

But *why* would he do that?

If he wants to flounce around town screwing everyone, why have a girlfriend at all, let alone a fiancée?

Otis gives a sympathetic shrug before admitting, "I don't think there's an innocent explanation, but maybe you should, you know, see if there are any other *babes* saved on that app."

I look and then gasp, because there's one more.

"There's another," I choke out. "GingerBeerBabe."

"Oh man, that's shitty. I think you need to text all of them."

"The women?" I ask, my voice quavering. "What would I even say?"

He shrugs again, then runs his hand through his shoulder-length light-brown hair. "I don't know, but you deserve the full story, and that dude's not going to be honest with you. When he found out I like disc golfing, he claimed he held a local record, but he doesn't even know what disc golfing is. He saw my pack and asked why I had so many frisbees."

"He does like to be the best," I say on an exhale.

"His own brother hates him," he adds.

"His brother's a dick."

Rob is Jonah's half-brother, from their father's first marriage. He's only a year and a half older than Jonah—thirty-one to Jonah's thirty. Rob's mother went to rehab for the first time when he was eight years old and afterward she only had visitation, so the two of them basically grew up in the same house. They didn't get along growing up, and they barely speak to each other now.

Rob's a musician—a "free spirit," Jonah's mother always says with a pinched expression. I've only met him half a dozen times, including at Christmas last year. I tried to be kind to him—and even sewed him a new guitar strap as a gift—but it's obvious his dislike of Jonah extends to everyone connected to Jonah. He calls me Pollyanna. At first, I figured he got my name wrong, but my great-aunt clucked her tongue and told me to use "that Google you're so fond of."

"That Google" informed me that a Pollyanna is a woman who puts a positive spin on everything. It was obviously intended as an insult.

He's not entirely wrong about me. After my life blew up when I was sixteen, I made a promise to get along and play nice. I've lived up to it, even though life has been full of more downs than ups. But he isn't right about me either, dammit, and every time I see him, I feel an inexplicable itch to prove it.

"Rob's not all bad," Otis says, scratching his nose. "We bumped into each other at Buchanan Brewery one time, and he bought me a beer."

"You only enjoyed yourself because you were both bad-mouthing Jonah."

"Maybe. But I've seen him at a couple of his shows, and he was nice then too." Otis takes another swig of his beer. His gaze lingers on my face. "You're not crying."

"I must be in shock."

"Or maybe the glass is shattering," he says. "You're realizing what Gram and I have known for months: that Jonah is a controlling douchebag. A liar."

I feel Otis symbolically tugging at my silver lining, and part of me is tempted to protect what's left of it. "There could still be an honest explanation."

"Text them," he says, acting surprisingly invested. "Do it now."

Hand trembling, I click into the SilverStarBabe chat.

> This isn't Jonah, but I have his phone. Who are you?

Three dots appear instantly.

Did you kidnap my boyfriend????? What do
you want?

I glance at Otis, who is unabashedly reading over my shoulder. "She says..."

"Tell her."

Finger shaking, I type:

I'm Jonah Price's fiancée, Sophie. We're
supposed to get married in four months. Who
are you?

She starts typing, but I switch to the chat with BigCatchBabe, because I know my cousin is right. I took one of those personality quizzes a couple of months ago, and it informed me I was an ostrich. If I stop digging now, before I have irrefutable evidence, Jonah might be able to talk me around. Because I really, really want to believe this isn't true.

Taking a deep breath, I send BigCatchBabe a message too.

This is Jonah Price's fiancée, Sophie. Who
are you?

There's a knock on the front door, and my eyes lock with Otis's.

"Hide the phone, man," he says. "Put it in the freezer, or stuff it in your boobs or something."

I look down at my flat chest, distracted for half a second before I shake my head. "I'm not hiding from this."

A surge of anger breaks through the shock and hurt. Jonah is always talking about the pressures of his job. He's always gone. Working, he says. But it's starting to look like the only thing he was working was me.

The phone buzzes in my hand, and I glance down.

It's SilverStarBabe.

That's not funny, Jonah.

So she doesn't know. It makes her blameless and him worse. Do the others know? I haven't texted GingerBeerBabe yet, but it feels like I've run out of time.

Another knock lands on the door as the phone buzzes with a new text, this one from BigCatchBabe.

Well, shit. I didn't know, but I should have. All the trips. The unavailability. I'm Hannah. Want to cut off his balls together?

A sound escapes me that's half sob, half laugh.

"Sophie."

I glance up at Otis as the knock lands again.

I hand him the phone.

His expression firms up. "I'll guard it with my life. He'll have to fight me for it."

It's a sweet offer, but I have a feeling Jonah would only have to look at him funny for Otis to hand it over.

"I'll handle this," I insist through a dry mouth.

I pick up my beer bottle, surprised to find it empty, even though I don't remember drinking more than a sip or two. Then I get up off the sticky floor and prepare to do something abnormal for me. I'm going to make a stand.

I try to harness the fire of BigCatchBabe as I make my way to the door. Inside, I'm teetering between devastation and fury. I want to latch onto the fury. I need it.

But when I open the door, Jonah's not standing on my stoop. It's his brother, Rob, dressed in a black band T-shirt and a pair of worn jeans. His dark hair is shaggy, his face unshaven. His eyes are hazel, like Jonah's, but more yellow than mossy green. He always looks like he's heading home from a bender or some woman's bed. He looms over me, several inches taller, even though I'm five foot six, hardly tiny.

Right now, he feels like the embodiment of his brother's sins. It's not fair, but I hate him. I loathe anyone with the last name of Price. I'm unimpressed by most people in possession of a Y chromosome, although Otis is currently exempt for being sweet and helpful. I want Rob to sink into the earth and drag Jonah with him. Their cold, intimidating father can join them.

I press a bracing hand on my hip and give him a cool look. I can feel the tears pressing at my eyes now, and I refuse to give into them in front of Rob, of all people. Swallowing all of the awful feelings down, I ask, "What are *you* doing here?"

CHAPTER TWO

ROB

I don't make a habit of doing favors for my half-brother. Jonah is and always has been a momma's boy. A complaining, self-aggrandizing baby. A user. A taker. An asshole.

He's still the kid who broke my stepmother's standing mixer and blamed it on me. The boy who ran down the family dog with his bicycle, breaking her leg, because he "wanted to see if he could." Did he cry afterward? Sure. He also cried after he ruined my life a decade ago. Minxy walked with a limp for the rest of her life, and Jonah's apology didn't do me any good either.

He'll never be able to give back what he took from me—and even if he could, I'd probably refuse on principle. I wouldn't willingly give him any more excuses to think well of himself.

But my father recently made a point of asking me to make nice with Jonah, so when my brother sent me an SOS text from an unknown number, saying he'd accidentally swapped phones with Sophie and was worried his wedding surprise for her would be ruined, I figured I'd come through for him.

My job doesn't start until afternoon, something he knows

and likes to remind me of. I played a late set last night, and his text this morning woke me with a jolt, my heart hammering until I saw it was just him. Waking me up early was his first sin, and that moment of panic was the second. I wanted to tell him off, but I came anyway, partly because I feel bad for Sophie. Sure, she's joined the Cult of Jonah and thinks he burps perfume and shits rainbows, just like his mother does, but Sophie comes off as an innocent. Naïve. Sweet. So accommodating she'd give someone her parking space at Trader Joe's.

The world isn't built for people like Sophie Ginnis. I should know—my mother's a bit like her.

A generous man would say it's to Jonah's credit that he wants to marry Sophie. She's pretty in a girl-next-door way. Wholesome. My first impression of her was that she probably thinks needlepoint is a fun way to waste a couple of hours and has a favorite pie she likes to bake. Her thick honey-brown hair is always pulled back primly, and she wears generic clothes that neither compliment her appearance nor take away from it. She's not a woman my brother would normally "honor" with a second glance. But I'm guessing he sees what I do, a girl next door with a sunny smile, a compliment for everyone, and the deductive reasoning skills of a smiley face drawn on the dirt of someone's windshield.

I don't admire or respect her for it.

Still, I like her a hell of a lot more than I like him.

So, here I am, on the doorstep of a blue Arts and Crafts style house that has seen better decades but bears a bright red door and shutters that reek of Pollyanna. I've come to do the decent thing, yet Sophie is glaring at me like I'm the spawn of Satan.

"Well?" she presses when I don't immediately explain my presence at her elderly relative's house at 8:30 a.m. on a Friday morning.

Okay, fair enough.

"Yeah, Jonah told me where you live," I say, shoving my hands into my pockets. "He said there'd been some mix-up, and you have his phone. He—"

"Did you know?" she snaps. Her sharp tone is like a jolt of caffeine to the system. I stand a little straighter. Study her more closely. Sophie usually looks soft, like the kind of woman an enterprising guy might pick up in the baking section at a grocery store, but there's something different about her today. Her hair is pulled back in the same ponytail as usual, and she's already dressed in a Buchanan Brewery shirt and khaki shorts, even though her shift is probably hours off. The expression in her eyes is almost feral, though, and her posture isn't gentle and accommodating but confrontational.

She also smells a little like...

"Have you been drinking?" I ask.

It was clearly the wrong question, because she bristles and spreads out her arms, taking up more of the doorway, as if she's worried I might barrel my way into the house. "Yes, Rob, I've been drinking. The last time I checked, it's perfectly legal for me to drink in my own home whenever I please. What are you going to do, tell on me?"

"Uh...no."

Her cousin Otis appears in the doorframe behind her and gives me a cautious wave. "Hey, what's up, man? Nice day, huh?"

It's not overly hot for early June, but he's practically sweating through his shirt.

Sophie's lips firm, and she shifts in the doorway, keeping her hands extended. "*Rob* has come for Jonah's phone."

"I know we weren't gonna give it to Jonah," he says, scratching the back of his head. "But what about Rob? He's a solid—"

"Rob is here on Jonah's mission of sin," she hisses.

A single bark of laughter escapes me. It's the phrase more than the meaning. *Mission of sin.* I'm guessing it's something her great-aunt says, and it's funny coming from a woman who hasn't clocked thirty.

Her eyes swivel to me, full of anger but also...

I've seen that look in a woman's eyes before. Sophie's sad. Heartbroken, even.

Suspicion bites between my shoulder blades. It probably would have come sooner if I weren't still tired.

Jonah would only ask me for a favor if he were truly desperate. Would he care this much about ruining a surprise for Sophie? Sure, he likes making his big gestures and getting the ego stroking that results from it, but I'm guessing Sophie would normally do him the favor of still acting surprised.

No, now that my brain's more fully awake, I can tell something else is going on here. My half-brother did something bad, again, and now he's panicking because he got himself caught and cornered.

"What'd you find on his phone?" I ask, my voice sounding harsh.

My anger is directed at my brother, but she turns back toward me and plants a hand on her hip. Otis is frozen in the background as if he's forgotten how to move.

For a second I'm distracted by the sight of Sophie's hand curled around her generous hip. Then she clears her throat, and I meet her gaze. "Are you pretending you don't know *exactly* what's on there? This is why you've been such an asshole to me, isn't it? You knew what Jonah was doing. You've probably known all along."

"He's cheating on you?" I ask. It's not the only bad thing I can imagine him doing, but I doubt she'd be this worked up over him lying on his taxes or stealing something from the grocery store to get a dopamine rush.

"You *did* know." The hurt in her gaze overpowers the anger, and she slumps against the side of the doorframe. "Why didn't you warn me?"

I open my mouth to say something, maybe *sorry for the Price men. I hate all of them too, mostly,* but she saves me from myself by adding, "*I* would have warned *you.*"

"I don't have a girlfriend right now," I point out. Again, the wrong thing to say.

"Of course you don't," she says tightly, shaking her head. "I'll bet you're out with a new woman every night."

I lift my eyebrows, letting her realize it herself. Jonah's the one who's been stepping out, not me.

And I instantly regret it, because her lower lip trembles. Shit. I can see tears welling in her eyes.

"Sophie?" Otis says, and when she turns toward him, he takes two steps backward, colliding with a wall and nearly taking down an aggressively ugly painting of a shepherd herding sheep that look like llamas. "Oh no. We need to get you back to the anger thing. The anger thing was good."

"I *am* angry," she insists in a wobbling voice.

I might not think much of her judgment, but seeing her like this is like a gut punch. It makes me want to deliver a gut punch to the man who's responsible.

My hand forms a fist as I think about punching Jonah. Something I have absolutely done before, and for good reason. I keep all of the times my fists have met his flesh in my memory bank to take out on special occasions.

But I remember something my mother said to me once. *Sometimes people don't want you to fix things for them, Rob. Sometimes they just need a hug.* So I step forward and wrap my arms around Sophie.

She's soft, and exactly the right height for her ear to be pressed to my heart when she's against my chest—a weird thing to notice, but let it never be said I'm normal. Her hair smells like flowers, and...

She stiffens as if I'd thrown a bucket of icy water over her. "Oh, no. You do *not* get to hug me."

I pull back, fighting a smile for half a second, because at least I got her pissed off again. That's better than sad and defeated. Shaking my head, I insist, "I didn't know, Sophie. If I'd known, I would have warned you."

"Me too," Otis pipes in.

"So you were just being an asshole because you're an asshole?" she asks, studying my face. I'd thought her eyes were brown, inasmuch as I'd given them any thought at all, but they're actually a deep, dark blue, surrounded by thick black lashes. It's a revelation so surprising that it takes me a second to remember she asked me a question. I decide to keep things simple and nod. It's not necessary to burden her with my side of the Price family drama. I'm guessing she'd like to shut the door on all of us permanently, and I wouldn't blame her. It would probably be the best thing that ever happened to her.

I glance at Otis, who looks like he's not sure where he should be but would prefer to be somewhere other than where he is. "So, where's the phone, bud? Seems like Soph should bring it back to Jonah personally."

Sophie flinches. "He's in a meeting with an important client—"

"Exactly," I say pointedly. "Wouldn't it be a pity if someone barged in and let the world know what an absolute waste of life he is?"

Otis gives a cheer. "I'm gonna go grab it from the freezer."

I don't know why the phone is in the freezer, and I'm not interested in asking. My focus is on Sophie.

I notice she hasn't agreed yet—and also that she still has Jonah's engagement ring on her finger. My gaze shifts to the little bungalow next door, where an elderly woman with purple hair is openly watching us from behind gauzy curtains. I wave, and she pops down as if to hide. I can still very much see her, but I let it go because I don't want her to break a hip trying to get fully out of view.

My gaze returns to Sophie. She seems to be waffling, and I don't want her to give up. I don't want her to give Jonah the chance to put one of his legendary spins on this.

"Follow your instincts," I tell her in an undertone as Otis appears with the phone, clutched in an oven mitt.

"She doesn't need to do that," he says, waving the phone. "She has evidence. Remember the evidence, Sophie. Don't let him dismiss what we saw. I took screenshots of everything before I put the phone in the freezer."

I'd like to know what they found. Then again, there's a possibility it's a photo of my brother's dick, and I already have trouble sleeping at night.

I also don't want to say or do anything that might unintentionally make Sophie cry.

Maybe this is a sign that I'm yet another Price man who's a selfish asshole, but I can't handle tears right now. It still isn't my normal wake-up time, and it's already been a crap day.

Her chin lifts as she takes the phone from him, immediately flinching from the cold.

"Sorry, sorry," Otis says, taking the glove off and handing it to her. She frowns at it. I'm hit with a sudden vision of her storming into Jonah's meeting with an oven mitt on her hand and dropping the phone into his lap. It's enough to make me smile—but as soon as I do, Sophie glowers at me.

"This is no laughing matter."

"Agreed," I say, wiping the look off my face.

She straightens her spine and hands the oven mitt back to Otis.

"Do you want me to come with you?" he asks in a tone that suggests he desperately wants her to say no.

She considers for a few seconds before shaking her head. "Just don't drink any more of those IPAs in case you need to drive."

"Is someone going to offer me a drink?" I ask, earning another dark look from Sophie. I lift a hand. "Kidding. Let's go."

"Wait, you want to come with me?" she asks, her expression shifting to shock. "But why?"

"Consider me your designated driver," I say pointedly, even though I doubt she drank enough to need one. Truth is, this is my way of ensuring she sticks to the course.

"Oh, that's a good idea," Otis says. "You definitely shouldn't be driving right now, Soph, and not just because of the beer. Remember when Grandma was so upset by that episode of *The Young and the Restless* that she hit a fire hydrant? I told her it was just a rerun, but she hadn't seen it before, and—"

"I'm perfectly capable of driving myself."

"So maybe I want to see this go down," I say, lifting my eyebrows. "Jonah pulled me into this, and I'd like to see it bite him in the ass."

She watches me with suspicious eyes, but then understanding filters into them. "You're worried I won't go through with it if I don't have someone with me."

I shrug.

"But are you sure you want to be involved in this? He's your brother."

"Yeah," I say. "That's exactly why I want to do it. If I don't help teach him a lesson, who will?"

I'm lucky I've learned to lie without flinching. Truth is, I don't think any kind of consequence exists that will transform Jonah Price into anything other than what he is.

Maybe I just want to see the look on his face when he's confronted with the truth of who he is, the way we all are at least once in our lives.

CHAPTER THREE

SOPHIE

Conversation with BigCatchBabe

> I'm bringing him his phone. He's in a meeting with the Silver Star owner.

Oh, yeah. It's going down. Spill a beer on him for me, will you?

> There are more of us. He also has a SilverStarBabe and a GingerBeerBabe on his phone.

Ho-ly shit.

I can't believe I have to miss this.

I'm sure I'll probably feel disappointed later by this proof that all men really are full of it, but right now I'm amped up on self-righteous adrenaline.

Hey, can we meet up so you can tell me how it all went down?

I turn the phone face down in my lap. I should probably answer her, but I don't know what to say—or how it'll feel to come face-to-face with these women who have been living parallel lives to mine for who knows how long.

My conscience tells me I should also message SilverStar-Babe, especially since I'm going to Silver Star and will probably see her, but she seems to genuinely care about Jonah, and if we keep messaging, we might both end up sobbing. Right now, I need to feed the other emotions festering inside of me. Because I have spent the past twelve years trying to avoid confrontation, and here I am, driving toward it.

Rob gives me a sidelong look as he cuts through downtown to get to the brewery. His car is a surprisingly clean Subaru, not an Outback like nearly every other person in Asheville possesses but a WRX with circular headlights. It looks like it has a smiley face—not that I'd ever tell him that, because I know what he'd say if I did.

Not everything has to smile, Pollyanna.

What a tool fictional Rob is.

We pass a couple of buskers, a group of lost-looking tourists with their phones out, and very little else. This is not a town known for its early risers. It *is* a town where people stay out late on Thursday nights.

The tasting room is in the South Slope, close to Buchanan's tasting room, so after I ruin Jonah's meeting, I can walk to work. Regrettably, I would be several hours early, but maybe they'd let me sit at the bar and stare off into nothingness for a few hours. Or scream into a pillow in the event room.

"So..." Rob says. I glance at him, taking in the dark circles under his eyes. No doubt he was living his own life of sin late into the night. For all I know, their father was doing the same. Maybe being a cheating jerk is a genetically inherited trait.

"Whoa, what's that look for?"

"Nothing," I say, wiping the disapproval from my face. That's exactly the sort of sentiment that could lead to an argument—and it's easier when everyone is acting the way they're supposed to.

Rob takes a turn, his gaze fixed on the road. Probably a good thing, since a couple of tourists just stepped into traffic, their eyes glued to their phones. He honks his horn, and one of them, a woman wearing oversized sunglasses and bright white sneakers, casts him a bewildered look, as if he'd just exposed himself in her living room.

After giving them an ironic wave, he shifts his attention back to me. "That wasn't nothing."

My first instinct is to hold my tongue, but it occurs to me I'll have no reason to interact with him ever again after this morning. Maybe my thinking is addled by my slight beer buzz, but why not be honest? "I was just thinking that I wouldn't be the least bit surprised if you were out carousing last night, too."

His lips twitch. "Carousing, huh? Don't you work at a brewery?"

"You know I do. The taproom always closes at ten, and I never drink on the job."

"Sure," he concedes, rubbing his chin.

We reach the brewery, and he parallel parks in a tight spot with enviable precision and no obvious anxiety. I *never* would have attempted that.

He glances at me as he activates the emergency brake. "I had a show. So, yeah, I was up late. Working. I don't drink on the job either. Not even when the nerves hit."

"*You* get nervous?"

He snorts. "I know, radical, isn't it? It feels good, playing for an audience, and it also feels like shit. Life's like that sometimes."

I know *all* about Rob's band. They're called Garbage Fire,

and they were voted best of Asheville twice in a row. Honestly, I haven't ever felt the need to listen to them, partly because of the name, and partly because Jonah told me they sound like a bunch of stoner teenagers. They've played at Buchanan Brewery before but never during one of my shifts.

"I haven't heard your band play. I guess I probably never will now," I say, and he raises a brow at me.

"Sorry," I apologize automatically.

"Are you?" he asks as he cocks his head, watching me. There's a challenge in his eyes, and it occurs to me that he's purposefully revving me up.

"I'm not sure," I admit. "It's what I was taught to say when I upset someone."

"Do I look upset?"

"No," I admit.

"I'm not. Doesn't bother me if you think I'm a loser. I know my brother does, and I couldn't care less."

"Why don't you like each other?" I ask. It's a stupid question —I know it, he knows it, the man dancing on the street corner probably would know it too, should we describe the situation to him. But I need to say something. I have to distract myself from what I'm about to do.

Rob smiles sadly and looks at the low-slung ceiling of the car as if he might find the answers written there. He seems enormous in the car, a giant stuck in a box. "I'm guessing he's told you why he doesn't like me. You're one of the people who knows him best. Can you guess why I might not like him?"

"Yes." I pause. "But why don't you like *me*?"

He glances at me, eyes wide. "I'm surprised you went there."

"Well?"

He turns up the air conditioner, which is a welcome distraction from the dancing man, who is now urinating against the side of a brick building in broad daylight. "I wouldn't say I dislike you."

"But you don't like me."

"Jonah doesn't need another person telling him how good he is at everything. He already thinks that."

"But he *is* good at a lot of things. And I try to focus on the positive. No one wants to be around people who keep pointing out everything they're bad at."

"No, but then they'll keep being bad at them. He thinks he's a god because his father's rich and he's a successful distributor, but—"

"You have the same father," I point out.

He laughs bitterly. "Now you tell me. It's my dad's money. It's never been mine. Never will be."

I'm not sure what he means by that, or how his situation is different from Jonah's. Their father is a wealthy financial planner, from a wealthy family. I know Jonah gained access to a small trust fund when he reached eighteen, and I'd assumed the same was true for Rob but that he'd blown it all on booze, blunts, and women, or whatever eighteen-year-old boys like to spend money on.

"Sorry," I say again, somewhat meaning it this time.

"There you go again."

"There you go being a dick again."

I cover my mouth after the words come out, which doesn't do any good.

Rob looks amused. "Well, at least we know you have no trouble being honest with *me*."

I watch as he runs a hand over his jaw. The coverage of the stubble is as perfect as if someone had painstakingly plotted it out on graph paper. Curiosity makes me want to brush my fingers over it, although of course I never would. Jonah's beard doesn't grow in like that—his is patchy, which is why he always shaves first thing in the morning. I used to think that sliver of self-consciousness was proof of a sweet vulnerability. But maybe that was something else I'd romanticized, making it into an endearing quality rather than a show of vanity.

"I never really knew Jonah at all," I reflect morosely.

"It's my turn to be sorry," Rob says with a sigh. "I suppose my brother's like all of us. He tries to put his best foot forward. He cares what people think."

"You don't."

He laughs, but I can't tell whether he's offended or genuinely amused. "The world could benefit from a little more honesty, don't you think?"

"A little more honesty," I repeat, letting the sentiment seep in. *A little more honesty.*

Yes, why yes I do.

I firm up my posture and exit the car. Rob gets out, too, but I don't look at him.

"I need to do this part by myself," I say.

There's a heavy pause, like he's preparing to object, but he says, "You're right. But I'll wait out here in case you need a ride. Or a getaway car."

Maybe he's only sticking around to make sure I actually go through with ruining his brother's morning, like he said before, but I'm not going to complain. It makes me feel less alone.

I suck in a breath of the warm summer air, then regret it, because it smells a bit like hot trash.

Garbage Fire.

The thought makes me sneak a surreptitious glance at Rob, who has returned to the driver's seat, though he's left the door open as if he's ready to jump out at a moment's notice. He winks at me, and apparently shock does crazy things to a woman because I feel something inside of me wink back. Metaphorically, of course. I have never possessed the ability to close only one eye upon command. It's like the universe solely bestowed that talent on men who would misuse it to make women feel things they shouldn't.

I glance away quickly, thinking of BigCatchBabe, Hannah, and kind of wishing she were here with me. Oh, who am I kidding. I wish she were dealing with this instead of me. She's clearly as addicted to conflict as I am allergic to it.

Gulping in another breath, regretting it again, I cross the road and approach the entrance for Silver Star...and realize the flaw in my plan when I see the "Closed" sign on the glass door. It's only nine a.m., at the latest, and they're not open for business yet. They probably won't open until noon, like Buchanan's tasting room.

I almost turn back. I have a valid excuse for not going in there. But I can practically see the look Rob will give me if I return to that car without even talking to Jonah. Disappointed but not surprised, like he was hopeful but didn't really think I had it in me. So I continue walking toward the building and then stand against the outer wall, next to an oversized potted plant that looks on the verge of death.

I consider my options.

Option 1: I could text Jonah, pretending to be Rob, and ask him to meet me at a side door so we can exchange the phones. But he probably doesn't have my phone on him if he's in the meeting. It would also eliminate my opportunity to embarrass him, and if I don't make a scene, he might be able to use his persuasion super power to get me to change my mind.

Option 2: I could text SilverStarBabe.

I pull out my phone, hands shaking, and send her a message.

> I know you don't believe me, but this is Sophie. I'm here at Silver Star to give Jonah his phone back.

> Will you let me in?

> If you're here, I mean.

> You'll see how he reacts when he sees me, and then you'll know.

There's a pause, and I'm contemplating reverting to Option 1 when she writes back.

> How do I know you're not some psychopath stalker?

I send her my Facebook profile. It says I'm engaged but not to whom. Jonah told me months ago that he has no social media presence and would like to keep it that way. He said he prefers to have real, in-person interactions.

I'll just bet he does.

> This tells me nothing other than that you work at Buchanan Brewery. We HATE Buchanan Brewery.

I look through the photos on Jonah's phone. He doesn't take many of them, but there's a photo of the two of us at his parents' house a few weeks ago. It was at an all-hands-on-deck family dinner, attended by Rob, who took the photograph with a smug grin on his face. Jonah has his arm around me, and my engagement ring is clearly visible.

A pained sound escapes me. We look content in the photo, and now that kind of happiness feels impossibly far away. To think...all this time, my silver lining was made of the kind of metal that turns your finger green.

Three dots appear and then disappear in the chat window. A passing car honks at me, and the man who urinated against the building walks past the brewery, muttering to himself loudly enough to set a very pale pigeon into flight. I glance over to check if Rob is still there—in his perfect parallel parking spot—and some of my unease drifts away when I see that he is. He's closed the door, but his window is open.

The phone buzzes in my hand.

SilverStarBabe: *I'll be there in two minutes.*

The next two minutes are probably the longest in my life. I almost leave, twice, to return to the safety of Rob's car. Finally, a woman in a bright green and blue wrap dress with feather earrings ducks across the street—not using the crosswalk but actually paying attention to oncoming traffic. She has thick golden hair down past her butt, and a gnawing feeling grows inside of me, because she's *beautiful.* Next to her, I feel like a mouse, perfectly average in every way.

Five minutes ago, the question was why Jonah would want someone else when he already had me, but now I wonder why anyone would want me if they could have her.

She walks up to me, her expression wary, and as she reaches me, her gaze drops to my engagement ring. Hurt ripples across her features, and I realize that this gorgeous woman probably feels the exact same way I do. The thought stokes the rage inside me again, thank God, and I firm up my jaw.

"SilverStarBabe?" I ask.

"My name's Briar," she says cautiously. "You're Sophie."

I nod.

"And you're really his fiancée?"

A ball of emotion lodges in my throat. When I break up with him, there's a chance she'll step in to pick up the pieces. Or maybe BigCatchBabe or GingerBeerBabe will. They could slip right into the role I've been playing and take over the wedding that never really felt like mine...

It doesn't matter, though. I've tried so hard to become a respectable person, and I'm not going to give up on it now.

"I was," I say. "How long were you—"

"About five months."

My mouth gapes open, and fresh indignation washes through me. "He proposed to me five months ago."

Her lips part, and I halfway expect her to call me a liar again. But she whispers, "That *jerk*. He...he told me he wanted to be exclusive. That he didn't have a lot of time to date, but he preferred to focus on forming a soul connection with one person at a time."

"He said 'soul connection'?" I ask in disbelief. The Jonah I thought I knew would never talk about *soul connections*.

She gives a wobbly nod.

"That *jerk*," I echo, feeling it so deeply in my bones it might as well be part of my marrow.

I want to tell her about the two other women. But that can come later. I need to confront him now. I need to do it while I'm feeling strong.

"I have to give his phone back to him, Briar."

She glances nervously at the building and bites her lip, and I remember what Jonah said about the Silver Star owner. How he's allergic to technology, even though his entire operation is reliant on it.

For a second, I think Briar is going to turn me down. There's uncertainty in her eyes, but she takes my hand and leads me around to a door she unlocks. We step into an office space with a couple of desks left out in the open like islands, a kitchenette, and a closed office door. I can hear a man behind it, laughing in deep gusts.

Then I hear Jonah's voice, so familiar but so wrong, and a shudder runs down my spine.

Briar and I exchange a glance. "You could just throw the phone in the garbage," she suggests. "He'd be able to find it with the Find My Phone app, probably, but he'd have to go through the trash. He'd hate that. He doesn't even like scraping dirty dishes off."

She's right, of course, although it's still hard to wrap my head around the reality that Jonah has spent so much time with other women, enough that they've eaten home-cooked meals together. Does he travel for work at all? Or did he make phone calls to me while crouched on other women's balconies or in their bathrooms?

"I'm going in," I say, stiffening my spine.

"He had your phone when he showed up?" she asks.

"Yeah," I say through my dry mouth.

Her lips press together. "I'll get it for you. I know where they're kept during meetings."

She walks away, and I can't help but notice that even the way she walks is elegant. It doesn't make me dislike her, though. None of this is her fault, or BigCatchBabe's fault, or even the fault of the mysterious GingerBeerBabe. There's one person behind this mess, and he's in that office.

That thought is enough to get me moving. I swing the office door open and walk in with Jonah's phone outstretched as if it has offended me. Both Jonah and the tall, rotund man behind the desk turn to stare at me. Despite the early hour, each of them is drinking from a flight of beer, the small glasses arranged in labeled wooden carriers.

A sense of indignation washes over me. Jonah must have known there was a chance I'd discover his lies, yet he still took this meeting. He sent Rob, whom he doesn't even like, to retrieve the phone. That's how much he cared. He's not just a cheater, but a lazy cheater.

I glare at him, my fingers squeezing the phone.

Surprise flickers across his face, followed by worry and then a fake wide grin. He's so handsome, with his big hazel eyes, closely cropped dark hair, and that perfectly shaved jaw, but his looks feel offensive now.

"This is my fiancée," he tells the big guy, who's scowling at me. "What a nice surprise, honey, but we're not quite done in here yet."

"Oh, I think you're done," I say, my voice thrumming with anger. "I think you're *very* done."

"Sophie?" Jonah says, reaching for my hand. "If you have something you need to talk about, we can grab breakfast in ten minutes. Why don't you wait for me outside? It won't be long."

Outside, like a dog.

Outside, like an umbrella abandoned after a rainy day.

People have treated me like that almost my whole life. I've spent my adulthood trying to absorb it like a sponge or make excuses for them, but no more. My fingers squeeze tighter around the phone.

I try to remember the breathing exercises I was taught in therapy. But I can't remember whether I'm supposed to breathe fast or slow to calm down, and—

"No phones allowed in here, sweetheart," says the man behind the desk as if he doesn't notice the chaotic energy thrumming through the room. "Bring that out there with you, will you?"

Something inside of me snaps, and I drop the phone on the floor and stomp on it. Once, twice. And again, feeling the glass crack satisfyingly under my orthopedic sneaker. Jonah's mouth drops open. He stares at me as if he's just this moment realized that he doesn't really know me.

I know what that feeling's like. Normally this is when my empathy would kick in, telling me to save someone else from something that has hurt me, but it doesn't happen.

I smile at him, probably looking like an insane person, and swing my gaze to the big boss. "Is that better, *sir*?"

He opens his mouth but doesn't say anything. Then he lifts one of the small glasses of beer and drains it.

"You'll apologize, Sophie," Jonah says, getting to his feet. He's five foot ten but consistently writes six-one on forms when asked for his height. He's capable of looking down at me, but not as much as he'd probably like.

"You're so much shorter than your brother, you know," I sneer. "I think he might *actually* be six-one. Maybe even six-two." I grab one of the little glasses from his display. I was going to throw the contents at him, but I notice at the last second it's their Elderberry Breeze, and I down it instead.

Surprisingly refreshing.

Jonah watches me with stupefaction now. Like he can't believe I'm the same woman who accepted his ring.

"Sophie," he finally manages to say. "Did you hear from your great-aunt?" He gives the big boss a *women will be women* look that infuriates me. "Sophie's elderly aunt just went into remission from a very serious illness. She's doing better now, but it's been a stressful time." Swinging his gaze to me, he adds, "But that's no excuse to make a spectacle of yourself, sweetheart."

"*You* have made an ass of yourself," I say. "What's your excuse?" I pick up another one of the small glasses of beer and face the boss man. He recoils a little as if he's afraid of what I might do, and for a second I quail. I know what happens when I break the rules. My mind pulls up a familiar memory. Sitting in the police station under the snapping fluorescent lights, my clothes smelling like smoke. But I swallow the old fear down. "Do you know this man has a girlfriend at every brewery in town? Every brewery." I gesture with the cup on the last two words, and a tiny slosh of beer splashes on his desk.

"There must be over a hundred," the boss man mutters, gazing at Jonah. Does he look *impressed?*

I'm tempted to add that one of them is here, in this brewery, but I don't want to unmask Briar, who's been nothing but helpful.

"He's also a liar," I say bitterly. "Do you want to work with a liar? You'll never be able to trust him."

He purses his lips. "I suppose it depends on who he's lying to."

I shake my head and down the beer in the little cup. This one's not as good. "You should go back to the drawing board for the tropical IPA," I say. "Ours is better at Buchanan Brewery. *Way* better."

The big boss slides his wheeled office chair back a couple of inches, looking like I just slapped him across the face.

Jonah, who's been staring at me in shock—a broken machine of a man—clears his throat and tells the big boss, "I think she's in the middle of some kind of breakdown, sir. I'm so sorry. We'll get her the help she needs, and it'll never—"

I slip off my engagement ring and throw it at Jonah's face. It bounces off the bridge of his nose and lands directly into one of the still-full cups on the tasting board. My lips part in surprise. I've never had good luck, but this is astounding. It's a hole in one. It's the kind of beautiful moment that will carry a person— for at least as long as it takes me to get out of here.

Not wanting to miss the chance for a perfect exit, I say, "I hope you choke on it, you...you...*ignoramus*. I never want to see you again."

Then I turn on my heel and leave the office, nearly colliding with Briar, who has been standing just beyond the doorway witnessing the whole thing.

To my amazement, I see that she's been recording it on her phone.

CHAPTER FOUR

ROB

I'm not leaving until Sophie comes out of the building.

It's a small thing I can do for her, so insignificant it's probably laughable. But I'm going to be there for her today, and then I'm going to beat the shit out of my brother.

Okay, maybe I won't do that. He'd probably have me arrested. But I'm owed something, aren't I? Both for what he did to Sophie and for roping me into this mess.

I'm daydreaming about how good it would feel to crunch my fist into his face when my phone rings. For half a second, I think it's going to be Jonah, calling me from Sophie's phone, but it's my buddy Travis.

To say Travis is a good guy would be as insufficient as saying my brother is a douchebag. Travis and I started Garbage Fire six or so years ago. He's the drummer, and I'm the lead on vocals and guitar. Our buddy Chance Bixby is on bass. We used to have another guy on guitar, but he quit a few months ago and hasn't been replaced yet.

Travis also pulled me into our other project: The Missing Beat, an after-school music program we run together. We teach the kids guitar, drums, song-writing, and singing, and they have performances around town. It fucking rocks.

Without Travis, I would have slid deeper into the dark place I fell into after what Jonah did to me. So, obviously, when he calls, I answer. I'd hide a body for him. Don't know how, but I'd figure that shit out.

"What's up?" I ask, picking up the call.

"You're awake."

"I'm awake."

"I figured I'd get your voicemail. Anyway...shit." He pauses, and I can imagine him rubbing the spot between his eyebrows—his go-to for when he's about to say something unwelcome. "Bix and I ducked into the Hot Spot last night, and Emil was working the register. That's why he hasn't been coming to the program anymore. His foster dad told him he has to contribute to the household. He's got him working so much the kid can't do his homework. And he's still not allowed to practice guitar at home. Not even if you give him one."

I swear under my breath.

Most people would tell you being a talented musician doesn't matter much. So few people are able to make a career of it. The dedicated are like us, part of a band that takes up the majority of our free time and only brings in enough money to pay a couple of utility bills. But this kid is magic on the guitar, and he writes his own songs. I truly believe he could make something of himself if he's given the chance.

The program wasn't costing his foster dad anything. Emil was one of our scholarship students, referred to us by the school music program. But I can't force his foster dad to send him.

Which is why I've had something cooking on the down-low.

"There's this idea I've been working on," I say.

My friend gives an easy laugh. "Why am I worried?"

"You probably should be. Look…I'll tell you about it later. I've gotta go. I'm Pollyanna's getaway driver."

He laughs. "Jonah's girlfriend has resorted to a life of crime?"

"Something like that. I'll fill you in on that later too."

"Nice. Have fun. Don't do anything I wouldn't do."

As soon as we hang up, I text Nelly, the caseworker who's helping me get approved as a foster parent.

It's a perfect solution. Emil's sixteen, nearly seventeen, and he doesn't really need another parent. He needs a place to stay with someone who's going to let him do his homework and practice guitar. I've got a spare bedroom that's home to nothing but my instruments mounted on the wall.

The guitars could go elsewhere, or they could stay—Emil would be over the moon to sleep beneath them.

I let Nelly know that Emil's foster dad has him working long hours, and she texts back seconds later.

> Crappy but not illegal. We got this. A few more weeks. Hang in there, my friend.

I hold the phone for a second, lost in thought, then tuck it away when I see Sophie hurrying out of the brewery with another woman, the same blonde who met her out front fifteen minutes ago. I've played sets at most of the breweries that host live music, so I recognize her, but I don't remember her name. Bixby calls her Goldilocks.

They open the back door, and they both slide into the back seat as if I really am their getaway driver.

"Go," Sophie says.

I don't hesitate or ask what happened, even if I really, really want to know. I pull away from the curb just as Jonah comes jogging outside. He waves his hand at the car, the gesture urgent.

Nope, can't let this go.

I park the car and turn to face the ladies.

"Please, Rob," Sophie says, leaning forward in her seat.

A few tendrils of hair have escaped her usual ponytail, and she has a wild, almost untamed look. I have the strange urge to reach back, not to tuck her hair behind her ear, but to tug the rest of it free.

"I'll be right back," I say. "Then we're getting out of here. I'll bring you wherever you like."

I climb out of the car and cross the road, making a beeline toward Jonah. He looks anxious, which I enjoy, but he clearly wishes to talk to me, which I do *not* enjoy.

In this moment, it feels like all the problems in the world are the result of Jonah and his devil-may-care dick.

"So you know," Jonah says as I get closer. He's dressed in a suit that's about as weather appropriate as wearing shorts in midwinter, and sweat has dampened the collar of his shirt. "Can you help me convince—"

I punch him in the face. His nose gives under my fist as pain bursts across my knuckles, and I'm not sorry. Not even if I've messed up my hand and won't be able to play right for weeks.

"What the hell?" he shrieks, lifting his hands up to cup his nose.

"That's for being just like our dad, you absolute piece of shit. How could you?"

"I...I don't know," he sputters. "I messed up. I'm going to fix it. I'm going to figure out a way."

"No. You're not," I say flatly. "You're going to leave her the fuck alone."

With that, I turn my back on him, knowing he could attack me from behind. Not really caring.

I cross the road to the car, from which Sophie and

Goldilocks are gaping at me. Sophie's face is practically pressed to the glass.

When I get to the car, I glance back. Jonah is still standing there, his hand wrapped around his bleeding nose, watching me with some sort of emotion written across his face. I'll be damned if I know what it is. I doubt he's learned anything from all of this, other than that he should be a better liar.

I slip behind the wheel, clear my throat, and say, "All right, ladies, where to?"

"You punched him," Sophie says in wonder, our eyes meeting in the rearview mirror. She doesn't look like Jonah's Sophie right now. The expression in her eyes is the same as it was this morning—fiery and vindictive—and it makes me smile.

"Since we've decided to be truthful with each other, Pollyanna, it felt pretty damn good."

It's only as I start the engine that I realize I may have just screwed everything up.

If Jonah calls the cops, I'll have a lot of explaining to do, and they may not agree that he had it coming.

FIFTEEN MINUTES LATER, we're sitting in a booth at Tea of Fortune, a tea shop picked out by Sophie. Apparently the owner is her next-door neighbor. The same next-door neighbor who was watching us from her window this morning.

I've seen Dottie Hendrickson around town before. She's the kind of person you can't help but notice. She must be in her eighties, but there's a spark in her eyes that makes her seem younger. Her white hair is always dyed a different color—a soft purple right now—and she wears colorful dresses that look like they've been seized from a fifties' diner. Today's dress has little clusters of hearts all over it.

The tea she selected is supposed to be a calming blend, but I've barely touched it. It tastes like the sachets my stepmother keeps in her bathroom closets smell, and it feels strange to drink something hot when it's warm outside. Besides, I've been distracted.

I can't stop watching the video of Sophie ripping Jonah a new one in front of his client, which her new friend sent to me so I'd stop hogging her phone. Never in a million years would I have thought she'd confront him like that. In that video, she's more of a warrior than a Pollyanna. The look on her face...the way the diamond ring pinged off Jonah's nose...it's *glorious*. I want it to play behind my eyelids when I lie down to sleep at night. Good God, there's nothing as intoxicating as seeing Jonah humbled.

It turns out my little brother probably had at least three secret girlfriends. One is Briar, the woman who took the video. Sophie texted the other two from the car after getting their numbers from her cousin Otis. One of them will be meeting us at the tea shop, and the other hasn't responded.

"Here you are, dear boy," Dottie says as she hands me a silicone bag full of ice and little fragrant specks that look like dried flowers.

"Oh, you didn't have to go to all this trouble," I say, taken aback.

I hadn't planned on requesting ice, but when the little old lady came around asking about what had brought us in, Sophie told her that I'd slugged someone in the face defending their honor and needed an ice pack befitting a hero. I'm guessing she's tipsier than I realized.

"No trouble at all," Dottie says as she pats my hand directly on my abraded knuckles. "Chamomile helps heal wounds in the body and soul."

She obviously means well, so I don't tell her it's nonsense.

When she leaves, I feel Sophie watching me—and what do you know? I press the ice pack to my knuckles.

"Good," she says, back to her slightly prudish, missish self. This is the Sophie who likes needlepoint and coordinating potluck dinners.

I'm kind of fascinated by the different sides of her I've seen today. Like she's a puzzle whose pieces fit together in dozens of different formations.

"This place has really good tea," Briar says. "Really good." She's still talking about the tea, probably some kind of nervous tic, when a short woman with curly bright-red hair comes through the front door.

"GingerBeerBabe?" Briar whispers.

Sophie shakes her head, her gaze on the redhead too. "Can't be. She never answered my text. I'm worried Jonah got to her first and is filling her head with BS."

The short redhead says something to Dottie and then approaches the table.

"Sophie?" she asks, her voice husky.

Sophie raises her hand and then starts laughing, either from the alcohol or nerves.

"I'm Hannah, from Big Catch. Oh good, we're drinking? I didn't think this place had liquor."

"It has tea," Briar says as the redhead slides in next to her.

"And you are?"

"I'm Briar," she says, picking at her manicured nails. "I'm another one of the...well..."

"She's SilverStarBabe," Sophie gushes. "She and Jonah were dating for five months. How long were you with him?"

Hannah snorts. "I wouldn't say we were *together* together.

But he *did* say he was single. Six months, maybe." Her gaze turns to me, her brow furrowing. "You look a little like him."

"I'm guessing I should. I'm his half-brother, Rob."

Her expression tightens, but Sophie wraps an arm around me before I can get my balls lopped off. Her scent surrounds me—clean with just the slightest hint of beer. "We like Rob. He punched Jonah in the face for us."

"It wasn't only for you," I feel compelled to admit. I'm done with her acting like I'm some kind of hero.

She tips her head at me, a silent question, acting like it's just the two of us in this whole place.

"My dad did the same thing to my mom with Jonah's mother. I've never thought much of Jonah, but after all the trouble our dad's cheating caused, you'd think he would have learned something."

A stricken expression crosses her face, her lips parting. "Oh, no. But his mother's so..."

She trails off, as if she can't find a word for the woman. Fair enough. I've been trying for decades.

I glance at the three of them, cozy around the table, and sense the obvious—it's time for me to go.

Sophie's arm is still around me, a testament to her tipsiness, so I turn to Briar, who seems like the type to have a cabinet full of tinctures at home, as opposed to Hannah, who almost certainly has a flask in her purse. "Can you make sure she gets home safely?"

"You're leaving, Rob?" Sophie asks, sounding thrown by it. "Will I ever see you again?"

This morning, I wouldn't have cared much about the answer to that question, but I'm invested now. I want to know how this plays out for her. And from the way she asked it, she cares about the answer too.

I smile at her. "We're playing at the Buchanan Brewery

tasting room in a few weeks. Maybe you'll be working that night. I'd buy you a drink if you hadn't already told me you don't drink on the job."

Hannah snaps her fingers in recognition and points at me. "Ah, you're the guy in that band. Garbage Fire."

"That's not very nice," Briar says, scrunching her nose.

Smiling, I say, "It's the name of my band, and no, it's not very nice. But it seemed like a good idea at the time. Don't get into too much trouble, ladies."

Sophie surprises me by hugging me one-armed before letting go. Peering into my eyes with those big blues of hers, she says, "Thank you, Rob. I think we restored some truth today, don't you?"

Something softens in my chest as I smile back at her. "Yeah, I'd say. I'm never going to challenge you to beer pong. You know, I'm starting to think you might be a wolf in sheep's clothing, Pollyanna."

I get up to leave with the ice pack pressed to my hand, but I find myself glancing back when I'm a few feet from the table. Sophie's talking to the other women, her hair hanging around her face now, more down than up. Her eyes are big and bright and full of life. She's going to be okay. For some reason, that's important, possibly because I don't want any more reasons to be ashamed to be a Price.

On my way to the door, I look for the owner and find her in the middle of a deeply personal conversation with a woman who's unloading about her stalled-out sex life. A middle-aged man is sitting at the table with them. Judging from their wedding rings, the conversation is about *him*, but he's playing blackjack on his phone while he disinterestedly eats a cookie.

I pause by the table, waiting for Dottie to notice me. She glances at me, and before I can even make a gesture, she lifts a finger and tells the woman, "Put a pin in that thought, dear. I have to help a friend, but I'm going to prepare a pot of jasmine tea for you. Very sensual. It should help you reconnect. And make sure you keep taking that supplement, Bradley."

He doesn't react whatsoever, which suggests apathy is the real problem.

Clucking her tongue, Dottie leads me to an empty table, then sits and gestures for me to do the same in the spindly wicker chair across from her, which looks like it has a fifty-fifty chance of disintegrating under me. This suggests a longer conversation than I was looking for. But I don't want to continue the Price family tradition of being a shitty person by ignoring an old lady. So I sit across from her and say, "I don't want to keep you, but I'd like to pay the tab for the table back there. Whatever they want."

I point to them, grateful to see there are still no tears. Briar's the closest to crying, I think, but I'm worried about what'll happen to Sophie once she's alone and the adrenaline of this morning runs low. She's a whole lot more complex than I thought she was, but she still has a soft side.

Dottie beams at me. "Oh, how *kind* of you. Which of the young ladies are you in love with, dear? No, don't tell me. I enjoy guessing."

I should stop her, but I don't. Call it curiosity.

She strokes the crystal pendant around her neck as she peers back at them, then nods in agreement with herself. She fans herself. "Dear me, it's *Sophie*, isn't it? I just love that girl."

"Uh...she was engaged to my brother," I say, scratching my chin. "I've never thought of her that way."

Dottie lifts her eyebrows, an amused expression forming on her face. "But you don't think of her as family, do you?"

"No, but that doesn't mean I want to...you know...date her or whatever."

"Give yourself time, dear boy."

I decide not to get into a circular argument that could last hours, so instead I pull out my credit card and give her the information.

Before I leave, she points to the ice pack I'm still holding. "When the ice melts, pour it into a teacup. Then slowly drain it until you're left with the dregs. Rotate the cup three times clockwise, and then gently tip it over to drain the rest of the liquid. Send me a picture of what you're left with in the bottom of the cup, will you?"

She scrawls her number down on the back of a Tea of Fortune business card.

I'm about to walk away with it when she surprises me by wrapping her hand around my wrist. I meet her gaze, her eyes a piercing light blue, and she says, "Everything happens for a reason. You remember that."

Her words shock me into silence before I realize what should have been obvious. "You're talking about Jonah."

She gives me a kind smile. "I don't know. I only knew you needed to hear it. Now, wait here. There's something else you need."

It would be rude to peace out, but I really hope she's not going to come back with promotional materials for a cult.

I have to swallow a groan when she returns carrying a yellow stone that's two or three inches long.

"It's golden calcite, dear," she says, placing it in my palm and pressing my fingers around it. "It'll help bring you joy. That crystal's for you to keep, from my personal collection."

"I don't really believe in that—"

I manage to cut off *nonsense*.

"I'll believe for you," she says, which feels an awful lot like cult talk. But she's a nice old lady, so I slip it into my pocket.

"Thank you, Dottie," I say. "Have a nice afternoon."

I can feel it adding weight to my jeans pocket.

"You too, my dear. You too. Remember what I said now."

My prickly side wants to ask her if she's talking about her attempt to get me interested in my brother's girl or the magic rock that's supposed to make me happy. But I know when to smile and nod.

As I turn to leave, I find myself stealing another glance at Sophie. She's laughing, her hand slightly lifted over her mouth as if she can't believe the laughter spilling out of her. In that moment it's hard to look away from her. Her hair's a mess, but she's never looked better to me.

Hell, there's something to be said for the power of persuasion.

I shake my head, amused at myself.

My phone starts ringing before I'm more than two steps beyond the door. I'm not at all surprised when I see that it's my father.

I might have gotten to hit my kid brother, but here's his sucker punch for me.

CHAPTER FIVE

SOPHIE

"So we're going to destroy this asshole, right?" Hannah asks, cracking her knuckles.

Briar rotates her teacup on the tabletop, peering inside hopefully. Dottie and her staff are trained to read people's fortunes in their tea leaves, although it's a mystery what that training actually entails.

My aunt isn't religious but is a true believer in everything involving mysticism. She and Dottie are in a Wise Women Group that Dottie started here at the tea shop, and from what I can tell, they discuss things like energy imbalances and auras and karma. It's probably ironic for a woman who believes in bad luck and curses to doubt the efficacy of such things, but I do. Mostly because I've tried to reverse my luck nearly every way possible and gotten nowhere.

"He was two-timing all of us. We can't let him get away with that," Hannah continues, taking our silence for a lack of agreement. Which I suppose it is.

It felt good throwing that ring at Jonah's face, and I wouldn't mind throwing other things at him, but revenge seems like a slippery slope. I don't to find myself back at a police station.

"We didn't," Briar says. "I let Sophie into the brewery, and she told him off in front of my boss." Her expression darkens into a look of dejection. "He's going to be so pissed."

"You won't get fired," I say, even though I obviously have no control over that. "You don't have to tell anyone how I got in. I doubt anyone even noticed you were there. And if your boss does give you a hard time, then you can confirm Jonah is a cheating a-hole."

She sighs and slides the teacup a few inches away from her. "No way. I'm not supposed to date anyone who works with the brewery."

"Come work at Big Catch," Hannah says. "I'm the taproom manager. We always need help, and I don't care who people are sleeping with."

"Isn't Big Catch owned by one of those mega-conglomerates?" Briar asks, her face puckering.

"Yes, and that's why we always need help. No locals want to work with us." She waves a hand at me. "Or you can go work with your other new best friend, at Buchanan. Or one of the other five hundred breweries in town."

"Yeah, don't let that jerk push you around," I say, getting into the spirit of it.

Briar fiddles with her teacup and then glances up at us. "He's...well...this is embarrassing to admit, but he's my dad. This is his latest business venture. He never sticks with them for long, and he's getting ready to move on. My own business tanked, so I'm supposed to take over the brewery soon. My mom doesn't want anything to do with any of it. She's a 'serious' writer. That's what she calls herself, anyway. She thinks the beer thing is demeaning. She's trying to get him to open a writers' salon so she can make friends."

I can feel my bad luck pulling at me, trying to drive me into more verbal missteps. "Oh my God. I'm so sorry, Briar. He seems...uh...he makes really good beer."

"He doesn't make any of it," she says sadly. "That's all our brewmaster, and he's always on the verge of quitting. Because my father *is* an asshole. I'm just hoping he hangs on until Dad leaves."

"You can hire my brother, Liam, if he quits," Hannah says offhandedly. "He's a pain in the ass, and the brass at Big Catch are always threatening to fire him. But he's also really good at brewing beer." She pauses. "But are you sure you don't want to tell your dad you were banging Jonah? He'd probably crush him like a tin can."

Briar shakes her head as she makes another rotation with the teacup. "No. I mean, maybe he would, but it wouldn't be worth it. I'd never hear the end of it."

"If your father gives you any trouble at all," a sweet but sturdy voice says, "you would be more than welcome to come work here, my dear." Dottie emerges from behind a couple who were standing next to our table. How long has she been listening?

She slides into the now-empty seat beside me, which doesn't surprise me in the least.

When my great-aunt went on her big vacation, she asked Dottie to keep an eye on Otis and me, as if we were children in need of tending and not two mostly functional adults in our twenties. Dottie has taken that role seriously. She stops by to check on us a few times a week, sometimes with her life partner, Bear—a sweet man with apple cheeks who runs a bakery and always brings over almond croissants because I mentioned offhandedly that I think they taste like Paris.

"Now, girls," she says, "did I hear you correctly? The young man who was supposed to marry Sophie was secretly dating all of you?"

"And at least one more. Someone he listed as GingerBeer-Babe on his phone," I say. "But we don't know who she is yet."

"We could find out," Hannah says. "There's only one ginger beer brewery in town. All we have to do is go inside and put up a dartboard with Jonah's face on it. See who uses it. Bam, we've got our girl."

"You don't seem very upset," Briar says to Hannah, frowning as she weaves a loop of golden hair around her fingers. She looks like she's trying to strangle them.

"Now, dear," Dottie says. "I want you to remember we all deal with things differently. You're going through something awful, but I have to say I agree with this young woman here."

She nods to Hannah, who introduces herself. If she's fazed by Dottie joining our table without invitation, it doesn't show.

"Oh, what a lovely name," Dottie says, reaching over and patting her hand. "Yes, Hannah made a good point. If you don't teach this young man a lesson, I'm afraid he's likely to repeat his mistakes again and again. He'll never become his best self, and goodness knows where it might lead for everyone else. We already have gonorrhea in the French Broad River."

I flinch. It occurs to me that I'm going to have to get tested for STDs. For all I know, Jonah's been fornicating *in* the French Broad River, double-exposing himself—and thus me, Briar, Hannah, and GingerBeerBabe—to contagion.

Hannah gives me a slight nod as if reading my mind. "We'll go together. All of us."

"The young rake must be exposed for what he's done, of course," Dottie continues. "But I dare say that won't be enough. He needs to know his behavior is deeply *unacceptable*. That punch in the face was well and good, but I suspect it won't teach him anything beyond a moment of humility in the face of a stronger specimen."

"What do you suggest?" I ask, grateful for the distraction.

After I leave this place, I'm going to start struggling. Shock and anger have carried me this far, but I can feel something dark oozing beneath them, threatening to suck me under.

It helps that I'm not dealing with this alone. I trusted the wrong person, but so did Briar, Hannah, and GingerBeerBabe. We made the same mistake, which means it must have been a reasonable one.

Dottie taps her bottom lip. "Once you get in touch with this fourth woman, you should confront him—in a public place, of course. He needs to face up to what he's done."

"Oh, I don't know if that's a good idea," I mutter.

"He'll never learn if you don't teach him," Dottie reminds me, tapping the table with her finger. "And he'll pull other innocent women into his depravity. They always do, dear. But if you teach him a lesson, you'll be helping him *and* those other women. Now, drink up. I'll read your leaves for you when you're done."

She rises from her seat. "That wonderful young man who was here earlier insisted on paying your bill. For every man who needs a lesson, there's a fine young buck who doesn't have to be led to water to drink."

With this, she winks and leaves.

"Do you think she just made an oral sex joke?" Hannah asks, smiling at Dottie's back. "I like her."

I give her a half laugh, murmuring, "So do I."

But my mind is stuck on what Dottie said—*Rob* arranged to pay our bill?

Surprise bubbles up inside me, chased by regret. I let Jonah shape my opinion about Rob as surely as if my thoughts were clay. He convinced me his brother was a deadbeat loser. And, sure, maybe Rob is a deadbeat—I truly have no idea what he does other than play with the garbage band—but he's not a loser.

He's *interesting*, and he cares about other people in a way Jonah is clearly not capable of.

What other horrible ideas has Jonah infected me with?

I clear my throat. "You know, Jonah never wanted to go to any breweries with me. He said it made him think of work, and he wanted to keep his home life and work life separate. He spent so much time traveling, working nights and weekends...I figured it made sense. But now..."

Hannah laughs through her nose. "He didn't want us comparing notes. Which means that's exactly what we should be doing. So what's the worst thing about him? You go first, Sophie."

My mind whirls, sifting through every little grievance I've stowed away like bugs in a spiderweb. "Uh...he'd say he didn't care about something, like where we went out to eat, or what favors we were going to give away at the wedding, and then he'd let me spin my wheels for hours, only for him to choose something completely different. Oh crap..." I bury my face in my hands, spearing my fingers through my hair. It was in a neat ponytail a couple of hours ago. It's an unholy mess now, and I honestly don't care. "I forgot about the wedding. I have so many arrangements to cancel."

"We'll help you."

I look up, surprised, because it was Briar who made the offer, her voice quavering.

"This isn't your fault, Briar. You don't owe me anything. He hurt you, too."

"I know," she says, still playing with her gorgeous hair. "But I want to help. Jonah *never* wants to help. He walked past an old woman lugging a stack of boxes into the post office, and he didn't even offer to hold the door for her. Not until I asked him to. That's when I should have known, but I made excuses for him. I told myself he mustn't have noticed."

A burst of air escapes me, not quite a laugh. "I know what that's like. I really wanted to believe he was what he seemed to be. So I ignored any evidence that he wasn't."

"What he is," Hannah says, setting down her tea, "is a bad kisser. Like seriously bad. We should all count ourselves lucky for escaping him. GingerBeerBabe too, if she has indeed escaped him."

I hug myself, worried for this woman I've never met. "I hope he didn't bamboozle her."

Briar smiles at me. "I haven't heard that word since I was a little girl. I like the way you talk. You called Jonah an ignoramus earlier."

"And I like your hair," I say. "You remind me of Rapunzel." A sigh seeps out, and because I'm still feeling the influence of one and a half high-gravity beers on a mostly empty stomach, I find myself saying, "You know, you're both stupidly hot. I don't understand why Jonah asked me to marry him in the first place. He's successful. Good looking. I work in a taproom and shop at big-box stores. I've never understood makeup...like, I bought a tube of lipstick at this makeup counter because the clerk promised it would change my life, and it was the same color as my lips. What's the point?"

Hannah, who was sipping her tea again, plunks her cup down so forcefully the bottom clinks on the wood table. Her expression is fierce. "You stop that, right now. We *all* work in breweries, and there's nothing wrong with that. I'm sure you have your own hopes and dreams. You're going to get them someday, but it won't be by stepping all over other people. Because you're not an asshole. And you're *also* stupidly hot, by the way. He's just stupid. But if you ever want to learn about makeup, I'll help you."

"Really?"

"Absolutely. I studied to be a makeup artist before I fell into the whole customer service thing. You need the perfect red lipstick. Every woman does." She glances at Briar. "You too, Rapunzel. I'll hook you both up."

Briar finally drops the lock of hair she's been messing with. She smiles at Hannah, then looks at me. "She's right. You're beautiful, Sophie. Your aura is too."

"You can see auras?" I ask, wondering if I believe her.

"I can't see them." She pats her hand on her very full chest. "But I can feel them. I felt yours the moment I met you."

"Not to be a naysayer," Hannah says, "but if that's true, why didn't you pick up on Jonah's aura?"

"You really know how to ruin a moment," Briar says, but she's smiling. Hannah and I both start laughing. It feels *good*. Maybe it's a just-for-now good, and later I'll slide back into that darker, oozier place. But I'm happy right now, and that's what matters.

"I like you both a lot," I say. "Isn't that funny? We all have terrible taste in men, but Jonah has fantastic taste in women. That's his silver lining."

"Maybe everything really does happen for a reason," Briar says, finishing her tea. "What if we were only drawn to him because he was supposed to bring us together?"

"An interesting theory," Hannah says as I lift my tea to finish it. "But it would have been a lot less traumatizing if we'd met after joining the same book club."

"But then no one would know the truth about Jonah," I say, setting my cup down. "What do you think about what Dottie said? I don't think I'm prepared to plan some sort of grand revenge."

Briar gives me a sympathetic look. "I'll bet it was exhausting planning the wedding."

"Actually, I had to let Jonah and his mother plan the whole thing. They sort of insisted on it."

Hannah snorts. "New idea. If they insisted on planning it, they can unplan it. We can make much better use of our time than doing their dirty work for them."

"You're right," I say, even though the idea brings on a wave of panic. No one likes it when other people give them work, and Mrs. Price only tolerates me because I let her have her way all the time. But it doesn't matter anymore. I no longer have anyone to impress. It's over.

It's over.

That thought pushes me closer to the sadness ooze, but I'm surprised by a feeling of...relief. I never really believed Jonah was mine forever. It always felt like I was on the verge of doing or saying something that would push him away.

"So are we confronting him?" Hannah asks. "How do we want to do it?"

"I don't know," Briar says, fidgeting with her hair again. "I try not to hold onto negativity. Besides, why would he agree to meet with us? If he gets his phone's data transferred onto a new device, he'll see the messages we exchanged. He'll know that his secret is fully out."

"GingerBeerBabe never responded," I point out. "Anyway, don't you think he's going to try to smooth this over with at least one of us? He obviously doesn't enjoy being alone if he has four girlfriends."

"He'll try to smooth it over with *you*," Briar says, almost sadly. "You're the one he wanted to marry."

She likely didn't say that to spike my anxiety, but my heart starts racing.

"I threw my engagement ring at his face. I shouted at him in front of your dad. You don't think he'll take that as a sign?"

Briar glides her hand over mine. "I think he's a man who's used to getting what he wants, regardless of what other people think about it. That's why he's so good at what he does."

The alarm on my phone goes off, reminding me I'm supposed to be at work in fifteen minutes. I stare at it in consternation. "I don't think I can go to work today. I'm a little tipsy."

"We should all call in sick," Hannah says.

Briar surprises me by agreeing. "You're right. My dad can't yell at me if I'm not there."

He can still do it later, but I won't burst her bubble. I understand the need for a silver lining.

I'm going to have to find a new one in this mess.

"Let's," I say.

Seconds later, before any of us have the chance to call in sick, Dottie bustles up to the table.

"Oh, delightful," she says, clapping her hands together. "You've finished your tea."

Without asking, she pushes in next to me again, bringing a scent of fresh lavender. "Who would like to go first?"

Briar glances at me with a glimmer of unease in her eyes, and I smile at her before saying, "Maybe we should push them all into a row."

We line up our cups, mine first, then Briar's, then Hannah's.

Dottie gets to work, rotating the cups, draining the excess liquid and then flipping them back over. Briar watches her as if she's performing emergency surgery; Hannah looks like she's rubbernecking. I'm studying them *and* her.

Finally, Dottie looks back up at us, beaming. "You all have the same symbol in your cups, in the same place. This very rarely happens."

"What does it look like?" Briar asks, on the hook.

"A dog at the top of your cup is a symbol of friendship."

I glance into the cups, a little dubious. The blobs just look like clumps of leaves to me. Admittedly, they each have a small clump attached to a larger clump, which could—with liberal imagination—be a dog.

"You are at the beginning of a beautiful friendship." She glances between each of us. "That's what you must remember, my dears. This is a beginning, not an end. You may not be marrying that young man, Sophie, but you're creating a much more important bond. With yourself and these other delightful women. All of you are. This is *your* time, my dears. Be happy for it. Paint and be young and make beautiful mistakes so you can learn from them. Oh, I'm excited for you. This is your opportunity to do everything you never thought you could. And you'll have each other for support, just like my Wise Women Group."

It's foolish to think she's professed words that are going to change my life, but that tingle traveling down my spine says otherwise.

"You know..." Dottie says slowly. "I usually don't read my own leaves, but this morning, I felt the urge to look. What do you think I saw in there?"

"Some damp leaves?" Hannah says with a smile.

"Yes," Dottie says with enthusiasm. "And they were in the very same shape and alignment as yours. I *knew* it was going to be a special day. I'm going to help you, my girls. We're going to forge ahead together. It's written in the stars."

"What do we do?" Briar asks, her voice full of the same uncertainty I feel.

"First," Dottie says, prompting me to lean forward slightly, as if all the mysteries of the world are about to be revealed. "First, and I feel this strongly, we need to get very drunk."

CHAPTER SIX

ROB

"Pass the potatoes, you thug," my stepmother says in her best ice queen voice. She's sitting at one end of the table, her stark blond hair combed back from her face, dressed all in black, no doubt mourning my presence. My father sits at the other end. He looks tired. He *always* looks tired at family dinners, and yet he's the one who insists on them.

My brother sits directly across from me, his eyes still surrounded by the remnants of yellow bruises covered with concealer. Maybe his mother did it for him—or one of his many girlfriends. I'm reasonably sure it wasn't Sophie.

It's Friday, exactly two weeks since the nose-punching incident.

Two weeks since I texted a photo of my chamomile leaves to Dottie Hendrickson, for reasons I can't put into words.

She texted back within five minutes:

Ooh, how interesting.

When she failed to follow up on that, I realized it was my turn to comment or question, and decided I'd rather not. Having a long, extended conversation with a woman who'd spouted mysticism and given me a phallic rock was beyond my current capacity.

Still. I would sooner die than admit this to anyone, but I've been carrying around the rock, moving it from the pocket of one pair of pants to the next so I always have it with me. It would feel like bad luck not to, especially since my home visit is coming up this week.

I dropped by the store where Emil works last night, and he didn't look good. He had circles under his eyes, and he admitted he was suffering from not being able to play. *I can't sleep, man.*

A lot of people don't understand that playing music isn't a hobby for a musician. It's a need. Especially for a kid who needs an outlet that won't hurt him or draw him into dangerous situations.

I've figured out a work-around—I bring a couple of guitars to the park on Saturday and Sunday mornings, when he's supposed to walk his foster parents' dog. But it's not enough. His needs aren't being met.

I shouldn't have told him what I was up to, but that look on his face broke me. I told him I was trying to get him out of that place for good. The kid practically teared up, and now I have a new sense of purpose: I can't do anything that might result in my application being denied.

My stepmother wanted to have me arrested for hitting Jonah. Thankfully, my father talked her out of calling the cops. She didn't back down out of any goodwill toward me, mind you, but because he pointed out it would create more family drama than anyone feels like dealing with. Jonah actually backed him up.

So here I am, gritting my teeth and playing nice.

"The potatoes," my stepmother prompts coldly, enunciating it carefully as if I'm too stupid to understand.

"I'd be delighted to be of service, Patricia," I say, passing her the dish of scalloped potatoes made by their poorly compensated cook.

She takes the dish but doesn't serve herself any potatoes before setting it down.

"Are you proud of what you did to your brother?" she asks, her dark eyes boring into me.

"Not particularly," I say. "But I'm not un-proud of it."

"Do you know he's had to go to meetings like this?" she asks shrilly, pointing at his face. The bruises are barely distinguishable at this point, but you'd think she's holding a smoking gun from the way she's talking.

"And I had to cancel one of my band's performances. We've all made sacrifices for Jonah's dick."

Jonah swears under his breath. "I swear to Christ, Rob. It's none of your business what goes on between me and my fiancée."

"Last I heard she was your *ex*-fiancée," I counter. "And you made it my business when you asked me to get your phone from her."

"It was a misunderstanding," my stepmother says primly. "It's unfortunate that we had to postpone the wedding, but I'm confident they'll clear everything up in time. It's not Jonah's fault that he has other young women interested in him. You might have more luck finding a steady girlfriend if you got a real job."

"How's your job treating you, Patricia?"

My father clears his throat, and I decide it's time for me to end this farce. I fold my napkin and place it beside my nearly untouched plate of food.

"Thanks for dinner," I say, pushing back my chair. "It was—"

"I have a plan for getting Sophie back," Jonah insists in a

tight voice, saving me from spouting a platitude I certainly wouldn't have meant.

"Why not just leave her alone?"

As far as I know, he hasn't seen Sophie since their show-down at Silver Star. The last time I saw her was the Sunday following the phone incident. I'd stopped by her aunt's house to give her a CD I'd burned for her. Yeah, a CD. Which was obviously a mistake, because she admitted she only has a CD player in her car. I had no business bringing Jonah's ex-fiancée gifts anyway, except I can't stop watching that video of her tossing the ring at him. I've memorized all of the details, including the look of disbelief on my brother's face. But my favorite part is the way Sophie changes on camera, transforming from a woman who always says yes to one who doesn't take shit from anyone.

That's what I was thinking of when I chose the songs for her CD. They were angry, mostly, meant to pump her up and keep her feeling strong. The worst thing that could happen is for her to go back to him.

I'm certain he's texted and called her, but if he'd made any headway, he would have said so.

Truth is, I'm glad to have gotten Sophie wrong, and not only because it's driving Jonah crazy that he's not getting what he wants. That's probably the real reason why he's hatched some half-assed scheme to charm her.

"She's my fiancée," he says tightly. "I'm not going to let a misunderstanding get in the way. I should never have texted those women and given them the wrong idea. That was my mistake. But they've obviously filled her head with lies."

I know he's full of it, *he* knows he's full of it, and my father undoubtedly knows the score too. But Jonah's mother would take his word for it if he said the Earth was as flat as a pancake. Hell, she'd tell him what a good boy he was as he drove them toward the nonexistent drop-off.

"What are you going to do?" I ask.

I half expect him to say *wouldn't you like to know?* But he actually answers.

"I'm going to make a grand gesture," he says. "At Buchanan Brewery."

I bristle at the thought. The Sophie on that video would have told him to go screw himself, but I have no idea what's happened to her since. What if she's been crying into her soup? What if she's close enough to cracking that Jonah showing up with an armful of red flowers and a mouthful of lies would convince her to accept the ring she threw at him?

I can't stand the thought. It would be impossible to look her in the eye ever again, because I'd know...

There's a fire inside of her, and she'd be smothering it to become my brother's compliant little wife.

Unease makes the back of my neck itch.

"Sounds romantic," my stepmother says, and it takes me a second to realize she's talking about Jonah's terrible grand gesture idea.

"Really?" I say. "I think it sounds a lot like stalking."

"Robert," my stepmother says in a harsh tone.

"*Patricia.* I thought you'd like some advice on how to keep your darling son out of the slammer."

She gives me a withering look, her lips squeezed into such a tight line there are little cracks running through them. "We certainly don't need advice from a delinquent like *you.*"

I got charged with public intoxication once, when I was in my early twenties, but it was dropped. She acts like I tried to bulldoze a group of nuns.

"Actually," Jonah says, apparently oblivious to every single thing that's been said since he last spoke, "I was hoping you'd help me, Rob."

A strangled laugh spills out of me. "Are you fucking serious?"

"Rob," my father warns.

"Sorry," I reply, my gaze still on my brother. My knee has started jiggling under the table. "*Are you serious?* The last time you asked for my help, you lied about what I'd be helping you with."

"So...this time you'd know everything. I was hoping you'd, you know, serenade her. I want to do something really romantic."

The injustice of this makes my ears burn, but I set my jaw and fist my hands, waiting for the worst of the anger to pass.

"No," I say flatly. "Travis and Bixby won't do it either, so don't ask them."

"I told you it was all a big misunderstanding. It was inappropriate for me to be texting other women, sure, but I wasn't cheating," he insists. "You punched me in the face for something I didn't do. The least you could do is help me fix this."

"No."

"I'll pay you."

"No amount of money could compel me."

Patricia apparently finds my last comment amusing, but I don't look away from Jonah. If I can't hit him again, I can at least tell him silently what I think of him.

My father clears his throat, and I'm embarrassed that I turn toward him with the rest of them, all of us recognizing who's in charge. "That's enough of that. Jonah, I expect you to make this right. Rob, you're not a teenager. Stop acting like one."

I've never wanted to throw a bread roll more in my life. But I'd prefer to leave than stay and argue. My father did me a favor; in return, I put in an appearance. Done and done. The sooner he realizes Jonah, Patricia, and I are never going to be friends, the better.

"You're right," I say tightly. "But I do have to leave." I force myself to glance at Patricia. "Thank you for dinner. It's been pleasant, as always."

She nods primly, her eyes full of her victory, and I've never been happier to leave a place.

I spent most of my childhood in this big, echoey house with its pillars and sculpted gardens—when I wasn't bouncing from one apartment to another with my mother—but it never felt like mine. The moment Patricia moved in, already pregnant, I became the visitor.

I'm in the car, on the way to my apartment, when I find myself driving to another house in the Montford neighborhood —old and blue, with windows that are likely older than my deceased grandparents.

I park on the street outside, feeling like a hypocrite. I just got done calling Jonah a stalker for planning to show up at Buchanan Brewery, but here I am outside her home. Isn't that ten times worse?

I don't have her phone number, though, and it would be wrong to let her find out about my little brother's grand gesture when he shows up at her place of work with a string orchestra. Because I doubt he's going to let my refusal stop him. He'll prob-ably hire an opera singer to deliver an aria while he throws roses at Sophie or jumps out of a cake, and the scene will end up on a dozen tourists' camera phones.

Maybe it'll be enough to pressure her into giving him a second chance.

The thought is brutal enough to propel me out of the car, even though I still don't know what I'm going to say. I find myself reaching into my pocket for the stone. My fingers wrap around it and squeeze.

When I get to the door, I knock twice on the worn wood. It swings open, revealing none other than Dottie Hendrickson.

She's wearing a fancier dress today—silver with sequins—and a flower tucked into her hair.

"Oh good," she says, beaming at my stupefied face. "You're just in time, dear. We're about to get started."

I glance inside, taking in the sight of Otis on the couch, dressed in a T-shirt with a tuxedo design and a pair of khakis. Hannah is with him, in a green dress, and they're drinking from flutes of what looks like champagne.

Otis grins and lifts his free hand. "Hey, man."

I suddenly, and absurdly, feel underdressed.

The floor is covered with a red satin cloth, and flower arrangements are strategically stationed around the living room, along with paper lanterns filled with lit tea lights.

"Uh..."

Sophie emerges into the living area wearing a fitted off-white dress with a flowing skirt.

My first thought is *wow*. Her hair is loose over her shoulders in soft brown waves, and she's wearing a shade of red lipstick that highlights the shape of her lips and brings out the deep blue of her eyes. The dress hugs her chest and hips, compelling attention to every dip and curve of her body.

She's a knockout. A perfect ten. An impossible twenty. No one would look at her and think Pollyanna, because they'd be too busy gaping.

My second thought is *what the hell?*

Because it's a wedding dress. Presumably the one she bought to marry my brother.

"Shall we begin?" Dottie asks with bright eyes.

CHAPTER SEVEN

SOPHIE

Rob Price is standing just inside the front door of my house in a band T-shirt and worn jeans again. It's like someone magically rewound the last two weeks out of existence. Except I wasn't at all happy to see him on my doorstep two weeks ago, and I *am* happy to see him today.

It felt like a bond formed between Rob and me the day of the great phone-off, and then Dottie called me the following day to say Rob's tea leaves had formed the same shape she'd seen in our four cups. Admittedly, his leaves weren't from actual tea, and tea-leaf reading isn't exactly a science, but it had felt *interesting*.

Then he came over with that CD two days later. To be honest, I've sat in my car listening to it for long stretches of time. So long that Otis once knocked on my window to tell me he'd read up about carbon monoxide poisoning and would be "keeping an eye" on me.

I'd informed him that was only a concern if the car was kept in an enclosed space with the engine running, and Aunt Penny's house had no garage, but he'd still looked worried.

It was the music that kept me in there, though. The songs

he'd chosen spoke to my angry, hurt soul, which was trying to piece itself back together.

I'd thought about reaching out to him, if for no other reason than to thank him, but I would have needed to ask Dottie for his phone number. Something she probably would have taken the wrong way.

But now he's here, like I'd manifested him.

"Hi," I say, smiling at Rob. "I've been thinking about you."

There's a confused, wary look in his golden eyes, which is when it hits me...

Oh, crap. I'm wearing a wedding dress. He must think I've gone full Miss Havisham, the jilted bride wearing her wedding dress continually until it's brown, moth-eaten, and full of holes.

I lift my hands in a pathetic and futile attempt to hide the dress he's already seen.

"I haven't been running around in my wedding dress crying," I say. "Or wearing it at all. This is an aberration. I mean, there have been some low moments, I'm not going to lie."

Otis nods silently, grimacing. I don't blame him. The other day, I cut up a bunch of photos and then accidentally got the shreds all over the kitchen floor. Another time, he walked in on me when I was crying while eating an entire pint of ice cream with a fork.

I didn't love Jonah, because I'd never really known him, but I still mourned the loss of Fake Jonah. Learning the truth about him had felt like losing the last of my innocence, and it was hard to face the world without it.

I force a smile. "But yeah...this isn't a cry for help. It's just..."

"She sunk all of her savings into that beautiful disaster, and she can't return it because she had to get it tailored," Hannah summarizes, lifting her champagne glass. "So we figured if she's only going to be able to sell it for a fourth of its value, she might as well get to wear it once."

"What she said." I point to Hannah, hopeful no one will mention the rest of the plan for the evening.

"And she's going to marry herself tonight," Dottie says with warm enthusiasm. She waves to indicate the setup we jokingly threw together with a few cheap grocery store bouquets, my crafting materials, and the big sheet of red satin material Briar had from a Christmas event at Silver Star last year. "We're so glad you arrived in time to witness it. Our poor Briar got called into work, but she insisted we push ahead."

Darn it. I didn't want him to know that.

Still, it's impossible to be mad at Dottie Hendrickson.

I *love* Dottie. After our afternoon at Tea of Fortune two weeks ago, she drove Hannah, Briar, and me back to my house and helped me break the news to Aunt Penny over FaceTime. That proved unnecessary because Otis had already told her everything. She was thrilled I'd finally realized Jonah was an ignoramus and insisted our little group should drink the peach schnapps she kept for special occasions.

It tasted like perfume, but we drank it anyway; it made it feel like she was there. Hannah, Briar, and I also shared our stories. Well, parts of them. I don't like telling anyone about my past. Aunt Penny knows, of course, and so does Otis. But even though Otis is usually more like a slice of Alpine Lace Swiss than a steel vault, he knows better than to talk about *that*.

Hannah has an older brother and a much younger brother. Her mom left a few months after her little brother was born, and they were raised by a single dad, who had taught them all how to brew beer by the time they were thirteen.

"Isn't it illegal for minors to brew beer?" I asked.

But Dottie had harrumphed and poured herself another shot of the terrible schnapps. "My nephew learned when he was a teenager too, and now he's the head brewer at Buchanan. Sometimes children are prodigies."

I wasn't sure I believed that, but there was no denying both Dottie's nephew and Hannah's brother were now brewmasters at two of the most successful breweries in the city.

Briar is an only child like I am. Her father had opened Silver Star a few years back, one of the many successful businesses he'd started, only to eventually abandon. She moved to Asheville last year to work under him after her handmade jewelry business went under. She seems to share her father's reticence toward technology, although she uses Etsy to sell her pieces.

Then there's Otis and me. Otis grew up here, graduated from Asheville High School, and has been waffling his way through dozens of odd jobs ever since. But he's twenty-one—waffling is expected.

I'm twenty-eight, I graduated from college six years ago, and I still haven't accomplished anything. My dream business is still just a dream.

I'd imagined leading messy, fun, immersive projects that parents would never want unleashed on their living rooms. I'd had a name for the business—The Crafty Monster—and I'd even purchased supplies and chosen a location. But the permits hadn't come through on time, and then my friend Lynn, who'd been all in to run the business with me, had gotten pregnant with twins.

She'd bowed out.

Then I'd moved to Asheville to help Aunt Penny, and that was that. My dream became hazy, the sort of dream you have at night but can barely remember in the morning.

I feel like I'm at a crossroads without a working compass. Which is why I'm glad Dottie has essentially appointed herself our life coach.

She's the one who came up with the idea of having a healing, symbolic wedding to myself.

I told her it was absolutely unnecessary, but when she takes a shine to an idea, it's hard to dissuade her. Especially since she convinced my friends to agree with her. Briar thought it was an "inspired" idea, but Briar also has a Siamese cat and sings in the shower. She makes jewelry from rocks she finds and tumbles. *Of course* she thought it was a good idea. I'd thought for sure Hannah would back me up, but no, she thought it was hilarious and had insisted she was going to bring me out for drinks afterward in my wedding dress.

In desperation, I appealed to Otis for help, but he'd fallen desperately in love with Briar the moment he met her, so of course he sided with everyone else.

Dottie insisted they wanted to celebrate me, the way we were supposed to on my wedding day, and it would have felt ungrateful to deny her. And I *love* arts and crafts. It had hurt to surrender all of the preparations for my wedding to Patricia. So I'd enjoyed making the lanterns and rearranging the bouquets. It had felt like a harmless distraction, a creative outlet I'd been longing for, and I also really wanted to wear the dress, dammit.

Now, though, with Rob Price grinning at me in that knowing way, I *really* wish I'd put a stop to this ridiculousness. Especially since Briar's not even here. Her dad had sensed she had plans and called her in to do inventory as punishment.

Rob sticks his hands in his back pockets, revealing another inch or two of his biceps.

"Do you want some champagne?" Hannah asks, startling me. I try to pretend I wasn't just staring at Rob's muscles. "We're going to eat cupcakes afterward. You in?"

He's still standing by the door. There's an inscrutable smile on his face, and I can't figure out whether he's going to stay or duck out into the obscurity of night. Please let him duck out.

His grin widens. "Wouldn't miss it, but I'm not really dressed for a wedding."

"There's no official dress code," Hannah says. "This is an informal ritual..." She pauses dramatically and gives us a wicked grin. "Until the blood sacrifice, of course." Then she gets up and disappears into the kitchen, possibly to get him champagne, possibly to grab a butcher knife. She likes to keep the mystery alive.

Rob rubs the back of his neck again, giving me another tease of his bicep, and walks a couple of steps inside.

"There now," Dottie says with a beatific smile as she waves him forward. "That's the right direction. Come right in, dear. We won't bite."

"Speak for yourself," Hannah calls from the kitchen.

"We could go play Xbox," Otis offers, pointing his thumb over his shoulder. "I have a pretty sick setup in my bedroom."

"Oh, quit trying to get Rob up to your room," Hannah says, returning with her champagne flute refilled and one for Rob. He immediately sets it down on the coffee table.

"I wasn't," Otis says, blushing. He gestures to the satin floor covering, the flowers, and the paper art. "It just seems like...you know. There's a lot of feminine energy in this room."

"There's nothing to worry about, dear," Dottie says with sweet sincerity. "Being exposed to feminine energy won't shrink your testes. If it did, my poor Bear wouldn't be nearly so potent in the bedroom."

Otis looks like he'd like to disappear into the couch, but he settles for draining his champagne flute, then looks hopefully at Hannah, who crosses her arms and stares him down, despite being so short he's practically taller than her sitting.

He sighs and gets up. "Would anyone like anything from the kitchen?"

Shock nearly freezes me solid. Otis never volunteers to do chores.

"Yes, dear," Dottie says, beaming at him. "I'd love to wet my whistle with a little of that schnapps from the other day."

I can feel Rob watching me, and another thrum of self-consciousness works through me. No, no way. I can't possibly go through with this silly ceremony if he's here. He'll think it's another instance of me being a Pollyanna. *My fiancé was cheating, but that's okay, I'll befriend his girlfriends and marry myself.*

Oh. My. God. Is he *right?*

"Hey, actually, I need a second alone with Rob," I say.

"*Of course*, dear," Dottie replies. "You two take all the time you need. I understand what it's like to have cold feet before a wedding."

Hannah guffaws.

Rob makes a sound in his throat that sounds suspiciously like stifled laughter.

It would seem impolite to ask Dottie and Hannah to make themselves scarce, especially since it's my house, so I lead Rob up the stairs and into my bedroom.

When I close the door behind him, he looks even more baffled than when he first saw me in my wedding dress.

"Oh my God," I blurt. "This isn't...I'm not trying to, like, seduce you by bringing you in here. I just wanted to beg you to please leave."

He laughs, his eyes crinkling at the corners, and I feel something completely unexpected—a fluttering sensation in my belly. My exposed skin tingles with heightened sensitivity, as if the temperature in the room just changed.

I'm attracted to Jonah's brother.

Jonah's *brother.*

Oh, this is bad.

"You've taken this truth-telling thing to another level," he says, rubbing his impeccably stubbled jaw.

I gulp, completely unmoored by my sudden awareness of him.

"Sorry," I manage.

He raises his eyebrows, his mouth twitching with amusement.

"Fine. I'm not sorry. But I can't possibly do this if you're here. You've got to understand that."

Something unexpected flickers in his eyes—hurt, maybe—and he shoves his hands into his pockets. "Sure. Yeah. I get it. I know we never got along before. I guess I figured something had changed. But—"

I grab his arm before he can leave, and then drop it, because it's thick and firm, which is embarrassing for reasons I can't express. "It *did* change. But this is unbelievably embarrassing, and I'm only going through with it because I promised them. I convinced Dottie not to bring her partner, but Otis lives here, so I couldn't very well kick him out. Look, I know you must think this is further proof of me being some Pollyanna who tries to please everyone, and—"

"I don't think that," he says, touching my arm.

He probably didn't mean to, but his warm touch sends a jolt of awareness through me.

We're in here alone, behind a closed door, and it suddenly feels improper.

His fingers glance off my skin, and I'm watching his face now, riveted. His eyes gleam in the dim light of the room, his hair overgrown enough that it's brushing his eyebrows. "I don't think that," he repeats. "It's cool that you've been hanging out with Hannah and Briar. Not every woman would. You've taken something positive from a fucked-up situation. I actually admire that."

"Oh, lucky me," I scoff, "I've earned Rob Price's approval."

I'm not sure why I'm baiting him. He's being kind. It's just...

I've drifted into territory I don't understand in a boat made of cardboard, and I don't have a paddle. Besides, he brings something out in me, a side I buried years ago without any last rites.

His mouth tips up at the corners. "Yes, you have." He gestures to the framed ABBA poster in the corner, close to my reading chair. "And also my curiosity. I need to know why you have a framed poster of ABBA."

"There's nothing wrong with ABBA." I'm pretty sure he's teasing me. I'm guessing Rob's not an ABBA fan. The songs on his CD were all angsty, and one of them was a Garbage Fire original. I'll admit that I looked up a few others.

Okay, all the ones available on Spotify.

They're good, maybe even great, but their songs aren't exactly bangers. Otis calls them rage anthems. That's usually not my thing, but ABBA doesn't do as much for you when you're filled with righteous fury. I've found myself listening to a few of Rob's songs on repeat, not that I'd *ever* admit it. His voice is deep and gravelly, and when I play the music loudly, I can feel it thrumming through me like a second pulse.

I look away from him, feeling my cheeks heat. It doesn't help that I'm in this dress, a gift wrapped for a man who'll never open it. A man I absolutely and emphatically no longer want.

"No, but having a framed poster of them suggests a level of fandom I find interesting. There are several things about you I find interesting, Sophie. Including your perfect aim at engagement ring beer pong. So, yes, I'd like an invitation to your wedding, if you wouldn't mind terribly much." His almost-there smile slips, replaced by a serious expression. "But that's not why I came over here. I wanted to warn you that Jonah is planning something. A grand gesture at the brewery."

I groan. "Seriously?"

"Has he been texting you?" he asks, sounding pissed.

"Yeah, until I blocked him," I say, my jaw tensing as I

remember his wheedling messages. He'd thrown Hannah and Briar under the bus, calling them liars. Saying he'd never slept with anyone else, only flirted, because he'd gotten cold feet, which his buddies assured him was super normal.

Never mind that Hannah, Briar, and I had compared notes about him, and there was no way they were lying.

"Here's the thing about my brother," Rob says. "If you don't give him what he wants, he'll try harder. The challenge is what he cares about. If you give in, he'll—"

"You really think I'd forgive him after what he did?" I snap, straightening my spine. I think of all the times Rob has called me Pollyanna with a knowing smirk on his face.

"He can be persuasive," he says, shoving his hands into his back pockets again. Once again, his biceps are on display, but I'm not going to be distracted this time.

"I didn't know him the way I thought I did," I fume. "But you know what, Rob Price? He didn't know me either, and neither do *you*. Just because I give people the benefit of the doubt doesn't mean I'll let them walk all over me. I think you should leave now."

He takes a half step toward me, his eyes full of remorse and lined by a surprising profusion of eyelashes.

"Sophie, I'm sorry," he says, his voice a low rumble. But I steel myself against his apology, his eyelashes, and his presence in my room, my life.

For one thing, he's a Price. For another, he's always treated me like I'm as interesting as dry toast.

"You've taught me how much apologies are worth to you," I say firmly. "Why would they be any more valuable to me?"

"I really am sorry. I just didn't want him to embarrass you at work."

"Too late," I mutter. Because everyone knows the engagement is off. Even if they don't know why it's off, it's still mortifying. They've all been so *nice*. And whatever Rob thinks of me and my Pollyanna kindness, their attitude sometimes makes me want to screech at the top of my lungs—or do something truly unforgivable, like empty a pitcher of beer onto a rude customer.

He shifts on his feet. "I don't want to walk away with you pissed off."

I exhale so sharply it comes out as a snort. "You don't get to choose how I feel."

"I know that. I wouldn't want to. But it wouldn't feel right to leave like this."

"I thought you didn't care what anyone thinks of you?"

His eyes hold mine, and I see something flicker in them. "I never said that. You did. Everyone cares what someone thinks, Sophie. Including me. I care what you think."

I sniff in disbelief. "Right. You know what the second thing you said to me was?"

"I'm Rob?" he asks, a glimmer of amusement in his eyes.

"No, that was the first thing—and you didn't say a word to me for the rest of dinner. The second thing you said to me was at the next family dinner. You said, 'Oh, you're still around?' Like you couldn't believe it."

"Because you were nice. I hoped he'd leave you alone."

"But not because you liked me."

He falls silent, working his jaw. When he finally opens his mouth to speak, the "Bridal Chorus" blasts deafeningly from downstairs. For half a second I think he's the one singing it into existence. Then I realize my guests have gotten impatient.

I feel a fresh surge of self-consciousness, my cheeks flushing.

"Look. You can leave, stay. I don't care." I look away from him. "They need me, and *they're* my friends."

I don't glance back to see if he follows me out of the room. I walk down the hall and descend the stairs, collecting a bouquet from Hannah, who's waiting at the bottom.

Her eyes dancing, she asks, "Are you ready to make the only kind of commitment a woman should ever make, Soph?"

"I am."

I step into the living room, where Dottie is waiting for me with a loving smile. Otis, who's back on the couch, burps loudly. He has his phone out and is recording this disaster.

"I think you mean *I do*," Dottie says, her eyes sparkling.

CHAPTER EIGHT

ROB

Sophie may have relented at the last minute, but she made it pretty clear that she wants me to leave.

I follow her out of the room, fully intending to make my way to and then through the front door, but I'm riveted by the way she's moving, the intention and resolve carrying her down the stairs, her shoulders primly set back. It has nothing to do with the long slope of her neck, revealed by the dress's sweeping open back, or the way the fabric is gathered just above her perfectly rounded ass, but once I've noticed those things it's hard to unnotice them.

I barely register that I'm passing Hannah before she stops me with a palm to my chest. I jolt to a stop, my eyes finding hers.

"She's the bride *and* the groom," Hannah says, looking amused. "If you're staying, you can sit on the couch. No crashing the proceedings or offering yourself up as tribute."

I feel my ears burning. "I was only—"

Following her like a kid chasing an ice cream truck.

I don't bother to finish the sentence. I just go over and join Otis on the couch. Because even if Sophie still wants me to leave, I'm not sure I can. My mind feels messy and confused, and the only not-confusing thought is that I want to see how this plays out.

Sophie doesn't glance back at me even once as she comes to a stop in front of Dottie, who's holding a crown made of woven flowers. But Sophie turns slightly, and I can see her profile, her hair tumbling around her face, cupping it in soft waves. The red lipstick that reminds me of a target: *kiss here.*

I shake my head at myself.

Otis murmurs, "I know, man. I know."

But he doesn't. I don't either. All I know is I can't look away.

He nods to the champagne Hannah brought out for me earlier, but I shake my head, my gaze still glued on Sophie.

"Oh, my dear girl," Dottie says, pressing her palms together. "I'm so honored to be here to conduct this ceremony. Self-love, when taken to an extreme, is an ugly thing, but we must accept and love ourselves if we're going to properly love our friends and neighbors." She gives Sophie a warm smile. "You, my dear, are making an important pact today. Do you, Sophie Ginnis, vow to love yourself?"

Sophie hesitates, like she's unsettled by this generic promise.

Again, my curiosity is stirred. Who *is* this woman?

Then she clears her throat and says, "I do."

"And do you vow to be true to yourself from this day forward?"

Again, there's a heavy pause as Sophie considers this standard aphorism with more intensity than it deserves. Finally, she nods. "I do. I will."

Dottie beams at her. "And will you, Sophie, support yourself through all of life's bumps and upsets with the dignity and respect we all owe ourselves?"

To my shock, Sophie's eyes look like they're shining as she nods. "I'll try," she stammers, then adds more firmly, "I will."

"Oh, my dear, dear girl. You don't know how happy I am to

hear you say that. I hope you chase after life's experiences and suck them down like nectar. All of them. And now, by the power vested in me by myself, I declare you your own life partner." She places the circlet of flowers on Sophie's head, and something in my chest melts.

Fuck me. It's so...*wholesome*. They're both emotional, and Sophie doesn't look quite real, dressed in that perfect gown that's shaped for her body, with a diadem of flowers resting on her thick, wavy hair. It's a travesty of justice that she usually leaves her hair up. It would have been a crime against humanity if she'd married my brother.

He never would have appreciated her.

He never would have seen her vulnerability as beautiful— only as convenient.

"Well, that was weird," Otis mutters as he lowers his smartphone and downs the rest of his champagne. "Can we go to the bar now?"

Hannah, who's been standing beside the couch, swats him lightly with her palm. "Have some respect."

I'd say something, but I can't talk. My mouth is too dry. I should probably leave, I know that, and yet...

"Here," Hannah says, handing me something. I take it without registering what it is, then look down and see a key chain—a circlet of dried flowers in resin.

"What is this?"

"Party favor," she says with a lift of her eyebrows. "Mrs. and Mrs. Ginnis made them. The paper lanterns too. She's shockingly crafty."

That's when the truth hits me like a stack of bricks. The guitar strap she gave me for Christmas...

She hadn't bought it off some vendor. She'd made it for me herself.

Dammit. I'm pretty sure I blew it off with an insincere

thank-you before shoving it into the back of my closet. I'd seen the gift as an offering from a woman who thrives on fulfilling obligations, but it was more thoughtful than I'd given her credit for. Way more so than the grocery store flowers I'd picked up for her and Patricia, who'd accepted hers with a sniff and almost certainly thrown them away before lunch.

"Wow," I manage, eloquence itself, running my finger over the key chain before pocketing it. "That's pretty damn impressive."

"Right?" Hannah asks with a wink. "If she hadn't already snapped herself up, I'd marry her."

I get up, possibly to leave, but Sophie approaches me, that flower diadem still positioned across her forehead.

She parts her lips, and I feel—

Well, I feel things you definitely aren't supposed to feel about a woman who was almost your sister-in-law.

"It wasn't that bad, was it?" she asks.

"It was beautiful," Dottie says, walking up behind her. "I'm sure everyone here will remember it always."

Otis mumbles something disparaging, but he doesn't seem like he genuinely minds much.

"I thought it was going to be dumb," I admit, surprised when Hannah's the only one who scowls at me. "But it wasn't. I wish my dad had done that instead of marrying his second wife. But if he had, I guess none of us would be here right now."

Hannah bustles out of the room, heading back toward the kitchen with purpose, and Dottie smiles at me. "I certainly wish I'd done that rather than marry my ex-husband. But I've had two great loves since, and I never would have met them if I hadn't suffered through that marriage. If we don't go through hardship, we don't have the wisdom to appreciate true happiness."

"That sounds like a crock," Hannah says, reappearing with a

plate of cupcakes. There's a little cake topper on one of them with two women in wedding dresses. "Let's eat these in the dining room."

We follow her into the dining area, connected to the living room by an open doorway.

"Grandma said we could use her china," Otis reports as he pulls the plates out of the glass-front cabinet positioned against the wall.

They're unsettling, porcelain plates with curlicues around the edges and giant eyes in the center.

"Gorgeous," Dottie says. "Simply gorgeous. I'll have to ask Penny where she got them. Set one extra, loves, so we can pretend our Briar is here."

"As long as I get her cupcake," Otis jokes, setting an empty plate at the end of the table. Its eye stares up vacantly.

We position ourselves around the table, Sophie sitting across from me and next to Briar's empty spot. I watch unabashedly as she pulls the topper out of her cupcake and sucks frosting off the end of it.

They're spice cupcakes with cream cheese frosting—another surprise, because I'd heard my stepmother say the wedding cake was vanilla upon vanilla, something I'd laughed about with Travis.

The others make small talk, but I keep quiet, lost in my head. After we finish, I nod to Otis. "Let's clean up, man."

His mouth opens, closes. "Jonah never cleans up."

"Which is why Jonah isn't getting married, or getting laid," Hannah says archly, tilting her head. Her red hair brushes the tops of her shoulders.

"I don't have any sexual prospects at this table," Otis replies.

She snorts in disgust, or amusement, I couldn't say which. "You wouldn't if Briar were here either, you know."

"And you won't have any prospects anywhere if you don't

learn to clean up after yourself," I say, figuring the kid could use some solid advice. I always cleaned up after myself. At my mom's, because she needed me to clean up after her too, more often than not. And at my dad's, because Patricia gave me a hard time when I didn't.

I can feel Sophie watching me curiously, or maybe suspiciously, as we clear the table of dishes before settling around it again.

"Oh goodness," Dottie says, her gaze flying to the clock positioned over the door. "I have to go home, my loves. Bear and I are babysitting for some of our grandchildren tonight."

She hugs everyone, ending with me. Before she pulls away, she says, "I can feel you've been carrying around the stone I gave you. I'm glad, my boy. Good things are coming your way. There'll be some bumps, but when aren't there?"

I gape at her as she turns and leaves, and the rock feels like it's become warm in my pocket. "She's..."

"*Brilliant*," Sophie says, with a warning note in her voice. It's obvious she won't tolerate anyone saying anything different.

"Yeah, I like her."

Silence hangs for a beat. The natural thing would be to leave. I delivered my warning, I overstayed my welcome, possibly by a lot. My job here is done.

"I'd like to buy you a drink," I tell Sophie before I can think twice about it.

"That's nice, Rob," she says. "But unnecessary. You already bought us tea the other day."

"And tea cakes," Hannah adds, lifting a finger. "We added those after you left and Dottie shared the news of your generosity."

"You wanted to go out in your dress," I point out.

"I still do, but we're a package deal," Sophie says, gesturing with her champagne flute at her cousin and her friend.

"You, yourself, and you, or you, Hannah, and Otis?"

"Both," she says, but she's smiling now. "I go nowhere without all four of them."

"So, let's all go. I'll be your designated driver."

"You haven't had any champagne?" she asks, sounding surprised. She looks for my flute but doesn't find it. Because I never claimed the one from the coffee table.

"No, I don't drink alcohol."

Sophie drops her champagne flute. It hits the porcelain plate beside her at exactly the wrong angle, and the thin, brittle porcelain cracks in half, leaving a fissure down the center of the eye.

"Oh no. That feels like bad luck," she murmurs. She looks shaken by it, like luck isn't a random thing, but a force guided by some invisible handler that's taken a disliking to her. I understand the sentiment, but I've stopped believing in things like luck. I've had to.

"Nah, old things don't last forever," I say. "They're not meant to."

"I don't know why anyone would want eyes staring at them in the middle of a special occasion anyway," Otis says. "We can get Gram something normal."

"So it was good luck," I add, smiling at Sophie. "You don't have to eat off a plate that's watching you anymore."

She laughs, but there's something off about her, an unease that's crept in. So I usher them out of the house and into my car. Otis calls shotgun, but I remind him it's sort of Sophie's wedding day. I open the door for her, and she looks up at me in surprise.

I have to laugh. "Let me guess. I'm an alcoholic, hard-partying loser who doesn't do anything good without an angle or for money."

She blushes as she settles into the seat, pulling in her lacy skirts after her. She looks like a cupcake. A greeting card. *An invitation to sin.*

I crush that last thought.

"I'm sorry," she says quietly. "I know he's a liar. I'm not sure why it keeps surprising me. I should just assume everything he said was a lie."

"It wasn't all a lie," I admit. "Some of the things he said used to be true, and it would suit him to believe they still are."

"He didn't even tell me he had a brother," Hannah interjects from the back seat. "He said he was an only child."

I'm not sure why I care, after everything, but that hurts too. It's like Jonah took an eraser and tried to rub out my existence.

"I knew he was a dick," Otis says victoriously, and I reach into the back seat and high-five him—only realizing mid-act that I'm leaning directly over Sophie, so close I can feel the whisper of her lacy dress and the warmth of her breath against my flesh.

I can feel my body responding to her, awakening, and it's disconcerting as hell. This is Sophie. *Pollyanna.* I remind myself of that fact again as I shut her door and circle around the car, sliding into the driver's side.

"Where to, gang?" I ask.

Hannah shoots Sophie a sly look from the cramped back seat. "The Ginger Station."

The Ginger Station is the only ginger beer brewery in town.

Sophie gasps. "No. We can't just ambush her."

"We don't even know who she is," Hannah says. "So ambushing her would be impossible. But if we happen to meet her..."

"*No,*" Sophie repeats. "I texted her from that app and my phone. She knows. What she chooses to do with that knowledge is up to her."

"What if he got to the messages before she saw them?"

She worries at her lips, her gaze out the window, before

turning back to Hannah. "I'm not showing up in a wedding dress. She'll think we're crazy."

Hannah shrugs. "Who cares. Maybe we are crazy. Besides, we don't have to talk to her tonight. It's an information-gathering mission, and I'd really like some ginger beer."

"It *is* refreshing," Otis says. "It tastes like soda, though, so you have to be careful. Grandma Penny drank one of mine by mistake when I got a four-pack. She got really sentimental about this framed baby picture, thinking it was of my dad. I didn't have the heart to tell her it had come with the frame."

I glance at Sophie, sensing the nerves radiating from her. "It's up to you, Sophie. It's your wedding night."

Personally, I feel like it's kind of a bad move to make any part of this night about my brother, however peripherally. But Hannah probably knows Sophie better than I do by now. Maybe she knows Sophie needs this.

One final woman to save.

Maybe I need to see it through too. To undo the harm Jonah has done to other people, since there's no undoing what he did to me.

She thinks for a moment, then nods, her hair dancing around the shoulders of her dress. "Okay. Let's go."

CHAPTER NINE

Everyone's staring at me.

Logically, I knew that would happen. I'm wearing a wedding dress, after all. But it didn't occur to me that if I showed up at a bar with a group, everyone would assume one of the guys was my new spouse.

I'll admit to being slightly offended that the bartender instantly assumed it was my cousin, in his tuxedo T-shirt, rather than Rob, who seems especially tall and virile tonight. Then again, the bartender is a pretty, dark-haired woman who seems to have a thing for Rob, so maybe it's wishful thinking on her part.

Or not-so-wishful thinking. He's single, after all. Maybe he'll go home with her. Maybe they'll fall madly in love, and we'll become the background of their story. The thought stings for reasons I can't begin to compute.

I'm still chewing on that thought a couple of drinks later, when Hannah comes back from a trip to the ladies' room with a satisfied smirk on her face.

"I put a photo of him up in the ladies' room," she whispers

as she slips onto her stool, glancing around to make sure no one's paying attention.

They are, but mostly to my dress.

"Of Rob?" I ask, distracted.

She frowns at me, her freckled nose wrinkling. "Why would I put up a photo of Rob in the ladies' room? We *like* Rob."

"We do?" Rob asks, grinning. "I thought the jury was still out. Sophie doesn't seem convinced."

I roll my eyes at him, but somehow manage to get distracted by the way his thick hair flops slightly over his eyebrow, as if he's from some '90s rom-com and didn't get the memo that most people choose either long or short, not this relentless, woman-slaying game of in-between.

I realize I've been staring at Rob and turn back to Hannah. "Why would you hang up a photo of Jonah? Did you catch him picking his nose?"

"It's a flyer that says he has STDs, and any women who have been exposed to him should immediately call the number on the flyer."

I feel like I should probably object to this, but instead I find myself snort-laughing. "And it's your number, isn't it? You're probably going to get hundreds of calls."

"Good. I'll inform them all that he has a diseased dick and they should make a run for it at the earliest opportunity."

He *doesn't* have a diseased dick, thankfully. Briar, Hannah, and I went to a clinic together to get tested. But it would be no more than he deserved if he did.

"Were you carrying those flyers around in your purse?" I ask, leaning in a little. "Have you posted them all around town?"

"In certain strategic locations." She looks so pleased with herself, I'd probably have smiled back even if I didn't agree. But I savor the thought of Mrs. Price finding one in the bathroom at her favorite wine bar.

"Can I have some too?" I ask. "And we should give Briar some."

Her grin stretches wider. "I like the way you think, and yes, of course. Let's put them everywhere. Let's make sure he never gets laid in Western North Carolina again. Give it to me." She holds her hand out for a fist bump, and I tap it with mine.

"Planning my brother's downfall?" Rob asks, clearly amused.

I turn on my stool to get a better look at him. He's not sitting too close, but I'm very aware of where his body ends and mine begins, and even the air between us. I'm still half stunned by the revelation that he doesn't drink.

Jonah told me Rob was a boozer in a band who spent every night drunk and with a different woman. I believed him, because Rob dresses like a teenager and looks...

Well, wanton.

I run a finger over the edge of the smooth bar, desperately aware of the blush rising on my cheeks. "Wouldn't he deserve it? He lied about your carousing."

He angles his head to get a better look at me. "He lies about lots of things. But like I said, it wasn't always a lie. I don't drink because I *can't* drink."

"You're allergic to alcohol?" Otis asks, his tone making it clear that this is the worst possible scenario he can imagine. He's been mostly silent since we arrived at the bar; in fact, he hasn't been particularly chatty since the whole phone mishap. I asked him about his unusual reticence yesterday, and he said he'd run out of weed gummies and didn't have enough cash to buy more, but I know that's a lie. He would have asked to borrow money if he'd run out.

"No, not like that," Rob replies. He doesn't expand on his response. I'd really like him to, but I'm not going to push him.

"I think alcohol is God's gift," Otis says, rocking on his stool.

"The world is really screwed up and weird, but if you're a little bit drunk, it seems okay, and everyone seems nice. They're probably still not, but booze makes it easier to pretend."

I lean over the bar to get a better look at my cousin, who's sitting on Rob's other side. "Are you okay? You didn't get fired again, did you?"

Otis has trouble keeping a job. I got him a taproom position at Buchanan Brewery for a few weeks, but he let a woman con him into giving her and her friend a private tour of the brewery. Her companion ended up getting injured, which could have gotten us sued.

My boss, Dylan, is a good guy and was very understanding. But Otis has a good way of finding people's boundaries and pushing past them.

More recently, he's been working for Honey Do, a service that lists odd jobs people want done and matches them up with the semi-employed. I didn't think you could get fired from something like that, but who knows.

"No," he says, slouching. "I think I'm just having a quarter-life crisis. Honey Do sucks."

"Why would melon give you a quarter-life crisis?" Hannah asks, leaning in to peer at him. "Just eat a different fruit, man."

I laugh through my nose. Hannah's obviously a little drunk, like I am. "D-o, not d-e-w. He's talking about the chore service. It's where he works." I glance back at Otis. "It's okay, Otis. I'll find you a new job. We can do the Myers-Briggs test to see what career would suit you best."

He smiles at me. "I just...you know...I want to prove I'm a man."

Hannah studies him quizzically. "Was there any question about that?" A second later, she taps her forehead dramatically. "Oh, you're still hoping to bang Briar. I'm sorry to tell you, buddy, but I don't think she's interested. In fact, she's so disgusted by this whole Jonah thing that I wouldn't be surprised if she gives up men entirely. I mean, the woman started crocheting. You don't pick up crocheting at thirty unless you're done with dick."

"She's a bit older than me *and* you," I tell Otis, who looks downcast. "But you never know. We'll find you a new job, and then we'll see what happens."

To my consternation, I can see Rob is frowning at me from the stool beside mine. He looks decidedly unimpressed.

"What's your problem?" I whisper-hiss, scowling at him.

Hannah, who either feels bad for popping Otis's balloon or wants to torment him further, vacates her seat and plants herself on the empty one beside him.

Rob leans toward me slightly and whispers, "He'll never get anywhere if you keep driving him around in a wheelbarrow, telling him how well he's doing on his free ride."

I glare at him. "How *dare* you. First you crashed my wedding, and now you're telling me how to—"

I catch myself before I can say *parent my cousin*, because he might have a point.

He arches his brows, giving me a slow smile I find infuriating, even if I have the impulse to trace the curve of it with my finger.

Oh, no.

I'd better get up and go to the bathroom. Maybe if I study that poster of Jonah, I'll see the resemblance between the two of them, and this madness will stop. I start to get up but move too fast and tumble off my stool, landing in a pile of lace skirts.

"Oh no, bride down!" someone calls out. "Bride down!"

They must have a protocol for drunk women in wedding dresses, because a woman is rushing toward me with a tall glass of water and what look like smelling salts before I can even get my bearings. Then Rob appears, leaning down and helping me to my feet, his hand so strong and warm—who knew a hand could feel strong?

"Are you okay?" Hannah asks, nearly her whole body stretched over the bar for prime rubbernecking.

"I'm okay, just a little woozy," I insist, mortified, because now everyone really *is* watching me. Including Otis, whose eyes are so wide and dilated I have to assume he not only has special gummies but ate one before we got in the car.

"Want me to take you outside for some fresh air?" Rob asks.

I'm embarrassed again, but not too embarrassed to agree. Fresh air sounds not only good but necessary right now.

"Yeah," I say, "that's a good idea."

The bartender gives me a dubious look, like she's afraid I'll vomit on the nicely polished wooden bar. The thought makes me a little nauseous, actually, so when Rob leads me to the back door, I'm relieved.

He opens it for me, and I step out into the warm night, stars speckling the sky above us. There's an expansive sitting area out here, with long wooden picnic tables. Farther back, there's a firepit with two empty Adirondack chairs next to it. There's no fire in the pit, probably because it feels like the inside of Satan's mouth out here—humid and hot and kind of dank—but the tables are packed with people.

I walk past them with purpose, needing to sit and wanting one of those empty chairs. I don't look back to see if Rob joins me. I'm not sure whether I want him to.

He follows me, though, and I hear a couple of people greeting him. A few others comment on my dress, but I ignore their murmurs. Even though it's not negative attention, I feel self-conscious. A bride without a groom is a curiosity. A question to be answered.

I lower into one of the Adirondack chairs, which is much less comfortable than I'd hoped. My head tips upward, and I sigh with pleasure. The night sky is even prettier from this vantage point, away from the fairy lights brightening up the back of the brewery. It's a velvet canvas stippled with glowing dots.

"The stars are so pretty tonight," I say.

"Let me guess, you like wishing upon a star, Sophie?" Rob asks as he sits next to me. His voice is teasing, as usual, but it's not condescending this time.

"I do," I admit. "You never know."

"What would you wish for tonight?" he asks. My gaze moves to him, taking in the gleam of his eyes in the night.

Awareness rocks through me. It's the way he's sitting in his chair, as if he's prepared to leap up at a moment's notice if I'm actually sick or need his help.

I swallow a ball of emotion, deciding to actually consider his question. There's a drone of conversation from the people at the tables, but we're distant enough that only occasional words drift through the mass of speech. *Tree. Dress. Herpes. Mushroom.*

"Something happened to me," I finally say, concentrating on his face to let the rest of those people fade into the background. "When I was sixteen. It was something I did..."

I pause, almost hoping he'll say something. Maybe hoping he'll stop me. He doesn't. His expression is thoughtful and intent. "Does Jonah know?"

I shake my head slowly. "Only that my parents don't really talk to me. I've spent my entire adult life trying to make up for it. But you can't rewind the clock, no matter how hard you try. Other than Otis and Aunt Penny, the people in my family all see me as the girl I was at sixteen. If I could wish for anything, it would be to reverse what I did."

He watches me intently. "I have to say, that's not very Pollyanna of you, Sophie."

I shake my head, feeling a surge of bitterness. "Because that's not who I am."

I turn to leave, but he gets to his feet and captures my arm, his fingers callused and strong. A gasp escapes me, although he didn't grab me hard. I could easily escape if I wanted to.

I meet his eyes, surprised by the intensity of his gaze.

"I know that. No one word could explain you. So why do you want other people to see you as something you're not?"

Is that what I've been doing? The hollow forming in my stomach suggests he might be right.

"I want them to know I've changed. That I think of other people before myself."

His hand brushes my arm with a soft caress, sending ripples of sensation through me before he pulls away. "It's nice that you want to think of other people, Sophie. It means you're a better person than most, but there's nothing wrong with letting people know you have an emotional range. If you don't...it's like listening to a singer who can only hit the high notes."

"Everyone likes Mariah Carey," I say stiffly. "She's the queen of pop."

He laughs. "Sure. *Everyone* likes her. Check out the comment section for 'All I Want for Christmas Is You' on YouTube."

"You should take notes from her. So many of your songs are angry. People enjoy being happy. They like things they can sing along to."

I expect him to storm off, the way Jonah would if someone said something he didn't like. But instead a slow smile forms on his face. "You've been listening to my music."

I shrug self-consciously. "You know what they say. Know thy enemy."

"We're not enemies, Soph," he says thickly, the sound of my

nickname sending a shiver through me. It's just that he didn't ask to use it, I rationalize. He should have.

I hold his gaze before finally admitting the truth. "No, we're not enemies. Did you write all of those songs yourself?"

"Some of them. My buddy writes with me sometimes."

I nod. "They're so...*sad*. The ones that aren't pissed-off."

His smile is sadder this time, regretful, backlit by the soft, warm lighting from the rear of the building. "I get stuck in the low registers sometimes, and you've glued yourself to the high ones. But your friend Dottie was right earlier. We're nothing without our pasts, Sophie. I don't know what happened to you, but whatever it was, it made you who you are. It's what got you here, to this moment. You'd be a different person if it hadn't shaped you."

"A better one," I say, the words bitter to the taste. "I wouldn't have lost everything."

He smiles at me, but there's still sadness beneath it. "Careful there, Soph. You sound like a sad song. But I'll let you in on a secret. People might like singing along to the happy songs in their cars, but it's the angry and sad ones they remember. If you let people see all of you, they're not likely to forget it."

I take a half step toward him without meaning to. Without really knowing whether I want to shove his arm or...

I don't know. I'm tipsy. Maybe even a little drunk. And he's *unexpected*. Normally, I'm not drawn to chaos. If you don't know what's going to happen, then everything can go wildly, horribly wrong, especially if you have haywire luck. But it's like I'm under a spell...

A warm breeze cascades hair into my face and rustles my skirts, reminding me again that I'm in a wedding dress. *My* wedding dress, which I'll never wear for real. My silver lining was made of tinfoil attached with a glue stick—the kind of craft I never would have rolled out if I'd managed to open my center.

I feel like the fool I've been and tears form in my eyes. I'm mortified, my gaze skating to those packed sardine tables so close to us, but if anyone was watching us, they've lost interest. My attention is drawn back to Rob as he reaches out and brushes the tear away with his callused fingers. There's an entreaty in his eyes, and I have to wonder if he's one of those men who has an aneurysm whenever a woman cries in front of him.

"You could tell me what happened, if you like," he says, cocking his head, the ends of his hair brushing the collar of his T-shirt. "I'd keep it to myself. And I'm not just asking because I want to have something Jonah doesn't."

"But would you write a sad or angry song about it?" I ask.

He smiles. "Any resemblance to real people, places, or things is accidental."

"'Oh Brother' is about Jonah, right?"

One side of his mouth lifts in a lopsided smile that would probably make his female fans swoon. "I'll never tell, but the title might give it away. If you're a woman who pays attention to such things."

I pause, considering the possibility of telling this man my secret. It would feel good to let it out, and I can tell that he would listen, really listen, in the way so few people do.

I even open my mouth to do it, but then I glance down and see a penny lying heads down. Bad luck.

I point to it. "They're bad luck when they're like that."

He gives me a disbelieving look. "You genuinely think a penny that's face down is bad luck?"

Feeling miserable and stupid, I nod. "If you have bad luck, you become familiar with the signs."

"I see," he says, frowning. He gives me a sidelong look that invites me to speak, to share everything. That penny feels like a reminder, though: *If you tell him, something bad will happen.*

After a moment, he says, "It's just a penny that fell from someone's pocket or wallet. Gravity made the decision. It doesn't mean anything other than what it is."

"Says the man who writes song lyrics."

He shrugs a shoulder and grabs the penny up off the ground.

"You shouldn't have done that," I say, hating the stupid quaver in my voice.

"Because now its bad luck will be attached to me?" He's giving me a challenging look, and suddenly I'm very aware of being alone with him.

"Yeah," I say softly. "And I think I've decided I like you."

He pockets the penny. "I've decided I like you too. Which is why I'm going to prove to you nothing bad will happen to me for collecting that penny." He smiles as he studies my face. "You think I've really jinxed myself now, don't you?"

Yes. No. I don't even know anymore. "You think I'm being silly."

"Maybe. But it turns out you're still charming when you're being silly. Lucky you. We can't all make that claim. I just turn into an asshole."

I smile at that, but I still feel an itch at the back of my brain, a worry. That he and Hannah and Briar and even Otis might be better off if they stay away from me and my bad luck. The thing is, I don't really want them to stay away.

Rob looks like he's about to say something else, but then my phone buzzes in my purse. And buzzes again before it starts ringing. I'm not an animal—my phone is almost always on silent —but I know it's ringing because the buzzing is more persistent. So I pull it out and check.

I frown at him, then glance at the back door. "It's Hannah. Maybe something's wrong inside. We should go see."

"Let's."

I'm deeply aware of him as he falls in behind me, as his finger grazes the small of my back, guiding me away from a stump that definitely would have sent me flying.

We reach the back door. When he opens it, I immediately hear Hannah's voice saying the word *prick*.

Rob shrugs. "We could always leave from the back," he says with a half-smile.

"We're not scoundrels," I say, which makes his smile upgrade to a grin.

"Sure, but let me go first."

I probably surprise both of us by allowing it. We walk inside, and I gasp when the tasting room comes into view ahead of Rob.

Hannah is standing in front of her stool, facing off with Jonah, who thankfully has his back to us.

"Oh bless my heart," I say, since no older Southern ladies are around to say it for me.

I guess I should have checked my messages.

CHAPTER TEN

ROB

What the hell is Jonah doing here?

Wait a minute…

He's obviously struck out with Hannah and Briar. Is he here to make a play on GingerBeerBabe?

What a total douche.

The old rage fills me, more self-righteous in flavor, because it's not just for myself this time.

"It's a free country, *Jonah*. I have every right to be here," Hannah tells him as I stop dead. Sophie runs into my back and then wraps her arms around my middle to avoid falling over.

Sensation strums through me as her hands grip my sides, her chest pressed to my back. The heat of her radiates through my T-shirt.

Does she think a penny foretold or did this?

She feels small, and maybe that's why I'm suddenly consumed by protectiveness. I want to turn around, sweep her up into my arms, and carry her away from this mess. But I don't want to help her avoid the ugly things in life. Like I said, it's the ugly parts that make the biggest impression. The bad luck pennies. The sadness. The wild grief and anger. Wipe those away, and what do you have left?

A fake smile, probably.

Jonah's back is to us, but he'll see us before long. Especially since Hannah is going to give us away with her overly dramatic *get the hell out of here* eyes.

"Why are you here with *him?*" Jonah asks, nodding toward Otis, who's sitting on his stool as if frozen, nursing his drink.

"We're on a date, you pompous prick," Hannah snaps. "I haven't been sitting at home crying over you. Otis is a *real* man. He realizes that a tongue should be used sparingly and women don't enjoy being slobbered on."

Otis drops the ginger beer he'd had halfway to his mouth. It was mostly empty, but his eyes shift into panic mode as the liquid spreads across the bar, and he pulls a tissue of dubious cleanliness out of his pocket to sop it up. Everyone's watching him, and he must feel it, because his cheeks are red.

Hannah sniffs primly "Now, if you don't mind, we're going home to make sweet, passionate love to each other."

Otis's face gets redder as Jonah shakes his head in disbelief. "No way. There's no way you randomly met this kid. Or that you wanted to date him. Have you been stalking my fiancée?"

Yup, that settles it. I have to get Sophie out of here, now. I start to turn, ready to hustle her out, when she surprises the hell out of me by pushing past me, her hands pressing to my chest to both reassure me and move me out of the way.

She was tipsy earlier, but there's no sign of it now as she stalks toward Jonah in her wedding dress.

It's the only time he'll ever get to see her wear it, and I'd be lying if I said I didn't take pleasure from that, because she is a fucking sight to see. As she slips past me, I take in the resolve burning in her big blue eyes and the firm line of her mouth.

She's a force of nature barreling toward Jonah, who still doesn't sense her.

Hannah's eyes are widening, but a pleased smile forms on her mouth as she watches Sophie coming.

"This woman's using you to get to Sophie," Jonah says, turning toward Otis on his stool.

"That's okay," Otis tells him. "I'm content with being used. More women can use me if they like." He looks around almost hopefully.

Just then, Sophie reaches Jonah and taps him on the shoulder as officiously as a Karen with a complaint.

He turns and lays eyes on her. I'm only about ten feet behind her, but he doesn't seem to notice me.

How could he?

He's staring at his ex-fiancée, who looks fine as hell in the dress she was supposed to marry him in. A sight like that would be enough to break most men. I'm not surprised when his mouth gapes open like a fish's, gasping for air. Someone pushes past me to make their way to the bar, business continuing as usual despite the entertaining scene playing out.

I consider moving in and intervening and decide I'll only do it if Sophie needs me. It's important for her to have this moment. To take her stand. To accept the parts of her that aren't as soft and accommodating as the Sophie I nicknamed Pollyanna.

"Sophie," Jonah finally manages. "Your dress..."

The look on his face...

I'm not too proud to admit I'm more tempted to drink his rage than I am by any form of alcohol.

"I'm not wearing it for you," she says, holding herself stiffly upright. "I paid for this dress, and I love it. I'm wearing it for me. Because I didn't want to hide it away in a drawer forever as if I'd done something to be ashamed of. And Hannah is here because we've become friends. Briar too. If anyone's a stalker, it's *you*.

You tracked me down with your Find My Friend app, didn't you?"

Or maybe my GingerBeerBabe theory is right. There's no way of knowing, and he certainly isn't going to be honest about it.

It only takes him half a second to recover. His gaze darts back to Hannah, who gives him a wave that would make Queen Elizabeth proud. Swearing, he shifts his gaze to Sophie. "She's just using you to get to me."

Hannah snorts. "Yeah, ego much?"

His eyes alight on me, widening in surprise and recognition, just as a little girl comes running out of the restroom with one of the Jonah flyers crumpled in her hand. "Mommy, what's an STD?" she asks as she hurries over to a woman seated with a group of other women in some armchairs arranged beside the bar. "Can I have one?"

The woman's eyes widen in horror, Hannah's gleam with glee, and Jonah, gaping at me, demands, "What are *you* doing here?"

I give him one of those Queen of England waves that Hannah pulled off. It feels good. Giving him the finger would feel better, but there's that kid to think about.

"I've decided to make friends too," I say with a smirk that'll hopefully piss him off further. "Looks like it's going better for me, and for Otis, than for you, bud."

He clearly would like nothing better than to storm toward me and list off threats, or possibly choke me, but the kid's mother stands and points at him. Her mouth forms an "O" like one of the pod people in *Invasion of the Body Snatchers*.

"That man's a pervert!" she shouts, shaking the crumpled flyer.

Honest-to-God laughter spouts out of me, because it's so

ridiculous, and also because I like this expression on my brother's face.

"What?" Jonah asks in confusion as a large, burly man with a shaved head approaches us from the back of the tasting room.

"What seems to be the problem, ma'am?" he asks the woman, before catching sight of Jonah. "You," he says in distaste. "You're not supposed to come around here anymore."

"Is this why?" the woman asks, waving the flyer. She covers her daughter's ears. "He's a p-e-r-v-e-r-t." I'm not sure why she bothered covering the kid's ears *and* spelling it out, especially since she's already said it out loud, but hey, maybe she's had some drinks herself. The other women in her party get to their feet, all of them looking aggrieved, like they'd enjoy taking their pound of flesh too.

"He's a what?" the bald guy says, scratching his head.

"He's a pervert," she says more loudly. "He..."

She trails off, clearly confused, just as Hannah slides off of her stool and grabs Otis's hand to get him up. She gestures furiously for Sophie and me to join them, but Sophie seems to have become a statue, staring fixedly at the man she almost married. A pang of fierce emotion unleashes inside of me.

I don't like that he hurt her. I like it even less that she still has the ability to be hurt by him. I press my hand to the small of her back and urge her in Hannah's direction as the bald guy gets closer, Jonah lifting his hands out, palms up.

"Hey," Jonah says, "no big deal. It was all a misunderstanding." He gives the woman a confused glance. His gaze narrows when he sees what's on the flyer. "Hannah did this," he barks heatedly, looking over at her as she leaves through the front, giving him a toodles wave. "She did it, she—"

I push past him with Sophie. He makes a grab at her, and a sound like a growl rumbles out of me as I lift her up and set her down out of his reach. I don't fully understand my reaction. All

I know is that I won't let him touch her. I wouldn't be able to stand it if he laid a single finger on her.

The big guy grabs Jonah by the arm. "We're going to get to the bottom of this."

Good for them. I hope it takes hours.

Sophie gives me a surprised look over her shoulder, and I wonder if I crossed a line, touching her like that. But then she reaches back for me, and I take her hand. It's more of a *we're in this together* gesture than anything romantic, but I feel a surge of energy when she touches me. Enough to get us out of there quickly, even as I feel my brother staring daggers at my back. Swearing at me.

It's only when we get outside, where Hannah is laughing, doubled over, and Otis still looks like a shell-shocked zoo animal, that I realize I'm probably in for it. Jonah hated me before all of this. Now I've punched him in the face and participated in his public humiliation. No way he's going to let that go.

Still, at the moment, it's hard to care. I laugh along with Hannah, who declares, very seriously, that she's going to pee her pants.

"We should go," Sophie says, casting a worried glance at the door. Is she worried for him? Or about what he might do?

She knows him well enough to understand he's a man who likes paying his debts back with interest.

"Yeah, we should," I say. Our eyes meet, and I feel a surge of...

Magic, Dottie would call it. The night *does* feel magical. Like the air is thick with possibility. It's not often I have a night like this. A lot of the time, I get bogged down in sadness and regret, but right now I feel like a helium balloon whose string has been cut.

On impulse, I reach for Sophie's hand and squeeze it on the

way to the car. Her fingers wrap around mine, her hand soft but strong. "You were something else back there," I say.

Amusement warms her gaze, her blue eyes sparkling. She's beautiful like this. It's okay to think it, because it's true, and also because I don't intend to do anything about it. "I certainly wasn't a Pollyanna."

"The look on his face..." Hannah says between wheezes.

We get to the car and all pile in, me behind the wheel.

As I'm driving out of the lot, I see Jonah coming out the front door, a look of white-hot rage on his face.

"Soooo," Otis says from the back seat. I glance in the rearview and see he's looking at Hannah. "Did you just ask me out? Because I have to respectfully decline. I realize that Briar may never see me the way I see her, but my heart is spoken for, man."

She shoves his arm fondly.

"One drop-off or multiple?" I ask as we approach Sophie's place.

"One," Hannah says. Glancing at Otis, she says, "Don't worry, Otis, I don't have designs on you, but if this isn't an occasion to stay up all night watching rom-coms and drinking, I don't know what is."

She leans forward in her seat. "Hey, did you guys catch what the bouncer dude said before everything went to hell? He said Jonah isn't welcome around there anymore. Do you think it's because of GingerBeerBabe?"

"Huh, probably," I say. "Or he just pissed them off by being himself."

"I think it does have something to do with her," Sophie contributes with a sigh. "But we may never know what."

"We should have thrown a handful of flyers through the door on our way out."

"But then *we* probably wouldn't be welcomed back," I say,

"and Sophie and I like wishing on stars in the back, don't we, Soph?"

She gives me an exasperated look that's at least partially fond. I'll take it.

I park in the driveway, feeling a pulse of regret that the night's over. Mind, I don't want to sit in front of rom-coms all night and watch these guys get drunk, but I was a part of something, and now I'm on the outside. That feeling of exclusion is an old one, baked into my bones.

Before they pile out, I say, "That was fun. We should do it again sometime."

Hannah laughs and starts to leave the car, but I ask her for some of the Jonah flyers first, and she comes through, bless her. Otis follows her out, mumbling to himself, but Sophie turns in her seat and grins at me. "Thank you, Rob. I'm sorry about earlier. I...you bring it out in me."

I don't know what possesses me, but I say, "I'm glad. And thank you for letting me stay. Dottie's right, I'll always remember it."

She smiles and then leans forward and presses her lips to my cheek. Shock roils through me at the press of her warm mouth to my face, her lips soft and giving. Generous. I'm hit with a whiff of the scent she always wears, gardenias. I used to think it smelled like old ladies, and it was something I'd smile to myself about after my visits with the happy couple, but now it fills me with warm affection.

I watch, still in shock, as she walks away, then look in the mirror and see the red imprint of her mouth on my cheek. It's like she branded me. The weight of the penny is still there in my pocket—almost nothing but not quite.

My hands grip the wheel, but I can't squeeze it hard enough to shake the feeling that what just happened will change my life.

CHAPTER ELEVEN

SOPHIE

Hannah and I decide it's a fantastic idea to drink some peach schnapps for "old times' sake." We also watch my absolute favorite rom-com—*10 Things I Hate About You*, followed by a delightfully terrible one. We each claim one side of the worn, plaid sectional couch in my great-aunt's living room, the floor of which is still covered in red satin. It's crazy late by the time we turn the TV off, considering that Hannah has to show up to work at noon, but she loudly proclaims it's Future Hannah's problem—right before she finishes the schnapps.

"Good God, that was awful," she says with a shudder.

I grin at her, feeling awash with pure fondness. "I'm sorry to say that's Present Hannah's problem."

"Hey, what happened with you and Rob, by the way? You were outside with him for a long time."

This is accompanied by a suggestive wagging of her eyebrows.

I snort-laugh. Hannah is delightfully ridiculous. "Nothing. He lectured me."

"Like in a sexy, stern daddy kind of way?"

More laughter. "Like in a he-thinks-he-knows-best kind of

way." I feel guilty even as I'm saying it, because that wasn't really what had happened. Our conversation made an impact on me.

Because he was right.

Who would I be if my life had all been smooth sailing?

I certainly wouldn't be the person I am, the person who'd stood up before Dottie, Rob, my cousin, and my new friend and pledged to love myself as I am. Doesn't that entail accepting what happened in my past? Maybe being grateful for it in some absurd way?

I'm definitely not there yet, but I can't deny he planted the seed of something inside of me. A new perspective.

I try to explain that, and Hannah starts laughing hysterically. "He planted his seed inside of you?"

So being drunk in the middle of the night in a wedding dress isn't the best time to have a serious conversation...

"I guess I'm trying to say that he's not all bad."

"No," she agrees. "And he's, like, *at least* ten times hotter than Jonah. Maybe twenty. It's too bad you don't like him like that. It would have been the ultimate queen-bee-level revenge for you to hook up with his brother."

"You could," I say, immediately regretting it, although not because I have a thing for Rob. Sure, he's a better person than I thought, and he's interesting and talented, and, yes, quite good-looking, but he's also the brother of the man I was supposed to marry. There are talk shows for that kind of thing.

"Nah," she says flippantly. "He's not my type. I have this pattern where I always date assholes and then act surprised and affronted when they turn out to be assholes. It's my thing."

We laugh and then fall asleep talking. It feels *good*. I'd forgotten what it was like to have a friend like this.

Sure, I had Jonah before all of this happened, but that was different. With him, I was always on guard. My happiness with him had felt tenuous, as if it could be snatched away if I failed to walk along the carefully marked line he'd drawn for me. I'd been so careful, and it had happened anyway.

I think again of what Rob said to me. If Jonah hadn't switched our phones that morning, none of this would have happened. I wouldn't have Hannah or Briar, and even Dottie would only be a sweet acquaintance, not a real friend. I certainly wouldn't be friendly with Rob.

Worse, I'd still be engaged to a man who was using me in the worst possible way.

So, yes, I decide I can be grateful for the phone swap. Even though I wish I'd kneed Jonah in the balls the day we met instead of giving him my number.

The thought makes me laugh softly to myself as I fall asleep.

When Hannah's alarm startles us awake in the morning, we're still sprawled out on the living room sectional, our feet touching because it's too small for two sleeping adults. I'm still in the wedding dress, which was never comfortable and is now less so. The stick-on bra I'd needed to wear with it has shifted and adhered to just below my collarbone, making me look like a Picasso. The empty bottle of schnapps lies on its side on the parquet wooden floor. At least we had the presence of mind to remove the red satin floor covering.

"I hate Past Hannah," Hannah groans, rubbing her forehead. Her makeup is smeared, and she's pale, but otherwise she looks okay. I'm sure I really do look like Miss Havisham now, and my mouth tastes like rotten peaches.

"I'm not fond of Past Sophie right now either," I say with a groan as I sit up.

"Why not?" Hannah asks with a grin. "She gave you a third boob. You're basically unstoppable now."

We laugh, then groan again, because it hurts to laugh.

After I change into sweatpants and throw the horrible sticky bra in the trash, I make us coffee and dry toast.

Hannah asks me to come to Big Catch for lunch, but I have a different plan. I don't have to work today. I took the day off because I had a feeling I'd be massively hungover. Go, past me! So I'm going back to the ginger beer brewery. First, because I realized last night that we never paid for our drinks, and I'm mortified that we stiffed them. Second, to ask some leading questions about Jonah and why he got banned from the brewery.

"Ugh. I want to come," Hannah says after I share my plans. She sets down her dry toast. "But one of the corporate overlords is coming by today."

Otis comes into the kitchen, wearing his flannel pajama bottoms and a Garbage Fire T-shirt. The logo is of, well, a garbage fire. But the dumpster has eyes. It's kind of a cute design, actually.

My cousin isn't an early riser, but he has a sixth sense for when other people have made coffee and breakfast.

"Did Rob give you that shirt?" I ask with a smile.

He nods with the stupor of someone who doesn't function properly without caffeine. "After one of his shows."

A sweet gesture.

I can't help but wonder what Rob would look like belting out his songs. But I shake off the thought; I don't like the strange way it's making me feel. Or the impulse to go on their website and check the schedule for their next show. He'd think it was weird if I just showed up and fangirled over them, wouldn't he?

Still, he mentioned they'd be playing at Buchanan sometime soon. I make a mental note to ask my boss about it.

Otis seems unimpressed by the dry toast I set in the middle of the table but shrugs and takes a piece. Then he pours himself some coffee and settles into the chair next to me, across from Hannah.

"Maybe I'll ask Briar to come with me on her lunch break," I muse, and Otis perks up like a golden retriever puppy offered a treat.

"Can I come?"

"You don't even know what they're doing. What if they're getting hers-and-hers colonoscopies?" Hannah asks with a laugh.

"They're not," he says, rolling his eyes. Then he looks at me. "You're not?"

"We're not. I'm going back to the ginger beer brewery to ask some questions."

"Like a private investigator?" he asks.

I consider it and then nod, deciding I like that thought. It feels *proactive*. "Yes. We're trying to identify GingerBeerBabe."

Hannah has been all in on the idea of tracking her down from the beginning, but I decide it's important to me too. Maybe GingerBeerBabe wants nothing to do with us. Maybe she's not eager to be a friend the way Briar and Hannah have become, but it's possible she feels as alone and broken as I did when I first saw those messages. Before I realized that even though it was the end of something, it could be the beginning of something too.

I think about Rob again, talking about accepting the past. He has a lovely way of speaking, is all. It's probably why he's so good at writing lyrics.

"You think she's hot?" Otis asks through a mouthful of toast.

"Yes, Otis," Hannah says dryly. "Maybe you'll get lucky, and she'll pretend to date you too."

I roll my eyes, then text Briar while I'm finishing my coffee. Unfortunately, she can't come unless we go tomorrow. I don't want to leave the bill unpaid for so long, so I decide to go without her.

Otis loses interest when he finds out she's not coming and leaves to do a Honey Do job, laundry for someone else, even though he has a mountain of dirty clothes in his room. Hannah finishes her coffee, groans a lot, and leaves to take a shower.

I take a shower and then prepare to leave. When I grab my phone to put it in my purse, I see a few notifications on the screen.

My heart beats hard when I see the first one, from an unknown number.

It's me.

Jonah.

I need a chance to give you my side of the story, Soph.

It's only fair, and I know you're fair.

> Do not, under any circumstances, ambush me at work.

I see my brother's been spreading stories.

> I'm blocking this number too, Jonah.

> I'd say have a nice life, but we both know you don't deserve it.

I love you, Sophie. I'm going to prove it to you.

This isn't over.

I rub the bridge of my nose after blocking this number too. His last words sounded ominous. I could have pointed that out, but it would have prolonged the conversation, which I didn't feel up to.

What if Jonah is camped outside of the ginger beer brewery, waiting for me? I checked last night, and it's impossible for a person you've blocked to use the Find My Friend app. So how did he know where to find me?

I take a couple of deep breaths and then head out the door. The moment I unlock the car with the key fob, Dottie's front door flies open.

"Wait for me, dear," she says, practically vaulting toward my driveway. I gasp, worried she'll break a hip or trip. "Please. I'll be right there."

I frown. She's acting as if we'd made plans to do something together.

"Did we make plans?" I ask as she comes to a stop on the other side of my Honda. She's holding an oversized Tupperware filled with something.

"Oh, no," she says. "You made an important vow yesterday, and I'm sure you spent a long night loving yourself, the way anyone should after a wedding. I didn't expect to see you until nightfall." My mouth drops open, but she continues, undaunted. "One of my granddaughters was at The Ginger Station last night, though, and she saw something most curious." Eyes glimmering, she says, "*Jonah*. And you were there, too, my dear, weren't you? With Rob and our other friends?"

"Uh, yeah," I say, feeling a throbbing pain developing in my temple. "Did you ask your granddaughter to go there to keep an eye on us?"

Was she one of the ladies with the kid?

"Of course," she says smiling, completely without qualms "I told your aunt Penny I'd keep an eye on you, and I intend to do a thorough job of it. What kind of friend would I be if I let you walk into a situation like that without any help at hand? Did Hannah put up those posters we made?"

"You..." I can't actually find the words to complete that

sentence. Dottie doesn't seem like the kind of person who'd help create something so inflammatory. "*You* helped her?"

"I tried to convince her we should say he has a dark aura," she says, clucking her tongue, "but she told me some young women would be drawn in by that. No young woman wants crabs."

That certainly sounds like Hannah.

I give Dottie a quick rundown of what happened last night, and she nods decisively. "Oh, dear me, yes, everything is happening as it should. I have a very good feeling about this. Let's go there now."

It's hard to say no to Dottie. I mean, I married myself just because she "suggested" it was a good idea. So I'm not surprised when I nod my agreement. "Okay."

I unlock the car, and she's sitting in the passenger seat before I even open my door. As soon as my butt's in the seat, she hands me the Tupperware, labeled with *Self-Love*.

She beams at me. "It's okay if you'd like to keep them all to yourself, dear. Once you've loved yourself long and well, you can think about giving your cookies to other people."

I'm not sure what that means, but it sounds sexual, so I pointedly change the subject, asking Dottie about her granddaughter, as I tuck the Tupperware into the back seat. I start driving to The Ginger Station, and Dottie tells me a long story about her granddaughter that takes us all the way to the brewery.

Once inside, we walk up to the bar together, but Dottie peels away, gravitating toward a couple sitting at the other end.

The bartender is the same woman who was working last night, although her brunette hair is pulled back in a tidy bun today.

My cheeks flushing, I try to get her attention.

"Hi, I'm so sorry," I say.

She raises her eyebrows. "For what?"

"I was here last night?"

Her face is still a blank slate. "And?"

I sigh "I was the one in the bridal gown who fell on the floor."

Her eyes widen. "Oh, you. Your friend put up the flyer that caused all that fuss."

"I know. I'm sorry for that too. Sort of. He deserved it, but obviously she should have been more careful. I'm here about the bill, though. I'm so sorry we ran out without paying."

She gives me a look that tactfully suggests I'm an idiot. "The guy you were with opened a tab. We never give out drinks without getting a card number first."

Rob.

I don't even consider the possibility that it might have been Otis. Because, let's be honest, it isn't a possibility.

A tide of emotion rushes through me, and tears spring to my eyes. It's not just this piece of kindness from Rob. It's that he was this kind to me when his brother, the man who was supposed to love me, treated me so poorly. My emotions are close to the surface right now, ready to well up in response to the slightest scratch.

The bartender's eyes widen. "Uh, it's not a big deal. You can buy him a drink another day. These things tend to even out."

"He doesn't drink," I say in a strangled voice.

"You can give him some of your cookies, my dear," Dottie says, stepping in beside me and taking my hand. "A piece of kindness at the right time, in the right place, can change a life." Turning to the bartender, she says, "Did you know that young man—the one from the flyer, I mean—was supposed to marry this dear girl, but instead he slept with her two best friends?"

Her mouth opens. Then shuts. "*Two* of your best friends?"

"Dottie," I chide. "They weren't my friends until after I found out."

"You became friends with them after you found out they were sleeping with your fiancé?" the bartender asks incredulously, oblivious to another customer's attempt to flag her down.

"They didn't know he had a fiancée," I say quickly, not wanting her to get the wrong idea about Hannah and Briar. "They thought he was single. He fooled all of us, and he's still lying about it."

A muscle at the corner of her jaw twitches. "That *bastard*," she says. "I just started here a few weeks ago, so I don't know him, but I know the type. My ex two-timed me, and I burned his underwear in the trailer park grill. This man doesn't deserve your tears, honey. They never do. Let yourself learn from it and move on. Move on big."

"Oh, that's not a bad idea," Dottie says sunnily. "As long as he uses cotton, it's a natural source of fuel. You could brown marshmallows over them and have a party. Do you have a key to Jonah's apartment, dear?"

I look at her in disbelief. "No."

I'd mailed it back to him without a note.

"Ah, oh well," she says, sounding disappointed. "We could have planted some crystals and herbs around to help reform his character before seeing ourselves out. Maybe Rob will let us in."

"You might be better off letting it go," the bartender says, pouring a couple of ginger beers. "I've got another friend who broke into her ex's apartment to put Nair in all of his shampoo bottles, and she got caught red-handed by the dog walker. Mind you, she ended up dating the dog walker, so it worked out okay. But he could have called the cops."

She slides the ginger beers across the counter to us and insists they're on the house.

"Thank you. But, uh...yeah I don't want that to happen.

Any of it," I say. "But I'm not sure *he'll* let it go. He texted me from a new phone this afternoon, saying he loved me. And last night his brother warned me that he's planning some big gesture at the brewery where I work. I don't know if Jonah changed his mind after last night, but—"

The bartender's shaking her head. "He's one of *them*."

"Them?"

"The kind who want you more when you're not interested."

"Yes, I'm concerned that may be the case," Dottie says, tsk-tsking. "I haven't wanted to trouble you with this, dear, but Bear and I had to send him away from your house the other day. It got a little heated."

"Bear really yelled at him?" I ask. Bear is such a kind older man, I wouldn't think him capable of it. He runs a support group in his free time and is always donating baked goods to every cause in town.

"Oh, no. Nothing like that. But I did tell him that his aura was very bleak. That might have been heavy news for him."

The bartender laughs. "You might want to let your friend here loose with her crystals. I doubt this guy's going to stand down easily."

A feeling of unease creeps over my neck, but I try not to let it show. I don't want to give Jonah that power over me.

"Oh good," Dottie says, clapping her hands. "I have a few lovely stones in mind. If they can't help him be decent, then nothing can." She purses her lips in thought. "In this case, I think we'd settle for mediocre."

I turn to the bartender, "Uh, on a related note, do you know why my ex was banned from this brewery? That's what the bouncer said last night."

"Bouncer?" she asks, laughing. "We don't have a bouncer. You must be talking about Pat."

"Is he here?" I ask warily. He looked pretty intimidating.

I'm not enough of a wannabe private investigator to want to interrogate him by myself, but I have a feeling Dottie would do fine with him. She could get a stone to talk.

"No," she says, "but I'll find out for you."

I consider telling her that I suspect someone who works at this brewery was also taken in by Jonah, but Dottie gives her head a firm shake. "Let's enjoy our drinks, dear girl," she tells me in an undertone. "Then we can call that *delightful* young man to pick us up. Why, we'll make a whole afternoon of it."

Something tells me she's not referring to Otis.

CHAPTER TWELVE

ROB

"Thank you, Rob," Sophie says for the fiftieth time. Or maybe sixtieth.

I picked her and Dottie up from the ginger beer brewery after she sent me an SOS text.

Or at least that had been the plan. Dottie had talked me into getting one of the nonalcoholic ginger beers and sitting with them "for a spell." To be honest, it hadn't been that hard for her to talk me around. "Come join me. Me and *Sophie*," she'd said, and I'd caved.

The part of my cheek that had been kissed by Sophie had kept me up half the night. It had felt like I could still feel her lips pressing against my skin. Still smell her sweet perfume...

The other half of the night, I'd spent raging about my brother, who'd also apparently been thinking about Sophie.

I hadn't gotten more than a couple of steps into my apartment last night before my phone started buzzing with pissed-off texts from Jonah.

Stay away from Sophie.

> Stop lying to her.

> I know you still have your panties in a twist
> about what happened, but it was years ago,
> and it was an accident.

> Grow the fuck up, and be a man.

Oh, the irony.

The real wonder was that I didn't get any icy calls from Patricia or my father. Jonah was thirty, sure, but it had never stopped him from tattling to Mommy and Daddy before. Maybe it was because he'd done something shitty and he knew it, and he was afraid even his mother would catch on eventually.

I could have taken the high road and left his unhinged texts unanswered. Instead, I told him to go fuck himself with a smiley face, and informed him that Sophie had a subzero interest in receiving a grand gesture from him.

He didn't respond, which doesn't mean he's not going to show up at Buchanan Brewery with a seven-string orchestra.

So I'd tried to go to sleep, mostly failed, and spent the morning keeping busy so I'd stop thinking about Sophie and the Jonah problem. I met Emil at the park with one of my extra guitars, as was our habit, then met up with the guys for band practice. It had almost been working when I'd received her text:

> If it's not too much trouble, could you possibly
> give Dottie and me a ride back to my place
> from The Ginger Station?

A Pollyanna message, but not a Pollyanna mission.

Why she'd wanted to go back to that brewery so soon after the little scene we'd fled from was a mystery—until Sophie and Dottie, who were both slightly tipsy off of one drink, didn't hesitate to tell me everything.

I wasn't sorry Sophie had asked for my help. It had felt good, like confirmation she didn't think I was the same as my brother. I *liked* that she trusted me. That she didn't care if I saw the parts of her that weren't always idealistic and upbeat—like the Sophie who went to a brewery in the middle of the day with her elderly neighbor, playing private investigator.

She was charming like this, even though she looked like she hadn't done much sleeping or paid any attention to the shirt she'd pulled on, from a fun run called *The Fun Onions!* More proof that she didn't care what I thought of her. Part of her charm, honestly, even though it was a reminder that I was background noise for her.

After we had sat for a while and talked, sipping our drinks, we'd left the brewery. Sophie had started in with the endless thanks before the car even left the lot, thanking me both for paying for her drinks last night and coming to pick them up. They didn't stop even when I pulled into her driveaway.

I'd had to leave band practice to pick them up, but I wasn't going to tell her that. She'd probably just end up thanking me again.

"I already said you didn't have to thank me." I put the car in park and turn toward her. Dottie had insisted on giving her the front seat. Nothing else would do. "The first forty-nine times were more than adequate."

"Give him one of your cookies, dear," Dottie says. "Go on."

"Oh, no," Sophie says, with a look of genuine horror. "I left them in my car at The Ginger Station. Do you think they'll be okay?"

"I don't think they're going to get up and walk away, if that's what you're concerned about," I tease.

"We'll get Bear to drop us off later so we can reclaim the car," Dottie insists. "Those cookies can withstand a hot car. They're filled with love. Love can withstand anything."

"Even being eaten?" I ask, and Sophie gives a delighted laugh. Even tired and hungover, she's hard to look away from.

Sophie holds my gaze and says, "Seriously, thank you, Rob."

"I'm going to start charging you for every tipsy thank-you."

"Money?" She cocks her head, her honey-brown hair spilling over the sleeve of her T-shirt.

"Stale car cookies."

"Oh, you," Dottie says sweetly. "Well, children, I'd better get home to give my love *his* cookies. But first, I wanted to give you this, my dear Sophie."

She hands her a rock, although it's not the same one that's sitting in my pocket. It looks like pink quartz.

"I can't take this," Sophie insists, looking pained by the thought of accepting a gift.

"Good luck with that," I tell her. "She's as good at taking no for an answer as you are at stopping the thank-yous."

Sophie's lips part in surprise. "You have one too?"

"Indeed," Dottie says, "and so do Briar and Hannah, although I had to hide Hannah's in her jacket pocket the other day. I didn't think she'd be happy to take it, the dear. But you all need them. I can see that very clearly. They'll help you believe in love again."

She's not looking at Sophie, but I see the pained face Soph makes. Yeah, she's not ready to believe in love again, but she's exactly the sort to believe in crystals. I try not to laugh.

Dottie gets out of the car, but Sophie lingers. Glancing at me, she says, "I'd like to see your band perform sometime."

I feel myself leaning toward her slightly. "Will you be in the front row dancing?"

"I might even throw confetti at you."

"Only if it's glitter confetti. I have standards to uphold. I think you'll get your chance, you know; we're playing at Buchanan on Friday night."

She smiles at me—and this smile is genuine and a bit fierce. I can imagine her saying, *You will be cheerful, Rob Price.* "I remember you saying something about that! I'm working that night. I owe you another drink. Nonalcoholic. Whatever you want."

"You'll get me another soda, then?" I joke. Some of the breweries have other options, but not many of them.

Her frown plants a furrow between her brows. "There isn't much, is there? I think we should do something about that. I owe you—"

I capture her hand and then release it quickly. She's my asshole brother's ex, and I've got no business holding her hand like some kind of p-e-r-v-e-r-t. "You owe me nothing," I insist. "You didn't owe me the ginger ale either."

"You have your ways, and I have mine. Are you going to get into trouble for what happened last night?"

"For paying your bar bill? Nah. I don't think the cops will take me in for that."

She gives me a level look. "You know what I mean."

I do. There will be consequences. With Jonah and my father's family, there always are. But I've decided I don't care. They don't have power over me anymore. When I was a kid, I had no choice but to live in my father's house. No choice but to try to get along, especially since my father paid for my mother to go to rehab the first time, and technically the second.

But I don't have to play their games anymore. Mom's doing well now, living in Montana with her second husband, a retired rancher, and a potbellied pig. I don't have to worry about her anymore, only about myself, and Jonah doesn't have anything I want. My father either.

"That's not for you to worry about," I tell Sophie. "The problems Jonah and I have with each other have nothing to do with you. They go back years. My father always sides with him, pretty much, because he likes getting action from my step-mother, who hates me. But I stopped worrying what any of them think of me a long time ago. It's easier that way."

"Well, I appreciate your help," she says, squeezing my fore-arm. "If there's anything I can do for you, name it."

"Same," I say as she reaches for the door to leave. "I want to be there for you."

She looks surprised by this, then her expression shifts to confused. *I'm* confused. I hadn't intended to get pulled further into her business or Jonah's.

Our connection probably should have ended two weeks ago, when I chauffeured her to Silver Star. It was likely a mistake to come when called today, but I know she's not a woman who asks for favors. She's usually the one who gives them without being asked. The fact that she asked me to come get her means something, and I couldn't say no. Didn't want to.

"I'm sorry, and *thank you*," she says with a wicked look, since she knows how I feel about apologies and has already thanked me endless times. Then she leaves the car, laughing, before I can tell her to take it back.

I watch her until she's safely inside. Then I check the time on my phone, finding a text from Travis.

Are you Pollyanna's chauffeur now?

Smiling, I type back:

Looks like. Are we still practicing?

No. Turns out the band sounds pretty bad with just a bass guitar and the drums. We're thinking of going tubing on the French Broad if you want to come.

I'd wanted to play for longer, but it's hard to be upset with the guys. I'm feeling positive. Upbeat.

I feel good about myself. I write back:

> Nah, man. I've got something else I need to do.

And I go home and work on a song.

It's a song she could dance to.

THE OTHER SHOE drops half a week later.

I had my home visit from the team weighing my application to be a foster parent, and it went great. Travis helped me clean up first, and the whole apartment smelled like potpourri.

But I get a call from my caseworker Nelly on Thursday evening, saying they'd received an anonymous tip that I have an alcohol problem and a sex addiction.

The first used to be true. The second? Total bullshit. Sure, I haven't had many long-term relationships, but that doesn't mean I'm bringing three women a night back to my apartment. I haven't even hooked up with anyone for over a month, not since I started the process of becoming a foster parent.

"My half-brother must have been behind it," I tell her, pacing up and down my apartment. "He's got something against me."

"So there's family drama," she says, her tone suggesting she's writing something down. Shit, that's probably not good.

"Not really, no. I don't have much to do with him." I lower onto the couch, feeling a headache coming on. "Emil would probably never even meet him. We're not close."

"Rob, it was a woman who called me."

The headache worsens. Did Jonah get his mother to do his dirty work for him? I'm tempted to ask if she sounded like a fifty-year-old finishing school student with a stick permanently lodged up her ass, but I have a feeling it wouldn't go down well.

"There's no truth to the sex addiction thing," I say firmly, embarrassed to have this conversation with Nelly, who's a sweet middle-aged woman who knits sweaters for preemie wards. "I don't...you know...any more than any other guy."

"And the other?" she asks, her tone gentle.

"I haven't had a drink in seven years, but yes, I was in AA. Is that a problem?"

"Not necessarily," she says. "Seven years is a long time. I'm assuming you can put me in touch with your sponsor?"

I cradle my forehead. "He's not sober anymore, and he moved years ago. But I have friends who can vouch for me. The guys in the band. They can tell you I don't drink. My buddy Travis is basically my sponsor at this point."

She hesitates. "Look, it's great that you have a two-bedroom apartment. Not many single people can afford that in this city. Especially in such a great part of town. But I have to be honest with you. It would look better if you were married or in a serious relationship. Especially given this other accusation."

I glance up at the brick wall in front of me, empty except for the mounted TV and a framed photograph of my mother and me. She'd given it to me, and I'd hung it up because I missed her. Because she'd always made me feel wanted, even when she was stuck in one of her downward spirals.

I want to provide Emil with that same security.

"Is it a no, then?" I ask thickly.

"I don't have an answer for you yet, sweetheart. But I know you're trying to do a good thing. Bless you for that. I'll make a case for you."

"Thanks, Nelly," I say, and hang up.

I have to be honest with myself. For the first time in years, I really want a drink. Because the last thing I can imagine doing is telling that kid it's a bust, and he'll only be able to play in stolen moments, when I'm able to meet him on his walks.

The thought fills me with shame, and enough rage that I'd like to pound my fist into the wall a few times. I'd like to call Jonah and curse him out, or show up at his doorstep and punch him in the face, again, the moment he answers the door. But then he really would have me arrested, and I'd have no one to blame but myself.

It's late, but I go to the gym and work out hard, until I'm tired, panting, and sweaty. When I sit in my car afterward, feeling alone, wrung out, and full of darkness, I find myself slipping a hand in my pocket to touch the stone Dottie gave me.

Then I slip it out and put it in the glove box. Because wishes and dreams don't do anything, whatever Sophie and Dottie have to say about it.

Travis calls me later, to ask if I have any updates on the Emil front. I feel a prickle of self-consciousness as I lie fluently to him, the way any alcoholic can, telling him the home visit went well and I'm feeling good about my chances.

"You ready for tomorrow night?" he asks.

"Tomorrow night?" Anything beyond today feels impossible or at the very least abstract. This whole evening has been about survival, one minute floating into the next.

He groans. "Don't tell me you forgot. We're playing at Buchanan. You can throw Pollyanna your shirt."

"Very funny."

"It would piss off your brother."

The thought hits a little too close to home, although I'll be honest. I'd fucking like to. I'd like to infuriate him so much he reveals the truth of who he is to everyone.

I shake the thought off and focus on the fact that Sophie will be there tomorrow. We've texted casually a couple of times since Sunday. For the most part, we've stuck to The Ginger Station situation, but there've been no real developments. I don't feel like I have the right to ask about anything else. Maybe I'm also trying to prepare myself for the inevitable. Maybe I'm also trying to prepare myself for the inevitable. I'm a reminder of the worst mistake of her life, and she's already told me flat out that she'd wish her mistakes away if she could, like dandelion fluff in the wind. It's pure hubris to think I wouldn't be cut loose alongside Jonah.

Still, after I get off the phone with Travis, I watch that video of her reaming out Jonah. Something I've been doing nearly every night.

I tell myself it's because I like watching Jonah getting schooled, which is true, but it's also because Sophie's transformation inspires me. It makes me want to write music.

CHAPTER THIRTEEN

SOPHIE

Conversation with Unknown Number

> Stop coming to The Ginger Station and asking about me.

> Who are you?

> None of your business.

> You do NOT want to piss off Pat.

> You're right. I don't.

"I'll have the Silver Star IPA," Briar says, twirling one of her long locks as she studies the menu. She and Hannah are sitting in one of the booths in my section at Buchanan Brewery. It's Friday evening, and they're both here for Rob's show. It's Briar's usual night off, and Hannah's playing hooky. Each of us are wearing our perfect red lipstick, chosen by Hannah.

"Seriously?" Hannah retorts, giving her the stink eye. "When in Buchanan…"

Briar shrugs. "If my dad found out I tried a Buchanan beer,

he'd probably have a heart attack. I'm not ready to run the brewery yet."

"Live a little," Hannah says.

Briar glances around as if worried someone's watching her and chronicling her choices. "Okay, maybe I'll have a flight."

"That's the spirit." Hannah claps her on the back. "I'll have the same, and you can choose the beers for us, Mrs. and Mrs. Ginnis. These are your stomping grounds." Her face puckers as if she's been sucking lemons. "But no ginger beer."

While Briar has accepted that GingerBeerBabe is obviously disinterested in being our friend, Hannah is adamant that the message I received from an unknown number could very well have been from Jonah himself. Or a friend of Jonah's. She's received a couple of texts that were obviously from Jonah in response to her STD posters. One of them said:

> He does NOT have crabs. I know that for a
> fact.

Which she'd responded to by saying:

> I never mentioned crabs specifically, how
> interesting.

I'm on the fence. Hannah's right, but so is Briar. It's perfectly likely that GingerBeerBabe knows all about Jonah's cheating and still wants nothing to do with us. I mean, I get it. I'm a woman who's tried to bury the past for over a decade. I understand if she'd prefer to be done with him and everything related to him. It's her God-given right. But I'd still like to meet her, or at least have confirmation of her existence. Hannah and I started down this path last weekend, and turning back now would feel like giving up.

On her, I mean. I gave up on Jonah weeks ago.

He definitely does not seem to have given up on me yet.

He sent chocolates earlier this week, which were melted and infested with ants by the time I got home from work. Then last night, we came home to a flower arrangement, or at least that's what Otis and I surmised. Some wild animal must have gotten at it after it was dropped off, leaving a trail of broken blooms and leaves across our front porch. All that was left was the mess and a chewed-up note. The only part that could be read said: *nah.*

It had felt like my bad luck was asserting itself. First there had been Great-Aunt Penny's plate, cracked in half, and then this...

I'd admitted as much to Otis. But he'd laughed and said it seemed more like bad luck for Jonah than for us.

Of course, he wasn't the one who'd cleaned it up.

As I head back to the bar to prepare my friends' orders, I glance toward the closed-off brewing area. Dottie and her partner came tonight too, but her great nephew River, our head brewer, brought them into the back to try his new Kölsch beer, and they haven't reappeared yet.

Otis would have come, but someone lost a rare albino pigeon and offered him—and presumably lots of other Honey Do employees—an obscene amount of money to try to catch "Fluffnut."

"It's just like what happened in *Ace Ventura*," he'd told me, excited.

He's still thinking of quitting Honey Do, especially after we did the Myers-Briggs test yesterday and Dottie did a crystal reading for him. Both results were in agreement: he'd do well working with children. Otis was excited and full of ideas. Still, he prefers to drift into new directions rather than force a change, so I expect it will be a while before he does anything about it.

I get my friends their drinks, and the evening carries on with a buzz of activity until Rob and two other guys emerge from the back with some sound equipment and their instrument cases. One of the band members is tall with longish, wavy black hair and a port wine birthmark on his forehead, and the other has reddish-brown hair and bright-blue eyes. I saw their photos when I looked up his songs, so I know the black-haired guy is Travis and the other is Chance Bixby.

A fizzy, excited feeling rises up in me. Because I really, *really* want to hear Rob sing. These last few weeks, my emotions have been waging a war of highs and lows. I can no longer walk the tightrope I'd gotten so good at toeing across. Watching the wrong commercial can lead to tears or mood swings. Acts of kindness are Superman-killing kryptonite that can send me into a chorus of sobs. It's like every emotion I've tried to suppress has come to the surface at once.

I wave at Rob, and when he sees me, he fumbles his guitar case, and Travis plows into his back.

Huh. That's strange. He's not usually clumsy.

I watch as the band members make their way toward the stage, people stopping them every couple of feet to say hello. Then Rob whispers something to them, sets his case down, and approaches the bar with a grin.

"We all came," I announce proudly, gesturing to the corner booth where I left my friends. But the booth is empty, and now I look like a psychopath.

"Oh, is that your wife sitting over there?" he asks with a lopsided smile. "Give Mrs. Ginnis my best."

I roll my eyes. "You're never going to let me live that down, are you? Hannah and Briar came, but they must have moved. Or maybe Dottie took them into the back."

"More clandestine brewery missions?"

"No, Dottie's family runs this place. That's how I found this job."

He smiles fondly. "Give her enough time, she'll be running the whole city. She's really something."

"Maybe she should be in charge. Everyone would be a lot nicer."

He raises his eyebrows. "You know how I feel about people who are always nice."

"Yes, we're terrible. We should all start pouring beer on people and then declaring the glasses half empty. Speaking of which, I owe you a drink," I add excitedly, because I've spent the last few days testing out nonalcoholic cocktails. My boss tried a few and agreed it might be a good idea to add them to the menu. It had made me feel useful in a way I hadn't since before my aunt left on her vacation.

Useful *and* creative.

"So you insisted the other day," he says lightly, but I notice he's giving me a funny look.

Suddenly self-conscious, I shift the skirt of my red dress with its pattern of golden stars. I've been wearing them lately. Dresses, I mean.

It's a hot, humid summer, and normally I'd breeze through it in a series of different cutoffs or khaki shorts and T-shirts, but Hannah and Briar have convinced me to diversify.

I've enjoyed trying out new looks. Until recently, I'd never experimented with clothes, the same way I'd never learned much about lipstick. I grew up an only child, and when I was sixteen, I was sent to reform school. The other kids had scared me, mostly, and I'd made friends with the house mother—a forty-eight-year-old woman named Ruth who made elaborate craft projects with me for the other girls. They were about as appreciative as Rob was of that guitar strap.

Ruth was great, but she'd owned the same shirt in twenty colors and wore only blue jeans. She'd never taken me shopping or taught me about makeup, and the girls at school who cared about that kind of thing were frankly terrifying. So I'd never really learned what I did and didn't like. I'd always been embarrassed to try. It would've seemed like I cared, and I'd learned that showing you cared was like throwing blood in the water.

Just ask poor Ruth. We'd spent hours creating handmade Christmas crackers for everyone my senior year, and one of the girls had thrown them into the indoor pool.

I told Hannah and Briar that story last week at a bar, although I described Rosewood Academy as a boarding school rather than reform school, and Hannah had put her drink down and said, "That's it. We're going shopping, right now. You don't have to pretend not to care because you're worried someone's going to make fun of you or throw your clothes into the pool. If anyone tries to pull that nonsense, you make fun of them right back, until they cry."

"I don't think *anyone* would try to make fun of you," Briar commented.

"Oh, they have," she said with a half-smile.

"And they cried?" I guessed.

She shrugged. "Sometimes they did. Sometimes *I* did. But if I was the one who cried, my brother Liam would roll in, and he'd turn around and make them cry. So either way they learned a lesson. You don't even want to know what happened to the kids who messed with our little brother. Now, we're going to shop, and you're going to get whatever the hell you want."

So I went shopping with my friends, and they helped me pick out some clothes that I actually liked. It was fun. But now Rob's giving me that inscrutable look, and I feel a prickling of the old self-consciousness. Did I overdo it? Do I look like one of those try-hard kids who got mocked mercilessly?

"Is it too fancy?" I ask. "I liked the color, but maybe it's a bit much. I—"

"Your dress looks good on you. Really good."

Something inside me glows at the praise, because I know he's a man who means what he says.

"Okay," I say, grinning, then slap the bar with my palm. "So, I've been experimenting with NA drinks all week, and I've come up with a few options that are really good. Do you want something fruity, aromatic, or fresh?"

"You did that for me?" he asks, sounding alarmed. He runs a hand through his shaggy hair, and I watch his arm as the muscles bunch, my mouth going dry.

"Dylan, um, he thinks we can put them on the menu," I stammer.

He gives a nod, followed by a smile that lights up his face, making those green-gold eyes crinkle at the edges. It feels like a metaphysical punch. "Surprise me, Not-So-Pollyanna. But I want it to be sweet."

I huff a laugh, shaking my head. "Sure you do."

"Heard anything more about your mystery?" he asks.

I tell him about the unknown-number messenger while I mix his drink. Then I pass it over the bar to him, our fingers brushing, and lean toward him in eagerness as I watch him sip.

I've never given it much thought, but there's something sensual about a man drinking. My eyes track his Adam's apple as he swallows the first taste.

"Well?" I ask. Conversation buzzes around the whole room and there's a few muted thumps from his friends setting up on the stage, but my attention is firmly fixed on him.

"Terrible." But his mouth is already twitching with a grin. "*You're* terrible."

"It's delicious, Sophie Ginnis. It tastes like an Aperol spritzer."

"Is it bad that it tastes like alcohol?" I ask, suddenly doubting myself. "I know, I mean, I guessed..."

"That I had an alcohol problem?" He gives me another half-smile. "I like the taste, but it's not going to drive me to a liquor bottle. Jonah's more likely to do that."

"What did he do?" I ask, horrified. I can tell from Rob's fixed jaw that Jonah definitely did something.

"I'm trying to become a foster parent," he says, and if I'd been holding something, I would have dropped it. Rob, a foster parent?

"Yes, I know. It shocked me too." He grins, shaking his head slightly. "But there's this kid, Emil, who was in my music program—"

"Music program?"

"Yeah," he says, grabbing the lip of the bar and leaning in a little. I see more people coming up to the bar, and I realize there are a few waiting not so patiently. My boss gives me a strained look, followed by a thumbs-up. I'm pretty sure he's just coddling me. Everyone at work has been so *nice*. They still don't know the details of what happened with my engagement, but I suspect the gossip circuit has put forth some pretty creative ideas.

After word got around, Dylan took me aside and informed me they wouldn't be using Jonah for distribution anymore, effective immediately. It wasn't his call, but I know he petitioned the Buchanans, who own the brewery, on my behalf. Knowing Dottie, I wouldn't be surprised if she'd had a hand in it too.

I know I'm not pulling my weight tonight, and I feel a familiar thrum of guilt. Still. I really, really want to hear what Rob's going to say.

"My job, you know?" he says.

"You have a job?" I gasp.

He laughs, strumming his fingers against the side of the wooden bar as if it's a guitar. "What did you think I did?"

"You're in a band." I point to the stage, where Rob's friends are still setting up. I guess he's shirking his duty, too, but I can't bring myself to say anything. I don't want him to walk away.

"Yeah, but we only do a couple of shows a week. What did you think I did with my time?"

I feel my cheeks flush as I think of all the comments Jonah had made about his derelict brother who spent all day eating corn chips and jerking off, living off their father's largesse. It obviously wasn't true.

Well, the jerking off part could be true...

The thought of Rob touching himself, of his head tipping back with pleasure, sends a fresh rush of blood to my cheeks.

Rob swears under his breath, then touches my hand across the counter. "You don't have to be embarrassed. No one in my dad's family is impressed by me. Travis—" He points to the guy I'd already identified thanks to my internet stalking. "Travis is my best friend. Has been for a long time. He's the one who came up with the idea. We run this after-school music program for middle school and high school kids. It's for kids who want to play music but not the traditional stuff like symphonies performed with woodwinds. We do string instruments. Drums. Rock mostly. But we've been swayed into some Taylor Swift covers by a few of the girls."

"That's awesome," I say, so bowled over I can barely summon the words. He works with children. He wants to be a foster parent.

This is *Rob*, the man who opened my heartfelt Christmas present and made a *huh* sound. How is this possible?

"I..." My throat feels tight suddenly. "I wanted to open an after-school craft business for kids. Younger kids, like elementary school. I had almost everything ready, but it fell through. The permits first, and then the friend who was supposed to run it with me dropped out, and then my great-aunt got sick."

"I didn't know that about you either," he says, his eyes on

mine. There's something curious and warm in them, and I feel myself melting a little. There are tears pressing at my eyes, which is frankly horrifying.

"Jonah never said?"

"No, but we're not exactly friends. Something like that would work in Asheville," he adds, nodding confidently. "You can't imagine how many requests we get from parents." He pauses, taking me in. "You'd be good at that. Your relentless positivity would be a plus."

My old dream tries to flicker to life inside of me, the image hazy. I attempt to shrug it off. "We'll see. I've moved pretty far from that old dream."

He glances down at his drink, his lips tipping up into a smile. Goodness. Has his smile *always* looked like that? It's like it was hand-sculpted by a higher power to make women want him. Surely I would have noticed before...

I focus on the tiny mole to the right of his right eyebrow. At least then I won't be fantasizing about what would happen if I leaned forward across the bar and—

"I don't know about that, Soph. Seems to me you invented a whole drink menu just because you thought I could do better than a soda. Those kids don't know what's coming for them."

"Thank you," I say, trying to swallow down the neediness that I hate.

It's just...I want to be the woman he sees when he looks at me. The one who wishes on stars and reaches for her dreams. I am, sometimes, but I'm so afraid of failure. Of being punished.

"I'm sorry," I say, and he lifts his eyebrows playfully, making me smile. "You were telling me about your job and I hijacked the conversation. I'd like to hear more."

"Sure, I'll talk about myself if you insist," he responds with a knowing look. He understands I'm being emotional, and also that I don't like it. "The kid I wanted to help, he's so damn talented. His current foster dad made him drop out of our program, though, and he's not allowed to practice at home, because the sound supposedly gives his foster mom headaches. Emil needs music, Sophie. I know because I did when I was his age. I could give him that, if I get to be his foster dad. But I don't think my application is going to be approved. Jonah had some lady call and tell them I'm an alcoholic and a sex addict, and now my caseworker thinks the only way they'll approve me is if I'm in a serious relationship."

My mouth falls open in horror. "He did that?"

"Look at what he did to you. He sucks. He's always sucked. The only reason I have anything to do with him is my dad, but to be honest, I feel pretty done with that whole side of my family. I've been thinking about taking a step back from them for a while now."

"I'm going to help you," I insist.

"By calling them up and telling them that I'm only a sex addict sometimes?"

"Are you?" I ask, biting my lower lip as I'm assailed by some very inappropriate thoughts. I see him noticing. I see him appreciating, and a shocking wave of heat swells through me.

This is what I felt the night of my wedding to myself. An attraction to Rob. It feels *very* real, but maybe it's only transference. I thought I was in love with Jonah up until three weeks ago, and Rob looks a bit like Jonah—*except ten times hotter*, I hear Hannah say in my mind—so it's natural I'd feel drawn to someone with a similar appearance. We've also been seeing each other a lot, and...

"Sorry," I say, shaking off that train of thought. "Sorry. I shouldn't have..."

I trail off as I notice a victorious gleam in his eyes and realize I'm arcing toward him, across the bar.

"You owe me some of those car cookies," he says.

"They're stale by now."

Plus, Otis and I ate them all while watching *Golden Girls* reruns. It was Aunt Penny's favorite show, and both of us used to complain about it, but I guess we kind of miss her, because we turned it on by mutual agreement.

"Maybe I like stale love cookies..."

Uh...what? Is he flirting?

I'm about to respond, but my words dry up, because Jonah just walked in through the front door. I haven't seen him in person since that night at The Ginger Station, and now he's here. Carrying a flipping boom box. Where did he even get it?

CHAPTER FOURTEEN

SOPHIE

I slip out from behind the bar and shove my way through the crowd, getting to Jonah just as he reaches for the play button.

I grab his hand, and he meets my gaze. For a second I feel the pull of the story I used to tell myself. It was a fairy tale, made of spun sugar, about this man saving me and making me respectable. About him loving me enough to make up for all the people who didn't.

It puts a knot in my throat, but I choke it down like the poison I know it to be.

"What are you doing?" I hiss.

Several people are gawking at us, but there's no sign of Briar or Hannah or Dottie.

I can feel Rob staring at us from his place at the bar. So I glance over at him. His eyes burn into me as he cocks his head: *Say the word, and I'll punch him again.*

"I'm going to serenade you," Jonah says, recapturing my attention. "The song from that *Ten Things* movie you love. I want to show you that I'm willing to embarrass myself for you. Anything to get you to hear me out."

I feel a twist in my stomach. He's being manipulative. If I don't hear him out, he's willing to embarrass both of us.

"Hey," I hear someone whisper to a friend. "Isn't that the guy with the STDs?"

"Should we warn her?" the friend responds.

Jonah's jaw tenses, but he doesn't move from his position, standing right inside the doorway, where people will need to squeeze around him. This feels like a statement too. *I will embarrass and inconvenience you at work.*

"Come with me," I say, my voice hoarse. Part of me hates myself for giving him what he wants, even if it's just a chance for me to tell him in more detail how deeply I resent him, but I can't let him serenade me in here. Sure, it would be more embarrassing for him, but it would still be a spectacle. It would be something people talk about for weeks, months, maybe even years, and I've already been a spectacle once in my life, and maybe a half spectacle last weekend with the wedding dress.

I lead him to the booth abandoned by my friends, who left enough of their stuff that their seats have not yet been commandeered by anyone else.

His posture stiffens, possibly because he recognizes their handbags, but he sits and sets the boom box on the tabletop, as if it's a perfectly usual thing for a person to have as an accessory.

"You're the type of person who forgives other people for making mistakes," he says.

Anger flares inside of me, so much of it I'm surprised my hair doesn't spontaneously turn the color of Hannah's.

"You don't get to tell me who I am."

Surprise flickers in his eyes, but he regains control of his expression quickly. "You've been different lately. I know it's my fault. But I need you to understand that nothing happened with those women except inappropriate flirting. I was having cold feet, I'll admit to that, but now I realize how stupid I was to jeopardize our future. Sophie, you're the perfect wife for me. You—"

Jonah cuts off abruptly at the sound of someone approaching. He glances toward the noise and tenses his jaw.

"You were saying?" Rob says conversationally, leaning against my side of the booth. He's holding the drink I made him. His body language is relaxed, bored almost, but something fierce is flashing in his eyes. I'm glad for it. I'm glad for him, being here, joining his strength with mine. I can practically feel it pulsing from him. I truly must be spending too much time with Dottie and Briar, because his energy feels friendly. Warm. Supportive.

"Don't let me interrupt you, man," Rob says, waving his glass. "You seemed really impassioned. It was just getting interesting. There are a few other people behind you who also want to see where you're going with this, right, guys?"

I peer over my shoulder and see a teenager's face raised over the back of my booth, but he disappears the instant our eyes meet, like a groundhog fleeing his shadow.

"I see you're drinking again," Jonah says in a withering tone.

Rob lifts the glass in a silent cheers. "Please, continue. Like I said, we're enjoying the show. I assume you came tonight on purpose, because I told you I thought you should leave Sophie alone, and you wanted to prove you could get her back, right? So, please. Prove it. I'm paying attention. Lots of us are. But there may be a plot twist you're not prepared for."

"You're shit-faced," Jonah sneers.

"I made the drink for him," I say, anger making my blood boil. "It's nonalcoholic. He's just being a good friend to me."

"Why are you hanging out with my deadbeat brother, anyway?" Jonah lashes out at me. "This is the second time I've seen you together. You know we don't get along." His voice is full of accusation, and the injustice of it sends goosebumps across the surface of my skin.

"It's none of your business who I spend time with," I say tightly. "I may be the perfect wife for you, Jonah, but you would *not* be the perfect husband for me. I'm really glad you thought I had to have exactly the same phone as you with exactly the same wallpaper, because otherwise I might have made the biggest mistake of my life."

"You're making the biggest mistake of your life right now," he says, standing.

It's uncomfortable to stand in these booths. Either the seat or the table digs into your legs, but a flash of intuition tells me he's doing it just so he can look down at me. He loves looking down at people. He even bought shoes with a two-inch lift so he could do it more efficiently.

Pure rage flash fries my Pollyanna side, and I stand up on the seat of the booth. So *I* can look down at *him*.

He stares at me in disbelief. It's the same stare he gave me that day at Silver Star, the *who are you and what did you do with the pushover I'm used to?* stare. The tasting room goes silent for half a second and then erupts into conversation.

I'm probably going to regret this. Possibly a lot. Seconds ago, I was worried about Jonah making a scene, and now I'm the one doing it. But something inside of me has burst, and I can't sit down. *I can't.* I wave at the crowd and then blow them a kiss. In the back of my head a panicked voice is screaming, but I shove it *down, down, down.*

My friends still haven't returned, but I'm certain it won't be long now. They'll have heard the uproar.

"Get down from there," Jonah says, his cheeks turning red. You're making a fool of yourself again."

"I thought *you* wanted that." I point to the boom box. "Go ahead, we'll perform a duet together. Heck, if you'll sing a duet with me right now, I'll agree to have dinner with you so we can talk about everything you totally didn't do. We'll even get dessert."

"But I'll be sitting in the booth behind you," Rob says with a laugh. "That's nonnegotiable. And I get to share the appetizers. I never want to eat all twelve chicken wings."

"Well?" I ask Jonah.

It's meant as a challenge, and it works. I can tell he never meant to serenade me. It was a threat, maybe even a bluff.

"Is there even a tape in that boom box?" I ask.

I can tell by the look on his face that there isn't. For some reason I'm more offended by this than the rest of his bullshit.

"I want you to leave me alone," I tell him, my voice rising with every word. "I never want to see you again. This is over. *Done.*"

Silence has descended on the bar, and I can feel dozens of eyes on me. I glance around. My friends still aren't around, and there's no sign of Dylan, which is probably why we haven't been interrupted. My coworker behind the bar gives me a shaky nod, like she's not sure whether she should intervene or support me through my public crisis.

"We are no longer engaged," I tell everyone. "This is over. *Permanently.*"

"It's probably because of all those STDs," I hear someone say.

Jonah looks so furious, I'm surprised he doesn't burst spontaneously into flame.

"I can have any woman I want," he says spitefully. "Any woman, anywhere, anytime. Why would I want a washed-up bartender whose own family doesn't want anything to do with her?"

The words are meant to stab me where it hurts, and they do. I become intensely aware of all those eyes on me, staring at me as if I were wearing a scarlet letter. Only I'm pretty sure mine is an L, for loser, instead of an A, for adultery.

My knees feel like they want to buckle, but I wrap my hand around the pendant at my neck and stand tall. It's the pink crystal from Dottie. Briar surprised Hannah and me by making our crystals into matching necklaces. It's a sign of love and friendship, and even though I was initially afraid of what it signified—moving on, trusting again—it gives me strength.

I refuse to sit back down.

"You'll want to be careful about the way you talk to her," Rob says from his stalwart position at my side of the booth. He stands up tall and straight, and suddenly he's pure menace, his arms loose at his sides and ready to do damage to Jonah.

"Why?" Jonah asks, giving a bitter laugh. "You never gave a shit about her until a few weeks ago. You have a sudden taste for my leftovers?"

Rob sets down his drink. It's obvious he's seconds away from punching Jonah in the face again, this time in front of a large crowd of people. He'd get into trouble for it, and I'm sure his chances of becoming a foster parent for that boy would be obliterated.

Oh, I *hate* Jonah.

I hate him in the way a person can only hate a dream gone sour. I don't want to think the best of him, or even try to improve him as a person with crystals, the way Dottie hopes to do. I want to destroy him. I want to make him feel as insignificant and unwanted as he made me feel. I want to watch him *cry*.

It's an awful, sickening feeling, especially when I've poured so much energy into being a glass-half-full person. A good influence. Someone who brings out the best in other people. But I don't want to deny the impulse. I want to grip it with both hands.

And then it hits me.

Hannah told me the best revenge would be dating Jonah's brother.

Rob said the only way out of the mess Jonah's created for him might be to jump into a serious relationship.

Plus, Rob made it pretty clear he doesn't want anything to do with his father's side of the family.

And Dottie said our fates were intertwined.

"Help me down, honey," I say to Rob, giving him a *please, for the love of God play along* look.

Jonah seems taken back, almost like he thinks I'm talking to him, and Rob looks like I just axed him in the head.

Rob recovers first, scooping me into his arms. I gasp as he pulls me into him. His chest is so solid and warm, and my whole body is suddenly filled with a different kind of awareness. Even here, in front of everyone, in front of freaking *Jonah*.

"Thanks," I say, peering up into his eyes. I silently will him to play along. "I think we'd better tell him."

His eyes are full of conflicting emotions, and for a second, doubt takes hold. I was impulsive again, first by getting up on the booth seat, and now this, and—

Rob dips his head to kiss me.

CHAPTER FIFTEEN

ROB

I promised myself I wouldn't lie anymore, that the lying was done when the drinking was, but I'll be damned if I'm not going to step up for Sophie, especially when it means I get to puncture Jonah's puffed-up ego.

It doesn't hurt that you've been thinking about kissing her.

When she stepped onto that booth seat, she was Sophie from that video again, a vengeful goddess full of fire and passion. My fingers itched for my pen, wanting to write another song about her. But I have to admit I was more interested in gliding my hands all over her. I wanted to learn the dips and curves of this perplexing woman who'd seemed so simple at first glance. I wanted to show her that I was a man who could appreciate a woman full of fire *and* honey, unlike my dipshit brother, who only wanted the sweetness.

When she called me "honey," it had felt like she'd reached into my head and pulled out the word.

It had felt natural to reach for her, to have her weight settle in my arms. To hold her against my chest in front of everyone, making a declaration. Then she'd looked into my eyes, hers alight with mischief and rage, and said, "I think we'd better tell him."

Damn.

This woman is so unexpected. Like a cherry candy with a spicy cinnamon center. One minute I have Pollyanna, the next a femme fatale.

Her lips are bright red tonight, the same color as the imprint they left on my cheek last weekend.

I can't help it. I lower my head and brush a kiss over them, soft and quick but deep enough to declare to my brother and every last person in this bar that this woman is now mine. Even if it's fake.

That's my intention, anyway. It lasts seconds longer than it should, because her sweet lips part and an electric feeling arcs between us, freezing my senses to everything except her and the places where we connect. The moment feels full of possibility and need. Now that I have my lips on her, I'm tempted to carry her out of here.

She's only pretending, Rob.

I pull back.

She stares up at me with those big blue eyes, which can look as innocent as a baby doll's one second and as fierce as the blade of a knife the next. "You can put me down now, babe."

"What the fuck?" Jonah says, finally sidling out of the booth. It's obvious he'd like to be the one to throw a punch this time, and maybe I'd let him—a punch for a punch—if she weren't in my arms.

I set her on her feet to give him his chance if he wants it. I'm surprised, and pleased, when she stays by my side, her body pressed to mine. Then she steps slightly in front of me, as if she can feel the violence brewing between my brother and me.

"We didn't plan for it to happen, Jonah," she says softly, firmly. "But Rob felt bad about everything that went down with the phone, so he checked on me a couple of times, and we got to talking, and what do you know? He and I have *much* more in common than you and I ever did. We're in love. So I'm thankful to you for cheating on me with several women—"

"Yup, he's the STDs guy all right," someone mutters, reminding me that we not only have witnesses but *a lot* of witnesses. My mind was so sandblasted by Sophie that it had erased all of them, leaving only fuzzy pencil imprints behind.

I glance up and feel all the eyes on us, hear the buzz of countless people talking in undertones. I tell myself it's no different than performing on stage.

My gaze darts to the stage, where Travis is gawking at me. I grin sheepishly at him.

Out of nowhere, a fist comes flying at me, clocking me in the face. I stumble, caught off guard. In my periphery, I catch sight of Sophie thrusting out a hand to catch herself, clearly having been knocked aside. And then there's Jonah, shaking out his fist with a look of shock on his face, like he'd forgotten there was an opportunity cost for throwing a punch.

Got to hand it to him, for a guy who doesn't know his way around the gym, he got in a good one. The pain radiates from the epicenter of the punch like an earthquake.

But I'm more pissed off than injured. He pushed Sophie. Not fucking okay. And no way am I going to let him get in a second punch, especially not with Sophie and dozens of other innocent bystanders hanging out around us.

Before I can react, Sophie pours the tasty nonalcoholic drink on Jonah. "You...jerk," she says. "I hope you choke on it."

I need to get her away from him. *Now.*

I go for him, and we scuffle—in a dance that's been familiar to both of us since we were kids—and I manage to get his arms pinned behind his back without much difficulty.

I glance around for Sophie, feeling the wild need to check

on her, and she's standing just behind me, wielding the empty glass as if preparing to thump Jonah with it.

She's okay. Thank God she's okay.

Blood is pumping through my head, in my ears, and through my injured nose.

"Oh *goodness*," I hear a familiar voice say. The crowd, which has moved back by a few feet, parts like the Red Sea to admit Dottie Hendrickson and a tall, built guy I recognize as Dylan, the tasting room manager and therefore Sophie's boss. He's a former Marine, and even though he's known as "the Gentle Giant," he's not a man anyone with half a brain would like to piss off.

Hannah and Briar are following in their wake.

"What happened?" Dylan asks with a slightly dazed look. "We have a strict no-violence policy, as you both know."

"Does that mean Briar and I don't get to knee Jonah in the balls?" Hannah asks.

"That's exactly what it means," Dylan says with an edge of annoyance in his voice. "Now, what happened?"

Most guys would threaten to call the cops, or tell us to take it outside, but Dylan's different. He likes to settle things himself to make sure people don't come back and make more trouble. Too bad this problem doesn't have an easy solution.

"Well," an old man says, wiping his mouth and standing up from his seat. His date tries to pull him down, but he persists. "This idiot"—he points to my brother, who tries to struggle his way to freedom and fails—"came in with a boom box, saying he wanted to serenade that pretty lady, but she was having none of it. She climbed onto the booth seat to try to get away from him, so this other young buck comes in and swoops her off her feet and kisses her. The idiot didn't like that much and punched him in the face. They danced a bit, and there you have it. You know, I wasn't sold on the live show, but it was actually pretty entertaining. Garbage Fire indeed."

A woman pipes up: "He's that young man who has all the STDs. I've seen flyers about him all around Asheville."

Hannah is shaking with silent laughter, while Briar looks like a deer in the headlights.

"Let. Me. Go," Jonah says.

I set him free and take a step back. Jonah's hair is dripping from the drink, and he's shaking out his hand. I know it must still hurt. Good. My face does too.

Sophie places a hand on my lower back, letting me know she's there, and I feel like we're back at The Ginger Station, when she first put her arms around me.

"You're fucking dead," Jonah snarls at me. "You're going to regret this." He glares at Sophie behind me, and I immediately sidestep so he can't get to her. Right now, I don't even want him looking at her.

"Oh, no," Dottie says. "I think he'll be quite all right. Looks like little more than a love tap, and I have just the thing to help him. I have something to help you, too, young man."

"*Dottie*," Dylan says, and then someone else, another man, calls her name worriedly from the back of the room.

But Dottie continues toward us without paying them any attention. My brother stands frozen in place as she slips a stone into his pocket and then lifts a hand to his cheek, giving him an actual love tap.

"There, now. If that doesn't improve your energy, then I don't deserve to call myself a crystal specialist. Try rubbing it for five minutes each evening and meditating. We'll see what that does for your emotional stamina."

Hannah starts snort-laughing, someone catcalls an insult, and a paper airplane soars through the air and hits Jonah in the cheek. He swats it down, but not before I see that it's one of the STD flyers.

This situation is getting wildly out of control.

My brother looks like he's about to blow an eye vessel. "Enjoy my leftovers, brother," he says, his jaw clenching. "But you're going to realize it's not worth what you just lost. She's vanilla in bed."

I hear the glass slip from Sophie's fingers, little sharp shards scattering across the floor as it explodes.

I start to lunge toward the door, rage eclipsing sense, but Sophie slips her hand into mine and holds on, her grip surprisingly strong. "*Don't.* He's baiting you."

"You're banned," Dylan calls out, losing his cool for the first time. He stalks toward the door, and Jonah, wide-eyed, backs away, his ass hitting the glass. Turning slightly to look at me, Dylan asks, "Do you want me to call the cops? You could have him arrested for assault."

"No," I say. "Fair is fair. I punched him a few weeks ago."

Dylan sighs, shifting his weight, and gives Jonah his attention again. "Don't come back here. If I ever see you in here again—"

"That man kisses like a dead fish," Hannah calls out as Jonah opens the door to the warm night. "And he's a bad tipper."

"He's rude to elderly people," Briar adds. "And he doesn't know much about beer."

Then the night swallows him, the door closing behind him. We're inside while he's left outside, a position I have never been in before with my brother. It's always been the other way around—me excluded, him treated like a golden god. I don't know what to do with myself. And now, Sophie's hand is in mine. Not Jonah's, but mine.

Ignoring the noise that's broken out all around us, I turn toward her.

"I'm sorry," she says in a feverish voice as she lifts her free hand to my painful face.

"There she goes again," I tease. "Does my nose look crooked?"

"I can't tell."

"It would be a good time for you to roll out some of that Pollyanna charm."

Her mouth tips into a smile, but it doesn't quite reach her eyes. "You look very handsome with a somewhat crooked nose, but I *never* should have done that without asking. I didn't mean to. I just thought…I really wanted to get back at Jonah, and I also hoped it might help you with your problem. You said they would be more likely to approve your application if they thought you were in a serious relationship."

My heart starts beating faster, something like hope rising inside of me, a feeling I don't want to attach any expectations to. From my experience, hope can plummet fast. "You'd do that for me?" I lower my voice to a whisper. "Pretend to be my girlfriend?"

You'd be lying, a voice in my head whispers. More lies. Deeper ones.

"Of course," she says, her eyes wide. "And Emil. I can't believe Jonah tried to stop you from helping him. I want to make that right, and to be perfectly honest, I also want to piss Jonah off. He deserves to be upset, don't you think? He shouldn't be able to do whatever he wants and get away with it."

"I won't disagree with you there. For how long?"

She squeezes my hand. "We'll figure that out later. You know, I don't understand what I ever saw in that…" She pauses, as if searching for a word that can adequately explain my brother. "Imbecilic asshole."

"You and me both, sister," Hannah murmurs, reminding me again that there are other people around us. A lot of them.

I glance around, finding the brewery full of confusion. Someone's sweeping up the glass, thankfully. Travis and Bixby are still on the stage, giving me *what the fuck?* looks. Understandable. I just got punched in the face. My hand is fine, given that I didn't fight back much, but I don't feel up to performing tonight anymore. I'm guessing Dylan doesn't much want me up there like this either.

My gaze finds Sophie's again. "You saw the best sides of him. You see the best in everyone."

Something warms in her eyes, and suddenly everyone else is gone again. No, not gone. They're in black and white and she's in warm, pulsing color—her dress and lips that perfect shade of red, her eyes oceans of blue that a man could lose himself in—and a sense of awe envelops me. She was here, all along, and I didn't notice.

Well, now I'm noticing. I can't seem to stop.

She holds my gaze for several long seconds, the connection feeling like my fingers strumming the strings of my guitar, and then looks away.

I can't read the expression on her face.

I can't really figure out what's going on in my own chest, other than that something significant happened here tonight. Something that's going to change everything that comes afterward.

"Here," Dottie says, returning from God knows where with a little lidded canister. The world floods back in. "Rub this all over your face tonight, my dear," Dottie instructs as I take the canister she's shoving at me, "and you'll wake up feeling like a new man. It should help with the bruising too. I *am* sorry I wasn't there to stop it from coming to fisticuffs, but I felt, very strongly, that Sophie needed a chance to confront him. I must admit that I kept the others occupied in the back to give our dear girl that cathartic moment."

Dylan sighs. "I should have known something was up when you kept asking about the names of the old beers. You had the Buchanans worried you were going senile."

It amuses me that she thinks she could have stopped Jonah from punching me in the face, but I don't say so. Turning to Dylan, who looks like he's doing breathing exercises to get back to his usual state of zen, I say, "I don't think I can play tonight, man. Can we make it up to you another time?"

He laughs ruefully. "Not a problem. I think we'll be getting more foot traffic for weeks because of this. The people around these parts have a taste for drama." Turning to Sophie, he says, "Sophie, can you work?"

That's when I notice all of the gawking bystanders are now lined up at the bar for drinks, and there's only one bartender working. She has a fixed smile on her face that makes her look like the *before* in a commercial for anxiety medication.

Hannah whispers something to Briar, who nods decisively and then says, "We all will, if you'd like."

"Really?" Sophie asks, her face full of wonder. "Wouldn't your father mind?"

"Oh, yes," she says, "but I think we'll have a riot on our hands if we don't start serving these people soon."

"I wish someone would work," says the grumpy old man who's decided he enjoys dinner theater. "I need a refill."

CHAPTER SIXTEEN

It's ten forty-five, and the brewery is closed.

Dottie went home soon after the brouhaha, saying her work here was done, but Hannah and Briar both poured drinks with me, Dylan, and the other staffer on shift until the bitter end. Rob and the guys from the band stuck around too. Even though Rob didn't feel up to singing with a swollen face, they played their instruments for a while for the *very full* brewery. My whole body had heated up at the sight of his guitar. God help me, he was wearing the homemade strap I'd sewn for him for Christmas.

At one point in the evening, Hannah had surprised us all by offering to sing a cover with them, and she has an amazing, sultry voice.

After closing, Hannah, Briar, and the guys in the band helped us clean up, and Dylan, who had to go home to his wife and stepkids, said we could stay and drink for a while if we wanted to.

Now my friends and I are sitting around a high-top table, drinking pints of The Bitter End while we chat with Rob and his bandmates, Travis and Bixby.

Because he kissed you.

Because he took a punch from his brother for you.

Because you asked him to lie for you.

Because you acted impulsively, and someone got hurt. Again.

Okay, maybe there are many reasons I'm hesitating, but it's the first one that makes me feel hot all over, even behind my ears. He'd gathered me in his arms like I weighed nothing and then lowered his mouth to mine. The kiss lasted no longer than a few seconds. But feeling the brush of his lips and seeing his face so up close and personal—those wolfish hazel eyes and that perfect-length stubble—did something to me. It's like a switch was flipped, and I can no longer look at him as just Rob.

You lost that ability days ago, a voice in my head argues, and I take a sip of my beer to silence it, trying to return my attention to the conversation.

Rob's watching me, his eyes pulsing heat into me, and I almost fumble my beer. His focus is disconcerting and deep—so different from the way other men have looked at me. It's like they saw only what I showed them, and he sees all the layers beneath.

Hannah would tell me I'm making myself sound like a Tootsie pop if I told her that, and I suppose she'd be right. The thing is, part of me actually wants to let him down to that last layer.

The rest of me is determined never to let anyone down that deep, so I pointedly look away.

Travis is telling us about his past. He went on tour with a major band just under eight years ago, after their drummer dropped out last minute. He'd decided to stay in Asheville for reasons he won't share, but he says there was some sign he should stay.

"What kind of sign?" Briar asks, getting caught up in the story.

"A literal one," Travis says. "I asked the universe for a sign, and there was a road blockage directly in front of me. They were just putting it up as I rolled to a stop. A tree had fallen."

Briar gasps. "No."

"Maybe the universe was trying to kill you," Hannah suggests with a low laugh. "Or the sign was meant for someone else, and you changed the whole course of your life because of a mistake."

Travis smiles mischievously. "So let's call it a happy accident."

"Nope," Rob says, lifting the fresh drink I made for him. "We've already got one Pollyanna in this group. We're not taking auditions for a second."

"You still think I'm a Pollyanna?" I ask, finding the courage to look at him again. The sight of his swollen nose makes me flinch. "Should you apply that cream Dottie gave you?"

"I'll do it later. It's not your fault," he says gently. "I punched him a few weeks ago, and he was paying me back. Karma at work. Honestly." He reaches across the table like it's nothing and pats my hand, the calluses from his playing brushing sensation across my flesh.

I draw in a sharp breath he misinterprets.

"We've probably punched each other hundreds of times."

"Boys," Hannah groans.

"What, you didn't punch your sisters to keep them in line?" Travis asks her, drumming his fingers against the tabletop. "I'm not sure I believe that."

"Because I'm a fiery redhead?" she asks, rolling her eyes. "Like I haven't heard *that* before. What a lazy stereotype."

"What a way to avoid the question," Travis says with a wry smile.

"I have two brothers, thank you very much, and I had no

problem controlling them without resorting to physical violence."

"I'll bet," Briar says with a sigh. "I can't seem to stop listening to your advice."

Hannah bumps shoulders with her, nearly toppling her from her stool. "That's because I give excellent advice. Admit it."

"If I say yes, I'll only be proving my point."

Bixby says something, but it barely registers in my brain, because my gaze has settled on Rob.

He smiles. "Yes, love of my life?"

Rob's joking, obviously, but I feel my cheeks burning. "We should probably talk about this some more."

"Probably," he agrees. "It's not every day a woman claims me in public."

I can feel Hannah smirking at that, and the heat in my face amps up, but I nod toward the booths. "Let's go sit."

He leads the way, then slides into the one where I made my stand, literally, earlier.

"Do we have to sit here?" I ask, immediately regretting it because I sound like a sulky baby.

"Yes," he says as he sets his drink onto the surface. "I have fond memories of this booth. It's where our relationship first started."

I swallow the lump that's formed in my throat. I know he's kidding, but a part of it feels...

Don't let a kiss turn you into a blithering idiot. Remember what happened last time you let yourself believe a man could save you.

"You're not going to make me stand on the seat, are you?" I ask.

"I'm not going to make you do anything," he says pointedly.

I believe him, and guilt pulses through my veins, because I kind of made him play along, didn't I?

This is what happens when I let myself be impulsive.

I slide in, setting my drink on the table's surface, and find him watching me intently in a way that disconcerts me.

"You didn't make me do this," he says, reading my mind. "Like you said, you'd be doing me a favor. Emil too."

"What about your father?" I ask, avoiding the impulse to chew my lip. It's a bad habit, one the bullies at Rosewood Academy made sure to mock me for.

"My father cheated on my mother with Patricia," he says flatly, leaning back on his side of the booth. "And then he started a family with her before the divorce papers had even been drawn up. He took me from my mom, because she was sick and needed help. It may not healthy to blame other people for your problems, but I'm happy to blame him for hers. I don't care if he's pissed. In fact, I hope he is."

"What if he thinks—"

He brushes his fingers across my hand splayed out on the top of the table. "I mean it. I don't care what he thinks."

"What about the money?" I ask. I know their father is loaded and has given Rob money in the past.

"You know about the trust fund?"

I nod.

"My mother needed to go to rehab again when I was in high school. I asked my father for help, and he said he'd let me use my trust for that instead of my education, but he wouldn't recommend it."

"And you did?" I ask with a gasp.

"Of course I did. I haven't gotten another penny from him, and I wouldn't take one. I don't need his money. Don't want it either."

"And when you were the one who needed help?"

He works his jaw. "My mom brought me to meetings with her, and Travis helped a lot too. More than my sponsor. He still helps me when I need it."

I'm tempted to ask him why he bothered going to any family functions at all, given the way he's been treated, but I don't. I recognize from the stubborn look on his face that he won't tell me. I also know how complicated family can be. How you can resent someone down to the marrow in your bones but still want them to love you.

"I'm—" I cut myself off before I can apologize.

"You were going to say sorry, weren't you?" he asks with a half-smile.

"You'll never know," I deflect, my gaze settling again on his swollen nose. "But I really don't like that you got hurt because of me."

"Jonah got hurt because of you a few weeks ago. Did you mind then?"

I decide on honesty. "No, not really. But you've made a point of being straightforward with me, and I shouldn't have backed you into a lie. Especially a lie that got you hurt." I gesture to his face as exhibit A, feeling my heart beat faster.

"I'll lie for you," he says.

"I don't want you to have to. Pretending we're together might be helpful to you, and I really do want to get back at Jonah, but I know honesty means something to you."

He shrugs. "So we can start sleeping together to make it truthful."

"Very funny."

"Oof." His lips curve into a smile that's devastating to my nervous system. "You know how to slice through a man's ego. Hold onto that for Jonah."

He must be able to tell I'm still feeling guilty because he reaches for my hand. I give it to him, my heart pounding now. "I don't like lying, but it's a little white lie. It's not going to hurt anyone, and it might do some good. Jonah lied about me, and to counter that lie, we have to stretch the truth a little."

"That still sounds a lot like lying," I say, remembering all the times he's told me he values truth. Am I corrupting *Rob*? I wouldn't have thought it was possible a few weeks ago, but now I'm a person who stands on booth seats and makes public spectacles. Plural.

He squeezes my hand. "Take a few slow breaths. In through your nose, out through your mouth."

I take his advice, breathing in a pattern that helps calm my heart, or which should. He's still holding my hand, and there's a bundle of confusing feelings squirming inside of me.

"What happened to you, Sophie?" he asks, holding my gaze. "You think you were at fault for something. The thing you said you'd change if you could."

"I *know* I was at fault," I say in a harsh tone. "Jonah was right. My aunt and Otis are the only people in my family who think I'm worth anything. My parents sent me off to boarding school"—reform school—"and moved to Florida to get away from me." My pulse speeds up again. "They only call me on holidays. I'm pretty sure they didn't want a child in the first place, and once they had me, they decided they definitely didn't want more. But that doesn't matter. It's all in the past."

"It does matter," he protests. "Otherwise you wouldn't be practically hyperventilating."

"But it doesn't have to mean everything. I don't want it to."

He shrugs, but his expression is a bit disappointed. Like he hoped I'd level with him, but I built a wall instead. That's true, I guess. But I don't know how to be any different.

"So," I say, "let's talk a bit more about...you know..."

He squeezes my hand and releases it, a smile playing at the corners of his lips. "Our fake relationship?"

I nod. "It was impulsive."

"It was worth it for the look on Jonah's face."

I study him, taking in the satisfied gleam in his eyes, and realize what I should have caught onto a long time ago. "He did something bad to you, too, didn't he? Other than repeating your father's mistakes, I mean."

He watches me for a moment before slowly nodding. "Yeah, he did."

I pause. "Aren't you going to tell me what?"

He smiles. "How about this, Sophie? I'll tell you as soon as you're ready to tell me what happened in your past. A past for a past. Then we can decide whether or not the past matters."

His words shake me. It feels like I'm on the edge of some greater truth, and one misstep could be fatal.

"Okay," I say through a dry mouth. "Should we shake on it?"

He extends his arm across the table. I shake his hand, feeling those strong, callused fingers against mine. Feeling...I don't know. Just *feeling*.

I clear my throat as I pull my hand back, trying not to do it too quickly. "What happens next? Will someone want to interview me? For Emil, I mean. I want to do everything I can to help. I mean it. It's my fault—"

"It's not," he maintains. "You want to blame anything else on yourself while you're at it? Climate change? Rising gas prices? The wart on Patricia's nose?"

I laugh, then reach across the table and shove his arm, the action feeling natural and comfortable until it doesn't. Because his arm is hot and hard, and I suddenly want to encircle it with my hand. I pull back instead. "She does *not* have a wart."

"But it would be fun if she did, wouldn't it?"

"It would," I agree. "She'd probably sell her soul to get it removed."

He snorts. "As if. The devil's already got that locked down."

"She's not going to like this," I say, feeling a tug of worry, not for myself but for him.

"Good."

"So...?"

"So I'll call my caseworker and let her know. She'll tell me what comes next, but if they do want to talk to you, we should discuss what we'll say first. Thank you, Sophie."

I smile at him. "Do I get to meet Emil?"

He pauses. "You want to?"

"Of course I do."

I'm desperate to, actually. I want to see more of this hidden side of Rob. Rob, the musician who's good with kids and teaches them music.

"We'll make it happen." His expression darkens. "Jonah had no right to say those things to you earlier. He didn't mean them either. If he didn't want you back, he wouldn't have shown his face tonight."

Hurt wells in my chest. But it's not really hurt specifically caused by Jonah. All he did was stir up old feelings, the pain of a little girl who was rejected by everyone who was supposed to love her. "I don't know. I guess it doesn't matter."

"It does," he insists. Then he surprises me by taking my hand again. "And I think we should make a point of parading our happiness in front of him. I know where he likes to hang out."

"Maybe," I say, biting my lip this time. "He would certainly deserve it. But do you think it would even upset him? You heard what he said about me."

"He was trying to save face. You're beautiful, kind, and smart—"

My laughter cuts him short.

He tilts his head in silent question, his hair tumbling a bit. "Did I say something funny?" he asks.

"You don't think I'm smart."

"Oh? What else do I think?"

"You don't," I insist. "You've always treated me as if I'm as dumb as a bag of rocks."

Guilt passes over his face. "I didn't think you were stupid. Just...basic."

"Ouch," I say, laughing.

"I was wrong, obviously. There's nothing basic about you."

"And you're not nearly as much of a bad boy as I thought you were."

He gives me a wicked smile. "You might want to reserve judgment on that one, Pollyanna."

I huff out a sharp breath. I thought we were done with this Pollyanna business. "Why are you still calling me that? You just admitted that I'm not basic."

"No, but you're still inclined to think well of people until they prove otherwise. It's one of the things I like about you."

"*One* of the things?"

He smiles and shakes his head. "Now you're just fishing for compliments. What would Mrs. Ginnis think?"

My mouth falls open.

"Am I allowed to touch you in public, Sophie? If you were my girlfriend, I would."

I search him for signs that he's teasing me. It's impossible to tell. He's looking at me like he could devour me whole, and the thought makes me squirm a little. Especially since I can still feel the brush of his lips against mine and his arm circled around me.

"You just did, didn't you?" I ask, straightening.

"I did," he agrees. "It felt pretty natural, didn't it?"

It had felt...*phenomenal*.

"You can't kiss me again," I blurt, even though part of me wants to ask him to do it again, right now, while our friends are distracted talking at that table. Kissing him was so confusing and exciting and—

"No, probably not," he says, straightening up. His eyes lose the gleam they had, and I'm sorry for it. "But I'll need to hold your hand, to touch your lower back. Little signals to show everyone you're mine. That'll drive Jonah crazy."

It's on the tip of my tongue to tell him Jonah never touched me like that. Not really. He'd put an arm around me sometimes, when we were at parties together, but he hadn't treated me like I was someone he cherished and wanted to protect.

Emotion clogs my throat. "Okay."

"Don't sound so happy about it," he says with a smile. "It's going to be okay, Sophie. It's all going to be okay. Someday this'll be a story you'll tell your kids. And they'll know, like I do, that there's nothing basic about Sophie Ginnis."

He gets up from the table, leaving me staring at him, my whole being arrested by him.

"Why do you care?"

A gust of air escapes him, like a laugh that didn't quite come into being. "You don't need a reason to care about someone. You of all people should know that."

It hurts, and I can't help but wonder if he meant it to. But he's wrong. I had plenty of reasons to care about Jonah. They were just the wrong reasons. I don't want Rob to care about me for the wrong reasons.

He waits for me to stand, and when I don't get up, he asks, "You need me to pick you up again?"

Yes.

"No," I say abruptly, standing so quickly I probably look like a jack-in-the-box.

He laughs softly to himself as we walk back to the high-top table, where Hannah is arm-wrestling Travis. She loses, obviously, but he seems impressed by the effort she put in.

"How'd it go?" Briar whispers to me as I slip onto my chair. Her hand encircles the crystal at her neck.

"I honestly don't know," I answer.

"Touch your crystal," she says in an undertone, but not enough of an undertone, because Hannah says, "Yes, stroke it *really* well. Dottie's convinced the one she gave Jonah can improve his personality, and if a crystal can do that, I'm sure they can do anything."

CHAPTER SEVENTEEN

ROB

Conversation with Travis

You've got it bad for Pollyanna.

She orchestrated this whole thing so she could help with Emil.

How does it help you with Emil if your caseworker thinks you're banging your brother's fiancée?

You mean dating my brother's ex, fuck you very much, and it'll help because it's an explanation for why he'd go scorched-earth and have his friends call in a bunch of BS complaints about me.

I dunno. Sounds like a mess.

Probably. We don't all have alphabetized spice cabinets.

I'm not even confident you own salt and pepper.

I'm totally not changing the subject. But let's talk about the way you were arm wrestling with the fiery redhead…

Let's not stereotype.

Uh-huh. You have a thing for women who can sing.

I love peace more.

That woman doesn't know the meaning of the word.

By the way, I'm not purposefully changing the subject either, but one of my friends called to ask if we wanted to play some '80s covers at the Orange Peel in a couple of weeks.

They're having a dance party.

It's on your biiiiirthday. What do you say, bud? Dance it up?

Are you serious with this?

Don't kill the messenger.

Over my dead body. Not my thing.

No, fun isn't your thing.

But your brother's girl is.

I start to set my phone down, then change my mind and shoot off a text to Sophie. She's my fake girlfriend, after all. Got to get used to pretending, and girlfriends expect check-ins. Or so I've heard from Travis, who's in the off phase of an epic on-and-off relationship that's lasted for years and is the reason Bixby says he's never going to date anyone for longer than three weeks.

> Goodnight, Sophie. Wish on a star for me, would you?

> That's awfully presumptuous.

I'm laughing, tapping my fingers against the side of the phone in a tic I can't kick, when her next message comes through.

> Please use that cream Dottie gave you.

> I will.

> Goodnight, Rob. Thank you for everything.

> Wait, am I allowed to say that?

> Sorrys, I have no use for. Thank-yous, I will hoard.

> But I'll still spare one for you. Thank you for making me special drinks tonight. That was thoughtful.

> And here's another: thank you for wanting to help Emil.

I'm smiling as I set my phone down. Humming as I spread that cream all over my face. It's thick and herbal smelling.

In the morning, I wake up from a dream about Sophie with a rock-hard dick.

It's not her, I tell myself. It's morning wood. No big deal.

I go to the bathroom to take a piss, but I'm distracted by the image in the mirror.

My face is *blue*. Not blue as in slightly pale with a blue undertone, but actually blue. Like a ripe blueberry. My pillow-case is too.

I fumble for the little container Dottie gave me, but the only label is a whimsical line drawing of a flower. That's not going to help me figure out how to make my face a normal color.

I bolt back into my bedroom and go for my phone, pulling up Dottie Hendrickson's number.

It rings three times and then goes to voicemail.

I try her again.

Same result.

Well, shit.

If I believed in karmic punishment, I'd have to wonder if this was a direct result of me breaking my vow to the truth last night.

I don't, but I can't escape the feeling that it's a kind of natural consequence.

I scrub my face with hot water and soap, but the color only fades a little. I still look unnatural, to put it mildly, and it hurts to touch my nose. Not good. I need to call Nelly, but I'm blue and have a bruised face. It seems like those two problems may outweigh my newly acquired fake girlfriend on her *is Rob worthy?* scale.

I check my phone. There's a text from my dad:

> Call me. We need to talk.

And a repetitive, uncreative threat from Jonah:

> You're going to regret you were ever born, fuckstick.

I avoid the childish impulse to respond that I already regret *he* was ever born, and opt for not responding to either of them. My face is blue, and that's the only thing I can focus on right now.

I google allergic reactions and blue faces and get a whole lot of nothing. So I try Dottie again.

She picks up this time, thank God.

"Hello, my dear. I was just thinking about you."

"Yeah, same...I'm blue, Dottie."

"Oh, you might not believe it, but I feel blue sometimes too. Even though life gives us wonderful gifts, it can take away things that are precious to us. But we have to focus—"

"No, I used that cream you gave me, and now my face is blue."

"Oh, dear," she says. "You know, I was in such a hurry to get you my restorative skin treatment last night, it's possible I made an error. Is there a cornflower on the label or a calendula?"

"I don't know," I say, trying to keep my temper under control. "I missed that day in gardening class."

She clucks her tongue. "Why don't you come to the tea shop? We'll get it sorted out for you. And then I'll make you a nice, soothing cup of tea."

I don't want a cup of tea. But I also don't want to still be blue when I show up at The Missing Beat on Monday afternoon. I have a feeling the teenagers in our program would never let me live it down. I'd probably be called Blue Balls until our middle schoolers graduate high school.

So I suck it up, pull on a baseball hat that doesn't do a thing to hide the fact that my face is blue, and roll out to Tea of Fortune.

I have to grab street parking a couple of blocks away, so I'm treated with a bunch of stares as I walk toward the tea shop. Might as well embrace it, so I grin and wave, either terrorizing or exciting a huge group of tourists speaking Italian.

They're excited, I decide, when they start singing, "Blue (Da Ba Dee)."

A few minute later, I reach the storefront. I walk in, and dozens of eyes find me. Two older women in particular are staring at me from a table near the front of the shop.

Dottie Hendrickson, who was pouring tea for a customer in one of the booths, clucks her tongue and starts toward me, nearly beaning someone with the kettle of tea in her hand.

"Oh goodness," she says as she reaches me. "It must have been the cornflower. My vision isn't what it used to be, I'm afraid. Bear keeps telling me to wear some readers, but I confess I can't keep track of them."

"What does the cornflower mean?"

"Oh, it's my hair dye. Homemade."

"You're saying I put hair dye on my face?" It makes sense, given the state of my pillowcase, but it's certainly not good news.

"Here, sit," she says, leading me to the table near the entrance where the two septuagenarian women are seated. There are a couple of empty chairs—one for me, apparently. "Drink some tea and try to relax."

She turns over the teacup on my table setting and fills it with whatever's in that kettle. I sure as hell will never know. Her cream turned my face blue; I won't be drinking her mystery tea.

"We'll get you sorted, dear, not a problem," she says, patting my shoulder encouragingly. "And I must say, blue *is* your color. Wouldn't you say so, Constance?"

The older woman seated next to me looks up from her crocheting project—either an ugly sweater for a dog or a kid's sweater gone wrong. The stitches are all different sizes, some too loose and the others much too tight. Her hair is crisply styled, her face wrinkled in a way that suggests she smiles more than it would seem based on her current demeanor. Despite the sweater she's crocheting, she doesn't give off a warm, fuzzy vibe. "No," she says, and laughs before returning to her crocheting.

Dottie gives a *can't please everyone* shrug and tells me in an undertone, "This is my Wise Women Group. Penny's not here, of course, given she's on her journey, and the group *does* feel incomplete without her. Odd numbers, you know. Still, we meet twice a week to share our wisdom. I was going to invite you to join us before you called me. It's kismet! But let's get your face sorted first."

Turning from me, she raises her voice and asks the room, "Does anyone here have baby wipes? This young man has an emergency, I'm afraid."

"Happens to the best of us," says the woman across the table from Constance. She has dark, barely lined skin, rainbow-rimmed glasses, thick false lashes, and a hearing aid. "My friend had so many accidents he started wearing Depends. You know, in the advertisements they use fine young men such as yourself. It was the first I'd heard of it happening to young men."

Fantastic. A roomful of women think I just soiled myself.

A young mother at a table in the back lifts up a packet of wipes. Dottie hurries over to her, praising her in the highest terms imaginable, and then comes padding back over to the table. Every person in the shop watches as she takes out a wipe and starts cleaning my face as if I'm her toddler child.

To my shock, the blue crap is coming off, appearing on the wipe. "I can do that," I say, taking the wipe from her.

"Use a circular motion," Rainbow Glasses says a little too loudly, getting into the swing of things. "That's it. You're doing it."

I scrub at my face, wondering why Dottie didn't just tell me to buy baby wipes.

But I don't need to ask, because she sits in the open chair across from me and says, "Now, we were just discussing what you can do to make Sophie realize your interest in her is genuine."

The baby wipe drops from my fingers into my lap.

"Who says my interest *is* genuine?"

Crocheting Constance snorts. "Who do you think, Einstein? I'll give you three guesses."

I fix a level gaze on Dottie. "Dottie, I don't want to discuss my personal business with a couple of—"*Old gossips.* "Ladies I don't know."

"Oh, my dear boy," she exclaims. "Strangers are just friends you haven't met yet."

Is someone handing out Pollyanna juice? I glance skeptically at the tea in front of me, and Constance gives another of those deep laughs. "That's what Ted Bundy used to tell women too, you know," she says. "Some strangers are friends you haven't met yet. Others are psychopaths. It's like playing the lottery."

I think I like her. I still don't want her to know that I'm fake-dating my brother's ex-fiancée.

"Uh-huh," says Rainbow Glasses. "It's exciting, isn't it? Like that movie about the simple boy and the shrimp. You never know what you're gonna get."

Glancing up at me, Constance points to her nose. "You still have some right there, son."

I start wiping again, groaning at the pain that radiates through my nose.

"Dear me, that's a real bruise," Dottie says. "Well, I have just the cream for that. We'll clear it up in two shakes of a lamb's tail."

"Let me stop you right there." I lift a hand. "I don't need cream. I don't need advice." I hold up the container of baby wipes. "This right here is all I need. So thank you."

"Have you been carrying the calcite?" Dottie asks, in the way of someone who knows I haven't. Rainbow Glasses leans over the table to get a better listen. "On your person, I mean."

"Did you break into my car and check my glove box for it?" I ask, feeling a surge of annoyance. This woman is well-meaning, obviously, but she's also disrespectful of boundaries. A busybody.

"No, but I can sense you haven't been carrying it."

"Then you should get a job at that psychic place in the strip mall."

She smiles beatifically at me. "Perhaps, because there's something else I see."

I sigh. "Give it to me. I can tell it's going to be good."

Ignoring my sarcasm, she says, "My dear boy. You may not know you have feelings for Sophie yet, but *I* can see it. We all could see it at the brewery last night. Pink light practically beamed from you. Why did you think your brother was so upset?"

"Because I kissed his former fiancée right in front of him?"

"Yes, that *did* upset him," Dottie says. "But if you ask me, what really upset him was that the kiss made Sophie breathless. Now, I've lived next door to that girl for over a year, and I've seen your brother give her *many* goodnight kisses, and I must say, her breathing never seemed the slightest bit impacted by any of them. Kissing him seemed to be as exciting for her as finding a good coupon."

Crocheting Constance sets the ugly sweater aside, giving us her full attention. Apparently I've been deemed worthy of notice. "Speak for yourself," she interjects. "I've never met a man as exciting as a coupon."

"But you have that dreamy paramour," says Rainbow Glasses.

"Yes, Ann, and I still prefer a good deal. A coupon doesn't need any blue pills to carry out its intended purpose."

"Neither do I," I put in, because it seems like a good time to interject.

"Give it another thirty years, son," Constance says. "You'll be singing a different tune."

"*Sophie* is a romantic," Dottie says pointedly. "And she just realized it last night."

I can't deny she's saying exactly what I'd like to hear.

Honestly, I don't know what I want to happen. I worry this whole fake-dating, for-real-wanting Sophie business is a bad idea. Messy, just like Travis said. It's possible I made my life a lot more difficult by deciding to play along last night.

This deal with Sophie might very well save me from having to engage in those miserable dinners with Jonah, Patricia, and my dad. But at what cost? I'm still lying, something I pledged not to do anymore.

I'm not going to back down, though. I refuse to let Sophie or Emil down.

"Are you sure you wouldn't like some advice?" Dottie stresses, giving me a knowing look.

"Advice about what?" I say.

"About your situation," Dottie says.

"I don't have a 'situation.' So I don't need advice about it."

"You're going to get the advice whether you like it or not, son," Constance says. "Might as well tear off the Band-Aid."

She may be bad at crocheting, but she raises a good point.

"Okay," I concede. "What would you do in my position, Dottie?"

"Well, a young man and a young woman who are pretending to be in love need to know each other very well, wouldn't you say? Spend quality time with her, dear. Ask her questions about herself."

That seems pretty obvious and straightforward. Definitely not worthy of the trip over here. "Yeah," I agree. "That's the plan."

"And the universe didn't bestow you with the voice of an angel so you could sing in that garbage band," Dottie continues. "Sing sweet music to her."

My lips twitch up as I think about the boom box last night. "We'll see. But, yeah, I figured I'd take her out."

"Would anyone else like to share advice?" Dottie asks the others, making an encouraging gesture with her hand.

"Be useful," says Constance of The Bad Crocheting. "No woman wants to spend all day working and then have to wait on a man. Show her that you're not afraid of getting your hands wet."

"You said get his shirt wet?" asks Ann, adjusting her hearing aid. "Yes, I see your point. He does seem to fill it out nicely. A wet shirt might seal the deal."

"Not what I meant, but you may have a point. Might even want to take it off. Especially if he has tattoos." Constance turns to me. "Do you have tattoos? My granddaughter's boyfriend has at least a dozen. I thought they were a lot of fuss and bother, but she can't seem to get enough of them."

"Maybe you should invest in a few if you don't have any," Ann suggests, as if a tattoo is as easy to acquire as a haircut.

"Oh, yes," Dottie says, taking a little notebook and pencil out of the pocket of her apron and scribbling furiously. "That could be effective."

"Yeah, I'll be sure to pick up a pack of temporary ones the next time I go to the drugstore," I joke. I have a few real tattoos, including the band's logo on my arm, but something tells me they might ask me to take off my shirt and give them a show if I tell them.

Constance snort-laughs, but Ann is nodding quickly, as if she thinks putting on a variety pack of fake tattoos is a grade-A strategy for seducing a woman. "And get her some scratch-off lotto tickets," she adds.

Constance harrumphs. "We all know what makes *you* drop your granny panties."

Ann shrugs, looking unoffended or possibly mis-hearing her.

"Well, all right," I say, pushing my chair back. "If I want to romance her, all I have to do is buy her some scratch-offs, do the dishes, and then pull off my shirt. If she doesn't have me arrested after that, I'll consider myself lucky."

"Above all, be yourself," Dottie says, rising to her feet. I stand, keeping the baby wipes, because I still haven't looked in a mirror.

"If you're an agreeable sort of man," Constance adds. "If not, you'd be better off pretending to be someone else."

Yes, I definitely like her.

"Is that for a dog or a kid?" I ask, pointing at the sweater.

"It's for Bertie." Which doesn't answer the question.

"A dog," Ann says, "but she treats him like a little king."

Constance makes a dismissive gesture. "If he shit scratchers, you'd treat him like a king."

Shaking my head in amusement, I take a step away from the table.

"Wait," Dottie says, her tone almost frantic. "You haven't drunk your tea."

"And I won't," I say, honestly. "I'm not in the mood."

"Suit yourself. But I feel, very strongly, that you need to carry the calcite everywhere. *Please.*"

How could I say no to that? I can't, so I smile and nod.

"Try wearing that hat backward," Constance says. "Women love a backward cap."

"And a doorway lean," Ann pipes up. "My granddaughter told me that's why she married her husband."

"Because he can't stand properly?"

"Because he's tall," she explains. "He's nice enough, but he has a face like a bunched fist and is about as smart as one. You seem much smarter, son." She winks at me. "Don't forget the scratchers. You may get lucky in more ways than one."

"I'll keep that in mind," I say, smiling. "Good day, ladies." I wave to the woman who gave me the wipes, and she waves back, a confused look on her face.

I've made it only a few steps from the tea shop before Dottie rushes out, stopping me.

"What is it?" I ask, turning toward her. Something in my heart softens. It's been a while since I've received this kind of regard for my well-being from anyone but Mother Hen Travis.

She reaches for my hand and squeezes it. "Help her realize it wasn't her fault, my dear. She needs to know."

It feels like a bolt of lightning just split me in half, leaving both sides charred and burned.

I know she must be talking about whatever happened to Sophie, the event she'd like to erase from her past.

"Do you know what happened to her?" I ask.

She nods once, her chin firm. "And she's been treated abominably, if you ask me. I hope you can change that, dear heart."

"It's a fake relationship, Dottie," I say with a resigned sigh. "She's just doing it to help me."

"Oh?"

A few people step past us with aggravated expressions. New Yorkers, probably. Tons of them have moved here from the big city and brought their big-city mentality with them.

I lead her over to a bench on the sidewalk. We sit, and I tell her about Emil.

To my surprise, Dottie blots her eyes with a little napkin she retrieves from her apron. "You're a good boy," she says, squeezing my hand. "My great-nephew didn't have the best childhood, but his mother left him with me when he was a teenager, and he grew to be a *wonderful,* upstanding man. He has a beautiful family of his own now. Sometimes, all a child needs is one person to believe in him. We all want the people we love to have what we didn't. If you need a character witness, you have one, my dear. I will stand up for you, and so will all of my friends."

She hugs me, and I let her. Then I walk back to my car, lost in thought. Because she was right. I'm trying to give Emil what I never received, and I didn't realize it until this second.

I take a few minutes to collect myself, and then I check the time—after nine thirty—and send a message to Nelly instead of calling, telling her about Sophie.

Five minutes later, she calls back and asks to meet my girlfriend.

This is happening.

CHAPTER EIGHTEEN

SOPHIE

"I missed all of that?" Otis asks, looking dejected.

We're sitting at the breakfast table at ten on Saturday.

It's a bit late, especially since my shift starts at noon, but I didn't sleep much last night. After leaving Buchanan Brewery, Hannah, Briar, and I went to Prohibition, a speakeasy-style bar, to get another drink so we could dissect our conversation with Rob and the other guys. Basically, they wanted to know everything Rob had said to me.

I told them most of it, including a suspicion I hadn't shared with Rob, that GingerBeerBabe might be helping Jonah. A woman had made that call to Rob's caseworker, and even though I didn't like Patricia, I couldn't see her condescending to do that.

"But why would he be banned from The Ginger Station if she's still into him?" Hannah asked, which was a good point.

"I'll check with that bartender," I offered, because apparently she and Dottie have been trading recipes.

The only thing I kept from my friends was my information-sharing pact with Rob. I trust Hannah and Briar, but I'm not ready to tell them about my past either. I'm worried they would judge me.

I couldn't bear it if they did.

"So he wants to practice pretending to be a couple?" Hannah said, wagging her eyebrows. "You know, you really should have seen the look on Jonah's face last night. It was the best thing that ever happened to me. I'm just gonna say it. You should definitely make him suffer more by sleeping with Rob."

"Hannah," I said. "That's a terrible idea. He's Jonah's brother."

Briar lifted a finger. "Agreed. I'm going off men for at least six months, and then I'm only going to date people who adhere to a very specific checklist."

"Eating granola?" Hannah asked. "Believing in crystals?"

Briar gave her the side-eye. "Not being a cheater or related to a man who cheated on me would be a good start."

I sighed. "Briar's right. If Rob and I got together, I'd have to see Jonah all the time. I wouldn't be able to escape him."

Hannah laughed, her eyes flashing with mischief. "Yeah, I'm sure the two of them are going to hang up Christmas stockings for each other."

That almost put tears in my eyes. "Did I ruin his relationship with his brother forever?"

"They hated each other anyway," she replied. "You said so."

I had said so. I'd thought so. I still think so. I'm ninety percent sure Jonah did something awful to Rob, something *unforgivable*, but the only way I can find out is by telling Rob my own story.

"What about his father?" I asked. "His relationship with him sounded complicated anyway. What if I've destroyed it?"

Hannah shrugged. "Shouldn't you leave that up to him?"

Maybe she was right, but I slept fitfully anyway last night. Then I got up and made pancakes for Otis, because he'd texted me to say that he'd accidentally captured the wrong pigeon and had claw marks all over his arms.

We glumly ate them while I told him all about what had happened at the brewery last night.

"I would've come if I'd known that would happen," he continues.

"Trust me," I say, pushing away my plate. "It was not fun. Catching that pigeon was probably more fun."

"It was kind of fun." My cousin sighs and runs a hand through his already-messy hair. "I had to use my wits to set the trap. But it was a bummer when I figured out I'd been chasing the wrong bird the whole time."

This feels a little too close to home for some reason. I get to my feet, grabbing my plate. I'm about to grab his, too, when I realize I'm doing it again. Parenting my cousin. Trying to take care of other people's problems so they'll think I'm helpful. So I leave his plate and bring mine to the sink.

Otis doesn't even hesitate to bring his things into the kitchen too.

"Are you okay?" he asks. "You seem a little, well...you're not going to do the fork-and-ice-cream thing again, are you? I mean...if you want more ice cream, I picked up some extra spoons you can use."

I hug him spontaneously, which seems to make him nervous, but what a completely Otis thing to do, buying more spoons instead of cleaning the ones we already have. Or buying the actual ice cream, for that matter. At the same time, it shows he cares and was thinking about me. "Thank you, Otis. That's wonderful. I'll make sure to use one later."

He pulls back. "Uh...okay. Do you want to talk about the Briggs Mayers thing? Maybe you should take it too?" He scratches nervously behind his ear. "I haven't wanted to say anything, but you're always making things." He gestures to the room at large, and I can't deny it's full of an unusual number of craft projects, even for me. Crafting is my nervous tic. "Are you fulfilled? Don't you want to do that craft business?"

Yes.

"I don't have the money to do that right now, Otis." Heat burns behind my eyes. "That wedding dress took out most of my savings, and I lost most of the money I poured into the business in Greensboro."

"Really?" he asks, looking perplexed. "How much could your dress have possibly cost? Two hundred? Three?"

"Much more," I say, touched by his naivety.

"Do you want me to try to sell it online for you?"

"You'd do that?"

"I just need to know how much it cost."

Embarrassed, I look away and mutter, "Eight thousand."

He drops his dish, and it shatters, spraying syrup and pottery shards everywhere.

"Sorry," he says. "But did you say *eight thousand?*"

"It's vintage."

"Is it a car?"

I'd never really bought myself any nice clothes before buying that dress. I'd thought it was wasteful and vain to focus on myself. But Jonah had proposed, and then it had become something I was doing for someone else. I didn't want him to be embarrassed of me, and he'd made a point of telling me to choose something fancy. So I'd tried it on, fallen in love, and it had felt okay, because it was for him, really.

It wasn't until I'd gone shopping with Hannah and Briar that I'd actually let myself buy things that were just for me. For no greater reason than that I liked how I looked in them.

My phone chirps with a text, and I'm grateful for the distraction. (And, yes, I may have turned the volume on because I was hoping to hear from a certain someone.)

Picking it up, I see Rob's name, and my pulse quickens.

What is happening to me? When I was with Jonah, I felt a sense of satisfaction, of having done well for myself, and I tipped my diamond ring into every shaft of light just to watch it sparkle. But I never felt like this.

Otis starts to clean up the broken dish. Part of me feels guilty, like I should put down what I'm doing and help him, or take over. But I muffle the feeling as I read Rob's message.

Dottie turned my face blue. But now it's only black and blue, so my day's looking up.

I gasp when I see the two photos he sent through. One of his face looking bright blue, the second of the black and blue radiating out from his nose.

I'm so sorry.

I'm the one who's sorry, Soph. It's not even eleven, and you've already exceeded your apology quota for the rest of the day. I'm not sure what you'll do with yourself now.

I suppose I could start thanking you. Or just give in and go to sleep so I can start apologizing again in the morning.

That's defeatist thinking, Pollyanna.

I spoke with my caseworker, and she said she'd like to meet you at my apartment. She's on vacation for a week and a half, but she asked if we could meet the Thursday after next. Would that work?

Sure, I can do that.

"Oh, good, you're smiling," Otis comments. "Is it Hannah? You always smile when you're talking to Hannah."

I hide my phone's screen with my hand, not sure why I feel

the need to conceal the truth, but slightly panicked. Another chirp sounds. "Yeah, it's Hannah. She's funny."

He grunts. "Well, think about what I said." He gestures to my handiwork again. "Crafting, I mean. Would you like me to list the dress?"

I think about what it felt like to wear the dress, like I was a desirable, beautiful woman. The kind of woman a man would be proud to marry.

But I bought the dress for Jonah. To impress him and make him proud. And now that I've had my one day with it, I don't want it anymore.

I nod. "Please. It's dead to me."

"Women are so melodramatic."

"Says the man who's so obsessed with Briar he turned down a fictional date with Hannah."

He sighs. "Touché." Only he pronounces it *toosh*.

He goes to leave, then pauses, giving me a sidelong look. "I think we're both going to be okay, Soph."

I smile at him, feeling a sweet warmth in my chest. I never had a brother. Or a sister. Or even a dog. So I wasn't sure what to do with Otis when I first moved here. But it feels like we're becoming closer, more like siblings. He's buying spoons for me, and I'm making him pancakes, and we're supporting each other's dreams. That's something. Maybe even a lot.

"Thanks, Otis," I say, and then I rush forward and hug him. He's sticky with syrup, and probably half terrified, but it feels good.

He pulls back and pats me on the shoulder with a goofy smile on his face, then leaves the kitchen. He missed a big shard of the broken dish, but at least he tried.

I clean it up and then retrieve my phone, carrying it over to the small kitchen table. My heart pumps faster as I get closer to the moment when I'll be able to check my messages, but I tell myself that's normal. It's only because I'm anxious about this mess I've created for myself.

I unlock the phone's screen and look at Rob's latest texts like they're a present I've unwrapped.

Perfect. That gives us time to prepare. Want to meet up after your shift tonight?

We could get a late dinner.

My heart beats faster, giving me away to myself.

Fake date.

Anything else would be impossible. He's Jonah's brother, for one thing, and for another, I just got out of a relationship that fell apart in a spectacular mess. I'm not ready for another.

Even so, my heart warms as I text him back.

We could. Should we?

Yes.

Jonah's favorite restaurant is Curate, but I don't know how late it's open.

Couldn't give a fuck what his favorite restaurant is. What's yours?

My mouth forms an 'O' as I try to process that. He'd said we should go places where Jonah might see us, but this...

He's asking me where *I* want to go. Admittedly, there aren't that many places open after ten, but there are some. I write:

I like pizza.

Thank God. I'd worry about you otherwise.

I know just the place.

I'll pick you up from the brewery.

What a good fake boyfriend.

Way to find the silver lining, Pollyanna. ;-)

To be clear, this isn't a date, is it?

Nope, but I'm looking forward to our Not-a-Date.

Me too.

I'm smiling to myself as I get dressed for work, choosing a pair of shorts and a top that's not Buchanan branded. Then I text Hannah and Briar to share the latest news.

Hannah: You stroked your crystal necklace, didn't you? This was a quick result. It sounds an awful lot like a REAL date.

Briar: It does.

Briar: Please be careful.

Briar: Rob's really nice, and so are his friends, but we can't forget he's Jonah's brother.

Hannah: You don't trust men in general right now.

Briar: True.

Hannah: Well, let it be known that I'm NOT encouraging her to marry Rob instead. But I do think you should have rebound sex with him, Sophie. You owe it to yourself.

Me: He's NOT interested in that.

Hannah: He's a man.

Briar: She has a point. Meet up before our
shifts tomorrow so you can tell us everything?

Me: Yes.

Briar's words give me hesitation.

Am I setting myself up for disaster again?

I remind myself it's a fake date. Sure, Rob isn't the man I thought he was, and I'm not the woman he assumed I was, but that doesn't mean we're suddenly going to be an item. We can be friends, maybe. Friends who are helping each other out in a very unusual way.

And maybe...

Well. He is *very* attractive, and I need to get my groove back. Maybe it wouldn't be the worst idea in the world to take Hannah's advice. Out of curiosity, I check a couple of message boards I've joined for scorned women to see what my fellow cheating victims have to say about rebound sex. Everyone seems very pro rebounding!

But no, no. I can't sleep with him. I shouldn't. Still, I change into a short blue dress that I picked out with my friends, feeling almost giddy—and very naughty—as I slip it on.

You're not going to sleep with him.

But would it be the end of the world if I did?

Something has changed between us, and it buzzes with possibility like a hive of bees, plenty of danger mixed in with the honey.

You're not going to sleep with him.

But I wear the dress anyway, and I feel good in it. I feel beautiful and wanted.

When I get to the brewery, I discover my coworkers have hung up a photo of Jonah behind the bar with the word BANNED scrawled across it in red. It puts a ball of emotion in my throat. Especially when the other server on shift suggests we hang it on the dartboard.

Dylan pulls me into the back and says, "We're family here. I wouldn't let that man distribute a pack of gum for me, Sophie. Doesn't matter how many contacts he has. And if anyone asks me, I'm going to tell them exactly what I think of him."

In the past, no one other than my great-aunt had stood up for me. No one. But suddenly I have a whole army of people in my corner. Still...it's hard to believe I deserve it, after everything, especially since I know Otis is right. I'm not fulfilled at Buchanan Brewery. I like working here, but it won't be enough for me, long term. It feels dishonest to accept their support when I know I don't plan on staying.

"Working here isn't my dream, Dylan," I blurt out. It's probably not the right time to admit that, given that he just did something nice for me, but I don't want him to burn any bridges for Buchanan Brewery if I'm only going to be here temporarily. Also, I can't stand the thought of lying to him.

He gives me a strange look. "Uh, yeah, pouring beer isn't most people's dream. This place may just be a stop in your journey, but that doesn't mean you're not part of our family. And, hey, I shared your recipes for the NA drinks with the owners. They want to put them on the menu. Good work. You can come up with the names if you'd like, but no swearing. The Buchanans will get on my case."

My heart swells in my chest as I get back to work, and it's a good night. A *crowded* night. But I won't lie. I'm happiest when my shift ends. I want to see Rob's golden-hazel eyes light up when he catches sight of me. I want to see his lips and remember what it felt like when they brushed over mine, lighting me up with a fire I didn't know I could feel with a man.

Which is why it really sucks when he doesn't show up.

I sweep the floors a second time. Wipe the counters a third.

I text him, but he doesn't text back. I call, but it goes directly to his voice message. I'm torn between being upset and worried that something happened to him. What if Jonah hurt him or his father did something to him or...

What if he realized this is insane, and he figured out another way to help Emil? Or maybe there never really was an Emil, and it was all a lie. He and Jonah may BOTH be liars.

Maybe he realized you want him, and he's embarrassed for you. Because you're too vanilla.

I pretend to clean some more, feeling like an idiot for putting on this dress. The staffers who worked with me probably knew exactly why I was wearing it and felt sorry for me, because I'm the last person any man would want to sleep with. Certainly the last woman any man would want to marry.

I inhale a few deep breaths and then close up the brewery and drive home.

I find Otis watching a dirty movie on the couch while eating burnt popcorn. It doesn't look like porn, necessarily, but it's definitely close—even if the dick the woman on screen is about to suck looks like a stack of quarters covered in Play-Doh.

"I didn't think you were going to be home," Otis says frantically. He fumbles to turn it off and somehow increases the volume, blasting the living room with deafening moans.

I press my hand to my chest to calm the lurching sensation there. The pull of bad luck must be more powerful than good fortune. Maybe this is the kind of mishap I'm doomed to suffer again and again. Thinking I'm going to have a late dinner with a guy I like and instead walking in on my cousin about to jerk off.

A voice in my head suggests that at least I got here before and not during, but it's not much of a silver lining.

Finally, Otis gets the movie turned off, and I grab a pint of ice cream from the freezer and a fork.

"What about the spoons?" he asks, his expression alarmed,

no doubt having flashbacks of all of my low moments over the last couple of weeks.

I sigh. "A spoon just doesn't have the same gravitas."

CHAPTER NINETEEN

ROB

Conversation with Sophie

Sophie? I'm sorry I'm late.

Are you still there?

You're not at the brewery.

I'm coming over to check on you.

Dammit. *Dammit.*

I missed my Not-a-Date with Sophie.

I didn't even have a good reason for it, other than that the incident at Tea of Fortune this morning had progressed into an epically bad afternoon.

My father had kept calling me, and finally I'd called him back after grabbing lunch with Travis.

He'd asked me to meet him for coffee, and I agreed. It was a highbrow place I hadn't been to before, where all the lattes are named after political figures and cost twice what they should. Fine, he was probably trying to put me in my place by making it clear that I didn't belong.

When I arrived, he was already there with two drinks on his two-top table, so apparently he'd already decided on my drink order.

I sat down across from him, feeling a familiar tightness in my chest. I used to want his good opinion, even though he didn't have mine. Part of me still does. Maybe it was my lot in life to always want the things I couldn't have. His good opinion. A successful career in music. My brother's girl...

I'd have to tell my father it was fake. I'd say Sophie was doing me a favor, and as soon as that favor was completed, I'd come clean to Jonah. Didn't mean I'd be doing him any more favors anytime soon, or attending a "family" dinner ever again, but at least it would guarantee my father the peace he always claimed he wanted.

"The Napoleon Bonaparte," he said, sliding one of the cups across the table to me.

"Win some, lose some," I told him with a shrug as I accepted the drink. I didn't really care what it was called as long as it had caffeine.

"Clever," he said with a nod.

"I have my moments."

"Was one of those moments last night?" he asked, angling his head and gesturing to the flesh around his nose. As if I could somehow have missed that my skin was still tinged blue, especially around my nose.

I took a sip of the drink, which was oversweet and tasted like a stale car air freshener.

"Yeah, I think so," I said after shoving the offensive drink a couple of inches away. "I suppose you heard that I'm dating Jonah's ex?"

"I understand, son," he said, surprising the hell out of me. My father had never really understood me. Not back when I'd used my trust fund to help my mom instead of going to college. Not when Jonah had blown up my life. And not now, when I was "wasting" my life playing at dead-end gigs in bars and babysitting kids.

"Oh?"

He sipped his own drink, and frowned, probably quite rightly. "Sometimes the heart wants what it shouldn't. I can tell you're a wreck over it. You don't look good. I understand that too. It's hard to disappoint people's expectations."

He reached out and patted my hand, his expression so fucking fatherly I wanted to punch *him* in the face. He was equating me standing up for Jonah's ex-fiancée with what he'd done to my mother.

Cheating on her.

Leaving her before I was even a year old for his pregnant mistress.

Getting married the day the divorce went through.

He was using me to shed the last of his guilt—if he'd ever felt any in the first place.

"I didn't *steal* her from Jonah, Dad. He lost her because he was unfaithful. If he's upset about it, he only has himself to blame."

"I get it," he said again. I'd never been so infuriated over someone trying to agree with me.

"No, you don't," I snapped. "Jonah was cheating on her."

He shrugged. "That's not the story he's telling. But what's done is done. It's how we move forward that's important." He sighed and looked up, probably trying to find inspiration from the line drawings of dictators on the walls. "Look, Rob. You've had your fun, and you've gotten back at Jonah. Cut the girl loose. She's nothing special. God knows Patricia and I tried to tell him as much when he first brought her home."

"Is that how you felt about my mother?" I fumed, getting to my feet. Really wanting to unload the Napoleon Bonaparte all over his expensive white shirt.

He looked alarmed. I can only assume he finally realized we were having a different conversation than he'd set out to have. I felt eyes on me, but I didn't care.

"Your mother's fine."

"She is *now*," I said, withholding the *no thanks to you*. "But you'll forgive me, *sir*, if I choose not to take relationship advice from you."

Anger flashed in his eyes. "You'd do better if you'd take all of my advice."

"Maybe so, but I wouldn't be very fucking happy. And just so you know, Sophie is worth ten of Jonah. He should have gotten down on his knees and thanked a higher power that she'd agreed to marry him."

He huffed a bitter laugh. "And how many of *you* is she worth? Thirty?"

"At least five. This is goodbye for now, Dad. I won't be coming to any more family dinners."

"You won't be invited," he sniped.

And then I left, having told him exactly the opposite of what I'd meant to.

So now he thinks the relationship with Sophie is real, and he'll obviously report back to Patricia and Jonah. Fine. I'd wanted Jonah to believe the lie anyway.

After meeting with my dad, I felt worked up. I almost called Travis immediately and asked for help. I wanted to lose myself in something, and I was in the kind of mood that could lead to dark places that had no ladder.

Instead, I went home, set an alarm for when I was supposed to get Sophie, and started playing my guitar. The hours hummed by the way they do when I'm in the zone, living in the music, the time streaming as quickly as water.

Losing myself.

Losing myself so much I didn't hear the fucking alarm go off.

Which was why I'd missed my Not-a-Date with Sophie. I hadn't eaten either. And when I finally surfaced, I was starving for the real world—for her, for food, for something that wasn't pretend.

I admit, I panicked. I was already late, and she wasn't answering her phone. I rushed to the brewery, but when I got there, the place was dark inside. She'd already left. So I got right back into my car and drove toward her house.

I'm there now, feeling hyped up and worried. Needing to fix this.

Otis answers the door, looking as solemn as his nature probably allows him to. "Sophie's pretty upset, man. She's eating ice cream with a fork again."

It's a metric I haven't heard of before, but it's obvious it's not good.

"I fucked up," I admit, feeling my heart thrum in my chest. "It was unintentional, but I know that doesn't make it okay. Can I see her?"

He scratches the back of his head, his expression conflicted. "Are you going to make it right?"

"I'd like to try."

He considers this for a moment and then nods. "I know you're a good guy, and it makes me sick that I missed everything at the brewery last night. But my cousin is...she's *awesome*, man, and she doesn't know it. It kills my grandmother and me, but I tell you what. I don't want anyone messing with her. I mean, I'm not challenging you to a fight or anything. We both know I'd lose, but be cool."

"I get it," I say. "I respect that."

"I'm, you know, the man of the house here. I've got to step up."

I hold back a smile, because he's totally serious.

"You're a good cousin, Otis. I'm sure Sophie appreciates you and all you do."

"All I do," he says with a laugh. "Yeah, I'm a regular captain of industry, me and my Honey Do job."

I remember what it was like to be his age, to think everything was the end of the world, that if my legacy wasn't established by thirty, I'd be dust. So I say, "Come on. You're doing all right. But if you're looking for other work, you could come help Trav and me at The Missing Beat sometime. Text me."

"Working with kids?" he asks, nodding thoughtfully.

"Yeah, it's the best." Even if Otis is little more than a kid himself. Maybe seeing our students find their passions will help him do the same.

"Count me in, but let me know if you ever see this bird." He flashes me a photo on his phone. "There's a huge reward."

"For that?" I ask, incredulous.

"Rich people," he deadpans. "Anyway, I'll go get her," he adds and then heads up the stairs and out of sight.

Sophie comes down a few minutes later, wearing pajamas: a loose Buchanan Brewery T-shirt and a pair of boxer shorts with hearts printed all over them. Her eyes are a little red, like maybe she was crying earlier, and it feels like someone's attacking my heart with a vegetable peeler.

I'm the one who did this to her, not Jonah. I'll have to remember she's sensitive. Sweet. She deserves more than he was able to give her. Truthfully, she might deserve more than I could give her too, which means keeping this thing between us fake is the right play.

If Jonah believes we're together, fantastic.

If Nelly believes? All the better.

But we should keep it at that.

Even if my impulse is to bury my hand in her hair and kiss her again. Kissing her last night had unlocked something inside of me, and I'd known instantly it was a place I wanted to explore and stay awhile. A place that would make music.

But looking at her now, all I want to do is make her feel better. "I'm sorry, Sophie," I say. "I could make an excuse, but I'm not going to. I should have at least texted."

"Your face..."

"Is slightly blue and moderately bruised. It's okay. Dottie accidentally gave me blue hair dye instead of bruise cream."

Her lips twitch slightly and then she turns serious again. "You know, I was worried about you," she says, crossing her arms over her chest. Some fire flares back into her eyes, and relief courses through me. "I was worried something might have happened to you. Or your dad—"

"Something did happen with him, but that's no excuse. I screwed up. Will you come with me now?"

She smooths a hand over the shorts self-consciously. "I was wearing a blue dress earlier. It was really hot. And short."

I hold back a groan. I would have liked to see her in that dress. To be completely honest, I would have loved to run my hands up her bare thighs under it. I'd happily forget all about my current dislike for the color blue. But I'm not knocking the view I have now. I like her like this, stripped bare of any pretense. All Sophie.

Shifting on my feet, I say, "And these make you look like you. And still hot. Let's take a walk."

She glances doubtfully outside. It's pitch black aside from the pools of light from a few neighborhood streetlights.

"Or we can sit on the porch for a minute."

"We'll walk," she says, then casts me a rebellious glance before slipping on a pair of Crocs that have seen better days.

"They complete the look," I say.

That earns me a dagger-eyed stare that lifts my spirits. She's still got her sassiness. Thank God. If I were the man who took it from her, I'd struggle to forgive myself.

She steps out into the warm night with me. The breeze plays with her hair, and I feel a pulse of longing so powerful it nearly brings me to my knees.

I'd like to be that breeze.

"What's wrong?" she asks, frowning at me.

"Everything," I admit as I brush my hair back from my face.

"You wanted to walk?"

No. I want to carry her upstairs so I can sink into her sweet heat and make an honest man of myself. So I can look my brother in the eye and say, *Yes, I stole your fiancée, and I don't have a single fucking regret. You're going to spend the rest of your life knowing I have what you lost, and I hope it hurts as much as what you took from me.*

But it's a ridiculous thought, and I know it.

"Yeah, let's walk."

We stroll side by side on the sidewalk. After a long moment of companionable silence, she says, "Your dad upset you."

"He always upsets me."

She gives me a sidelong look, then shocks me by slipping her small hand into mine and squeezing. The next second, she releases me, but my hand remembers. It wants. So when her hand swings close again, fingers brushing mine, I catch it and hold on.

At her sharp inhale, I give her a pointed look. "You're my girlfriend, right? Watching eyes."

I know at least one person will be watching, from the little purple house we just passed. In fact, I'm pretty sure I noticed the shades moving.

I have to smile at that. Smile and move my fingers over the stone in my other pocket. Dottie told me to start carrying it again, and I'd listened.

"We should probably know a little more about each other," Sophie says at last, her small hand still clasped in mine. "Before next Thursday. What's your mother's name?"

I glance at her, taking in the way the breeze is still playing with her thick hair. "Patricia."

"Your *real* mom, I mean."

I smile. "My real mom is also named Patricia. Let it never be said my father doesn't have predictable taste."

Her eyes widen, and she stops walking. "Are you teasing me?"

"Always. But that's really my mother's name. You can imagine her confusion when she heard about the other woman."

She shakes her head, her lips tilting up at the corners like she's not sure she should laugh. "I'm sorry. That must have been awful for her."

"It was," I tell her honestly. "A lot of things were. But she's doing fine now. She remarried a really solid guy, and they're living on a ranch with a bunch of sheep and a potbellied pig. Look, I don't want to talk about my family right now, and I'm guessing you don't want to talk about yours."

"No, not really. I already told you. They don't like me very much."

"Otis does." I gesture back toward the house. "He practically offered to fight me if I upset you."

"He did?" she asks, her eyes full of warmth. "Oh, bless him."

I grin at her. "You did good. Your little boy is growing up. Before too long, he'll be smoking cigarettes and stealing your car."

She shoves my arm playfully. "You're a jerk. But I did almost walk in on him masturbating earlier. It was the cherry on my crappy sundae."

I laugh, but I'm not willing to let this go yet. "Now, embarrassing encounters aside, why the hell would anyone in your family not like you? You're the most likeable person I've ever met."

"You didn't used to think so," she challenges, looking away, as if the bushes lining the sidewalk are incredibly interesting.

"I always thought you were likeable. I just don't enjoy being told what to do."

"I can see that," she says, smiling softly.

There's a pause, and for a moment I think she might spill her secrets to me on this public sidewalk, where we've been standing for so long the people in the house across from us probably think we're casing the joint. We've only made it a few houses down from hers.

I want her to tell me. Something inside of me requires it, even though I've only known her, really known her, for less than a month.

But then she shakes her head softly. "They have their reasons. But Otis and Aunt Penny are exceptions to the rule, thank goodness."

The evasion shouldn't burn the way it does, but I want to know her. I want her to trust me enough to tell me everything.

That's probably a big ask given I broke my word tonight.

"You know..." She pauses and takes a deep breath. "I didn't think it was going to feel like that when you kissed me."

If she wanted to distract me, she's doing a good job of it. I take a slight step toward her. "Like what?"

"So *good*."

I laugh despite myself. "There you go being honest again."

A stricken look fills her eyes, and I run a finger over her soft lips. "Don't say you're sorry, Soph. Don't be sorry. I want you to be honest with me, even if we have to lie to other people."

"Did it feel good for you too?" she asks.

My blood rushes south, because this woman I've been thinking about for weeks is peering up at me in the dim glow of the streetlights asking if I enjoyed having my mouth on her.

"Yes," I admit. "It felt good. It felt like bliss. I fell asleep with a smile on my face and woke up looking blue. And you want to know what? I still felt pretty good, right up until I saw my father."

She smiles, but it falls a second later, a crease forming between her eyebrows. "Do you think it only felt so good because we were doing it in front of Jonah? Because we were getting back at him?"

"No," I say bluntly, wrapping my hand around her hip. "But it certainly didn't hurt."

Lust flashes in her eyes, so blue I could drown in them. It's a wonder I didn't fall into them the first moment I saw her.

But I can tell she's scared. Hell, I'm scared. It feels like we're stepping into unchartered territory.

"I don't bite," I say, smiling. "Unless you want me to."

She shoves my chest with her open palm, then leaves it there, the fingers moving gently across my shirt. They send bolts of sensation webbing through me, and then she shocks me by grabbing a handful of my shirt in her fist.

"Yes?" I ask, trying to act composed—and like I'm not suddenly imagining backing her against the lamppost and showing her that our kiss was no aberration.

She glances at her hand fisting my shirt, her eyes widening, but she doesn't let go. "I..." She pauses. "I think the only way we can know for sure is if we kiss again, when he's not around."

"A sound scientific principle," I say, backing her toward the nearby lamppost.

"We're in public." Her tone is slightly scandalized but also a bit husky. She likes the thought even if she thinks she shouldn't.

"It's just a scientific kiss," I say, barely even paying attention to the words now, because Sophie's still gripping my shirt, my hand wrapped around her hip like it doesn't know how to let go. Another step brings us to the lamppost. Her back collides with it, and she releases a breathy gasp that makes my pulse pound. Even more so when she lifts her head to me, her lips parted.

They're pale pink tonight, but they're no less tantalizing.

"I'm wearing boxer shorts," she comments, self-consciousness riding the remark.

"As long as they weren't Jonah's."

She grimaces, and honestly, that should be enough to wake me up to some kind of sense. I'm here with my brother's ex—Sophie, the woman he almost married. But I don't back away. Not even the slightest part of me wants to. "I like them," I say breathily. "I like looking at your sexy legs."

"Then you would have *really* liked that dress."

"Too bad. Maybe we could go back to your house, and you can take all of your clothes off and put it back on. I'll watch. For scientific purposes."

She smiles up at me, a wicked glint in her eyes, her features glowing from the streetlight. "You're bad."

"I warned you about that last night." I tuck a glossy lock of hair behind her ear, soaking her in.

"Well?" she says after a second.

I laugh as I lower my head to her, my hand flexing on her hip. I'd like to lift her up so I can have her legs around me, but I don't want to rush her. Or to take things too far in her neighborhood, where Dottie could very well be filming us for her Wise Women Group.

Our lips brush softly at first. But then she pulls me closer with that little fist tugging my shirt, standing on her tiptoes. I'm lost as her mouth moves against mine, and I push her into the lamppost so I can get closer as our tongues move together.

She's sweet and spicy like this too, all soft lips and insistent hands. She holds me close, gripping my shirt tightly, while her other hand reaches up and burrows into my hair. Her head tips back, and I leave her mouth to kiss the column of her neck, sucking for a few seconds under her ear, which pulls a glorious sound from her that makes my dick hard. Harder, I should say, because my body responded to her the moment she brushed her fingers against my chest.

I want to leave a mark on her, I decide.

I want Jonah to see it, and to think she's mine.

She must feel my dick, but instead of backing away, she pushes into me, and I claim her mouth again, half-crazed. Last night something sparked between us when we kissed, but it wasn't like this. This is...

I feel like I could kiss her for hours, and it wouldn't be enough. I'd like to kiss her until my lips stop working. Until we fall to the ground from exhaustion. The little sounds she's making, and the sensation of her fingers in my hair, only make the desire stronger. I let my hand slip under the back of her shirt, feeling her soft skin. It sends a shudder of need through me. My other hand is still at her hip, but I dip it down to her butt, feeling the curve of her beneath those boxer shorts that don't hide anything. And when her response is to push closer, a sense of delighted wonder courses through me. It's—

There's a rustling sound behind me, and I pull away from her, feeling a surge of protectiveness, just as an apple-cheeked older man with a hound dog turns the corner.

From the way he looks at us, I suspect he's well aware of what we were doing.

He nods at Sophie, smiling kindly. "Night, Sophie. Say hello to your cousin for me."

She barely manages a nod back, her hair mussed, her eyes glittering. She looks slightly scandalized—by us, I'm sure.

He walks past, whistling to himself, and a few moments later turns to enter the little purple house next to Sophie's.

"Shit," I murmur. "Is that Dottie Hendrickson's boyfriend?"

To my surprise, Sophie starts laughing softly, her hand gripping the lamppost. "Yes," she says. "And we're never going to hear the end of it."

CHAPTER TWENTY

SOPHIE

I just got caught making out with Jonah's brother against a streetlight. Who *am* I?

Part of me is fearful that I'm not behaving the way I'm supposed to, and there will be consequences. There already have been. Bear saw us together, and he will certainly tell Dottie, but I'm surprised by how little I mind the thought. She obviously likes Rob. The worst she'll do is buy me a box of condoms.

Besides, I did all the right things with Jonah, and I still had bad luck.

Maybe I should be panicked, but the truth is I feel powerful for once. I wanted to kiss Rob, *really* kiss him, and I did. I made it happen.

And it was so good. So, so good, in a way that kissing never has been before. I feel giddy and wild, and even though part of me thinks I should send him home, I take his hand and lead him back to my aunt's house. He gives me a sidelong glance as he walks with me, his gaze amused and appreciative.

Goodness, has he always been this hot?

His chest is warm and hard, like his thick arms, and his mouth is so talented. Like he was playing my body the way he plays his instrument.

"Soooo," he says slowly as we walk, his hand swinging with mine as if holding hands is natural for us. Is he doing it for show, so Bear and Dottie will see and spread the word? Or because he wants to? "Scientifically speaking, what are your thoughts?"

"What are yours?"

"For the record, I asked first," he says, his mouth quirking up. "Although I don't think this one's up for debate. That kiss was definitely better than the first one, and Jonah wasn't watching."

I beam at him, caught up in a giddy feeling, as we continue walking. "Would it have been better if I'd been wearing the blue dress?"

"There's only one way to know. And I'm suddenly very committed to the scientific process. Who knew."

I'm laughing as we reach my steps. He stops me there, his hand holding mine.

"I'm not coming in," he says.

Disappointment tugs at me. "Why not? I could put on that dress..."

"You'd never get it on," he says, his eyes seeming to darken and absorb the shadows around us. "I..." He reaches up with his free hand and rubs his jaw. "If we're continuing with the whole straightforward thing between the two of us, I really want to fuck you, and I'm not sure it's a good idea."

My mouth drops open, as much from the language as from his honesty. "Are you trying to shock me?"

"Maybe."

"What if *I* want to...fuck *you*?" It comes out awkward, and from the glint of amusement in his eyes, he knows I don't use that word often and finds it funny. But I can tell he liked hearing it. I steel myself, then add, "People say it's a good idea to have rebound sex after your wedding is called off. Hannah said so, and I looked it up on the internet. Everyone seems to be in agreement."

I expect him to tease me for that, but instead he tightens his hand around mine. "And you're saying you want to have rebound sex with me?"

"Yes."

"Because of Jonah?" he asks, holding my gaze. His eyes are a deeper, earthier color in the dark.

"Because you make me feel good."

"I could make you feel even better," he says, leaning closer. He places a kiss on my neck that sends spiraling need to places I didn't even think of as erogenous until this very moment.

"Big talker," I tease, trying not to show him what he's doing to me, how a kiss to the neck is already making me feel like I'm going to fall apart.

"That's not the only part of me that's big."

I laugh and shove his chest, loving the way it feels against my hand. "You're so cheesy."

He gives me a wicked smile, but it slides away, and his expression turns serious. "Let's get you inside and to bed."

"With you?" I ask as he guides me up the porch steps.

He doesn't answer, just holds my hand and walks to the door with me. He waits for me to unlock it, then closes and locks it behind him.

"I hope that means you're staying," I say.

His lips twitch, like he's suppressing a laugh. "I need to get something to eat. I haven't eaten since this morning."

"Oh no. I'll make you something." I start to walk toward the kitchen, but he catches me with a big, broad hand across my waist.

"You know what? I'll raid your kitchen later," he says, turning me toward him. "There's something else I'd like to eat."

Holy crap. No one's ever said anything like that to me before. No one's made me feel irresistible either. Maybe Hannah was right about this whole rebound thing.

Before I can respond, Rob reaches down and sweeps me off my feet and into his warm arms. He carries me with such ease that I'm both breathless and speechless as he whisks me up the stairs and toward my bedroom.

"How do you remember where it is?" I ask in an undertone.

"Oh, I never forget an ABBA poster," he says, pushing the door open with his leg. After he carries me through, he shuts it the same way, then sets me down on the edge of my bed. I remove my Crocs, feeling almost shy now that I've managed to get him up here. He removes his boots too.

"Take off those little shorts, Sophie."

"Why don't you?"

"Because I want to watch you do it," he says. "I want to know you're thinking about me burying my head between your legs."

"Oh goodness."

"Your grandmotherly phrases have have no place here, but they certainly won't stop me. The only thing that will stop me is a no."

I inch down my boxers, trying to make it look sexy even though I begin laughing uncontrollably, like I don't know how to stop.

He grins at me, shaking his head a little, but then he freezes, and his gaze becomes intense as I shove the shorts down my legs and let them fall to the floor. Now I'm wearing only my Buchanan Brewery shirt, no bra, no shoes.

He swears. "You weren't wearing anything underneath them?"

"The better to seduce you with," I say, even though I'd planned nothing of the sort. I'd put them on for bed, thinking he'd blown me off.

The thought has the tartness of a lemon, and I feel a wave of doubt. Until he gets down on his knees in front of me. I'm still sitting, so his head is about level with mine, and he leans in to kiss me softly.

I'm glad he's here. I'm glad I'm with him. I just need to keep reminding myself to stay in the moment, not to let my thoughts veer off into any dangerous tangents.

"Are you sure about this?" he asks, pulling back slightly. His face is only inches from mine.

"Not a great time to ask." His smile is close enough to kiss, so I do. "I'm sure about it," I say, sounding more certain than I feel.

He traces a finger down the side of my face. "You don't seem like the kind of woman who'd want no-strings rebound sex."

For a second, I feel a nervous tension radiating through my chest. Is that what this is? Is that what I want it to be?

The fact that he's asking the question suggests it's what's being offered, and that's almost certainly for the best. After all, Rob is Jonah's brother, and from what I can tell, he's not someone my aunt would call *a serious prospect*. I've known him for almost a year, and even though we only saw each other a few times, he never once brought a girlfriend around or mentioned one. It was a Price family joke that he was never with the same woman twice. Then again, that might have been another way for them to drag him down, something they obviously enjoy doing.

Over the past few weeks, I've realized Rob is a good man. Funny and talented and interesting. And he cares about helping people.

I like him. *A lot.*

He's also crazy hot, and I definitely want to have sex with him.

I'm not ready to consider anything more meaningful either, so why worry about what I might want in the future? Shouldn't I just live in the now?

So I swallow my worry and say, "You don't tell me what I want. Besides, I've asked Mrs. Ginnis, and she approves."

He flashes me an impish grin. "What if I'd like to tell you what to do?"

Damn it. My body likes hearing that. A lot. "Maybe I'd allow it, under very specific circumstances."

"Spread your legs for me."

They open without bothering to check in with my brain. He glides his hands up my inner thighs, and the roughness of his calluses against the skin there drives every last worry out of my mind. "Your hands are so rough." He laughs, and I rush to add, "In a good way. From playing, I guess. That feels really nice, and—"

He leans in and kisses my inner thigh—very close to where I'm aching for him—and then lightly bites it. My eyes flutter open. Goodness. No one's ever done that there before...

My legs open wider in silent invitation. I run my hand through his hair, grabbing on, as he spreads my legs wider and kisses his way inward, switching between my legs so neither gets lonely. It feels so otherworldly, so deeply good that the ache might kill me. Literally. He's playing with me, toying with me, and I need his mouth on me. Now.

"*Rob.* You're in the wrong place."

"Lie back and think of England," he says devilishly as he tugs on my legs, pulling them over his shoulders.

Oh. *Oh.*

He sucks me in, his mouth so clever, and I bury my hand

deeper into his hair, needing something to hang on to, because he's really good at this.

Or are you just really into him? an aggravating voice asks, trying to steal me from the moment.

But I have to admit both things are true. If it had been someone else with their head between my legs—a stranger from a bar—it wouldn't feel like this.

And then I can't think anymore. Sensation and pleasure have so thoroughly taken hold of me that I can't process anything but the feeling of his mouth on me and his soft, shaggy hair clutched in my hand. I'm overcome. I'm—

"I'm coming," I whisper, shocked, because usually it takes much longer than this, and my words have him sucking harder, moving his tongue in a way that makes me release a shocked moan as pleasure tightens its grip.

My body tenses and then releases, and I'm left with a feeling of serenity that's frankly amazing.

He leans back, letting my feet drop to the floor, and makes a show of licking his lips.

I *know* I have to be blushing. "That was...wow."

He smiles. "Good. Wow is my baseline. Anything below it, and I'd have work to do."

I don't like thinking about that, about all the other women he must have been with. The thought doesn't last, though. I feel too good. And from the way he's looking at me, he's not done yet.

I reach for him and pull him on top of me. His body feels incredibly warm and big and firm. *Very* firm.

He kisses me and trails a hand up my shirt, and self-consciousness catches me unaware. My boobs have always been small—*but perky!* Hannah said when I brought it up. They're a source of embarrassment and have been ever since I had to change in front of other girls in gym class. My exes never paid them much mind at all.

"You don't have to do that," I say, moving his hand.

"Does that mean you don't want me to," he asks, "or are you just informing me that I don't have to?"

"I know they're small. It's not like I'm blind or anything." I never would have been so direct with another man, but Rob has made it clear that this is a no-strings situation. Besides, I don't feel nearly as self-conscious with him as I've felt with other people.

He lifts himself up so he can look me in the eye and very pointedly lifts the hem of my shirt. I let him help me take it off, but now I feel my cheeks burning.

"You have to take yours off too. It's only fair," I say.

His answer is to pull his shirt up by the hem—his arms flexing with the movement—and reveals a very nice, defined chest that I instantly want to run my fingers and tongue over.

I must say so out loud, because he says, "Me first."

He caresses my breasts, then lowers his head to suck one nipple at a time, the sensation making the heat from my cheeks invade every inch of my body.

"They're perfect," he says, lifting his head again. He sounds a bit angry about it, frankly.

"They're not—"

"They are. They're absolutely perfect, exactly the way they are. I could write a song about your nipples."

"Please don't," I say. And then he's grinning at me in that teasing way of his, and I feel a rush of fondness. It twines with the need I feel, driven by the sensation of him against me—his mouth and hands on me and the feeling of him hard and demanding inside of his pants.

I lower my hand below his waistband and trace the hard length of him. Excitement spirals through me, especially when he releases an impatient moan, bowing his head to kiss my throat, then my lower lip, while his hand caresses my breast. Treating it like it really is perfect.

"Do you have a condom?" I ask, my whole body tingling at the thought of having him inside me. I need that. *Now.*

"Uh, no," he says, pulling back. "I didn't come over here thinking you were into that. I wasn't sure you'd even talk to me."

"You don't keep one in your wallet?"

He lifts his eyebrows. "Do you?"

I suppose he has a point.

He runs a hand through his hair. "You don't...you know, have any here?"

He means from when Jonah and I were sleeping together. "Oh, no. I threw them all away as part of my purge."

His lips form a half-second smile, but it drops quickly, probably because I'm still moving my fingers against his hardness, unwilling to stop.

It's just, he's here in my room, and suddenly I can't get enough of him.

I don't know if this is ever going to happen again, and it's horrifying to think that I might not get the Rob Price experience in full.

"I could ask my cousin," I say, inspired.

"You're going to ask your cousin for a condom?" he asks flatly.

"Yes."

"You're that desperate for my dick?" He moves over me, pressing it into me, and the truth tumbles out:

"Yes."

He swears under his breath, then kisses me beneath my ear. "That's incredibly hot. You drive me crazy."

I feel giddy with a sense of victory. He's a very sexy man,

undoubtedly very experienced, but I drive *him* crazy. That doesn't sound vanilla, now does it?

"I'm going to do it," I say, bucking my hips so he's pressed where I want him, separated only by his pants. "I really am."

He groans as I give him a final squeeze before getting up.

His gaze lingers on me, as if he's mapping me inside his brain. "You're gorgeous."

I feel it.

I throw the shirt on quickly, followed by the shorts. I probably look insane, and I'm never going to live this down. But I need this to happen. If it doesn't, I don't know what I'm going to do with myself. Probably eat more ice cream with a fork.

I leave the room, shutting the door behind me, and march down the hallway to Otis's room. I lose steam as I reach his door. I mean. I don't know anything about Otis's sex life beyond that movie he was watching earlier. What if he's a virgin? Will he be offended if I ask him for condoms?

Then I remember Rob between my legs, my hand gripping his messy hair.

I want his dick. I think it's the win I need tonight.

I gather myself and knock on the door. Otis opens it, releasing a billow of skunk smell.

His eyes widen, either because of my sex hair or because he realizes that I must know what he was doing in there—breaking one of Aunt Penny's edicts against any kind of smoking in the house.

"I'd appreciate it if you wouldn't tell my grandmother," he says, scratching the back of his neck sheepishly.

"Tell her what?" I ask.

He grins, then glances down the hallway. "Is Rob still here?"

"Uh...I need to ask for a return favor."

"You want some pot?" he asks, shoving his hand into his

pocket. "I'll give you some, no problem, but it's not very good. It's kind of skunky, and—"

"I need a condom."

He looks like he's about to choke on his own spit. And I feel a surge of regret that I'm hoping will dissipate the second I get back to the smoking hot man in my room.

"Uh...are you sure about this? He's a good guy and all, but you were pretty upset with him earlier. I mean, I figure it's for you and Rob, but maybe I'm making assumptions. I guess you could have had someone else come over after he left, and—"

"It's Rob. But you can't tell anyone."

He stares at me silently, and I'm so embarrassed I think I might actually transcend my body. Finally, he says, "I thought Rob was your fake boyfriend. Don't you *want* people to think you're sleeping together?"

When he puts it that way, it does sound like a tangled web. "Yeah, I guess, but you know, maybe don't make a point of mentioning it to anyone other than Hannah and Briar. I'll have to tell them."

"I don't discuss your sex life with my friends, Soph. But, you know, sure."

He pops into his room and returns seconds later, dangling a row of brightly colored condoms. There must be fifteen of them.

Oh, thank goodness. It would have been so much worse to make this request and get nothing out of it.

"You know," he says, handing me the condoms, "I listed your wedding dress earlier."

"You did?" I say, my heart feeling gooey. He said he was going to do it, of course, but in the past he hasn't always been great about following through.

"There's already been some interest, but you know, Soph..."

"Yeah?"

"Be careful. I've learned as much about wedding dresses as I care to, so I'd rather not have to sell another." He pauses, fussing with his hair. "I guess what I'm trying to say is that I don't want to see you get hurt again."

Emotion balls in my throat. "Thanks, Otis." I lift the row of colorful condoms. "And thanks for these. Let's never, ever talk about it again."

"Talk about what?" he asks with a goofy grin.

CHAPTER TWENTY-ONE

ROB

I should probably be thinking about what a grave mistake it is to have meaningless rebound sex with a woman I'm starting to have real feelings for. But she *asked* me to fuck her. It would be ungentlemanly to say no.

It would also be impossible.

She deserves to be worshipped in bed. It's obvious from the way she reacted to me feasting on her that she hasn't been. And I'll be damned if I'm going to walk away without giving her everything. It doesn't need to be awkward or weird. She wants a rebound bang; I'm going to give it to her. If anything, it'll make our fake-dating act more believable for Nelly, Jonah, and anyone else who needs to buy into it.

Besides, my dick is aching to sink into her, especially after feeling how ready she is for me. How *needy*.

I really hope that kid has condoms. I hope he has hundreds of them, the way I did when I was his age and grabbed hopeful handfuls from every giveaway bowl I came across as if they were Halloween candy.

I take off my socks and my pants but leave on my boxer briefs, feeling like it would be too presumptuous to go fully nude. Even though she's asked for sex and is seeking out condoms, she might still change her mind.

A grin stretches across my face when she knocks on the door to her own bedroom. At least I hope it's her.

"Can I come in?" she asks in a voice that's surprisingly shy given what she's asked of me. Then again, that's Sophie for you: sweet and spicy.

I open the door a crack, taking in the multicolor condoms she's gripping. The sight nearly makes me laugh. It's a very early-twentysomething stash. "What if I say no?" I ask, raising my eyebrows.

"You won't get to..." She glances over her shoulder. "Fuck me," she whispers.

I could never get sick of hearing her say that, her slight embarrassment overridden by the defiance that's been blooming inside her. Damn. This woman.

"You make a good argument," I say, tugging her inside.

I close the door, lock it, and press her against it. This time I pull down her little shorts while she loses the shirt, the condoms still clutched in one hand.

"Winner's choice," I say, nodding to the colorful row. "What's your favorite color?"

"I refuse to tell you."

I smirk. "It's pink, isn't it?"

Her answer is to tear off the pink one. Yellow's next. Then red. Then green. I'd like to use the whole rainbow.

"Will you take off your shorts?" she asks.

"Since you asked nicely." I push them down one-handed, my other hand pressed against the door above her head, and my dick springs up, very ready for her. Her little gasp is gratifying.

"Put it on me," I say, leaning in to kiss her jaw, her lips.

She opens the condom and then takes my dick in her hand—

the feeling of her hand around me, nothing between us, nearly my undoing—and slowly rolls the condom onto it.

Damn.

Glancing up at me, her hand still wrapped around me, she says, "Can we do it against the door? I was thinking about you doing it, you know, against the lamppost outside."

Damn, damn, damn.

"How about the wall?" I ask, picking her up by the waist and lifting her, her hair swinging a bit from the sudden motion as I set her back down on her feet. "I'd like to fuck you just beneath your ABBA poster."

"You have an obsession with ABBA," she says, sounding breathless.

I'm tempted to tell her that I'm starting to have an obsession with *her*, but I must still have a thimbleful of blood left in my brain, because I don't.

Her hand finds my dick again and pumps rhythmically as I back her into the wall, my head bowing to suck on her nipples. Perfect. Fucking perfect. And I have a feeling I know who made her feel like they weren't.

It makes me want to punch a wall, as much good as that would do.

I reach down to feel her, and she's still so wet. Pressing my mouth to hers, I capture the little sound that escapes from her lips.

"You still want this dick?" I ask, partially because I want to see her blush for me.

She does, but she doesn't look away to try to hide it. "Yes."

"Do you have any high heels?"

Her eyes widen. "The ones...the ones I was supposed to wear for the...well..."

Her wedding.

"*Perfect,*" I say. "Put them on."

A naughty gleam enters her eyes, and she walks to her closet, nude, and pulls out a pair of sparkly four-inch heels. Not tall enough that I won't need to lean down, but they'll do.

I fist my dick as I watch her sit on the bed and put them on.

"Turn around and put your hands on the wall."

She does what I've asked of her, pushing up her butt. It's a sight I want to memorize, but there are other things I'd prefer to do right now. I run my palms over her butt and her lower back, the arc elegant—

I can't wait anymore.

I crouch slightly to get the angle right, and I line myself up, gripping her hip. Slowly, I sink into her. The feeling is so over-whelming it ignites an instant tingling at my lower back that tells me this isn't going to last as long as I'd like unless I start forcing myself to think dismal thoughts. Using her hip as a handhold, I push deeper and lean in toward her ear, kissing the side of her face.

"Is this okay?" I ask.

Her response is to push back, taking in more of me. "You feel so good," she says, her voice shaking slightly. "So good."

She angles her head to the side and kisses me as I slowly thrust the rest of the way in, giving her time to adjust to me. The feeling of her body squeezing my dick while she kisses me is so intense I can barely stand it, but I need to move. I start to thrust in and out while she balances on those sparkly, spiky heels, her hands still raised on the wall for me. Because I asked her to put them there.

I swear into her mouth, her hair. I kiss her. And I slide my other hand between her legs, making sure I'm giving her what she needs, because she is *definitely* giving me what I need.

"Does that feel good?" I ask as I thrust in hard, her tits swaying with it.

"Yes," she says, her voice breathy, "but I want to see you when it happens. I want to see your face."

I pull out and turn her around. Something in my chest melts as I take in the sight of her, completely naked except for the heels she bought to wear for my brother.

I lift her up by the hips and back her into the wall. Her mouth parts as I adjust myself and thrust in deep. And she wraps her legs behind my back as I bottom out. Holy hell. I'm not going to last, so I'm relieved when I feel her clench around me.

I capture her lips with mine and thrust in again, and again, and I can feel myself going over the edge as she releases a sweet gasp into my mouth. I come so hard my knees go weak, and I barely manage to carry her over to the bed, still inside of her, before collapsing onto it, with Sophie on top of me.

"Oh goodness," she says as I finally pull out.

"That's one way of putting it," I say, my voice ragged. "You're extraordinary."

She smiles, shaking her head. "I'm incredibly ordinary."

"Nope. And if you keep denying it, I'll definitely write a song about it."

"You wouldn't."

"Oh, but I would. Someone keeps telling me that all the stuff I write is too depressing and pissed off. Blissed-out would be a nice change."

I kiss her shoulder before getting up to deal with the condom in the en suite bathroom. Thankful as hell there is one, because I don't want to face Otis right now. I come back with a damp cloth for her and help her clean up. Then I pull on my underwear and pants. My shirt. And she tugs on her Buchanan Brewery shirt.

"Are you leaving?" she asks.

I don't know if I'm imagining it, or if there's really a thread of sadness in her voice. But I'm supposed to leave, aren't I? That was the deal. Rebound sex isn't cuddling and sweet whispered words. It's hard and fast and good, against a wall.

"Yeah," I say. "I need to get something to eat." Her eyes widen, but I put up a hand. "You don't have to take care of me, Soph. I can feed myself. Get some rest. You deserve it."

She has a compulsion to take care of everyone and solve their problems, and I don't want to be one more person she can be of service to.

Her lips purse. "Do you have anything in your fridge?"

Probably some seltzer water and stale bread.

"That's a little intrusive, don't you think?" I tease.

"Well, you could make yourself a sandwich in the kitchen downstairs. You did say you'd raid the fridge."

I smile at her. "You can't help yourself, can you?"

"I'm just providing you with the information. What you do with it is up to you."

She sounds a little pissed, though, and I don't want to leave her like that, so I decide to give her my gift.

I pull them out of my pants pockets—a bunch of folded-up scratchers, just like Ann said to bring.

"Scratch-off lottery tickets?" she asks, clearly confused.

I shrug. "I had a pretty weird experience with Dottie and her friends this morning."

"Uh, you're not getting away with just saying that..."

I was going to leave, I *should* leave, but I sit on the side of the bed. I tell her nearly everything, leaving out only Dottie's conviction that I've got a thing for her.

"So you got me lotto tickets?" She's grinning now.

"The drugstore had some temporary tattoos, but I wasn't sure Hello Kitty would be sexy to a twenty-eighty-year-old woman."

"You downplay the influence of Hello Kitty on women of my generation."

I smile at her and run my open palm across her bare thigh, needing the feel of her again. I'm allowed that, aren't I?

"You think you're unlucky, but luck's a game. It doesn't care who you are. I figured you'd probably at least win a couple of bucks off ten scratch-offs. It could be our luck fund."

She gives me a look that reaches into my chest and holds on tight, and it feels like I'm in some trouble here. Maybe deep trouble. She gets up on her knees, still naked aside from that shirt, and says, "Do you have a coin?" Her eyes are bright with excitement, like a kid on Christmas morning.

"Coins. Condoms. What do you take me for? A convenience store?" I joke.

"I don't think I have any," she says, her expression crestfallen. "I get cash tips sometimes, but no one leaves coins."

"I've got something you can use." I pull my wallet out of my back pocket.

"You kept the bad luck penny?" she guesses.

Yes, actually. I've kept it tucked away in my wallet. I can't bring myself to spend it or throw it away. It feels like it's become part of this thing with Sophie. But I don't tell her any of that. "I have something else in mind."

Releasing a breath, I pull out my lucky guitar pick. I'm not a man for superstition, but Travis got me this one when we first started the band. I don't use it for its intended purpose anymore, but I carry it around always. "It's my lucky pick," I admit.

"You believe in luck," she says, her tone almost accusatory.

"Right now? Hell, yes, I do."

I can tell this, at least, was the right thing to say. She takes the pick from me, our fingers brushing, and leans over the side of the bed to the desk, pressing the scratcher onto the flat surface.

She looks up at me, her eyes eager. "Do you think luck can change, Rob?"

"Yeah," I say, feeling a little choked up. "I'm starting to think just about anything can happen if you keep your mind open to it."

She looks lost in thought for a moment, but then she leans down to scratch the ticket. Her lips form a pout. "I think I lost, but it's a bit confusing."

I scoot over next to her, our thighs pressing together. "Oh, you definitely lost."

We make our way through seven of the tickets before we get to a winner.

She glances up at me, her eyes huge. "We won ten bucks!"

I laugh as she gets up on her bed and starts jumping around, clutching the winning lotto ticket in her hand. Her hair dances around her face, and her joy is infectious. Ten bucks. Less than what I paid for two of them, but totally fucking worth it for this. I'd spend hundreds to see her this happy.

"Come on," she urges, reaching down to pull me up with her.

"I'd rather break your bed for a different reason," I say with a grin.

"I might take you up on that," she says in a singsong as she keeps dancing around.

The last two tickets are losers, but it's hard to care. We're still riding high from the ten-dollar win. Sophie tosses all the losers in the trash and then makes a big show of attaching the lucky ticket to the metallic side of her desk with a smiling-face magnet. It seems like a good note to end on, as much as I don't want this night to end. But it's time.

"I've gotta go," I say, dropping a kiss on top of her head. "But first, I really, really want to know which ABBA song you love so much you got that poster."

She scrunches her nose. "It's embarrassing."

"You did just dance on your bed after winning ten dollars off a lottery ticket. I think embarrassment flew out the window long ago."

She swats my arm playfully but then holds onto it, her fingers wrapping around my bicep. "You have such incredibly nice arms."

"Stop trying to distract me."

She sighs. "Fine. It's 'I Have a Dream.'"

Not a dance song, then. A wistful song for my Pollyanna.

"Here I was thinking you were about to say 'Dancing Queen.'" I stroke her hair with the gentlest of touches, feeling a tenderness toward her that surprises me. "I can't make fun of you for that. I like your dreams."

She smiles at me. "It's a bit lame, but it used to make me feel better when I was...you know..."

When she was struggling. I'd like to ask her why, but it's her secret to keep or share. "It's entirely lame," I say, leaning in to kiss her head again, "but it's also cute. Goodnight, Sophie."

I get to my feet, feeling her watch me. Liking it.

"I'm pretending you're definitely going to make yourself a sandwich downstairs."

"I probably will."

"When am I going to see you again?"

"When do you want to? We can spend our ten dollars like high rollers."

She beams at me. "I'd like that. But can we go see Emil?"

I nod slowly, trying to figure out how I feel about that. I'm not totally sure. I don't want to lie to the kid, so I'll have to tell him she's just a friend—no need to mention *with benefits*—who offered to help us out.

Her smile is slipping, and I definitely don't want that to happen, so I say, "Sure. They have him walk the dog on weekend mornings, so we might be able to catch him at the park tomorrow. I usually hang out with an extra guitar so we can get in some playing. It's the only way he gets to practice these days."

"You'll let me come?"

"Yes, light of my life. I'll even play a song for you."

I'm halfway out the door when she calls my name. When I look back, she's holding the pick out to me. "You forgot this."

And I do something that surprises me. I say, "You keep it, Pollyanna. I want you to have it."

CHAPTER TWENTY-TWO

SOPHIE

I wake up to the doorbell ringing. My first thought is that Rob has come back, and a giddy, stupid feeling fills my chest. It's eight, half an hour before my alarm was set to go off. I slip on a pair of sweatpants and practically race downstairs to answer the door, tripping on the last step and catching myself on the banister. Good grief. I'm desperate *and* a klutz.

But it's not him.

It's Hannah and Briar, with a bag of pastries and a tray of coffees. Normally, I'd be happy to see my friends, but I can't deny my mood deflates like a punctured balloon. I'd been hoping *he* would be the one bringing me breakfast.

Then again, Rob and I had agreed on rebound sex and a fake relationship. I probably shouldn't blame him for giving me exactly what I'd asked for. Or for not wanting me to wait on him last night.

It's just...I've started to want more.

Hannah raises the coffee tray. "You have to let us in. We come bearing gifts."

I yawn. "Isn't it a little early for all of us?"

"Yes," Hannah says, "and you're entirely to blame for my

lack of sleep. I'm as invested in your sex life as I would be in a terrible show on the CW."

Briar just smiles and shrugs. "I wake up to do yoga every morning at six thirty, so I was already up."

"I'm stunned that I don't hate you." Hannah nudges Briar with her shoulder, a small smile on her lips to show she's joking.

It occurs to me that we all could have hated each other, like Rob said. We could have decided to be jealous, but instead we've built something beautiful.

"Come in," I say, and follow them into the dining room.

They set their offerings on the table, and I grab us some of the scary eye dishes and napkins. Then Briar serves us each a muffin.

"Soooo," Hannah says. "I hear that Rob was super-duper busy last night."

"She's been texting with Travis," Briar says pointedly.

"Oh?"

"This isn't about me," Hannah says dismissively. "And I only asked for his number so I could get some intel about your boyfriend."

"Fake boyfriend," I correct, which feels strange when I can still feel the phantom ache of him between my legs, and hear the echo of his voice telling me to put those shoes on for him.

But I have to remember that Rob didn't ask for any of this. Our fake relationship was my idea. Last night was a fluke. Just a thing that happened, which wouldn't have happened if I hadn't set the ball rolling.

I can feel my friends watching me, probably reading every expression passing over my face.

"Yes. Fake. *Obviously*," Hannah says. "Did you give yourself fake sex hair too?"

I give myself away by self-consciously touching my hair.

"I told you," Hannah says triumphantly to Briar, who nods.

"Look," I tell them, glancing toward the stairwell to make sure Otis isn't coming down. The last thing I need is for him to join in and tell them all about the strip of condoms I begged him for last night. "You're the one who told me I should have rebound sex with him. It's no big deal, right? I mean, it doesn't have to be one. Lord knows, he's probably slept with dozens of women. Maybe even hundreds." I pause, dwelling on this thought, and feel my heart beating faster. "Do you really think it could be hundreds?"

If so, it probably meant nothing to him. It would be like flossing—a thought that's horribly embarrassing.

Hannah laughs. "No. I don't think he's slept with *hundreds of women*, Sophie. Or at least Travis doesn't think so. He says Rob's always been a bit of a loner."

"Gosh, how long were you texting with him last night?"

"Let's circle back to you having rebound sex with Rob. How was it?"

"She doesn't have to say," Briar interrupts, glancing at me. Tugging on one of her long blond locks, she adds, "But I think we would both appreciate a general idea of whether it was good."

I feel my cheeks heating up. "It was really good. Like, I feel like I didn't really understand what good sex was until last night. I..." I dart a look at the stairs again, then whisper, "I wore my wedding shoes."

Briar sighs contentedly. "That's so romantic."

Laughing, Hannah bumps shoulders with her. "You think it's *so romantic* that he fucked her in the shoes she was going to wear to marry his brother? Mind you, I'm not knocking it. It's definitely hot."

I roll my eyes, but it feels nice to have friends like this. Friends I can talk to about anything, even the elephant in the room: the fact that we've all slept with Jonah, so we know exactly what mediocre sex feels like.

"He was just trying to help me."

Hannah gives me a disbelieving look. "You think he had sex with you because he was being nice?"

I shrug, feeling the thought burn into my brain. I don't really believe it, at least not all the way, but an old voice whispers in my ear, *He felt bad for you. He left...*

"It *was* very nice of him."

"I don't doubt it, but that's not why he did it," Hannah says.

"You're beautiful, Sophie," Briar says firmly. "And you're glowing this morning. We would have known what happened even without Hannah's invasive texting. Heck, we've known he's interested for weeks. Hannah says he couldn't look away from you when you were wearing your wedding dress, and he's kept popping back up—"

"Because he feels guilty about what Jonah did," I say. "He's trying to make amends."

"Men don't fuck women to make amends on behalf of their cheating brothers," Hannah scoffs. "They do it because they want to. *He wanted to.*"

I think back to last night, to the way Rob looked at me, like I was a feast he wanted to gorge himself on.

"Okay," I concede, rubbing my forehead. "You may have a point. But he still left afterward. It mustn't have meant that much to him."

"Did you want him to stay?" Hannah asks, lifting her eyebrows. "Did you *ask* him to stay?"

"No." I lean back in my chair, feeling stupid now. "But I *am* supposed to meet up with him and Emil today at the park."

"He's introducing you to Emil?" Hannah asks. "It's obvious Emil is super important to him. Travis told me all about it."

Briar and I exchange a split-second knowing look.

Hannah laughs. "I'm not into him. If I were going to fuck anyone in that band, it would be the one with the weird name, but everyone knows two redheads can't sleep together. There'd be a supernova."

"You like Bixby?" I ask. "He barely said two words the other night."

"Thus the basis of his appeal. I'm done with men who talk a lot. My bullshit threshold is very low. Plus, I'm not into him either. I was just making a point. I'm definitely not sleeping with anyone in your kind-of-fake-kind-of-real boyfriend's band. Our web is tangled enough, don't you think?"

I can't deny that.

"Sure, but if you really want to sleep with Bixby, I'm not going to get in your way. Maybe we can all rebound with the band."

I'm mostly joking, trying to make light of something heavy.

"No, thank you," Briar says. "I meant what I said. I'm done with men. Even if I get another cat, it's going to be female."

Hannah laughs. "We'll see how long that lasts. But let's get back to the fact that Rob asked you to hang out with the kid he wants to foster. That's sort of a big deal."

"Yeah, but I asked him for that too."

Hannah gives me a pointed look. "Ask and ye shall receive. He doesn't need to give you what you want, you know."

"This brings us back to him trying to make amends," I say.

"He doesn't even *like* Jonah," Hannah says. "I don't see him going out of his way to make amends for something his brother did. Look, I'm not saying he's your one true love or any of that bullshit. But he likes you. He wants to be your friend and enjoy those sweet, sweet benefits. Nothing wrong with that."

"But why?" I ask. I'm not fishing for compliments. I'm honestly not sure. I've acted like a complete nutcase around him, getting on his case one minute, begging him to have sex with me the next.

"He sees in you what we see," Briar says simply, as if it should be the most obvious thing in the world.

Suddenly I feel burning behind my eyes. "What if *I* don't see it," I ask in an undertone. "I...I've been trying to, like I promised to last weekend. But it's hard. My whole life...no one's ever wanted to keep me." It feels like I just peeled back my skin and showed them my insides, but I force myself to keep going. "I thought Jonah did, and I felt so *grateful*. It makes me sick to think about it."

Briar takes my hand and squeezes it, her grip surprisingly strong. "You're not getting rid of us."

"Even if you wanted to," Hannah agrees. "We'll keep showing up with muffins, and it will be a whole stalker situation." She's her usual Hannah self—not a big feelings talker like Briar—but she presses a hand to my back, then adds, "And if you can't see it, then it's our job to remind you. Just like you're always throwing compliments at us. Telling Briar you love her ridiculously gorgeous hair and all her rocks. Telling me how much you like my big mouth."

"I think she said she liked your lipstick," Briar says with a soft smile.

"And the smart mouth underneath it," I say, with tears still welling in my eyes. "I like *everything* about both of you. You know, Rob told me something last week that I've been thinking about a lot. He said our past makes us who we are, so we can't resent it. I'm glad that all this crap happened with Jonah, because if it didn't, then I wouldn't have you two. It's been a long time since I've had a real friend."

"Me too," Hannah says, squeezing my shoulder.

"And me," Briar adds.

"Speaking of," Hannah says. "Did you hear anything from that bartender at The Ginger Station?"

"I haven't reached out to her yet," I admit. "The whole Rob thing kind of took over."

Briar gives her a quizzical look. "Why is this so important to you?"

"No one gets left behind," she says. "It was one of our rules when we were kids. Probably because my dad was totally crap at keeping an eye on us. That's why I'm working with Liam. He needs someone to keep him in line."

I realize I felt the same way about Otis, although that feeling has been shifting. The more space I've given him, the more he's grown. "You don't like working at the brewery?" I ask.

"Eh, it's okay," Hannah replies. "You know me. I like being around people, and the team is pretty good. But it's not my dream job, no. I'm there for Liam."

Interesting. I haven't met Liam yet, but from what she's said, he has a short fuse. It's hard to imagine Hannah shaping her whole life around a man, even her brother. "Does he know that?"

"No," she says, giving me a piercing look. "And he won't. Ever."

"I'm not going to tell him. We haven't even met him."

"Can we meet him and Connor?" Briar asks, Connor being Hannah's younger brother.

"Oh, you don't want to meet Liam. He's an asshole."

I laugh. "We don't want to meet the big brother you love so much you're working at a job you only sort of like so you can keep an eye on him?"

She laughs, shaking her head. "Look. You're going to meet him at some point, but I want to make sure you're inextricably attached to me before you do. Connor's great. The life of the party. But he lives in Boston."

"We want to meet Liam *and* Connor," I say. "We're already very attached to you."

"You also told me I could hire him if my brewer quits," Briar points out. "Which is almost certainly going to happen, because my father just announced he's not giving anyone more than two consecutive days off until the end of the summer, and our brewer's girlfriend lives across the state."

"You'll both meet him," Hannah says, waving a hand. "We'll have a beer together sometime, pinky swear. But I'm with him at work all day, and honestly it's good to get a break sometime. Anyway. We've let things wander too far from the point, which is that it bothers me that we don't know what GingerBeerBabe's deal is. If she *is* on Team Jonah, I feel like we should know, especially after Sophie and Rob just declared World War III on him."

"Crap, you really think we did?" I ask, biting my lip. "I don't like conflict."

Hannah smiles at me. "You stood up in a booth and told a roomful of people exactly what a cheating jerk he is. He's going to try to bite back. So we have to bite harder. I'll follow up on the whole GingerBeerBabe situation."

I glance at the clock, and my pulse leaps. "On that ominous note, I have to get ready. I'm supposed to be at the park in twenty minutes, and it's at least ten minutes away."

Briar stands up. "We're helping you."

"I'm just going to the park," I say. "It's no big deal. It'll probably be boring." But when I think about seeing Rob again, my pulse picks up, and butterflies start fluttering drunkenly in my midsection.

I don't know what I want from him, but I have to be at least this honest with myself: I want something.

"Your self-esteem is a very big deal, actually," Hannah says as she gets up and puts a hand on her hip. She's shorter than me, but she knows how to strike a pose. "And we're going to help you feel beautiful. Because there's a confident, badass bitch inside of you—we've all seen it—and you need to keep feeding her if you want her to show up more."

"Is this because I'm meeting Rob?" I ask, laughing through the knot of emotion in my throat. "You should have seen the lame getup I was wearing last night. He didn't seem to mind."

"Exactly," Briar says emphatically. "Because he sees you for who you are."

"But you don't," Hannah says. "So we're going to help get it through your thick head if it's the last thing we do."

CHAPTER TWENTY-THREE

ROB

Conversation with Dottie

I hear things have progressed.

I'm DELIGHTED!

The Wise Women have some ideas for you. Meet us at the tea shop on Wednesday morning. Eight thirty. We all agreed it's urgent for you to be there.

I'm just helping a friend, and vice versa. It's no big deal.

That may be how it started, my dear, but that's not how it has to end.

I'm busy Wednesday.

Yes, busy meeting with us.

This morning at the park, I'm thinking about Dottie, and her pals, and baby wipes, and about a beautiful woman who begged her cousin for a condom last night just so she could fuck me.

I'm thinking about Sophie moaning. Sophie dancing. Sophie smiling at me like I hung the sun.

"So, this woman's your girlfriend now?" Emil asks, looking at me like he knows exactly what's going on in my head.

I stop playing the guitar mid-strum. "Huh?"

We're sitting beneath a large maple tree in Montford Park, each of us with a guitar. He's tall for his age, like I was, and all skin and bone with a mop of dark hair. I guess I've gotten to the age where teenagers look like toddlers, because he seems so young to me. So innocent and impressionable. But I know from experience how easily it could all go off the rails. He's smart, but even kids who know better can screw up

He'll be okay. This too shall pass.

The hurricane that messed up our town over a year ago did a number on this park, but it's reviving. Things do. Time is the great and only equalizer when it comes to trauma. Loss becomes part of a person, or a place, but with enough time, it's no longer the whole story. I'm hoping time will help Emil too.

He has the dog's leash wrapped around the maple's trunk, and the mutt's lying in the grass, soaking up some sun. I like dogs, but I don't like that this one is treated better than Emil, with its expensive collar and organic dog treats.

"Fake girlfriend," I correct. "But that's between you and me, because I promised I'd never lie to you. It's not for anyone else to know."

He whistles and strums the opening notes of one of the songs he wrote. "Man, your brother's gotta love that."

"You've seen the bruise on my face. That's about how much he loves it," I say, laughing. But there's an edge of uneasiness to my voice, because Sophie's not here yet. She's five minutes late, and she's more of a five-minutes-early type.

Is she having doubts?

Did I inadvertently piss her off?

Or maybe she wanted a quick and easy way to get back at Jonah, and she decided fucking his brother was just the ticket.

Nah. Sophie would never do something like that. She wouldn't use another person as a means to an end, even if I'd basically given her a blank check to do it.

Besides, sex aside, we're...*friends* doesn't seem like the right word, but we're becoming something to each other.

I sigh and set my guitar down, leaning back in the grass next to the dog, who licks my face.

"You're in a strange mood," Emil comments, his fingers still playing music like he can't bear to stop.

"You've heard about my week. Sure you still want to come stay with me?"

He huffs a laugh. "Yeah, man. It won't be boring. And you own, like, four guitars."

"Five, but who's counting."

"Plus I miss Travis and the other kids at the Beat."

"We miss you too, buddy. Everyone's been in a funk without you."

The sun beats down on me, chasing away some of the darkness and the specter of a sleepless night. A consequence of having come home from Sophie's and staying up late working on the song I'd started the night of her wedding to herself. My happy song.

All night, I couldn't get that image of her jumping on the bed out of my head. I wanted to see her do it again. I'm only a man, so I also kept thinking of the way her head had arced back as she came, the sweet sound she made its own kind of music.

I'm soaking in the memories when Emil whistles and stops strumming. "Is that *her?*"

I sit up. And gawk.

It *is* Soph, and she's walking toward us on the path, wearing a little blue sundress that fits her like a dream, flaring out at the knees. And...shit. She's wearing the shoes.

"*That's* your fake girlfriend?" Emil asks in an undertone. "What are you thinking, man? You've got to do something about that."

I have to laugh. He has a point. I don't know what I've been thinking. I don't have a complete thought in my head right now, other than that I have another song to write. One about a little blue dress and a pair of shoes she bought to wear for another man.

Her face lights up when she sees us, and...

You know what? She's supposed to be my girlfriend. I have every reason to greet her like one. There are plenty of people around to be our audience.

I get up and stalk toward her with purpose. When I get close, she says, "I know it's a little much, but—"

I reach for her waist and twirl her around, and she starts laughing. "You're wearing the little blue dress," I say as I set her down, crowding her a little so my words are only for her. "You were talking it up so much, I thought it couldn't possibly live up to its reputation, but I'm glad I was wrong."

"It's not the same one I wore last night," she says as if I might actually care about her laundry habits.

"So you've decided to wear nothing but blue to match my face? Are we one of those couples who color-coordinates?"

She gives me a playful nudge, and I lean my forehead down to hers. "And the shoes," I whisper. "Are you wearing them to taunt me?"

"Maybe," she says with a wry twist of her mouth.

"It's working." I kiss her cheek and pull back, taking her small hand in mine. "I'm happy to see you. I was worried things might be weird because of last night."

Maybe I shouldn't have put it out there, like a cat dropping a mouse at its favorite person's feet. But there it is. I was worried she wouldn't come, or that she wouldn't be herself around me anymore.

"Nope. No weirdness." She checks out her sexy little dress and the heels. "Actually maybe this *is* weird. I should have worn a T-shirt and shorts. I feel really embarrassed suddenly. Who even goes to the park like this?"

"Women who are so sexy they have to marry themselves so they don't lower their standards."

She lets out a single bark of laughter, then covers her mouth, her eyes wide but delighted.

She really is charming. I feel my mood lifting just from being around her.

Releasing my hand and crossing her arms over her chest, she says in an undertone, "I let Hannah and Briar help me get ready. They were very insistent."

"You look good," I say, caressing her arm. "But you always look good."

"I know I don't." She stiffens. "I know I usually dress plainly. But it's because I always feel so self-conscious when I get dolled up. Like I'm playing dress-up."

Vulnerability lines every word, and I run my fingers up and down her arm again, reminding her I'm right there with her. "Did you feel self-conscious in the wedding dress?"

"Of course I did. It's a wedding dress. But I knew I looked good in it, and at least we were at a place people go to celebrate. We're at a park, but I look like I'm going to the prom."

This time I'm the one who laughs. "You went to prom in a sundress?"

"I didn't go at all," she says. The look on her face suggests this is part of the past she'd rather hide from me.

"You can wear whatever you want, and the only reason people are going to notice or care is because you're pretty. A lot of people here are wearing sundresses," I say, nodding toward the field next to the path. Emil gives a salute before returning to his strumming, his smile smug.

I lean in closer, toward her ear. "I grant you, most of them aren't wearing fuck-me shoes, but I'm the last person who's going to complain about that. You probably won't be able to play frisbee in them, but who cares. Frisbee sucks. Now, come meet Emil. He knows the truth, by the way. I don't lie to the kids in my program. That's a hard line for me."

Guilt flickers across her face as she smiles at him. "I'm—"

She stops herself, which makes me grin. "Look at you, cutting apologies short. I'm proud of you, Soph."

"Because I'm less polite than I used to be?"

"You've never been overly polite with me, just overly apologetic. And before you try to apologize for not being overly polite, I should probably mention that I hate polite people. They're the worst."

"Yes," she says, her eyes dancing, "damn them and their kind ways."

I raise my eyebrows. "Kindness and politeness are not the same things."

She eyes the field and then her shoes, looking uncertain.

Fuck it. I sweep her off her feet and start carrying her toward the maple tree, and if people weren't already watching, they are now.

"What are you doing?" she asks, laughing, and I'll be damned if she doesn't kick her feet. It's up there with watching her jump around on the bed, especially since she's cradled in my arms when she does it.

"I'm being kind but not polite. Saving those shoes I've become so fond of."

She doesn't say anything else as I carry her toward the tree, but she leans into my chest. I like the feeling of her there a lot more than I should.

I like *her* more than I should, but I tell myself it's a problem for a different day. I'm here with her now. I'm with Emil. And I have my guitar. There's not a whole lot to dislike about the moment.

I set her on her feet as we reach Emil, who shifts from jamming to playing "Here Comes the Bride."

"Very funny, bud," I say. "This is Sophie."

He sets the guitar aside and gets up to shake her hand like a man. I'm proud of him, and of her. A warm feeling fills my chest as they smile at each other.

"You're really good," Sophie says, pulling back. "Would you play something else for us?"

Music to his ears. He plays and sings softly for another fifteen minutes, then glances mournfully at the dog, who's comatose in a sunny patch. "I'd better get back"

"This'll be done soon," I say, hoping it's true.

He grins at me. "Hey, let me take a photo for you. You can use it for social media."

"Oh, joy," I say dryly. "You know how much I love sharing my private business with complete strangers."

Sophie gives me an apologetic look, and I hold up a hand. "Don't even think about saying you're sorry," I say. "We're going to take this photo and post it."

"Arms around each other," Emil says, gesturing. "Stand in front of the tree."

I give him my phone, and we submit to the photo shoot. Sophie stands in front of me, I wrap my arms around her, and she leans her head back so her hair tickles my chest and neck.

He takes five photos, being fastidious about it, as if he's secretly joined the photography club, then hands the phone back.

"She's a total natural. You, not so much."

"How kind of you," I say, smiling, and scroll through the photos. There's a funny feeling inside me as I study the third one. Sophie is glancing over her shoulder at me, I'm looking at her, and...

It looks real, is all.

"Yeah, definitely use that one," Emil says.

It's a shitty reminder that these are for other people, not for us, just like this lie we've told.

"Can you send it to me?" Sophie asks, inspecting the photo. There's an unreadable look in her eyes, and I wonder if she's thinking the same thing I am. Or if I just want her to be thinking it.

I send the photo to her, then say, "Are we going Facebook official?"

Emil laughs and murmurs something about old people.

"Let's," she says with a sparkle in her eyes. "He won't like that."

No, he won't.

"Let me call my mom first to let her know the score. I won't lie to her either."

She nods, her expression serious, and I know there's an apology on the tip of her tongue. I'd like to kiss it away, but it doesn't feel like it would be in keeping with our arrangement. She wants to have some fun and put on a show, but that's not the kind of kiss it would be, and I know it.

"I gotta split," Emil says.

I nod at him. "Same time next Saturday?"

"Yeah." He gives me another salute, then actually bows to Sophie.

"Smooth moves, Junior," I say with a grin. "Don't outshine me."

"Don't listen to him, Emil," Sophie interjects, laughing. "Don't you dim your shine for anyone."

He gives me a smart-aleck grin. "You heard her. She's smart *and* stupid-hot. Don't screw this up."

He's talking about Sophie, not the situation with the caseworker, but uneasiness settles inside my chest. What if I'm screwing it up right now? What if I've made everything worse by lying about my relationship with Sophie?

If Nelly finds out it's a lie...

Only, how would she?

Sure, Jonah could call in another anonymous tip, but his word won't mean much if Sophie insists she's with me. Besides, we've got a whole brewery full of people to back us up, plus Emil.

Emil hands over my guitar reverently, as if it's his woman. The look on his face is so full of longing, it physically hurts.

I set the guitar aside as I watch him go, feeling helpless.

Sophie turns to me as he walks out of view with the mutt. "I like him. He's really smart."

"You just think that because he said you're hot."

She shakes her head, her eyes crinkling slightly at the corners from her smile.

"Okay, maybe *I* just think that because he said you're hot. Want to make out for twenty minutes like teenagers?"

She laughs. "Out here? Won't we get arrested for public indecency?"

I shrug. "Maybe. It's also very possible word will get back to Jonah, so I think we owe it to ourselves to make a full and enduring spectacle."

"Well, when you put it that way,"

I pull her onto my lap and kiss her. We make out beneath the maple tree, the warm breeze wafting around us, making her hair tickle my arms and face as my lips move with hers, both of us seeking and finding something, it feels like.

Finally we break apart, panting. And the sight of her lips, a deep pink from our kissing, stirs something inside of me. I feel inspired, you could call it.

"What do you say, Soph? Should we make it Facebook official? I'll text my mom a warning and have a lengthy phone call with her later."

She grins at me. "Let's do it."

I take out my phone. After I send a text to my mother about the favor I'm doing for a friend, I connect my Facebook profile with Sophie's, adding the photo of us as my profile picture.

"Isn't that a bit over the top?" she asks, still cradled on my lap, which is causing me a problem she's got to feel.

"Yes, that's the point. Let's rub our love in their faces and hope it feels like sandpaper." As I say it, I caption the photo: *With my girl at the park. Summer lovin'.*

Her subsequent laughter has her body bouncing on top of me, and dear God, she needs to move now, because my problem is only getting bigger.

"All right, Pollyanna," I say, lifting her off and trying to pull my shirt down over the bulge in my pants. No go. I try to think deflating thoughts. "We have work to do. That ten bucks isn't going to waste itself."

She laughs. "You want to blow our money?"

"It's been burning a hole in my pocket since last night."

Angling her head, she asks, "Do you have plans for it?"

"Oh, I have plans for it."

Her eyes widen. "We shouldn't waste it on condoms. I still have the rest of that rainbow strip."

A laugh escapes me. "Not what I was thinking, but it's good to know the rebound isn't over."

She gives me a long look that has my blood running hot

again. Must think more deflating thoughts. *Jonah. Patricia's fake wart. My dad's dictator coffee shop.* "Not for me. You know...if you're okay with that," she says.

I get up and hold my hand out to her to give her a boost. "I'm more than okay with that. But, as it happens, I have a different plan for our money. You up for an outing?"

She glances at her shoes, then slips them off one at a time, my gaze riveted to the view as she does it. Carrying them one-handed, she says, "I can hold one of the guitars if you'd like."

"I'd like," I say, because the only thing sexier than Sophie barefoot in the grass wearing that dress, with her fuck-me pumps in her hand, would be Sophie holding one of my guitars.

A voice inside suggests this definitely isn't going to end well, but we're supposed to be putting on a show, aren't we? And people *are* watching. I don't blame them. She's a sight to see in that sexy blue dress, her hair loose and flowing, and her eyes bright.

This can't last, whatever Dottie and her club would like to believe, but it's a glowing moment. It's now. And it's *good*.

Maybe that'll be enough.

The lyrics of a new song start taking shape in my head, humming through my brain.

A beautiful girl who never got her prom...

A stolen moment...

When we reach the parking lot, she slips the shoes on. We tuck the guitars into the back of my Subaru and then climb in.

"Where are we going?" she asks.

I turn the car on so I can crank the air conditioner. Then I shift in my seat to get a better look at her. "You never went to prom. We're getting you a corsage."

"What?" she asks, laughing. "They don't just carry those at the grocery store all year round."

"No, but I know a crafter who can make something out of

anything. I was thinking we'd get a Trader Joe's bouquet, some ribbon, and make one ourselves. We can do a boutonniere too, if you want."

"Really?" she asks. "Did you go to prom? I saw a few old photos of you at your parents' house—"

"My dad's house," I correct, feeling like a bit of a dick because it came out harsher than I'd intended. "It's my dad's house."

She nods, understanding flickering in her gaze. "Sorry. I know that. Did you go?"

"Nah. I was a loner mostly."

People pass by my car, giving us curious looks through the windshield. I suppose it is unusual to sit in a hot car talking, when we could be out there under a tree in the warm summer breeze, but it feels like we're alone in here. It feels...intimate.

"Did you already play in a band back then?" she asks."Yes." A phantom ache throbs in my hand. The old anger isn't far behind, but I swallow it down.

"Garbage Fire?"

"Nah..." I rub my chin. "I was in Bad Magic."

Her hand lifts to her throat. "*The* Bad Magic?"

I nod again, my throat tightening. "I was the rhythm guitarist."

"How did I not know that?"

Bad Magic made it big nine years ago—after I was forced to quit because I couldn't go on tour with them. They're a local fucking success story, and their lead singer is famous. I could have been too.

It's been hard to let that one go. Every day, going about my business, it whispers in my ear.

That could have been you.

But there's plenty to like about my life now, things I wouldn't willingly let go of.

If I'd gone on tour with the band that summer, I'd be richer. More successful. But maybe not better. Maybe the drive to drink would've hit me anyway, and it would've been harder to stop with no one around to tell me no, or to give me a reason to think I should.

"Jonah has his reasons for not wanting to talk about it," I say, clutching the wheel hard enough that it hurts. "I have mine."

She reaches for my hand, grasping it. As I release the wheel to weave my fingers through hers, an awful, aching need fills me. Oh, this is no good. No fucking good at all.

My eyes find hers again, like I can't help myself.

"It was his fault," she says. "Jonah's." In her tone I can hear how much these last weeks have changed her. She's on my side, no questions asked.

"Are we telling each other?" I ask gruffly.

She knows exactly what I mean, and a look of panic flashes across her face, cutting the tension with the efficacy of an obsidian knife. "Not yet."

I'm disappointed but not surprised. She didn't share her secret with Jonah, and she'd almost *married* him. Why would she tell me? We're just having fun together. Making Jonah jealous. Helping Emil.

"All right, sunshine," I say, clearing my throat, trying to pull myself up out of those low registers. "Let's get you those flowers."

She squeezes my hand. "I'm afraid you'll look at me differently once you know."

I try to smile, but I don't quite manage it. "Don't start caring what I think now, Soph. You might give me the wrong idea."

CHAPTER TWENTY-FOUR

SOPHIE

We get the cheesiest-looking bouquet we can find. We have just over four dollars left. It's hopefully enough to buy the ribbon, but there aren't any available here, so we have to cross the street to a different grocery store to continue our quest.

There are only a few rolls, and the cheapest—gray—costs $4.99.

"What are we going to do?" I ask.

Rob tsks. "I know you want to have some bad-girl fun, Soph, but I'm not shoplifting with you."

I glance around nervously, my heart pounding, to see if anyone heard, and notice an older woman looking up at us from a display of faith-based birthday cards.

"He was kidding," I say, feeling my cheeks heat.

"Nope, definitely not kidding. She's a *very* bad girl."

The woman stuffs the card into the pocket of her coat and hurries away.

"You think she just shoplifted because of us?" Rob asks conversationally.

I surprise myself by laughing, giving his chest a playful

push. The feeling of it beneath my fingers is familiar now, and an ache forms between my legs.

"You're terrible," I say.

"And yet you keep coming back for more. Do you happen to have any ribbon at home?"

"It would ruin the game."

"What if we buy another scratcher to see if we can add to our fund?" he asks with a sly grin. "If we win, we'll still be using our luck fund."

He's willing to play along, and a delicious warmth fills me. There's no question he's doing it for me.

"Okay, but we have to buy the ticket with the leftover money. It's essential."

"If you insist."

We buy a single lottery ticket. The moment the cashier hands it to Rob, I swipe it out of his hands and dash to the nearest flat surface, a wall just a few feet away, and pull out Rob's lucky guitar pick.

He watches me, grinning when he notices the pick.

"I'll give it back," I say, unconsciously wrapping my fingers around it. "That's why I was carrying it around."

"I don't want it back," he says. "I want you to carry my luck for me, Soph. I trust it more with you."

My heart tries to grow. "Do you still have that penny? If so, you're holding onto my bad luck. That hardly seems fair."

He grins at me. "That's a lot of significance to put on a penny, but you're right. It's in my wallet, and nothing could convince me to part with it."

Maybe he wouldn't say so if he knew everything. But I keep that thought to myself. Because if he were to blame me the way my parents did...

I don't think I'd have the strength to share my secret with anyone else, ever again. At the same time, I *want* him to know. I want Hannah and Briar to know too. In some ways, they won't feel like they're fully mine until they do.

"We don't have all day, barkeep," he says, and I realize I've been standing there like a statue, the lotto ticket pressed to the wall.

I read the instructions, which feel overly complicated, and then get to scratching.

Turning toward Rob, I toggle up and down a little on my feet, feeling carried away by the current of him. "We won five dollars, and it only cost two-fifty. We can buy the ugly ribbon."

He barks out a laugh, pulls me to him one-handed, and kisses the top of my head. The gesture is so natural, so sweet, it undoes me.

Jonah *never* touched me like this. His displays of affection were always about showboating or initiating sex. Isn't it ironic that this thing with Rob *is* a show, basically, with a sprinkling of friends with benefits, but it feels more real?

"Lead on, Soph."

I collect the money from the cashier, who doesn't seem impressed with us, and then buy our crappy ribbon. I can't seem to stop grinning, even when we get back to the car and find that the flowers have wilted in the heat, and we now have only forty-five minutes before I need to leave for work.

By the time we collect my car and get back to my house, we only have twenty minutes to work on the corsage and boutonniere.

"We'll have to do this quickly," I say, leading him inside to the kitchen.

"Aye aye."

I pause, because there's a note from Otis on the small kitchen table:

I'm making another attempt at catching the

pigeon, Soph. She's been spotted in Biltmore Village. I've got her favorite snack to lure her in. Also, there's something I want to discuss with you. Can we talk later?

Rob gives me a wicked grin and waves the note at me. "You think this is about the condoms?"

"Yes," I say, setting our purchases down, and bury my face in my hands. "He'll probably never let me hear the end of it. I can't believe I did that."

He pulls my hand away so I can see his smile. "I can. Just like I believe you can make one hell of a corsage in eighteen and a half minutes."

"Why, Mr. Price. Did you just issue a challenge?" I say.

"Oh, *absolutely*."

"Well then. I *accept*." I give him my sauciest grin and hurry into the kitchen to grab the scissors, floral tape, and a safety pin from the junk drawer. Am I stretching my own rules by using a couple of things I already have? Assuredly. But I'm having too much fun to care.

"But there's a complication," he tells me, his tone thick with mischief and intent. "You have to do it from my lap."

The scissors clatter as I drop them onto the table, and the safety pin settles without a sound. The green floral tape rolls for a second before tipping onto its side.

"*Oh*. Should I get the yellow condom?"

He swears, a smile turning up his lips. "Yellow's next?"

"Yellow's next. We'll have to be quick, though."

"I'm not going to stop you."

I run upstairs to grab it, then hurry back down to find Rob sitting in a chair in front of the flowers, waiting for me.

"We have less than fifteen minutes," he says, taking my

hand and pulling me to him. "Seems like you'd better get going with those flowers."

I climb into his lap, my whole body vibrating with awareness of him. The rough texture of his jeans. The heat of his hardness pressing into me. I rock back against it, and he groans, then slides the chair in toward the table.

"You really want me to work on these?"

"Fourteen minutes," he says, his voice strained as he wraps a hand around my hip, pinning me in place.

So I get started, taking the flowers out of their wrapping and choosing matching sets for the corsage and boutonniere. I've just gotten the flower selection sorted when he flicks up the skirt of my dress and parts my thighs with his other hand.

I can feel him getting harder underneath me.

I peer back at him. "Yellow condom time?"

But he shakes his head. "Keep going, Soph. You've got this."

"So you're going to torment me?" I ask.

His laughter radiates through me. "I'm tormenting myself too, so at least it's fair."

But even as he speaks of torment, his touch dips closer to where I need it, to where I'm so eager for him I can barely remember what a flower is, let alone how to arrange it.

I turn my head and brush a kiss against his cheek. "I don't think I care about the flowers."

"Ah, that's too bad," he says, slipping his fingers past the strap of my underwear and brushing them over me. Then I feel him tugging down the fabric, and I lift up for a moment so he can get the underwear past my butt. They drop and get caught on the heels, and I shake them off my feet. "Because I'm only going to put the yellow condom on if you finish."

He's playing games with me. He must be able to feel how much I like it, because he makes a sound of pleasure, tightening his grip on my hip, and dips his fingers inside of me under the dress. He moves them so skillfully and with such purpose that sweat beads on my forehead as I try to trim the flowers to the correct length. I start working with the ribbon.

Almost done.

I've done this before, but my fingers feel clumsy and sluggish, as if I can only pay attention to one sensation at a time, and this is not the one I want to waste any brain cells on.

He leans in close as he thrusts his fingers in deep, the palm of his hand pressing against a place that has me writhing against him. His hair brushes my neck before his lips press against the skin beneath my ear. He sucks on the flesh softly, his hand still working me while his other hand pins me down to his lap, showing me exactly the effect this is having on him—and what reward I'll get if I finish the flowers.

I make almost inhuman noises as I tie a clumsy knot around the flowers. It could, with imagination, be considered a corsage. It's probably the ugliest thing I've ever made, but I don't care. I'll wear it. I'll wear it every day until it wilts if he'll just give me what I want.

I start on the boutonniere as he moves his fingers, curling them up to stroke a spot I didn't know existed, his lips still on my neck. Pleasure ripples through me.

I'm clumsy as I fumble with the tape and the pin, but I get it done, and I don't look at the clock. I don't even look back at him. I grab the yellow condom and turn toward him, silently pleading.

And the way he's looking at me...

No man has ever looked at me like this before.

My whole body feels like it's on the verge of erupting. His fingers move inside of me.

"Take off your pants, please," I plead.

"So polite."

He smiles at me as I get up, and I watch, hungry, as he

pushes down his pants and underwear. My mouth goes dry as he pumps a hand up his dick once and then rolls on the condom. "Sit down," he says, his voice velvet. "Just like before, Sophie. Your back to me."

As I start to lower down, I feel him position himself, and then I sink down onto him, slowly, the feeling exquisite. His hands reach up to cup my breasts as I move on top of him, my hands gripping the edge of the table for support.

"So beautiful," he breathes into my neck. "So good at taking my dick."

No one's ever spoken to me like that before. Part of me clutches her pearls even as I move more quickly on top of him, taking more of him. Wanting him deeper.

"And you make such gorgeous flower arrangements," he whispers into my ear before capturing the lobe in his teeth.

I'm shocked that I can laugh right now, with him inside of me like this, at the kitchen table, but it's such a ridiculous thing to say. The flowers are all at awkward, rushed angles. Because I wanted him too much to be anything close to rational.

"I was on a tight schedule," I say as I push into him, taking him so deep it feels like my eyes will roll back into my head.

"So am I, Sophie. I only have five minutes to make you come. Do you think I can do it?"

His hand moves between my legs, and the feeling of him stroking me there while I take him in deep, out here in the kitchen, is enough to drive me crazy.

"I believe in you," I say as I grind into him, his hips bucking up to meet me.

It grabs me all at once this time, and it takes far less than five minutes. Pleasure bursts through me, so fierce it almost hurts, radiating all the way down to my fingers and toes. To the nerve endings on my scalp.

He groans, and I feel him pulse inside me, which only drives my pleasure higher, even more so when he leans in and kisses my neck with an open mouth.

"With time to spare," he whispers into my ear.

I get up, and he groans before climbing to his feet and taking off the condom.

"Crap," I say, checking the clock. I have to leave for work in three minutes. I hurry to the bathroom, and he follows me at a more leisurely pace, knotting the condom and throwing it in the trash. It looks so dirty in there, like an accusation. So I crumple some tissues and throw them on top. Then I hurry to run a brush through my hair.

"Let me do that," he says, watching me in the mirror.

My heart skips a beat. "You want to brush my hair?"

"Yeah," he says, scratching his head. He looks a little sheepish, almost embarrassed. I hadn't thought Rob Price could be embarrassed. He's always seemed so untouched by other people's opinions. My chest feels gooey now, but also raw.

I rub my fingers over the cage holding my heart. "Okay."

He takes the brush from me while I grab my makeup bag to put on lipstick. Then he watches me in the mirror as he glides the brush carefully through my thick hair, working in segments. Something *strange* is happening to me. I almost feel like crying. And at the same time, I want to jump into the air and throw my hands to the sky. I want to kiss him too. Softly. Lovingly.

The lipstick's the only thing that stops me.

When he finishes, he leans in to kiss my neck before setting the brush down. "There's nothing vanilla about you, Sophie Ginnis," he says, his eyes twinkling. "I've got plans for the red condom. And for the boutonniere. I'm wearing it to my show today."

"You're not," I say with a smile. "It's awful."

"Don't tell me what to do. I'm going to pin it to my T-shirt. You know, you promised to wear yours too."

"I will," I say with a small laugh. "But I'm going to feel stupid."

"Don't. Every time someone asks you about it, you can think about what happened at the kitchen table."

He grins at me in the mirror, so painfully handsome with those golden eyes and his dark hair a beautiful mess around his face. And then he leaves, giving me thirty seconds of privacy so I can try to make myself look like I didn't just have mind-blowing sex in a chair at the kitchen table.

A few of his last words echo through my head as I change into comfortable shoes.

There's nothing vanilla about you.

That's a good thing, obviously, a compliment, but what he said...it connects this morning, and last night, back to Jonah.

It's foolish to feel bad about that, because Rob wouldn't have been here with me if not for Jonah, but I don't want Jonah to have anything to do with this. With this rebound or whatever it is we're doing.

And yet...Jonah is Rob's brother. Rob hates him and would probably do anything to get back at him.

Am I the *anything* in this equation?

CHAPTER TWENTY-FIVE

SOPHIE

Hannah texts me in our group chat an hour into my shift:

> HOLY CRAP. YOUR FAKE-LATIONSHIP IS
> FACEBOOK OFFICIAL. HAS MAMA PRICE
> PUBLICLY SHAMED YOU AND STRICKEN
> YOU FROM HER FEED YET?

Patricia Price doesn't need to, because I already unfriended her. Actually, I'd also unfriended Jonah, so it's very possible neither of them will see that I've changed my relationship status to "in a relationship" and posted the photo with Rob.

I say as much, and Briar responds:

> Yes, but Rob is probably still connected to them.

That makes the guilt return.

Then again, it's always there, an ocean with waves rolling in and out.

Playing idly with the corsage on my wrist, I take down the photo and the relationship status. No one asks about the corsage, although plenty of people take notice of it.

I don't check my phone again until after I'd poured maybe a dozen beers. And I find a message waiting from Rob.

> Is this your way of dumping your fake boyfriend, Soph? I expected at least a Post-it note. Or my good-luck pick bounced off my face into a cup of NA beer.

Smiling to myself, I type back:

> I had second thoughts. We don't need to be social media official for the caseworker to buy our relationship, and I don't want to cause more trouble for you. Maybe it's better not to rub Jonah's and Patricia's faces in it.

> Ah, but I'd like to. And we both look really, really good in that photo. Isn't that what social media is for? Bragging to strangers and getting them to gossip about you?

> Has anyone asked about the corsage?

> No. But there have been plenty of curious glances. They probably think I'm making a fashion statement.

> I'm about to perform at One World Brewery with my boutonniere on. Wish me luck.

I pour some more drinks and practice making one of my NA recipes in a delicious pocket of downtime, nestled into the afternoon like a chocolate chip in a cookie. When I check my phone again, there's an alert on my phone.

Rob Price wants to be in an "It's complicated" relationship with you. Accept?

My heart thumps as I press accept. Then I click through to Rob's page and read the comments beneath the photo. There's one from Travis—moony heart eyes—and another from someone I don't know.

Whoa. Isn't that your brother's fiancée, Sonya?

Rob's already responded—*That's Sophie to you. And she WAS my brother's fiancée. She's my girlfriend. I'm one lucky man.*

My heart is racing now. Obviously, he's just doing it to get a rise out of people. Rob *wants* to upset his brother and Patricia. He's said so. And I can't deny I take satisfaction from the thought too. But it still makes me anxious. It feels like he's taking a stand for *me*, and it might cause trouble for him.

I promise myself we'll talk about it later. I'll convince him to back down if necessary.

I tuck away my phone again, promising myself I won't keep checking it for my whole shift. It's just...

I feel myself slipping into deeper waters than I expected with Rob. He's so thoughtful and funny and deep, and every moment we've spent together has embedded itself in my memory. I know he's been having fun, too, but it's possible our new friendship-with-benefits means less to him. Maybe even very little.

I don't want to believe that, but the anxious thought keeps pestering me, like a mosquito with a taste for my blood.

About an hour before my shift ends, Dottie Hendrickson sweeps in, dressed in an adorable summer dress covered in smiling cups of tea. I know why she's here—or at least I think I do—but I'm still happy to see her. Dottie always lifts my mood simply by being herself. By being *kind*.

She greets half a dozen people by name before reaching the bar. She sets a zippered case down in front of her. "My dear girl," she says with a broad smile. "What a beautiful corsage. Did you make it yourself?"

"How could you tell?" I ask wryly.

"Those flowers are such a wonderful choice." She studies my corsage with much more attention than it deserves. "Honeysuckle for devoted affection and a red camellia...very sensual. I couldn't be happier for you, my girl."

I smile, because of course she's the only person to actually address the silly corsage. But she didn't stop there. She made it feel like something beautiful.

I adore her. Blindly. Truly. I would follow her into a lion's den. "Why are you happy for me, exactly?"

A dumb question, but I'd rather hear what she already knows before giving her more information.

"My dear man saw you and our mutual friend together yesterday evening, of course. And then I saw that lovely photo you posted. I can't tell you how pleased I am for you young people. Why, the very first time I saw you together, I could tell there was something special brewing between you."

I give her a disbelieving look. "Dottie, the first time you saw us together was the day I found out Jonah was cheating on me."

"And the sparks were already there," she says in a knowing tone. "Two more beautiful auras, I never saw. And your star signs are in gorgeous alignment."

"You know when my birthday is?" I ask, surprised. I've never told her.

She looks almost offended. "Of course, my dear. I marked it down in my calendar last year. I mark down all of my young people's birthdays."

Emotion clogs my throat. "I don't know when your birthday is."

"And you needn't," she says. "I stopped counting at eighty. But let's not get off topic." She clasps her hands against her chest. "Pisces and Cancer are a lovely match. Very compatible."

I tilt my head. I'm a Pisces, which means Rob must be a Cancer. I have no idea how Dottie would have come by that information—Rob doesn't strike me as someone who'd give out his birthday—but I don't doubt her. "Cancer. That ends in July, right? So it must be coming up soon."

"Indeed, my dear. His birthday is coming up in a few weeks." She rattles off the date. "He didn't mention it to you?"

No, in fact. I shouldn't be surprised by that. Rob doesn't seem like the kind of guy who'd make a big deal out of his birthday. But it does make me feel a little twist of sadness.

She clucks her tongue. "He wouldn't, would he? Our boy is surprisingly reticent for the lead singer of a band. It's as if all the ego went to his brother. Still, I *do* hope Jonah has been stroking his stone. It should help expel some negative energy."

I smile, thinking about how Hannah would react to that statement. "Yeah, I'm sorry, but I don't see him doing that."

"Me neither," she says, her tone mournful. "But all we can do is present a person with opportunities to be better, my dear. We can't do the work for them."

It has the weight of truth to it, and we both let the words sit between us for a moment before she pushes the zippered case toward me. "I've brought you a little gift. For the rest of your shift, we're going to work magic together."

I smile at her. "I have to work, Dottie. I've already been distracted."

"Oh, don't worry one bit. I've cleared it with Dylan already. We're going to practice some alchemy and make your new drink menu even better."

That sounds fun and creative, and I'd very much like to do it. But I've dawdled too much as it is, checking my phone multiple times during my shift. I purse my lips, debating what to do.

"Just a second," I say, and walk over to the curve in the L-shaped bar so I can catch Dylan's eye. He glances over, taking notice instantly, and walks toward me.

"Are you really okay with me spending the rest of my shift mixing drinks with Dottie?" I swallow nervously. "I feel like I've already created so much fuss..." I trail off in response to the severe expression on his face.

"I want you to mix drinks with Dottie because the owners and I think the NA menu is a great idea that will make everyone money. This isn't me cutting you a break, Sophie. But even if I were, there wouldn't be anything wrong with that. We like having you around here, for as long as you'd like to be part of the team."

They want me here. They like what I'm doing. They think it has worth...

"Thank you, Dylan," I say, my voice slightly wobbly.

He gives me an awkward nod, probably noticing that I'm on edge. "Thank *you*. And have fun. I figured you could practice at the staff bar."

Based on what I've heard from Hannah and Briar, the fully stocked staff bar in the back might be a purely Buchanan Brewery phenomenon. Briar says it's one of the things her father, who is allergic to fun, hates most about Buchanan Brewery. Dottie and Beau Buchanan used to throw the most memorable staff parties when they were a couple. Beau passed away years ago, and Dottie doesn't technically work at the brewery anymore, but their grandchildren have carried on the tradition.

I convey the information to Dottie, and she slings the bag over her arm and heads into the back with me. It turns out she's brought several varieties of iced tea from her signature blends at Tea of Fortune, and we have a lovely time creating together. Including naming all of the drinks.

I feel the lovely itch to do more of this. To make something.

Before I know it, my shift is over.

"Go on home, my dear," Dottie says, her eyes shining. "I feel impassioned by our work, don't you? Perhaps you should invite your young man over."

I consider it and find I *would* like to share this with him, to make him a Man About Town and watch him while he drinks it. To ask him for his help conceptualizing and naming new drinks.

But he's not really your boyfriend, a voice in my head whispers. *It's mostly pretend.*

"We'll see," I say with a forced smile.

Dottie notices, of course.

"You *will* see," she says, patting my face gently. "It'll all work out, better than you'd thought possible."

I reach into the pocket of my sundress for the little guitar pick, running my finger over it, and for a moment I let myself believe her.

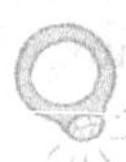

WHEN I GET HOME, Otis is sitting on the couch with a beer and, thankfully, no pseudo-pornography on the television. He perks up when he sees me. "You're home."

"Did you catch the pigeon?"

He sighs and slumps a little more. "No. But I staked her out for an hour and a half in an oak tree. Then she followed me halfway to the house, and I felt sure I had her. She swooped down to grab one of the treats, but as soon as I tried to grab her, she shot up into the air and pooped on my head."

I smile at his damp hair. So that's what it takes to get him to shower regularly. "Sorry, but they say a bird pooping on your head is good luck."

More knowledge I've tucked away about luck.

"It didn't make me feel very lucky." He pauses, surveying

me with a glum look on his face. "There's something I'm not sure if I should tell you."

"You've already gotten halfway there," I say, feeling a twinge of unease. "Might as well pull off the rest of the Band-Aid."

"When I got home, there was a big box on the doorstep. It looks like your stuff, but there was also a boom box in there. I think maybe we could sell that to a nostalgic boomer on eBay."

My mind skips backward to Jonah bringing a boom box to the brewery. I clear my throat. "Was there a note?"

"It was five pages long. I..." He glances sheepishly into the kitchen. "I kind of...threw it away."

"You threw it away?"

"Jonah said a lot of mean stuff and accused you of being the cheater, and I figured you didn't need to read that, Soph. So, yeah, I threw it away."

I pause, trying to process that, and then nod. "Thank you."

"But I figured you might want to go through the box by yourself. There's, like, an old toothbrush and a few paperbacks, some clothes." He blushes. "Uh...like underwear. Stuff like that."

"*Oh.*"

"So...I brought it up to your room."

The thought of going through those things alone sucks, but maybe I can get Hannah and Briar to sift through them with me in a few days. Or I can dump the whole thing out.

"Want me to set it on fire?" he asks. I flinch, and he swears.

"Sorry, Soph. Bad choice of words. I didn't mean—"

"Thanks, Otis. You definitely deserve that beer. Or..." I pause. "I have something better in mind."

"Better than *beer*?"

I grin at him. "Yes."

Dottie supplied me with some of the iced teas from her case, and I take them into the kitchen to mix him one of our specials.

I tell him all about my experiment with Dottie before he takes his first sip.

He puffs his lips out, looking thoughtful. "Don't take this the wrong way." He proceeds to pour some vodka from the top of the fridge into his cup. I've tried to convince my great-aunt not to store her spirits up there, but it's impossible to tell Great-Aunt Penny anything she doesn't want to hear.

He sips it again and nods to himself. "That's the stuff."

"You had something you wanted to tell me?" I ask.

"Yeah, let's sit down."

I eye the kitchen table. There are still stalks and leaves and flower petals all over it, but Otis hasn't commented on the mess. I sweep it up and throw it in the trash, then lower into the chair. Yes, the chair.

I did clean it right before I left the house, with bleach wipes from under the sink, but it still feels special. And sitting here, I'm transported back to earlier, to the feel of Rob behind me. Inside of me.

I feel *good*.

"What's up?" I ask.

"I sold your dress."

"You did?" I ask, astounded. "That was quick."

"Look, I know it was worth eight grand or whatever. But I got four for it. I think that's the best we can do based on what I've seen online."

"You did that for me?" I ask, feeling a little emotional all over again.

"Yeah, Soph. Just like you took that Myers-Briggs thing with me and got me that job at Buchanan. I mean, the job didn't work out, but I knew you had my back. You have everyone's back. You shouldn't be so shocked if we want to have yours." But he gives me a knowing look, because he understand my struggles in a way other people don't. "You're my family."

"Don't make me cry," I say, even though the tears are already welling.

"So we have four grand." He claps his hands together. "What if we started a business together, Sophie? We could combine our Myers and Briggs talents and knock it out of the park, Ginnis style?"

"You want to do that with *me*?" I'm so surprised, I don't immediately know how to respond. Maybe I should tell him no. Otis isn't always the most reliable person. But then again, he's taken initiative lately. He sold my dress. He took that test...

He's been trying, really hard, to catch that pigeon. There's a little notepad in the kitchen chronicling all of his attempts.

Maybe he just needs someone to take a chance on him. Maybe that's all both of us need.

"You want to open The Crafty Monster together?"

"Hell, yeah, I do. It sounds dope. I'm going to help out at Rob and Travis's place as practice. He offered the other day. I was checking out their socials, and I can tell I'm going to love working with those little bastards."

Oh, my heart...

Leave it to Rob to give him a chance before I even considered it. "I hope you don't call them that."

He mimes zipping his lips. "You saw my Briggs results. Working with kids is my thing. Yours too."

"I think we should workshop ideas together," I say, trying not to get too excited. "But I'm afraid four thousand dollars might not go very far. We'll have to save up, probably for a while."

"So we will," he says, sounding like he really means it. "I have some ideas for making money. Other than catching Fluffnut, I mean. He's one wily bird."

"They don't involve selling drugs, do they?"

He laughs. "Soph. What do you take me for?"

I grin at him, feeling a sense of belonging that's still very new to me. "I take you for my cousin, whose room smells like cheap pot, but who is very good at purchasing spoons. Let's use them to eat some ice cream."

"I don't know," he says. "I've become very fond of forks."

CHAPTER TWENTY-SIX

ROB

It's Saturday morning. Just over a week has passed since Sophie and I announced our fake relationship to the world.

A number of things have happened since then, some good, some...well, I suppose it depends on perspective. For starters, Jonah called me and told me I was an asshole. Patricia unfriended me on all the major social networks and then informed me via text, which surprised me because I hadn't realized our accounts were connected in the first place. And then my father officially uninvited me to Thanksgiving, which is several months away. I wasn't going anyway, since I'd already told my mother I was coming to see her in Montana.

I should probably be upset by some of that stuff, but I'm not. I'm surprised by how much I'm not.

It's actually freeing, being lifted from the obligation of trying to get along with them. I've known for a while now that my father would never be proud of me. It's not in his makeup. My successes aren't the kind that mean anything to him.

The situation with my family *has* upset Sophie, however. She's been a nervous wreck, thinking she ruined my life with her fake-relationship scheme. No amount of reassurance has worked, even though she knows how important it is for me to get approved as a foster parent.

There's probably only one thing that will convince her. I need to tell her everything. But we made that bargain, and I'm not sure she's ready to share her story with me.

On Wednesday, Sophie and I met up after her shift to get a pizza. It was one of those places that had a make-your-own-pizza option for kids, and I convinced the server to let us do it. Of course, Sophie gave the thing a smiley face with olives and pepperoni.

While we were making it, Jonah's friend walked past the window. I noticed because he paused and did a double take. Naturally, I leaned in and kissed Sophie, making it a good one. He snapped a photo, I gave him a one-fingered salute, and that was that.

Afterward, we went back to her place to hang out with Otis for a while, spitballing ideas for possible locations for The Crafty Monster.

Sophie and I used the red condom that night, followed by the green. I didn't stay over, because staying over would have meant we were something besides friends having a good time, and that's all we'd agreed to. The rest was for show.

It was the following morning that I got the official Thanksgiving kiss-off, so I guess our little performance got noticed.

Then last night, Travis, Bixby and I got together with Sophie and her friends after our show. We talked and laughed, but I could tell something was weighing on her. Guilt, it seemed like, probably over my exclusion from a family event I'd never intended to go to. From what I can tell, she always feels guilty about something.

After I drove her home, something I insisted any good fake boyfriend would do, I asked her why she felt she needed to apologize for herself all the time. She insisted she didn't anymore and then pulled me into her room to make use of the blue condom. I didn't object. If she wants to keep using me for pleasure, or to get back at my brother, she can.

But I'm starting to think I want more.

Which is why I got up early this morning to attend the Saturday morning meeting of the Wise Women Group. To be totally transparent, I went on Wednesday morning too. Constance was the one who recommended the pizza place.

What can I say? I don't have a sister, my mother's in Montana, and this isn't the kind of thing you talk to your buddies about, even though Travis is already getting on my case about my "weird thing" with Sophie. Not a relationship, and not really a fake relationship either. "A situationship," Bixby called it, which I guess is the closest description. Although I didn't like him using the same word he uses to describe his half a dozen friends with benefits.

"I knew she'd warm to the lotto tickets," Ann says, shaking a finger at me. "No woman alive wouldn't like it if a man showed up with some scratchers. Now, throw a Powerball ticket in there, and that woman will be taking your last name instead of your brother's."

"You mean the same last name?" Constance says gruffly, looking up from today's crochet project. This one appears to be an ugly scarf, the same color gray as the ribbon Sophie and I bought last weekend.

I wore my boutonniere all day last Sunday, catching tons of crap from my friends about it. They knew there was no way I'd suddenly started making flower pins for myself.

"Huh, at least it would make it convenient for her if she'd already had stationery made."

"Honestly, Ann, young people don't have stationery made for themselves," Constance says with a snort. "The majority of them have probably never handwritten a letter."

Dottie furrows her brow. "What a sad thought. I have a drawerful of passionate letters from all of my beaus."

Ann adjusts her hearing aid, then says, "You tie them up with bows? Does your man like reading them? Rufus always liked reading my dirty letters. It made him proud to be the man I chose when all those other men wanted me."

Constance snorts. "You've got that dagnab thing in your ear, but you never turn it on."

"I think we're getting off topic," Dottie says, then reaches out and squeezes my hand. "Did you try the other techniques we've discussed?"

"Yes, what about the wet shirt?" Ann asks. "We mentioned it again at our last meeting."

"Does no shirt count?"

She considers this before shaking her head. "No, sometimes subtlety is better."

I smile and rub the stone in my pocket. "Uh. I think we should clear something up first. I'm not out to marry her. I mean, she was just engaged, for one thing, and for another...I'm not at that point in my life."

Another snort from Constance. "You're, what, twenty-five?" Glancing at the others, she says, "Young bucks that age don't settle down. It's not until they're thirty or so that they get half a brain in their head."

There's a teasing glint in her eyes, and I'm pretty sure she's messing with me. "I'm thirty-one, actually."

She makes a *humph* sound. "You'd better get on that."

"We don't need to discuss marriage," Dottie says, which is both surprising and a relief. "What you want is for her to know you love her."

The words hit like a fist to the gut, and I can feel sweat beading on my forehead.

"I wouldn't say I *love* her," I tell them, forcing a laugh. "I mean, we've only been getting to know each other over the past month. These things take time."

"Son, when you get to be our age," says Constance, "there's not much time left, and you start thinking about what's really important."

"Like winning the lottery," Ann says with a smile.

"Or spending time with dear friends," Dottie adds.

"Or giving advice to a young whippersnapper who's probably not wise enough to take it," Constance puts forth. "If you *like* the girl and want to continue 'getting to know her,' tell her. It's that simple. No need to pussyfoot around the issue. And don't text it to her. Tell her face-to-face, like a man."

Damn it. I don't like that she's got a point.

"A grand gesture wouldn't hurt," Dottie says. "A grand gesture can really sweep a woman off her feet."

"Oh, I wouldn't try to kidnap her," Ann says, either mishearing or misinterpreting. "That only works out well in those books."

"When you're right, you're right," I say, tapping the table with my hands. "I'm going to ask her over for dinner tomorrow night."

I can't tonight. It's one of the rare Saturdays that Travis and I are working at The Missing Beat.

Sophie doesn't get off until late on Sundays, but she has to eat at some point, right? I'm supposed to show her the apartment soon anyway. Our meeting with Nelly is coming up, and Sophie needs to seem comfortable in my place. At home.

"Do you know how to cook, my boy?" Dottie asks, taking my hand. From her tone, she's not confident I could successfully follow the instructions on a box of mac and cheese.

"Sure. I've been living on my own for over a decade, and I haven't died of starvation once."

"That doesn't sound good," Ann says, making a face. "We'd

better help him. I've seen what my teenage grandsons eat, and it's not pretty. If he greets her with a bag of orange chips and a pile of taco meat, she'll hightail it."

Constance scoffs and looks up from her work. "What he doesn't need is this girl thinking he can't do anything without a woman to do it for him. Who wants to be romanced by a man who can't boil spaghetti, for God's sake?" Waving her crochet needle for emphasis, she says, "Make something you know how to make, and make it well."

"But we *will* provide you with dessert, dear," Dottie says. "I must insist on that."

"Speak for yourself, Dottie," Constance retorts. "I've got my own date to prepare for."

"I am, dear. And I have something for you and your paramour too."

Constance gives her a fond look that shows her grousing is at least partially an act. "I won't say no, and I imagine our young friend here won't either."

"I won't," I agree. "I might be able to cook, but I can't bake."

"It's true there's no perfect man," Ann says with a sigh. "But you should pick up some of those temporary tattoos. That will help."

You know what? I think Sophie would find that pretty fucking funny, especially knowing that the Wise Women recommended it to me. Truth is, I have a thing for making her laugh. She's got about a dozen different laughs, from soft and sweet to so unrestrained she can't breathe. I've taken a liking to all of them.

Dottie excuses herself and comes back with a huge box from the bakery next door, which is run by her very pleasant, very bigmouthed boyfriend. And I walk away with what feels like a whole cake before stopping at a couple of stores to find the fake tats I want.

It's only once I'm back in the car that I realize I haven't even asked her to dinner yet. I've been assuming she can come—that she *wants* to come. Sure, it's tomorrow, not tonight, but most people plan farther ahead than that.

Smooth move, Price.

I feel surprisingly jittery about writing the simple text, even though Sophie and I have been so easy together.

> Dinner tomorrow, my place? I figure it's a good idea for you to get comfortable there.
>
> I'll cook.

I drum my fingers on the wheel, waiting for an answer that doesn't come. Okay, so she's busy, or she hasn't woken up yet. Her shift doesn't start until noon. But the buzzing anxiety has set in, digging claws into my brain.

I go about my business, meeting up with Emil the way we've taken to, and then help one of Bixby's friends move.

By five o'clock, several hours later, I still haven't received a reply from Sophie, It's all I can do to ignore those claws digging ever deeper into my brain and meet up with Travis to prepare for our Parents' Night Out. We hold the event once a month—parents leave their kids with us so they can go out on date nights, and we play music with them and then get pizza and watch a movie. Sometimes the movie is music themed, like *School of Rock*. Sometimes we let the kids take a vote.

We've got a nice spot for our program, a unit in an old warehouse in a neighborhood that's not quite convenient to anything, and therefore slightly less expensive. Which is not to say inexpensive. Everything in this town is so much pricier than when I was a kid. We won a grant, though, because Travis is knowledgeable about any number of things, grant applications among them. The sound in here is sick, the acoustics so perfect it could make a man weep.

I fucking love my job.

This and Garbage Fire saved my life. When Bad Magic blew up, the bitterness over what could have been mine was hard to let go of. Hundreds of bottles of whiskey and beer did nothing to blunt the feeling. They only made me hate myself for being weak enough to develop the same disease that had nearly killed my mother. The only thing that helped was making something of what was left of myself.

So usually it's not hard to fully immerse myself in this place and my role here. But apparently I'm acting like a psychopath, because it only takes my buddy five minutes to ask, "What the fuck's gotten into you? You're acting like you just took five shots of espresso."

I swipe my hair back from my face and glance out the window.

"I'm the one talking to you, Price, not the window.

I roll my eyes at him but admit, "t's just...I'm a little worried about Sophie. She hasn't answered my text."

"Have you tried calling her, bro?" he asks, giving me a look that says he knows very well that I haven't.

"I suppose I could."

He laughs, shaking his head. "Speaking of. I got a crazy call last night."

"From who?"

"This woman Lilah. We had a thing, like, nearly eight years ago, when I was on the road. I'm shocked she still has my number."

"She wanted more of your Travis charm?"

"I don't know what she wanted. It was pretty weird. She asked me if I still lived in Asheville, then *where* I live in Asheville. I figured she was in town, you know, like she wanted to get together, but then she basically hung up on me."

"Huh, that is weird. You think she's going to send a flaming bag of shit to your doorstep?"

He laughs, but I can tell he's still chewing on it. "Nah, man. She was a lot, but she's the one who ended things."

I shrug. "Keep one eye open, I guess."

"Go call your girl. We gotta be fresh by the time the kids get here. There's been some drama between Stephen and Grant."

Stephen and Grant are brothers, and they get along about as well as Jonah and I do.

"Oh joy."

I duck into the hallway and dial Sophie before remembering she'll be at work, too. I leave a voicemail and then another text, feeling needy and not liking it. But she'll get back to me eventually.

Unless Jonah got to her...

It's a stupid impulse, but I check our social media profiles, breathing out a sigh of relief when I see they're still linked, that photo of us front and center.

Reflexively, I trace my finger over Sophie's face on the screen, and feel like a real idiot.

I tell myself what I've been repeating for a couple of days now. *It's just a rebound. Don't get hung up.*

But I am, obviously, and I don't even know why or when it started. Maybe it started the moment I saw the video of her throwing that ring at Jonah's face. It's certainly been building ever since.

I remind myself that the important thing is for Sophie to show up next week for the meeting with Nelly. No matter what happens, she wouldn't bow out before that. I know she wouldn't.

Rubbing my temples, I head back inside, in a pretty awful mood, to be perfectly honest.

My mood doesn't improve after the kids show up. Stephen and Grant keep bitching at each other, and it takes twenty minutes for us to settle on a movie to watch. *School of Rock*, which we've already seen about a dozen times.

After the last of the kids take off, we straighten up the room, both of us quiet.

"You want to go out for a bit?" Travis asks as we finish, but I can tell *he* doesn't want to go out for a bit.

It hits me that he's not looking so great either, like maybe he didn't sleep last night. His eyes are heavy, his hair a bit messy for him. Trav's the only type A drummer I've ever met. It's like all the chaos in his soul goes into his music, and he's got nothing left. That, or he's always setting the beat for his own life. Maintaining order helps with his anxiety, he says.

"You okay?" I ask.

He laughs and lifts one shoulder in a half-shrug. "I don't know. It was kind of jarring, hearing from her. Last I heard she was pregnant and marrying some old rich guy. A producer."

"The one she dumped you for?" I say. "Harsh."

"Yeah. Hearing from her put me in a funk, I guess." He gives me a knowing look. "You're in a weird state too."

"Yeah." I tap my fingers against my arm. "It's this thing with Soph. She hasn't gotten back to me all afternoon." I swear. "I sound like one of our kids."

"Let's sit for a minute." He nods to the couch in the corner of the room. We carry over the leftover pizzas and a couple of seltzers and settle into it, facing the floor-to-ceiling window overlooking a parking lot. Like I said, the unit was relatively cheap, and relatively cheap places usually don't come with views.

We shoot the breeze about everything but Lilah and Sophie

for a while, eating some of the cold pizza. I ask if he's still been texting with Hannah, and he gives me an *oh, please* look. "If Lilah was a tornado, that woman's a hurricane."

Maybe we're both avoiding going home, knowing there's nothing much to greet us there—unless Lilah really did send him a flaming bag of shit. Travis is like me. He doesn't even have a goldfish, let alone a cat to sit by the fishbowl. He likes his space, but I can tell the solitary nature of his existence gets to him sometimes, just like it does with me. My friend and I live parallel existences, intersecting plenty, but always returning to the baseline. The empty apartment. The feeling of missing something that isn't there and maybe never has been. The tug toward *something more*. He has a sister he keeps in touch with, but she lives in New York City and doesn't visit much. His dad, who was already sixty when he was born, passed away years ago; his mom is on her third husband and living in Europe.

Eventually, Travis forces me to circle back to the topic of my family. And I rehash all the crap they pulled this past week.

"Look, man," he says. "There's no easy way to say this, so I'm just going for it. You're better off without them. Your dad and Jonah only bring you down. You don't need that."

I nod, because he's right. My feelings about my father have always been complicated, but up until recently, there was still a part of me that hadn't let go. I felt it loosening its grip at the coffee shop last week, and it felt fantastic. I tell him as much.

"That's right," he says, clapping me on the shoulder. "We've got *this*, man. We've made something great here. Better even than Bad Magic." His mouth purses to one side. "They suck anyway. Have you heard their latest single?"

Have I heard it?

Of course I have. I follow their every success and failure. I'm only human. Besides, their lead singer, David, was my childhood best friend. *Was* being the operative word in that sentence.

He took it personally when I couldn't come on tour with them. He acted like it was a choice, not a decision that had been ripped from me. We've talked a few times since, but it's been years since the last time we exchanged a word. He hasn't looked back, only forward, and who could blame him?

I smile ruefully. "You know it was fucking good."

He cocks an eyebrow. "We're better. But I'm glad no one outside of this area knows it. Being on tour sucks. And the music should be just about the music, not about what's popular or what other people want, you know? We've got everything we need."

I can tell he means it—or has convinced himself he does—but it's not true for me anymore.

He gives me the amused look of a man who knows me well. "I like her. Now, *she's* good for you."

I smile at him. "Thanks, man. I'd like to be good for her too."

"You will." He hesitates before adding, "Have you told her what Jonah did?"

I think about my deal with Sophie—a past for a past. But maybe that's unfair. She might need me to show her the ultimate trust before she can do the same. "Not yet," I say. "Maybe it's about that time."

He grins at me. "You *do* have it bad. Just don't start writing pop music. I can't take it if you become a pop music guy."

This makes me laugh, because the songs I've been writing recently could probably be classified that way. "I have a couple of new ones for our next practice. They're gonna make people want to dance."

Hopefully, they'll make *her* dance.

The thought plants an idea in my head. "You said the show at the Peel is on my birthday."

"It is, and you said you wouldn't do it. I believe the words 'over my dead body' were used."

"I've changed my mind. If Bixby is down, let's tell them we're in."

"Oh, the mercurial artistic temperament. Let me guess. You want to see Sophie in leg warmers?"

I roll my eyes. "Seems fun. That's all."

It also seems like a banner opportunity to give her a real prom experience, though I'm definitely not admitting that yet.

"Yeah, right," he says with a laugh. "But I do want to see Bixby in fluorescents. I'll see if the Peel still has room for us."

CHAPTER TWENTY-SEVEN

SOPHIE

Up until now, this week has felt so dreamy and delicious. It was like the luck from those two small winning lottery tickets was carrying me along in a cloud. Or maybe it was the rainbow of condoms that was carrying me along. I've been so excited about the present that it felt like the past and future couldn't touch me. Rob and I were in a bubble, but that changed yesterday, when he told me about the whole Thanksgiving thing.

And then today...

Well, today has felt cursed from early this morning, and no matter how many times I rub my fingers over Rob's guitar pick, it doesn't seem to get better.

First, the woman who bought my wedding gown emailed Otis a plea to cancel the transaction because her fiancée was cheating on her. Talk about bad omens. Of course we said yes, but that leaves us back where we started financially.

Second, I got my parents' RSVP for my wedding this morning. Well, I suppose it must have arrived yesterday, but Otis and I aren't particularly good at gathering the mail.

They RSVPed yes and ordered the fish.

Poor choice. It was cooked sous vide, whatever that means, and Patricia is the only one who'd liked it.

Their RSVP card didn't even have a message on it. Just the penned circle around fish.

That's how close I am with my parents. They think I'm still marrying Jonah Price.

It made me feel a sharper stab of unease about driving a wedge between Rob and his dad. Because even though he insists the damage to their relationship was done long ago, I suspect part of him still wants to repair it.

I got Rob's text about dinner tomorrow while I was still stewing about all of this, and my first reaction was to start bouncing on my feet. It sounded like he was asking me out *for real*. But then panic set in...

It took me a while to figure out why I was panicking, but my ultimate conclusion was this: I'm going to have to tell him everything if we move forward, and also, he may have to give up half of his flipping family for me.

So I held off on answering him but spent all day thinking about it, hyperaware of my phone in my pocket. The only enjoyable moment of my shift was when Dottie came in to hone our drink offerings.

After work, I got home, only to find Otis was off on a bird-hunting mission. Texting Rob was the obvious next move. I wanted to do it, too, but I went up to my room to change and ended up tripping over the box Jonah had left on my doorstep last weekend.

It felt like a physical manifestation of my crappy past, and I had the firm conviction that unless I did something about it, I'd never be free to move on.

So I asked Hannah and Briar over to help me. Now we're sitting on the floor of my bedroom with beers, going through it. It's a big box, and we're only half done.

"Uh. This isn't mine," I say, lifting up a lacy thong with a pencil.

"It's mine," Briar says, blushing, then pulls the big trash bag closer. "Bin it."

"What a shithead," Hannah muses as she flips through the paperback she'd claimed from the box. "He couldn't even be bothered to sort through all of his various girlfriends' crap."

She's not exaggerating. We've already found several things that don't belong to any of us. A pretty pen with a jeweled top, an expensive-looking bra, and a journal with a list of rom-com movies inside. There is also a toothbrush that's unfamiliar to all of us, but we figured it was some kind of trap. *Please, use this toothbrush that looks deceptively new. I totally didn't clean my toilet with it.*

"Do you think this stuff belongs to GingerBeerBabe?" Hannah asks, gesturing to the unidentified belongings. "We could bring them to The Ginger Station and ask. She might want this stuff back."

Hannah made a follow-up trip to The Ginger Station last week, but no one would tell her anything about Jonah's possible fourth girlfriend. And she'd been warned to stop hanging up the STD flyers.

"Yes, whatever will she do without her bucket list of rom-coms and her sparkly pen," I say dryly, recognizing this as evidence of Hannah's leave-no-one-behind mentality. She's looking for excuses to get involved. "I think we should throw it all away. In fact, I'm done looking through the box. Unless you two want to comb through the rest, I'm tossing it."

"No," Briar says, wrinkling her nose with disgust. "I'm done too. I don't want any of this stuff back. It would only remind me of him."

"I'm keeping the book," Hannah says with a shrug. "And the rom-com list. I want to know if GingerBeerBabe has good taste."

"You know," I say, "I have a box of Jonah's crap in my closet. Do you guys?"

"I only had one of his T-shirts," Hannah says. "I burned it weeks ago."

I try not to flinch. "Briar?"

She shrugs. "I have some mementos I boxed up. It's..." She looks down, shrugging again. "I've been meaning to toss it, but there were some good memories. It's hard to process that all of it was..."

"Bullshit," Hannah finishes for her, springing to her feet. "Get your box, Sophie. We're taking Briar's car. She's barely sipped her beer."

"Where are we going?" I ask, caught off-guard by her shift in mood.

"Jonah's house. We're throwing that shit at his house. All of it. Do you have some eggs to throw too?"

"Uh, eggs are expensive these days. What about toilet paper?"

"Yes. Let's do it. I haven't toilet-papered a house in years."

I haven't done it since I was a teenager, before *the incident*. The bewildered look on Briar's face suggests she's never done it.

"We need this," Hannah declares with conviction, and I can't tell her she's wrong. There has been something raw building in my chest all day, ever since I saw that RSVP card. *Fish.* I'm not sure whether it's rage or grief, but it needs an outlet.

"Okay," I say.

"I don't know about this," Briar hedges, glancing at the box of our things combined together, as if we were one person to Jonah. Completely interchangeable. Somehow that infuriates me more than anything. Possibly because it's still easier to be angry on someone else's behalf than my own.

"I do," Hannah insists. "You're not just sad, Briar. You're angry. Be angry."

She considers this for a moment, her expression serious, then nods. "You're right. There's a time and a place for anger."

"Damn straight," Hannah roars.

We gather my Jonah box from the closet, plus some of the gross one-ply toilet paper Otis buys whenever I fail to come home with the nicer stuff, and pile into Briar's car.

"We deserve justice," Hannah fumes, a war general if ever there was one.

"It's not really justice to toilet-paper his house and throw his stuff around," I admit as Briar makes her way to his house, following my directions.

Apparently, he told her that he had a mold infestation so it was better if they spent time at her place; he invented a loud roommate for Hannah.

"No," Hannah says, "but it will make us feel better. The real justice is you banging his brother, the way he was banging your friends."

Even though they didn't become my friends until afterward, I have to laugh. "Yeah, that can't be great for his ego. I just worry about getting between Rob and his family."

"It might be a blessing," Briar says. "I wish someone would get between me and my parents."

Hannah laughs. "You act like you don't have a sense of humor, and then you hit us with some real zingers."

My skin feels itchy and hot as we get closer to Jonah's house, where I spent so many hours. Where I thought I would live with him after the wedding...

That marriage doesn't feel like a dream come true anymore, but a nightmare that almost became my whole reality. If Jonah hadn't swapped phones with me that morning, I wouldn't have found out he was a cheater until much later. Until we were married, probably, and I wouldn't have my friends, or even Otis. I *definitely* wouldn't have Rob.

Rob, who wants to make me dinner.

Rob, who touches me just because, even though he's not my real boyfriend.

Rob, who makes me feel cherished.

Rob, who's waiting for my text...

I'm feeling so many thing at the same time. Grief and rage, and a shocking glimmer of gratitude nestled into them. Because I'd escaped that fate I'd signed up for so eagerly. For once I'd gotten lucky.

"I'm feeling some big feelings," I confess.

"I hope rage is one of them?" Hannah asks.

"Oh, it definitely has a presence."

"Was there any shampoo in the box?" Briar asks practically. "It would be nice if there was something that would make a bit of a mess."

"Yes, and it's that expensive stuff with biotin," I say. "Because he's worried about losing his hair."

"I hope he does," Briar says. "I hope he loses everything but a funny little rim around the sides that makes him look like a medieval monk."

We're still laughing as I direct Briar to park on the curb in front of his house—a little crazy, a lot mad, and strangely... *happy*. His car is in the drive, but all of the lights are off. The house looks different tonight. Drab. Cramped.

"I almost lived there," I mutter.

"Huh," Hannah says, clearly disappointed. "I was hoping it would be a real villain lair. This just looks like—"

"Someone's great-aunt's house?" I ask, laughing. Because it is basically the same model as my aunt's house, only updated and with better amenities.

"But your aunt's house is bright and inviting," Briar says, hugging herself. "This place has a dark aura."

"You know what?" Hannah says. "I'm gonna agree with you on that one. Let's get this done."

We've already assigned ourselves roles. Hannah is the toilet-paperer, and I'm going to chuck the contents of my box at his house while Briar launches the contents of hers. She has fewer things, so once she finishes, she'll help Hannah.

"Ready. Set. Destruct," Hannah says, grinning like a banshee.

My heart in my throat, I open the box and begin yanking out its contents. I throw the sweatshirt he gave me, and it gets snagged in a tree. I open the biotin shampoo, then hurl it at his porch, and watch it bounce and spill its contents everywhere. I throw his toothbrush. His nail clippers. His special pillow.

Just a few feet from me, Briar makes quick work of emptying her box, throwing her own collection. Ticket stubs. A sweater.

When she finishes, she starts helping Hannah, who's running around, slinging toilet paper streamers, and I feel almost gleeful. Maybe this isn't justice. Maybe it's juvenile. But he deserves to have to clean up a mess. He deserves to have an imprint of us on his perfect little postage-stamp yard and his well-maintained house and—

"Who's out there?" a man shouts from the porch of the house next door. I know him a little. Alfred is kind, a bit over-weight, and overly talkative. Or at least Jonah used to say so. I always brought him cookies whenever I baked a batch, and I liked hearing about his children, because he's such a doting parent.

"Shit," Hannah says, dropping her latest roll of one-ply.

Panic grasps me in its claws, and *not again, not again, not again* runs through my head.

I broke the rules.

He could have us arrested. He could...

He puts a hand on his hip. "Is that you, Sophie?"

"It's me, sir," I say, "and a few friends. We were..."

He waves me off. "You go ahead and do what you need to do, sweetheart. Don't let me get in your way. I'm just going to come out here and enjoy a beer while I watch you finish."

Apparently Jonah is a worse neighbor than I thought.

Tears well in my eyes at this man's kindness, but the anxiety in my stomach doesn't quit.

"Thank you, sir," I say.

Then I bring what's left of the box up to Jonah's doorstep and stomp what's inside of it twice for good measure as my friends unspool more toilet paper.

Once I'm done, I wave to Alfred. "Have a good night."

"You too, honey. You tell your aunt hello from me."

"She's in Mallorca."

"Well, I don't rightly know where that is, but I hope she has herself a good time there."

"Sir," Hannah says, hurrying over to him, out of breath from her gymnastics around the yard. "I would be ever so grateful if you could take a video of Jonah discovering the mess and text it to me."

"He done you dirty too?" he asks her.

"Yes," I say. "All of us."

"And more besides, I'm sure. You've got it, honey."

Hannah gives him her number, and we pile back into the car, breathless, a little dirty, and agitated.

Or maybe that's just me.

"That felt good, didn't it?" Hannah asks as Briar pulls away from the curb cautiously, the way she always drives. Not at all like we're in a getaway car.

"It did," Briar agrees. "I didn't realize those things were weighing on me, but I feel lighter. Sophie?"

I just swallow and nod. "Yeah."

Hannah gives me a curious look but doesn't press me. Just as I haven't pressed her for more information about the situation with her brother Liam, which is obviously more complicated than she's wiling to let on.

Hannah's phone chirps when we're halfway back to my house. "It's from that cool old guy," she says, excited.

"Don't watch it until we get back to Sophie's aunt's place," Briar says. "We need to watch it together."

She actually goes three miles per hour above the speed limit to get us there. As soon as we arrive, Hannah leans in from the back seat and presses play.

We watch together as a car I don't recognize pulls up to Jonah's house. Jonah gets out in a burst of energy, swearing loudly enough to be picked up by Alfred's phone camera. Hannah snickers as we watch him weave his hands through his hair.

Then a woman exits the car and joins him, placing a hand on his arm.

I can hear Alfred laugh. "Damn. Got himself another one. She'll be the next to toilet-paper his house."

Jonah must have heard him, because he comes stomping over. "Are you filming this?"

"It's still a free country, last I heard," Alfred says as he lowers the camera. "Are you going to introduce me to your friend?"

"Who did this? Was it a little redheaded bitch?"

Briar gasps, but Hannah only laughs, shaking her head. "He couldn't conceive of you playing a part, Sophie."

But I'm barely paying attention anymore. It feels like all my muscles have seized and I'm in fight or flight. *Fish. Breaking the rules. Getting caught...*

"I need to go inside."

Hannah drops the phone and wraps her hand around my arm. "What's wrong?"

"You're not upset about the woman, are you?" Briar asks.

Honestly, no. It hadn't even occurred to me that I should feel upset.

"Nice to meet you," a woman's voice says, tinny from the phone's speakers. "I'm Nora."

Hannah's eyes widen, and I know she'll do an internet search as soon as she can.

"I don't care about her," I insist. "And you shouldn't either. We have to let this go."

"But she looks familiar," Hannah says. "I've seen her somewhere before. I need to know if she's GingerBeerBabe. And if she knows the whole truth."

"I don't care anymore," I say flatly. I realize I'm trembling slightly. "I should...I need to text Rob back. I haven't texted him all day."

"How dare you have a life," Hannah says with a small, encouraging smile. "What are we up to? Purple?"

"We?" Briar laughs. "It's not a team sport."

"You guys know way too much about my sex life." I turn away from Hannah's stare. "I think he wants to talk. He invited me over to dinner tomorrow night. He said he's going to cook."

"That sounds nice," Hannah says slowly, eyeing me in the dim light from the car's ceiling. "Why do you sound so terrified?"

I could tell them everything. I could tell them right here in my great-aunt's driveway, as if it's nothing. As if all of the pain and guilt I've carried around is the kind of baggage that can be stuffed in a box and left on someone else's doorstep. But the thought makes me want to hyperventilate.

"Take a slow breath in and out," Briar says softly. "It'll help."

I do, and then I say, "Rob and I have been having fun. A lot of fun. But I don't see how we can have a future. When I think about it, it feels like my chest is caving in."

"So don't think about it," Hannah insists. "Just enjoy the fun you're having and the present will become what you now see as the future. You don't have to fix everything right away."

She's right, probably. That's basically what I've been doing, and I've been enjoying myself. In a strange way, the last month of my life has been the happiest in...probably over a decade.

That doesn't say anything good about the way I've been living.

"I'm afraid," I admit. "About everything. That we're going to get arrested for TPing Jonah's house, that Rob's going to drop me, that you're going to drop me—"

Hannah reaches forward and squeezes my arm lightly again. "Jonah would *never* tell a policeman he thinks his mean ex-girlfriends ganged up on him to make his house messy. They'd make fun of him, and he hates it when anyone makes fun of him. So that's not gonna happen."

"But what if he retaliates in some other way?"

She shrugs. "Then we retaliate back. My neighbors actually like me. And we've already established you can never get rid of us, so you can toss that fear right away."

"And Rob?" I ask, my voice quavering.

"I think it's time for you to talk to him about that, don't you?" Briar asks sweetly.

"I thought you'd given up on men," I say in disbelief. "You said you wouldn't even adopt a male cat."

"That's me," she says. "It doesn't mean I've given up on men for you."

CHAPTER TWENTY-EIGHT

SOPHIE

Conversation with Rob

> Sorry!

> You know what? We're texting, so I can say it as many times as I like. Sorry, sorry, sorry.

> This was a weird day. A hard day.

> And there's been an interesting development. Can I call you?

Come over. I need to see you.

> Isn't it a little late?

Stay over.

> I'm with my friends. It'll be a while. Are you sure you'll be up?

I'll be waiting for you.

I still feel off as I drive to Rob's apartment. Nervous and guilty and *wrong*. But I'm also deeply curious about what his apartment looks like. I want to see it, and to see inside of him. To know him. I want...

Things I have no business wanting, even if it's starting to seem like he might want them too.

I park the car in the underground lot, surprised by how nice the building is. They're loft apartments, the kind that probably cost a bundle to rent. I ascend the stairs but pause before knocking, because he's singing.

Dear God.

I've always appreciated his voice—throaty and low and *very* sexy—but this isn't one of his usual angry or sad songs. It's... beautiful.

Like sunshine and fire.

It's her I desire...

I want to soak it up and internalize it, so it can play in my head while I go about my day, my own personal earworm.

I find myself pressing my ear to the door.

I don't fully register the sound of the stairwell door opening across the hall until I notice a teenage kid skulking in with shifty energy. His eyes widen when he sees me looking like a weirdo with my ear pressed flat against Rob's door.

I pull away so abruptly I almost trip. "I won't tell if you don't."

"Are you a stalker?" he asks, hanging back near the stairwell door.

"No. I'm an invited guest. Were you out drinking and smoking pot?"

The look on his face says it all.

"I'm guessing you weren't supposed to do that," I say as the music inside cuts off.

The kid gives me a dark look. "You're a narc?"

No. More like I know where that kind of thing can lead. I'm

tempted to warn him, but I plant my feet and say, "You could get into big trouble creeping around at night."

If I'm a hypocrite for saying it, so be it.

"And you could get into big trouble listening at people's doors. I'm not going inside until I know you're not a stalker."

Holy crap. I did not need another thing to go wrong with my day, but I nod my acceptance of the teenager's terms and knock on Rob's door. Seconds later, it swings open, revealing Rob in a purple T-shirt and a pair of gray sweatpants that deserves an award. My lips part in surprise. Did he wear that shirt because we're up to purple?

"Do you know this woman?" the teenager asks sternly, pulling his shoulder-length blond hair back into a loose ponytail.

"Yeah," Rob says, with a slow grin spreading across his face. "This is my friend, Sophie."

"She had her ear pressed to your door. That's a red flag, my man. And then she tried to bribe me into silence."

Rob looks like he's holding back hysterical laughter. Meanwhile, my face is burning.

"Thanks for looking out, but I like red flags. Have a good night."

Rob tugs me inside and shuts the door behind us before pushing me against it. My breath catches in my lungs.

"Look at you, Pollyanna," he says with an amused curl of his lips. "Feuding with teenagers. What's next? Are you going to declare war on Dottie's Wise Women Group?"

"Stop," I say, laughing despite myself. "I was embarrassed. He caught me in the act."

He runs his fingers through my hair and then dips them behind my ear. My nerve endings practically purr in delight.

"You were listening to me sing. I like that. Even if you were being super creepy about it."

"It was beautiful," I say, the truth tumbling out. "My favorite of your songs."

"Because this one was written for you." He grins at me, and I feel my heart quaking in my chest, so afraid and full of wanting. "But don't worry. This one's not about your perfect nipples. I'm keeping that one just for us."

I give his chest a gentle shove. "You didn't write a song about that."

"I did, and I'll play them both for you, but there's something I want to tell you first."

He takes my hand, and I let him lead me over to the couch, a leather futon. Across from it is an exposed brick wall with an alcove, where there's a photo of Rob and a beautiful older woman next to the TV.

"Is that your mom?"

"The other Patricia Price," he says with a half-smile. "Now Patricia Aycock. You can imagine how much she must hate my father to have willingly taken her second husband's name. Can I get you a drink? I've got some soda and iced tea."

I grasp his hand, feeling awash with nerves. "Actually, I brought us something special to drink. Dottie and I have finalized a couple of the drinks we've been working on."

"I'll get us a couple of glasses," he says, squeezing my hand before releasing it.

I take the few seconds he's gone to search around, soaking in the old bookshelves pushed up against the wall, filled with fat paperbacks. There's what looks like a setlist lying out on the coffee table, next to a lined yellow pad covered in pencil scratch. There's a thick rug underfoot, over a hardwood floor, and exposed beams overhead.

It's warm and cozy.

"Go ahead," Rob says, emerging from the kitchen with the glasses, which he sets on the coffee table. "Continue your mission of stalking. My underwear is in the top right drawer of my dresser."

I roll my eyes and pull the two bottles out of my bag. "I'd prefer them off."

He smiles but doesn't reach for me. He doesn't tug me off my feet and bend me over the couch.

My heart starts thumping faster again. We really are going to talk, then, and I'm not sure if I'm ready to. I'm not sure about anything other than that I'm happy to be here with him.

I think about what Hannah said: *Let the present become the future.*

"This is the Sunshine Spritzer," I say, pouring some for each of us before sitting next to him, our thighs pressed together.

He whirls the drink around in his glass, smiling at me with a spark of appreciation in his eyes, and then lifts it for a sip. His smile spreads. "Holy shit, this is good. Do you know how good this is? It tastes like you bottled up all your positivity and gave it to me."

I feel some of the heaviness of the day lifting and smile back at him. "It is, right? They're putting my drinks on the menu starting next week. I think we really have something here."

"Are they paying you extra for this?"

I cringe a little, because the thought honestly hadn't occurred to me. Isn't it enough to get the recognition from Dylan? The help from Dottie? "I'm sure they'll do something if it's successful."

"You don't know what you're worth," he says, nudging my knee with his.

It feels like he's gripped the hurting place inside of me.

"I'm worth two fish entrées," I say, the words seeping out of me the way they always seem to with him.

He frowns. "I'm not following, but I feel the need to point out that the fish on a menu is usually the most expensive."

"This is bad fish," I say, my voice quavering. "Rubbery."

"Not ideal, but I bet we could work with it. Add a little parsley and lemon. Are you coming to dinner tomorrow night? We could give it a go."

I pick at the collar of my T-shirt, a plain one today, from my old stash. This morning, I hadn't felt special. "I should tell you what happened today. It's about Jonah."

A cloud passes over his face, and he sets his drink down. "That's funny. I wanted to talk about Jonah too."

"Oh, did you hear about the toilet-papering?"

He gives me a quizzical look, which slips into amusement. "Did you really toilet-paper his house?"

I duck my head into my hands, embarrassed. "Yeah, it was unplanned." I tell him everything, including about the video his neighbor sent us. "Hannah thinks it might be GingerBeerBabe and that they're together now."

His gaze turns sharper, harder. "I don't give a fuck who he's seeing. He could be dating half this town for all I care, as long as he's not dating you. Do *you* care?"

He sounds almost jealous. My pulse skips a beat, and I wrap a hand around his leg. "No. Not like that. I don't care about this woman, but Hannah does. She doesn't think he deserves to be happy."

"He doesn't," he says, his jaw tensing. "You asked what he did to me..."

I feel like water starting to bubble on a hot burner. He's going to tell me, and then I'm going to have to tell him.

"You don't have to tell me what happened when you were younger, Sophie," he says with a knowing look, reading right through me. "Not yet. But I hope you'll want to. I don't know how we can ever hope to know each other unless you do, and I *want* to know you. Just like I want you to know me."

I swallow nothing, feeling lost. Feeling hopeful too.

"What did he do?" I finally ask, squeezing his thigh, needing the solid feel of him.

He lifts his right hand and shows it to me. I'm intimately familiar with it. Its calluses, its long, clever, well-formed fingers. The little white scars.

He points to the scars with his other fingers.

"I told you I was in Bad Magic. We were supposed to go on tour ten years ago. I was twenty-one. It felt like the beginning of everything. My life finally taking off. My mother was doing well…" His hand starts to tremble, and I take it in mine, feeling a rumble of foreboding.

"Jonah slammed my hand in a door. So hard it broke. He says it was an accident, but I saw the look on his face. He wanted to hurt me. Maybe he didn't set out to break my hand, but he did it on purpose."

I squeeze his hand, tears pricking in my eyes as horror blasts through me.

"I had to get surgery," he continues, softly. "I couldn't play for months. The doctors weren't sure I'd ever be able to play the way I used to. Sometimes I think they were right. Anyway, I couldn't go on tour with Bad Magic, so David, our lead singer, found a guy to take my place. The next summer they blew up. I cowrote a few of their first big singles with David, so I got a good amount of money from that. Still do. But that was it for me. I… we'd started the band together in his garage when we were in high school."

Jonah had always acted like Rob was a loser, a leech, a burden on their family, and yet he had taken something precious from his brother. Worse, my heart told me that Rob was right. That Jonah had done it knowingly, maybe out of jealousy, and was only sorry afterward.

"That *asshole*," I say tightly. Then I remember what Rob told me a few weeks ago about regret. How regretting the bad parts of the past would mean forsaking every good thing that had happened since. "What you said the other night...do you really not regret it?"

He gives me a faint smile, his gaze far away. "Depends when you ask me. I went through a pretty dark time after that happened. I drank away three years of my life. I'll always be ashamed of that, after having watched what my mother went through with alcohol. I knew what would happen, and I did it anyway. At the time, I didn't care. But then I met Travis, and he saved my life. I'm proud of what we've built. I wouldn't have any of that if I'd stayed with the band.

"So no, I don't regret being here, with you. I don't regret the life I've made, and I wouldn't dismantle it for all the money Bad Magic has made. I still get royalties from some of their songs anyway, so I was able to buy this place and contribute to The Missing Beat. Otherwise it would all be on Travis."

I feel tension building inside of me. He told me something that obviously wasn't easy for him to share.

We made a deal...

Rules matter to me. They have ever since I broke one.

I take my hand away, feeling my whole body trembling.

"You don't have to tell me anything, Sophie," he says.

"I think I want to."

Smiling, he says, "You don't sound like you want to."

"You understand."

"I do." Then he surprises me by pulling me onto his lap, his arms wrapping around me like they did when we took that photo the other week. "Maybe it'll be easier like this," he says into my ear.

I nod, feeling the familiar shameful burning in my eyes. "I got an RSVP from my parents this morning. They conde-scended to attend my cancelled wedding, and they'd both like the fish."

"Some pieces of the puzzle are clicking together," he says, nestling my head beneath his chin, his arms gripping me tightly, letting me know that I'm not alone.

I'm shocked to realize that I feel safe. I've never shared my story lightly, and it's always been done with fear and tension, but I feel at peace in Rob's arms. Cherished.

"I did something stupid when I was sixteen."

"You and most teenagers."

I swallow down a tide of emotion. "Most teenagers don't burn down buildings."

I expect him to say something, maybe *no way* or *holy shit*, or something glib like *leave it to you to cause a fire.*

But he just listens quietly, his arms still tightly around me.

"My parents were always busy," I say. "I was an only child, and they never seemed to have time for me. I got in the way. So when I got a bit older, I started doing things to see if they'd react. Drinking from their liquor cabinet. Skipping classes. But they only seemed to care when it interfered with their schedule. Like if my mom or dad had to come pick me up early. I was an inconvenience. My school counselor told me I was getting in my own way, and she was right, obviously, but it was like I couldn't stop. I needed something to happen." I glance down at his hands, crossed over my chest, and the little white scars on his fingers give me the courage to continue.

My voice shaky, I say, "We always used to go to my grandparents' cabin in the summers. Near Boone. Great-Aunt Penny would come too. And Otis. And a few other cousins. It was a whole thing. My parents made such a big deal of the importance of behaving myself at the cabin, like they suddenly cared, but I knew it was only because they saw me as a reflection of themselves. So I brought a pack of cigarettes I'd bought off an older kid. I didn't even like smoking." Tears prick at my eyes. "I didn't put the cigarette out properly, and it was so dry that summer...

His arms tighten around me as a sob rips out of me.

"The cabin burned down," he says softly.

I nod, tears coursing down my cheeks. "But it was worse than that. The fire spread through the woods before the fire-fighters could stop it. No one died, thank God, but my grandfather was hospitalized for smoke inhalation, and the cost...

"My parents had to pay over a hundred and twenty thousand dollars in fines, and they sent me to reform school as part of a plea deal. But I don't think it was just because they had to. They didn't want me anymore. They still don't."

I'm crying uncontrollably now, and he turns me in his lap to face him, his eyes so soft and warm that I cry harder. He rubs a soothing hand up and down my back. "And you've spent the last decade trying to make up for it by pleasing everyone. By serving them."

"I didn't please you," I sniffled.

He lifts his fingers to my cheek, tracing the tears. "You please me, Sophie. You please me a whole hell of a lot." He pulls me closer and presses a soft kiss to my lips, then to the tear tracks beneath my eyes. "You made a mistake, that's all. We've all made mistakes."

"Did yours burn acres of forest?" I ask, making a congested sound that could only very generously be called laughter.

"You were unlucky. That's the only difference. But luck isn't something that sticks, Soph. It's not something we carry with us or lose. It's random. And from what I can tell, you've paid for it. You've changed because of it. So why go on blaming yourself, honey? What good does it do anyone?"

I'm shaking as if I'm freezing, the tears still coming hard and fast. He wasn't supposed to understand. He was supposed to send me away...

I'd been preparing for it.

"They never forgave me," I say in a ragged voice.

"They sound like assholes, if you'll forgive me for being blunt." He strokes my hair from my face with one hand, pulling me closer with the other. "But I'll bet all of this brought you closer to your aunt. Your cousin."

"When I heard she was sick, I had to come help her. She was the only member of my family who still treated me like a person," I say through gasping sobs. "The only one who still loved me."

"Otis seems to like you a whole lot."

"I don't know why," I admit. It still came as a shock, Otis wanting to help me, Otis caring. Otis thinking we should try running a business together.

"Because he's sensible enough to value you. Your aunt too. We all make mistakes. It's how we respond to them that makes or breaks us." He cups my jaw with his hand, our faces inches apart. His fingers are wet with my tears. "And you, Sophie Ginnis, are a strong woman. You're a kind woman. And you're so fucking brave."

I start shaking my head, but he stills the motion.

"Thank you for telling me, Soph. Thank you for letting me in."

"I like you," I blurt out, my heart hammering.

He smiles at me, his eyes crinkling at the corners. "Jesus, I'd fucking hope so."

"I mean I *like* like you." Embarrassment and shame swirl inside of me, telling me to shut up, but it's too late. The floodgates have opened. "The way I'm not supposed to. It's terrifying."

"I like you too." He presses a soft kiss onto my wet lips. "I like you just as much as I'm supposed to. Because there are no rules for this. We're in unchartered territory, so don't you think we should make our own rules?"

"Oh goodness, I really want to. I want you." Emotion surges

inside of me. I'm happy, but I'm also worried about what that happiness might cost. "But I don't want to take you away from your family. I know…" I have to pause to regain my voice. It doesn't help that he's pressing soft little kisses to my face. Or that I'm cradled in his lap, where I feel so safe. "I know what it's like, to be at odds with people who are supposed to love you. My grandparents never spoke to me again. They're gone now, so I'll never be able to fix that."

"You were a child when that happened," he says disapprovingly, gripping me from behind and steadying me on his lap. "They should have offered you forgiveness."

Fresh tears surface from the seemingly bottomless well inside of me. "But what about your father?"

"Forgiving someone doesn't mean letting them continue to hurt you. Besides, you said Jonah is seeing someone else. Why should they care if you and I are together?"

"You really want to be with me?" I ask, stunned.

He laughs, though there's a look of frustration on his face. "Yes, Sophie. I figured that's what all of this was about. I want to be with you. There's something special between us. I don't want to let that go without exploring it. Do you?"

"No," I say. "Definitely not."

"Thank God," he says, and then he kisses me deeply, holding me to him with his hand in my hair.

I pull away slightly. "I didn't bring the purple condom."

"I've got a purple condom."

I laugh, feeling a surge of joy. "You bought multicolored condoms so we could continue with the correct color order?"

"Yeah," he says with a smile, smoothing his thumb over the side of my face. "I think I did. I got us some fake tattoos too. I went all out."

"Is that why you're wearing a purple shirt?"

He laughs, glancing down. "No. Let's call that a happy accident."

I kiss him, and I kiss him again and again and again, pausing only to take off his purple shirt so I can trace kisses over the band tattoo on his upper arm and the tat of his lucky guitar pick on his chest. I want to kiss him everywhere. I want to show him the way he makes me feel...

Not vanilla. Not biddable. Just me. Sometimes Pollyanna, and sometimes a bitch, the way any woman should be allowed to be.

So I get down on my knees in front of him and say, "Stand up and take off your pants, please."

"Again with the manners," he says with a slight smile as I lower his sweatpants. I reach for the elastic of his boxer briefs, and he stops me, clamping a hand around mine. "Hey," he says gently, "you don't have to do this."

For a second, horror turns me to stone. I realize I must look horrible. I've been sobbing, and there are probably makeup trails down my face. My eyes must be red and puffy and hideous. "I could wash up first."

He squeezes my hand before I can get up. "That's not what I meant. You look beautiful to me. You always do. You just...you do so much for other people. I don't want you to think you have to do that for me, if it's not going to bring you any pleasure."

"It will," I say. "I want to. I've been thinking about it."

"You've been thinking about sucking my dick?" he says with a cocky grin.

"A lot."

He swears, and I pull his boxer briefs down, stroking him with my hand for a moment. He's so hard for me. So big and beautiful. It's still difficult to believe that he wants me. For so long, I thought no one could want the real me. That if they knew what I'd done they'd turn on me.

Looking up at him, I find his eyes on me, his mouth parted in pleasure. I stare at him as I take him into my mouth, moving my tongue over him, learning this part of him with my mouth.

Groaning, he tips his head back. Then he weaves his hand into my hair and watches me. The knowledge that his eyes are on me right now is delicious.

I keep sucking him in deeper, in and out, unable to take all of him at once but giving it my everything, and his hand tightens in my hair, a strangled sound escaping him.

Then he's lifting me to my feet. Tugging the hem of my T-shirt. We undress like wild animals, throwing clothes, stepping on them, laughing, and he backs me toward his room, kissing me the whole way, passionate, open-mouthed kisses. My whole body is consumed by a deeper yearning than I've ever experienced with anyone, including him. I need him tonight. I need him to claim me, to thrust in deep, to show me that I'm still the woman he wants. That what I did is not the sum of who I am.

Maybe he feels the same way, because he won't stop touching me. When we get into the bedroom, he backs me against the bed, and I fall back onto it, laughing and so full of joy I could float. Until my head collides with something hard.

I turn to touch it, surprised to find a three-inch crystal.

Sitting up in his bed, I grin at him. "Dottie gave you this, didn't she?" I ask, holding it up. "You pretend to think her woo-woo stuff is BS, but you've been sleeping with it under your pillow. You've been *stroking* it, haven't you?"

He gives me a slow, lazy grin and lowers his hand to his dick for a single, rough stroke.

Oh. My...

Yeah, I was asking for that, and I don't regret that I got it.

"I might not believe in it," he says, taking a step toward me. I fall back onto my elbows, the crystal still clutched in my hand. "But I figure it makes sense to cover my bases. So, yeah, I've been carrying it around off and on. You want to rub your fingers over it while I have my mouth on you? It's my turn to get a taste."

Without any other warning, he pulls me down to him, hooking my legs over his shoulders, and—oh, *goodness*.

Every feeling is so heightened that it's only seconds before I'm panting and begging, glancing around wildly for the purple condom. The crystal falls from my fingers onto the blanket, forgotten.

"I really need your dick," I say—it seems like a time for honesty—and Rob swears against my flesh before sucking me in one more time.

Then he pulls away, giving me a wicked grin. "Good, because it really needs you."

He climbs off the bed, but only to put on the condom. It should look funny, seeing him encased in purple. It doesn't, though. It didn't look very funny when it was any of the other colors either. No, it looked like something I was desperate to have inside my body.

He climbs over me, his eyes hungry, and my body arcs up to him—wanting him to conquer, to take, to fill me. *Wanting him.* He adjusts himself and then thrusts in so slowly the pleasure is almost painful, making me frantic for him. But it's slower tonight. Reverent, even. And he kisses me slowly, deeply, taking me at the same leisurely pace, working me up to an orgasm that's so overwhelming I see stars at the edges of my vision.

"That's it. Give it to me, Soph," he says. As if I weren't already willing to give him everything.

CHAPTER TWENTY-NINE

ROB

She's so beautiful, with her eyelashes flat against her cheek, her legs tucked up, her arm slung across her chest.

Fuck, am I the kind of creep who watches women while they sleep? I guess I am now. I don't think I mind too much either.

Last night changed me. Just like the night I met Travis all those years ago. It was at an open mic night, and I was falling-down drunk. I played one of the songs I cowrote with David, and Travis told me I'd covered it better than Bad Magic played it. I told him my whole sad story, something I remembered none of the next morning, and he told me we were going to make something great together. Better than my old band. I told him all I could make right then was a garbage fire.

Game. Set. Match.

I want to build something great with Sophie too. I'm not sure how yet, but I figure most great things aren't built in one night. We're off to a good start, though. We've given this thing between us a foundation of truth, and if you ask me, that's the strongest foundation possible.

I decide to make pancakes, then realize I only have flour and eggs, so I settle for eggs and toast. And coffee, obviously.

I'm in the middle of making breakfast when I get Travis's text.

> We're all set for your birthday. Did you go see about a girl last night?

> I did. Thanks, man.

Sophie comes up behind me while I'm still at the stove. I turn toward her, and she wraps her arms around my neck. I think to myself, *I could get used to this.*

Then I notice she's wearing one of my band T-shirts, and I like it. My God, how I like it. My T-shirt. My woman. *Mine.*

"I stayed over," she says into my ear, her breath soft on my neck.

"You did." I set the spatula down. "Could you please leave now, before it gets awkward?"

Her hair is mussed, and the lines from my pillow are pressed into her face. It's as if my bed has decided she's ours too. I pull her closer and kiss her neck, her cheek. I try to kiss her lips, but she pulls back, smiling. "I have morning breath. You really will want me to leave if you kiss me."

"I won't, but there's an extra toothbrush under the sink, if you'd like to use it."

She glances down at the shirt, then folds her arms over her chest.

"Uh-oh," I say. "You're about to insist that you really need to leave. Your arms tell the whole story." I shrug, soaking in those pillow lines and the sight of her in my band's T-shirt. That does things to me.

"No," she says, dropping them abruptly. Then she laughs.

"Okay, maybe. I just...I have a shift later, and I haven't had a chance to shower. I feel grubby."

"You look absolutely delicious in my T-shirt. It's giving me all kinds of ideas."

"Really?" she says, sounding pleased and plenty surprised, which she really shouldn't be. I figured it was common knowledge that if you want to drive a guy crazy, you wear his band's shirt.

"*Really.*"

She lifts her eyebrows. "Did this just become my shirt?"

"Sure. You can have my whole wardrobe."

She smiles. "That's unnecessary. But I'd be happy to eat some burned eggs."

"How dare you. These eggs are undercooked."

"Were undercooked." Her smile turns wicked. "You've been distracted."

Of course, that's when the charred scent reaches my nose. "Burned eggs coming right up."

Laughing, she leans in and kisses my cheek.

I take the eggs off the burner, inspect them, and throw them in the trash. "I have cereal or cold toast."

"I'll have coffee," she says.

I watch as she pours it, looking at home in my kitchen, very much like she belongs there.

"I have to go meet Emil at the park, but why don't we stop at Dottie's place for breakfast?" I say, speaking like a man who wasn't there yesterday morning. I don't want Sophie to leave me yet. I'm not ready to release the spell that was cast last night.

She looks at me with an amused twinkle in her eyes. "First the crystal in your bedsheets, and now you want to go to Dottie's place for breakfast?"

"I know," I say, shaking my head theatrically. "It's like I've been drinking Pollyanna juice, or eating Pollyanna p—"

Laughing, she presses her hand to my mouth. "Don't you dare."

I kiss her palm. "Wouldn't dream of it."

She laughs harder, pulling her hand back. "Yes, you would."

"You know me well."

She glances thoughtfully into her coffee cup, as if it's full of tea leaves that might spell out the future for her. "I'm still worried about standing between you and your family. I don't want you to regret—"

I brush my thumb over her cheek. "What I'd regret is if I didn't give this a real shot because of them. If I let them stand in the way of something that could be really great. Besides, you're the person who's going to help me form a new family." Her eyes widen, and I realize how that sounded. "Don't worry, Soph. I was talking about Emil. But if you're really desperate for me to knock you up, I'll give it a try."

She laughs, but I still see the worry in her. I feel it.

"Listen, I'm better off without them. Every time I'm around my dad or Jonah, I get dragged down. Depressed. Isn't that a good reason to stay away?"

"Yeah," she says quietly. "But it shouldn't be final. It should be...don't you want to leave the door cracked open?"

I give her a sad smile, because I'm feeling her losses, which she spelled out for me last night. The parents who pawned her off on a reform school. The grandparents who never said their last goodbye. "That's the way the monsters creep in, or slip in an RSVP card with fish circled."

She smiles back, her expression just as rueful. "I guess I'm projecting. You're right. My parents are never going to change, so I need to stop wanting it. I've got Aunt Penny, and Otis is... we've become really close now that I'm no longer trying to steer him away from making my mistakes."

I rub my thumb over her cheek again, then lower my head to kiss her. "Don't you dare forget Mrs. Ginnis."

She pulls back to meet my gaze. "That wedding really made an impression on you."

"Damn straight. And it changed you too. You made a promise to be good to yourself, and you have been. You've started accepting yourself, and it's been beautiful to watch."

"Rob...I don't know if that's true. I don't even know who I am anymore." There's a warning in her tone. Maybe I'm a fool for ignoring it, but I'd be no less of a fool if I let her push me away because she's worried I'll leave her.

"It's all jumbled together," she continues, swallowing hard. "I almost had a panic attack last night, after we TPed Jonah's house. I felt like I was that girl again, the one who'd done something stupid and caused so much trouble. It's like I'm struggling with who I was back then, who I've tried to be, and who I am beneath it."

"I like all of them."

"You didn't," she says, her voice serious. "What if—"

"I like *all* of them. I'm fucking floored that you're still able to see the positive side of things after what happened to you. That's magic. Even if being optimistic is something you've done consciously."

"You mean after what I did. It didn't happen to me, Rob. I did it."

"I've made hundreds of mistakes and nearly ruined my own life dozens of times. I'm not going to judge you for that. You took responsibility for what you did, and you grew from it."

Her eyes well up with tears. "Fuck me," I say. "I didn't mean to make you cry again."

"They're good tears," she says, smiling. "Like rain on a sunny day."

"Who the hell wants it to rain on a sunny day?"

She leans in to kiss my cheek. "Me, I guess. There's something beautiful about the mixture of happy and sad. I...I still wish the fire hadn't happened. I'll always wish that. It caused so much harm, even though no one was seriously hurt. But I wouldn't willingly say goodbye to the life I have now. To the friendship I have with Hannah and Briar. And Otis. And...I wouldn't have you." She looks into my eyes, and I can see different versions of the future in them, each of them with us front and center.

"Damn, Sophie. It's like you're begging me to write a song right now."

"Maybe I am," she says softly, smiling even as tears course down her cheeks. "Maybe we're writing one together. It's a song I'd like to listen to."

"Me too. I guess we should get on that." I trace the tracks of her tears, then kiss them softly, my hand burrowing into her hair. Then I kiss her lips, wet from her tears. "I'm falling in love with you, Sophie. I didn't expect it, but that's the truth. I think it started the first time I saw that video of you throwing the ring in Jonah's face. I've watched it a thousand times."

Her eyes widen, and I wonder if I've pushed her too far. "If that's saying too much, you can blame my council of elders," I say, hoping to recapture some levity. "The Wise Women Group were very insistent that I should tell you how I feel."

"They were right," she says, getting onto her tiptoes to press a soft kiss to my face. "But will you give me a little time to figure all of this out?"

"All the time you need."

I kiss her neck, her cheek, her lips.

She makes a soft sound. "I should really take a shower."

"Me too," I say. "Want to be water-efficient?"

"Yes."

I lift her up, and she wraps her legs around my waist—completely bare aside from that T-shirt.

I push open the bathroom door with my back, my mouth on hers. If she had any real worry about morning breath, it's evaporated, thank God, because she's kissing me back just as feverishly. I set her down on the bathroom counter so I can pull my clothes off, and she watches me, her gaze hot, her legs splayed open. I step into them, accepting the silent invitation.

"It would be a pity to take that T-shirt off." I slide my hand under it, caressing. Squeezing. Appreciating.

Her head tips back, giving me access to her neck, and I press a kiss to it, gratified to see the mark I left there who knows when.

"It would be more of a pity to leave it on," she says huskily, and when she's right, she's right.

I step away to turn on the shower, and remember we still need the next condom from the strip in the bedroom. When I turn toward the door, she thrusts out her leg to bar my path. "You're not allowed to leave me in here."

"You can't shower alone?" I tease.

"Not anymore. There's a spot on my back that's very hard to reach."

"I'll be happy to assist you. But I need to grab the neon green condom."

She keeps her leg in my path, firmly pressed against me, "I'm on birth control. And I've gotten tested, you know, since...

I feel like a firebomb just exploded inside of me. That asshole. That fucking piece of shit. Imagine having Sophie and deciding she wasn't enough...

I grit my teeth and force myself to concentrate on what she's telling me. Because, oh, fuck...

"I've always used condoms," I say.

"I want you inside of me now. Without anything between

us." She lowers that sexy leg. "If that's okay. I mean, if you really want to make it through the rainbow, we can. I don't want to destroy our goal by—"

I lean in and kiss her hard. She opens her legs wider for me, and is it strictly necessary for us to make it into the shower? Because I want her here, in my shirt. I press closer to her, and she makes a sound deep in her throat, angling her head back far enough that it touches the mirror, her long hair a tumble down her back. Her legs cinch around me, pulling me in close.

I reach down to touch her, finding her ready for me, so damn ready, and the strangled sound that releases from her lips into mine tells me it's time. So I line myself up and push in—slowly at first, enjoying the difference in sensation, the fierce pleasure of being inside her like this, skin to skin, raw. And then I can't take it anymore, so I drive in deep. Sophie rocks forward, taking me deeper, her heels urgent against the small of my back.

"Oh my," she whispers.

Oh my indeed. I pull out and thrust in again, grabbing hold of her hair. Needing the feeling of her to engulf me and change me even more than it already has.

"You feel like a revelation," I pant into her ear. Then I tug at the hem of the shirt, because she's right—as good as it is on, it'll be better off. She helps me tug it off over her head, and then I carry her—still buried inside her—into the shower stall, where the warm water rains down on us.

Like rain on a sunny day.

The words sing inside of me, another addition to the record of us, as I press her back into the wall. My mouth and my hands and my dick are all desperate for her. She's soaked with water, soft and wet and so beautiful it hurts.

So beautiful it hurts.

That's part of our song too, part of us, and I drive into her again, and again, feeling her clenching around me, falling apart.

The sight of her like this—lips parted, eyes closed, neck taut and hair a wet tumble—shoves me over the edge into a kind of abyss. Pleasure spirals and curls around us as I clutch her to me. I don't want to let her go, but everything in life has an ending. It's what makes this time we spend alive so special. So painful.

I gently set her down on her feet, my arms still around her, and hold her as the water cascades over us, until we've recovered enough to actually use the shower for its intended purpose. And then I clean that spot between her shoulder blades, determined to treat her every bit as well as she deserves.

"Wow," she says, pressing her face into my chest beneath the constant stream of water.

"Wow," I repeat. "I may be unqualified to offer a scientific opinion, but I'd say this scientific experiment has had pretty definitive results."

"It's my unscientific opinion that you're right. I've been feeling pretty lucky lately. Do you think it's because of your lucky guitar pick?"

"Or maybe your unlucky penny. Maybe we should keep carrying them around just to be sure."

Laughing, she slicks my hair back from my face. "I'll make a Pollyanna of you yet."

Maybe she already has, because it feels like we're floating along on a cloud with no care for the miles of open air just beneath us.

Before we leave, I slip away for five minutes, saying I have to discuss the band's rehearsal schedule with Travis, which is enough time for me to call Dottie and make some arrangements.

When we get to Tea of Fortune, Dottie is waiting for us. So is the rest of the Wise Women Group.

"Didn't we do this yesterday?" I ask.

"None of us have lost our sense of time yet, young buck," Constance says. "But we weren't going to miss out on the fun."

Sophie looks confused, but before she can start asking questions, I hurry to introduce her to all of the women, giving Ann credit for her excellent taste in scratch-off tickets.

Dottie leads us to the booth directly next to their table, then hurries back moments later with two partially full cups of milky tea. "Now, drink those down, my dears, and I'll read your fortunes."

She stays glued to her spot, and it's obvious she has no intention of walking away to give us a private moment. Fair enough. I glance across the table at Sophie, who looks confused but a little excited. Like she knows something's up but sees the glass as half full.

Sophie finishes her tea first and then gasps as she sees what's written at the bottom of her cup. She turns to me. "Rob?"

Like clockwork, Ann brings over a bouquet of flowers, and Constance turns on ABBA's "I Have a Dream" on her phone, most likely suppressing an eyeroll.

I offer the flowers to Sophie with a flourish. "Will you go to the prom with me, Sophie Ginnis?"

That's what's written in the bottom of her teacup, more or less, space permitting.

Sophie laughs. "Are you asking me to crash the high school prom with you next spring?"

"We could try, if you insist. But that's not what this is about. I'm playing at the Orange Peel a week from Thursday. It's an eighties' cover party, and our set is short. I figured maybe we could treat it like the prom. Give you the experience you never had. We can rent a limo, bring your friends. We'll dance, Sophie."

She's gaping at me, looking mostly pleased, thank God, and then she says, "But that's your birthday."

"Did Jonah tell you?" I ask, shocked by the thought. It definitely doesn't seem like something he'd say or even remember.

"*I did,*" Dottie says, still beside our table, overseeing the promposal like she's our conductor. "I've always made a point of knowing when you young people have your special days."

I smile at her. "Thanks, Dottie. I think I've got this from here."

I half expect her to sit down next to me, but she joins her friends while I turn to face Sophie. "Yeah, it's my birthday, and this is the way I want to spend it."

She beams at me, then leans across the table to kiss me. Which causes the older women next to us to cheer, although I hear Ann shouting, "Did she say yes?"

The three of them invite us to eat with them. They pull up an extra chair, and we have breakfast at their table, while everyone but Constance fusses over us. When it's time to go, Dottie gives us a to-go container stuffed with treats for Emil. Despite never having met him, she's adamant that "great things" are in store for him. I can't say I don't like hearing it.

Then Sophie and I meet Emil at the park. He's feeling confident about our chances that I'll be approved to foster, and so am I. Right now it doesn't feel like anything could pull me down from this cloud.

Emil and I serenade Sophie. I've come to appreciate the wholesome kind of fun she likes to engage in almost as much as her dirty side. So when she suggests that the three of us put on the temporary tattoos I've had in my glove box for the last couple of days, I don't say no. I just ask who has a bottle of water so we can apply them.

Before Emil leaves with the dog, he asks me if we can have a talk, man to man. So I walk a ways away with him while Sophie sits under the tree with a paperback she had in her purse.

"It's not fake anymore, is it?" he asks when we're far enough that she probably can't hear.

"No," I admit. "Doesn't feel fake at all."

"You should do something nice for her," he says, drumming a fist over his heart.

"You're right about that." I glance back at the tree, at Sophie with the breeze ruffling her hair. I turn back and we continue walking. "I gave her a promposal."

He laughs. "Aren't you kind of old for that?"

"Absolutely. But if I can't handle making a fool of myself for her, then I don't deserve her."

I explain what I did while he regards me with serious eyes. Then he nods. "All right. I'll remember that. You've got some moves, man."

A little later, I drop Sophie off at her car. I spend a couple of hours working on my new songs in the park, and then I meet Travis and Bix at the Beat to practice. They share a few knowing headshakes over the tonal change in the new songs, but they like them.

I sense something's still off with Travis, though. He has that hollow-eyed look he gets when he hasn't been sleeping right. I ask him about it when Bixby is in the bathroom, but he just shakes his head.

"It's nothing."

"Doesn't seem like nothing."

He shrugs, glancing out the window at the parking lot beneath us like he's thinking of pulling a runner. Then he looks back at me with worried eyes. "I'm going to sound like one of the old geezers in a prison movie, but I think a storm's coming."

"Because of that call from Lilah?"

He shrugs, his expression helpless. "I don't know. It's just a gut feeling, but I'm having a hard time shaking it."

Storm's coming.

For the rest of the day, that phrase keeps repeating in my head, and it stays with me as I go to bed. If I were a more superstitious man, I'd say it's downright ominous.

CHAPTER THIRTY

SOPHIE

"You're sure it's her?" I ask Hannah.

"Yes, I used a Google image search, and the article I'd seen popped up."

"Smart women do foolish things all the time," Briar says resignedly. "Look at us."

The smart woman in question is Nora Leigh, the brewer at The Ginger Station. Hannah had recognized her because she'd seen an article about her in *Get Local* magazine. Female brewers are few and far between.

We've spent the last several minutes discussing Nora. Hannah, Briar, and I are at Buchanan Brewery. It's closed today, but Dylan told me I could bring them by for a taste test. I poured each of us flights of all six NA cocktails I've been working on. My friends are sitting across from me in high-top chairs, and I'm standing on the other side of the bar, anxiously awaiting their opinions on my drinks.

I've felt edgy all day, as if something's squirming just beneath my skin. *You're falling in love with Rob*, a voice inside of me whispers. *It's too fast. He's going to change his mind. He's going to realize his family's more important than you, even though Jonah sucks.*

I've tried to quiet the voice that has been telling me for years that nothing could possibly make up for the harm I've caused. For being the child who cost her family so much money and stress.

I wouldn't willingly admit this to anyone, but before my friends showed up at Buchanan, I spent several minutes poring over the texts Rob's sent me over the past few days, trying to convince myself that I'm not imagining things. That he really cares about me.

"You seem distracted," Briar comments. "Is it because of Nora?"

"Nah," Hannah says. "She's not hung up on the genius Jonah tricked into dating him. She's thinking about Rob's dick." She lifts one of the little glasses as if to cheer me on. She doesn't take a sip, though, which sets me on edge. What if they hate my drinks? What if they're bad? She's spent years working at Big Catch. She knows what people like. She'll know whether or not Dottie and I have been wasting our time.

"I'd probably be distracted too," she continues. "It's been a while since I've had any."

"Since Jonah?" Briar asks.

Hannah huffs a laugh. "Yeah, right. I took home a one-night stand the night I found out. I needed a palate cleanser, just like I told Sophie to find one. But Sophie being Sophie, she had to fall madly in—"

"I'm not in love with him," I lie. "It's only been, I mean...a month ago I didn't even like him."

"But you still must have secretly wondered what he looks like naked, right? I mean, he's a looker."

"No! Wait, do *you* secretly wonder what Rob looks like naked?"

"Yes," Hannah says carelessly, "but not because I want to sleep with him. I secretly wonder what everyone looks like naked. It's the great equalizer, don't you think? Without clothes on, you can't hide anything."

"Except for a black soul," Briar says darkly.

Hannah waves one of the tiny drink glasses at her, the Sunshine Spritzer, the one I'm proudest of. "Yeah, but you said you can see auras."

"It's an imperfect science." From the small smile on Briar's face, she's obviously trying to needle Hannah.

I feel a swell of fondness for both of them, but I narrow my focus on Hannah, because she's finally trying the drink.

"There's no alcohol in these?" Hannah asks, eyebrows nearly to her hairline.

"Not a drop. What do you think?"

"It's good. Really good," she says, eyes gleaming with approval. "They'd be even better if you poured some vodka in them, but—"

Briar gives Hannah her best disapproving-teacher look.

"Okay, fine, they're great exactly the way they are," Hannah says, rolling her eyes. "Plus, people need to sober up at the end of the night, but you still want them ordering drinks. This is brilliant, actually."

I pause, weighing my next question. I feel dirty even thinking about it, but Rob said I shouldn't downplay my contributions. "If I, you know...if they put my drinks on the menu, and they're successful, should I ask for some kind of recognition? Rob seemed to think I was selling myself short by not asking."

"Yes," Briar says briskly. "Especially since this could be the starting point for something bigger."

I part my lips, ready to argue, but Hannah interjects, "Exactly what I was thinking. These flavors are great." She gestures to one of the glasses. "What if there was, like, a beer and an NA drink with the same flavor profile? You could do a tasting with a friend who doesn't imbibe. It would be fun. A hook that would bring people in."

"Wow," I say, amazed. "I hadn't thought that far ahead." In the beginning, this had been just a fun project, a way to make sure Rob had something to drink other than flat soda. It's developing into something larger, mostly because I've let other people help.

Hannah snaps her fingers. "That's why you have us. Briar's really good at business stuff, and I know how to entertain people."

I look at her and then Briar, feeling tension form a knot in my gut. There's another reason I asked them here...

Dropping my gaze to the bar, I trace the woodgrain with my finger. "So, I had another reason for luring you guys out today."

"Yes, damn you and your delicious free drinks," Hannah jokes. "I knew there'd be a catch. If this is about the prom thing, then yes, obviously we're going. Travis texted me about it too."

"He asked you to prom?" I ask, excited even though she'd made a point of saying she wasn't interested in him.

"No." She rolls her eyes at me. "He just wanted to make sure we're coming, because it would probably be boring for you while they're playing if you're by yourself."

I beam at her. "Rob's going to get a limo to pick us up. It'll be like a real prom."

She laughs. "So some inexperienced eighteen-year-old is going to try to feel me up in the back seat of a Buick?"

Briar smiles at us. "It'll be fun." She sets her hand on mine for a second before pulling away. "But you were going to tell us something, Sophie. I don't think it was about the show."

I inhale in a deep breath, reminding myself of how much my connection with Rob has deepened because I let him in. I want the same for my friendship with these two women, my fellow babes of brewing.

"I...I think maybe you've realized I had a weird adolescence."

"Were you in a cult?" Hannah asks. "We have this bet going."

Briar gives her another stern-teacher look. "It's not a bet. You asked me if I thought she'd been in a cult, and I said maybe. 'Maybe' does not constitute a bet."

Of course they've been wondering.

"I did something bad," I say, tears welling in my eyes. "And for a while, I thought I'd ruined my life. It felt like everyone had abandoned me, and maybe they were right to."

Hannah nods in acknowledgement. "You can tell us anything. I already told you my mom took off when I was little. I know how it feels to be left behind. Briar does too."

"I do," she agrees. "My parents sent me away to boarding school when I was six."

"Oh Briar," I say, pressing a hand to my heart. "I didn't know that."

She shrugs. "You met my father. It was probably for the best."

"I'm sure it doesn't hurt any less," I say softly, fully understanding. I massage the back of my neck, which has tightened with tension. "I was sent away to reform school when I was sixteen. I've barely seen my parents since."

"*Reform school?*" Hannah asks. "What'd you do, compliment someone to death? Strangle them with handknit scarves?"

Feeling numb, I say, "No. It's bad. Really bad, actually."

I take a deep, shuddering breath, suppressing the old sense of panic attempting to flood back in. *They won't judge me*, I tell myself. *They won't leave me.* Then I release the captured breath and speak in a rush, telling them everything. It's hard, but it's much easier than I thought it would be. I know it's because I already shared the truth with Rob.

They both hug me from across the bar, and then Hannah comes over to my side and grabs the vodka bottle from the top shelf. We all laugh as she tops off all of our glasses.

"Let's carry these to a booth so you can sit with us," Briar says. "It feels weird having you across the bar from us."

Once we're all comfortably situated in a booth, Hannah lifts one of her glasses. "To Sophie. For being a brave-ass bitch and telling us her secret."

"To Sophie," Briar echoes, and I feel my cheeks burning as I lift one of the little glasses and drink with them.

It feels like I'm letting go of a weight I've been carrying for years, the effort breaking my back and sapping my strength.

As we set our glasses down, Briar asks, "Does Jonah know?"

"Who cares about Jonah?" Hannah says. "Does Rob know?"

"He does." I tell them. "But Jonah doesn't. I knew I should tell him, but I couldn't bring myself to do it."

"Maybe you subconsciously sensed his aura," Briar says, playing with her hair. "I think I did too. That's why I felt so uncertain all the time. You can't be uncertain of yourself if you're a woman in business."

"So you think we all subconsciously knew he was an asshole?" Hannah asks her. "That tracks. You know, it's for the best that he never knew about the fire, Sophie. I'm guessing Rob was cool about it?"

I think about Rob's heartfelt reaction to my confession, and I can hardly contain my smile. "Yeah, more than cool. He's been through some hard stuff too."

I consider whether he'd want me to share what Jonah did to him and decide not to. It's his private business, and it's up to him who he shares it with.

"Well, let's hoist one up for Rob," Hannah says with a

mischievous twinkle in her eye. She lifts one of the taster cups. "For not being a complete and total asshole. I'm so done with assholes."

"Did Jonah get on your case about the TP thing?" I ask, frowning.

She gives a hearty laugh. "Oh, he tried. He texted me from an unknown number and said if I ever come near him or his house again, he'll call the police. And that I was lucky his girlfriend convinced him not to press charges."

"What a dick," I say, scowling.

"So I told him I'd give my brother his address if he ever comes near any of us again. I have a feeling he'll be keeping his distance."

"Is Liam that scary?" I ask in disbelief.

Jonah's shorter and not as well-built as Rob, but he's hardly shrimpy.

Hannah considers this, then says, "He's a big, grumpy guy who's made his dislike of Jonah very clear. Plus, he's in this amateur boxing club. Jonah's terrified of him." A sigh seeps out of her. "So is management. He's squabbling with them again, and I'm sick of being the intermediary."

"Maybe you should stop," I say, knowing it's not that easy. But I would have kept quiet in the past, and I'm learning to express my opinions. To value them, even. "I was hovering over Otis, and once I stopped, he's actually stepped up. It's awesome."

Hannah shrugs. "Otis is a golden retriever. Liam is like...a grumpy old dog who barks at people to get off his porch, then barks at them for leaving."

"And you're the kind of woman who barks back," I say.

Hannah smiles. "I'll drink to that."

"Me too," Briar says, lifting one of her cups. "But I have a feeling the trouble isn't over."

Same.

CHAPTER THIRTY-ONE

ROB

Monday passes in a blur of band practice, work, and Sophie. A pretty good blur, if you want to know the truth.

Travis seems more himself, Bixby is in a good mood that won't quit, and the kids are mostly behaving themselves. Sophie is...

She's delightful. She's funny. She's sweet. I mean...she invited the kid down the hall over for ice cream because she felt guilty about their squabble over the weekend.

He told her he knew very well what happened to people who accepted free ice cream from strangers, so clearly he hasn't warmed to the Sophie Ginnis charm, but there's no denying the effort was adorable.

It's hard to forget what Travis said on Sunday, though. I can still feel that storm on the horizon. I try to tell myself it's just nerves over our impending meeting with Nelly, but it feels bigger than that.

On Tuesday night, my dad texts to say he needs to discuss something with me. *Urgently*. I write back to say we can hash it out over Thanksgiving dinner.

He responds by telling me it's time for me to stop being a

smart-ass and rely on people who are more seasoned than me and have my best interests at heart to make the important decisions, and I tell him I'm done talking to him for now. Because he's clearly trying to rip Sophie and me apart, and I won't allow that. Not even the effort. It feels good when I add his number to my block list.

But I'm still on edge.

My dad knows something, or thinks he does. Maybe he's going to do something about it, too, like when he had my mother's custody of me revoked for "your own good."

I go to see the Wise Women Group on Wednesday morning and share my fears with my elderly friends.

Constance pats my arm. "You did good cutting the cord. My ex-husband was an ornery old coot who thought he knew what was best for everyone. Wish I'd gotten rid of him twenty years earlier. I'd have saved myself a world of trouble."

"We won't let them hurt your dear girl," Dottie says staunchly, as if she could stop an army with a mere look. "We're on your side."

"We are indeed," Ann says, beaming. Then she rifles through her purse and hands me a couple of scratchers, patting my hand. Some older women carry hard candies; Ann carries scratchers. "No one messes with our grandchildren."

"Quite right," Constance says firmly.

I'll be damned if my throat doesn't tighten over these three older women claiming me as theirs. I have an awful lot more to protect than I used to, more than enough to make up for the things I've supposedly lost.

"Thanks, Ann. If I win big, I'll buy you some fake tats."

"Convince your friends to wear wet shirts for her," Constance says, setting today's crocheting project aside. "That's what Ann really wants."

I leave feeling better, but the sense of impending doom

doesn't disperse. It hangs around me all day like smoke. So I'm not surprised when I come home from the Beat and find an oversized box of matches on my stoop.

There's no note, but the meaning's so obvious, I feel like a fucking idiot for not seeing it coming. Sophie did something horrible unintentionally, and someone—my brother or maybe my father—knows. They're pointing out, ever so unsubtly, that it's not going to look so good if Nelly and the others reviewing my file find out. They'll think I'm an alcoholic with an alleged sex addiction, and my girlfriend is an arsonist.

Fuck.

Fuck.

I go inside, swallow down the urge to punch the dry wall, and pace until my heart rate slows. Then I unblock and call Jonah, my number one suspect.

"You got my message?" he says, his voice smarmy and so fucking satisfied with himself.

"You talk in code now? How adventurous of you."

"Sophie pulled me in too," he says. "I was totally fooled. I had no idea she was a pyro, but Dad hired a private investigator to look into her past. We were all concerned about you."

"Bullshit," I say, squeezing the phone. "You wanted to mess with me, just like you did when you had your girlfriend call the foster agency."

"Not everything's about you, Rob. Mom and I have valid concerns about you being a foster parent. We were doing our civic duty."

So it was Patricia, not his girlfriend. Sophie and her friends will be happy to hear that, at least.

"Yup, you're such an Eagle Scout. Well, you'll have to use your compass to find your own asshole if you go anywhere near my girlfriend again. Leave her alone. Same goes for Dad. From what I hear, you've managed to convince one of your other girl-friends to give you another shot. Let it go. Be satisfied with what you've got."

But I know he won't. Maybe he can't be satisfied. Even if he doesn't want Sophie anymore, he can't stand for her to be happy with someone else, especially me.

"Sorry. I can't knowingly put you or that kid in danger. If you don't break up with her, I'm going to have to make another call and tell them everything I know."

"What's your deal with me?" I ask, because I've never really understood. There are plenty of reasons for *me* to resent *him*, beyond his shitty personality, but why does he resent me? Our father left my mother for his, and Dad's always shown a strong preference for his son with the "right" Patricia. The kid who went to college, got a job in middle management, and did things the "correct" way. "Why do you want to mess up my life?"

He laughs. "You think I care about your life, Rob? Please. Not everything's about you. This is about doing what's right."

"You go on telling yourself that."

"Break up with her," he says, "and you can have that teenage boy move in with you, not like that's weird at all."

"Fuck you," I shout, feeling a vein throb in my forehead. My rage is at a ten. A twenty.

"No, Rob," he says, his voice perfectly calm. "Fuck you. You thought you could steal my fiancée and flaunt her around town? No. You deserve this, man. You dug your own grave. I hope you rot in it."

Then he hangs up.

My whole body is trembling with rage. I'm filled with the need to act. To hit him. To drink. To destroy something, even if it's myself.

He's jealous, my mom has told me. Although I can't begin to understand why, other than that he's never had a passion beyond the drive to be the first, the award winner, the golden boy.

Regardless, I don't doubt that he'll do what he's threatened. He'll reveal Sophie's past to Nelly, maybe to everyone, if I don't step away from her.

CHAPTER THIRTY-TWO

SOPHIE

I was supposed to spend the night at Rob's, but he isn't picking up his phone or answering my texts. I've tried three times and left two messages, which seems excessive, but he almost always answers his phone.

"You're going to wear a hole in the carpet," Otis says, using one of his grandmother's favorite expressions. I feel a rush of longing for her, but she's having the trip of a lifetime, and good for her.

I'm ready to live my best life too. It feels like I'm on the cusp of something wonderful. But when you're on the cusp, you're also in a precarious position, in danger of teetering toward total disappointment instead.

I glance at my cousin, feeling a swell of affection when I see he's sketching logos for The Crafty Muncher.

I'll have to correct him about the name at some point, but it's the thought that counts. I'm happy he's so interested. It'll probably be a long time before we're able to open it, but I'm starting to believe it *will* happen.

He sighs and sets down his pencil. "I have to warn you. If Rob did something fucked up, I'm absolutely not capable of beating him up. The best I could manage is a dressing-down, and even then, it might be hard. He's pretty cool, for the most part."

I give him a fond smile. "You're pretty cool for the most part, too. He told me you threatened him the other day."

He lifts up both palms defensively. "Whoa, let's not exaggerate. I just made it clear that I didn't want anyone messing with you."

Walking up to the couch, I lean down and give him an awkward backward hug. "I don't want anyone messing with you either."

"Does that mean you'll grab me a beer from the kitchen?"

"Absolutely. I could use one myself."

We've just settled down on the couch and uncapped the beers when a knock lands on the door. We exchange a look, and Otis nods toward the front of the house. "I'm guessing it's for you. I'm still on the hunt for Fluffnut, but pigeons don't knock."

I go to the door, nervous but determined. Then I open it to find Rob standing there.

Something's wrong. I would have known it from a hundred paces away. There's no trace of his usual smile, and there are hollows beneath his eyes. He looks like he's been dragged into a dark place.

"Will you come take a walk with me?" he asks in a low voice, and my heart flails, because I know this will be a very different walk than the one we took a couple of weeks ago.

Otis peers at us over the back of the couch, scowling, like he knows he might be called upon to deliver his dressing-down and he'd really rather not.

I wave to the two bottles on the coffee table. "You can have them both."

He perks up a little, which might have made me laugh under other circumstances.

I follow Rob out into the warm night and look at him, taking in the hard lines around his mouth. "Something's wrong," I say, deciding to call it out. "Let's sit on the porch and you can tell me."

One corner of his mouth lifts, but it's such a fleeting smile it barely registers. "You're right of course." He sighs and then sits down on the top step, lowering his head into his hands and combing his fingers through his hair. I sit beside him, pressing close enough that our legs touch, because I need to be anchored to him right now.

He places his palm over my thigh, and I'm so relieved I nearly tear up. Whatever's happened, he still wants his hands on me.

He turns to get a better look at me. "I've cancelled the meeting with Nelly tomorrow."

"What?" I ask, floored. "Why would you do that?"

He pauses for a long moment. "I withdrew my application to become a foster parent."

I feel myself teetering on the edge as I wait for him to reply, because I already know his answer will everything to do with me.

"Jonah left a box of matches outside of my apartment earlier. I called him, and he confessed that he and my dad had a PI investigate you. They managed to access your juvenile record, and Jonah threatened me with it." He runs his hands through his hair again, agitation radiating off him like sparks.

And there I go, tumbling off the edge. I was a fool to think I could leave my past behind.

This is all my fault. If it weren't for me, Jonah wouldn't have arranged for that initial call to Nelly. I'd thought I was helping by offering to pose as Rob's girlfriend, but of course I wasn't, because even though the files were sealed, my secret wasn't safe. Someone found out, and they used the truth of who I am to hurt

Rob and Emil. And now Emil won't be able to play his music except on those stolen weekend mornings with Rob. And Rob...

Oh, Rob.

My whole body begins trembling as if it might shatter into tiny pieces, nothing but atoms and molecules. "Tell her we're not together. Tell her you discovered the truth and dumped me. Say—"

He takes my hand, fixing his gaze on mine. "I'm done lying, Sophie. I shouldn't have lied in the first place."

A sob breaks free of my chest, and he runs his fingers over my cheek, his touch so gentle it hurts. "I'm not leaving you, Soph. But if we stay together, there's a chance they could release this information anyway. They could hurt you. Jonah wants to hurt me."

"He already *has* hurt you." I slip my hand into my pocket and find the guitar pick. I run my finger across its pointy tip, poking myself. It's stupid, but it feels like it betrayed me. Still, I run my finger over it again and again, hoping for a Hail Mary I know will never come.

I've taken Rob's family from him, and now they've turned on him.

I've ruined his chance to become Emil's foster parent.

I've ruined *everything*.

"This was supposed to be fake," I say, my voice quavering as tears track down my face. "Maybe we should have kept it that way."

"Are you being honest with me right now, Sophie?" he asks, his golden eyes focused so purely on me that I feel like more than just a speck of a person on a speck of a planet. Being this important in his eyes is really something. Maybe it's everything. And it makes my heart feel like it's bleeding out, because the right thing to do is walk away, isn't it? I draw in a long breath as I think of how to answer him, and whether I even can answer him.

"We promised to be honest, with each other at least," he continues.

I open my mouth, still unsure of what to say. I close it and lick my lips. And then the front door of the house bursts open.

"Hey," Otis says, his voice harsh. "I warned you, man."

My heart bleeds a little more, and now I'm crying for both of these men who've put so much on the line for me. Lifting a hand toward my cousin, I say, "No, Otis, it's not like that. It's Jonah who did something awful."

"Oh, thank God," Otis says, pressing a palm to his chest. "I didn't know how I was going to follow up on that. But I slugged one of those beers for courage before I came out here, and now—"

"Why don't you sit down, bud?" Rob says, nodding toward the porch chair.

But Otis comes around and sits down on the other side of me, on the broad front steps. "What did he do now?"

"He—" I fall silent as the front door of the little purple house next door creaks open.

"Yoo-hoo," Dottie says, waving from her stoop. "Who would like some fresh-baked cookies?"

I'm guessing what she really wants is some fresh gossip. However much I love Dottie, I'm about to tell her no, but Rob is already waving her over. "Sure. Yes," he says. "I think we could all use some fresh-baked cookies."

"Rob," I whisper as she slips back into the little purple house. "We can't avoid this. We need to settle it. *Now*."

"It's been settled," he says with that firm jaw covered in perfect stubble. "I made the call. Even if I told Nelly it was over between us, it wouldn't help. The damage is done. My application is dead in the water. And I'm not willing to give you up. I'm not."

"This is my—"

"I swear to God, Sophie," he says with a flash of anger. "Don't say it was your fault, and don't you dare apologize. It was my brother. I'll have to figure out something else for Emil. I *will* figure it out."

My heart breaks for him all over again. He's not going to give up. He's going to do everything he can for that boy—because when he needed someone to step up for him when he was younger, no one did. "Rob..."

My mind is spinning, my soul reeling. I know Rob is going to do everything in his power to make sure these wrongs are righted, but it's hard to let go of the thought that this wouldn't be a problem in the first place if not for me. Emil would probably be practicing guitar in his room even now.

Rob wraps his hand around my chin, tipping my head up. "This is no time to stop thinking Pollyanna thoughts. Let's settle it this way. I'll toss my unlucky penny, and if it's heads up, we invite Dottie inside, and we tell her and Otis everything. If it's tails?" He shrugs. "We do things your way. We'll let the little fucker keep us apart, even if it's not going to fix anything."

"Uh, are you willing to take a fifty-fifty chance on that, dude?" Otis says, scratching his head. "That's a bet you don't want to lose."

"You're right," Rob says, his eyes on me. "But I'm not going to lose. I'm going to believe the glass is half full. Are you going to believe with me, Sophie?"

The look of hope in his eyes makes me want to knit my broken heart back together.

"I want to," I sniffle. I watch in horror and excitement as he pulls the unlucky penny out of his wallet. "*I want to.*"

The last time I say it, it's a whisper. A prayer.

"I do too," he says.

"So do I," Otis adds. And somehow it feels exactly right that he's a part of this moment, just like he was that first day when Rob came over for a phone that was stowed in the freezer.

I suck in my breath and hold it as Rob flips the penny into the air. Then a snow-white bird swoops into the penny, knocking the coin out of sight.

The breath gusts out of me in disbelief.

"No fucking way," Otis says as the bird lands and pads across the front porch.

Otis reaches into his pocket and pulls out a handful of sunflower seeds, meaning my cousin has either been walking around with snacks loose in his pockets, or he is very committed to finding this pigeon.

The bird hops directly to him, and I watch in disbelief as he gently strokes her feathers and then picks her up, his eyes aglow.

"It's her. I did it. I really did it," my cousin says.

I turn to Rob, my whole heart reaching for him. "We need to find that penny."

"It's gone," he says, getting up as Otis retreats into the house with the bird.

Dottie exits her house with a huge square container, humming absently into the night air as if my universe hadn't just been torn apart and possibly pieced back together.

She pauses on the sidewalk halfway to our house and stoops to pick something up. My heart lodges in my throat. Could it be...?

When she reaches us, she lifts it up with a grin, the copper shining in the dim porch light. "Find a penny, pick it up."

My heart seizes. Everything inside of me is frozen. "Dottie, was it heads up when you picked it up?"

"Facing up, dear," she tells me with a beatific smile. "Always facing up."

I'm not sure what to make of that. A coin is always, technically, facing up, no matter how it lands. The knowing smile on Dottie's face suggests that's as much as she's going to tell me. And I get it. She wants me to decide which side was turned up, heads or tails.

I take a deep breath, and then I turn toward Rob and take his hand. The love in his eyes makes my decision.

"It was heads up."

And then I kiss him.

CHAPTER THIRTY-THREE

ROB

We bring Dottie inside as Otis comes down the stairs, carrying the pigeon in a cage. The bird is munching on some sunflower seeds, acting as if she didn't have the adventure to end all adventures.

"This is some night," he says, shaking his head. "*Miracles* are happening."

"How wonderful," Dottie says, clapping. "Take a cookie, please, my young friend. Even miracles need to be fed."

He takes two in his free hand. Before he can leave, presumably to return Fluffnut to his owner, I grab his arm. "Take an uber, would you, bud? You just chugged a beer."

He gives me a thumbs-up. "Way ahead of you. They're picking me up in five." Then he turns toward Sophie and lifts the cage. "We just got this much closer to the Crafty Muncher, Soph."

She beams at him and doesn't correct him for using a porn-star version of her dream store's name. Or point out the reward probably won't go far enough.

Once Otis is gone, we gather around the dinner table. As we eat some delicious cookies, Sophie tells Dottie everything.

When she gets to the part about the matches, Dottie clucks her tongue, her face a mask of disappointment. "That boy hasn't been stroking his stone."

I laugh, feeling so much lighter than I did an hour ago, when I'd left to come here, knowing there was a distinct possibility I might lose Sophie. But that bird descended at exactly the right moment to change the trajectory of the coin, and it felt like a sign. A twist of fate. *Something.*

"You'll be pleased to know Rob's been stroking his," Sophie says with a mirthful glance at me. "He sometimes even keeps it in his bedsheets."

"Which means you've seen them," Dottie says with a wide grin that makes *me* blush, dammit. "Congratulations, children. I couldn't be happier for you. I knew you were destined for each other."

I don't argue. I like that she still thinks it, and I *love* that Sophie's not arguing. Taking her hand under the table, I give it a squeeze.

Before I came over here, I spent several awful hours pacing my apartment and then my neighborhood, fighting the darkness welling inside of me. Knowing that if I gave into it, I'd just be giving Jonah what he wants.

I knew Sophie would blame herself. She'd spent twelve years blaming herself, and most of the people around her had encouraged it. That kind of negativity helps set the grooves of a bad habit. So I knew she would try to break what we were building, and my fear of that told me one thing:

I couldn't let it happen.

So I came over to make a pitch for myself.

It didn't go the way I'd expected, but I was getting used to that. Some days life sinks you down so low you don't think you could swim or crawl your way out, and then there are moments of grace, like what happened today. So damn beautiful it makes your throat catch and your notion of what is possible expand to fit the unknown edges of the universe.

Still, this isn't over. I'm not going to let Jonah hurt someone I care about. If Emil can't come live with me, then maybe Travis could start a foster parent application. It would throw things off by a few months, which is unfortunate, but it's better than nothing. I'm not going to go to that kid, hat in hand, and tell him I have nothing for him. Too many people have let him down already.

"It does sadden me that some people don't want to improve themselves," Dottie says with a sigh, setting a half-eaten cookie down on her plate. "But there must be consequences to unrelenting bad behavior, don't you think?"

"I do," Sophie says with purpose in her eyes. "And Jonah Price is going to feel them. TPing his house wasn't nearly enough."

I smile, because there it is again. The spicy side of my sweet, caring woman.

"But first we need to get Emil into a good home until he graduates." Dottie's gaze finds mine. "You leave that to me, my boy. I'll get it sorted in no time. I know a few people who have been foster parents before. Good ones. I'll knock on some doors."

This woman has half of Asheville in the palm of her hand, and I don't doubt she can follow through. More of the darkness I've been carrying lifts. I might not be the one who gets to help Emil, but I'll still be giving him what he needs. I can make peace with that. "Thank you, Dottie."

"You're welcome, my dear. Now, what shall we do about your wayward brother?"

"Something tells me you already have an idea," I say, cocking my head.

"That's because you've been stroking your stone." She

smiles in delight. "It's made you more attuned to the energy around you."

Sophie squeezes my leg under the table, giving me a wicked look, and I layer my hand over hers.

"Have *you* been stroking your stone, Sophie?" Dottie asks.

Sophie blushes. "Not really, but I've been carrying around Rob's lucky guitar pick."

"Indeed," she replies with a twinkle in her eyes.

Sophie's blush deepens, making her even more irresistible. "I mean that literally."

"*Of course* you do, dear. Now, I think we'd better bring in the other girls for our discussion, don't you? Tomorrow morning at the tea shop, perhaps?"

"Yes," Sophie says. "Yes, they need to be a part of this."

"It *is* a pity about the young woman who's connected herself with Jonah." Dottie tsks. "But it may be that he's bamboozled her. I've been bamboozled myself. Men with silver tongues can be very convincing."

I'd already told Sophie and Dottie about Patricia making that first call to Nelly.

Dottie purses her lips and then nods. "We'll discuss this further tomorrow, but I still believe that young man needs a public truth-telling. In front of that young woman."

"He'll sue if we don't have our bases covered," I say, because it wouldn't be the first time Jonah or my dad used the world *lawyer* to get out of trouble. "There's nothing he cares about more than his reputation."

"So we'll make sure we have all of our bases covered," Dottie says. "I was thinking we could make your prom *very special*. It's just over a week away, so we'd have plenty of time to prepare."

"How will you get him there?" I ask, smiling a little at the thought of Jonah with an eighties' mustache. "It's not exactly his scene."

"Leave that to me, my dears," Dottie says. "But I have no doubt of my success."

Again, neither do I. She's proven, over and over again, how much she'll do for the people she cares about. And from what I've seen, that includes just about everyone.

It's largely thanks to this woman that Sophie and I are here now, together. Dottie convinced Sophie to make a commitment to be true to herself—and Sophie has. And Dottie convinced me to indulge in some Pollyanna thinking of my own.

"Thank you, Dottie," I say, taking her hand and squeezing it. "I can't say it enough."

She stands and says, "You already have. Seeing you happy gives me great joy. Have a good night, my dears. We'll talk soon."

Sophie and I walk her to the door and stand there together as she makes the very short trip home. Her partner meets her at the door, greeting her with a loving smile that moves me.

"That could be us someday," I say, looking down at Sophie.

Her eyes widen. "Really?"

"Yeah," I say, nudging her into the house and shutting the door behind us. Then I gently push her against it. "I think I'll still be looking at you like that when we're both old and gray, Soph. And let's be honest. You'll definitely be dying your hair purple."

"Maybe I'll try now," she says, raking her hand through my hair. "Maybe *you* should try it."

"Is that your next scheme, Sophie? Because I'll do it. Anything you want to try, we'll try together."

She smiles up at me, her whole being shining with it. "I think you mean that."

"I do, baby. I do."

"Then...fuck me against this door, Rob."

I grin at her, then lean in and kiss her neck, her jaw. "How hard was it for you to say 'fuck,' Soph?"

"You wouldn't believe it," she says.

"I'm in love with you," I admit. "I know that wasn't what you asked me for, but it's what happened, and there was no fighting it. I didn't want to."

"Thank God," she says, wrapping her arms around me and squeezing as if I might disappear if she doesn't squeeze hard enough. "Because I'm desperately in love with you."

CHAPTER THIRTY-FOUR

SOPHIE

"Are we sure Jonah's coming?" Hannah asks, glancing out the window of the limousine. It's Rob's birthday, and also the night of the "prom."

The past week has been a whirlwind of activity.

First, someone called Dylan, anonymously, and informed him about the fire, saying I was an arsonist and a menace.

Dylan pulled me aside and told me about it. He said he'd informed the person that if they came into the brewery talking smack about any of his employees, they'd find an ex-Marine's boot print on their butt.

That had made me hug him.

I'd intended to talk to him about the NA menu, but his sweet gesture made me "chicken out" (Hannah's term). I assured Hannah that I was still going to do it, someday soon. At the moment, the drinks were on a paper specials menu, but they're going to add them to the laminated menus soon.

"Jonah's coming," I say, adjusting my corsage. It's a gorgeous one, made by someone who wasn't on a delicious time crunch. Rob brought it over this morning, along with corsages for Hannah and Briar, because he's *amazing*.

"You're mooning," Hannah accuses without heat.

"I am," I agree, grinning. "I'm desperately, sickeningly in love."

"Let the record show that you're the one who said it was sickening."

We took the eighties theme to heart. We're all wearing eighties-era prom dresses we found at a thrift store, and Hannah teased her hair so it's as big as a lion's mane. Briar crimped hers, and Otis fell all over himself praising it. He only caught a glimpse of her all decked out at the house before he had to leave. Unfortunately, he didn't get to ride in the limo with us, as he had to get to the Orange Peel early, having volunteered to help with the band's equipment.

I'm not altogether sure his help was needed, or even wanted, but Rob acted grateful anyway, bless him.

"It *is* sickening," I reply. "I'm happier than I have any right to be."

Hannah scowls at me. "Take that back."

"Yes," Briar agrees. "You're exactly as happy as you should be."

Maybe they have a point.

Either way, I've decided to embrace these good feelings.

I haven't emailed, texted, or phoned my parents to let them know about my cancelled wedding. If they neglect to call anyone else in the family, they may very well be boarding a plane soon to sit in the wedding venue alone. If I find out they're over there at the pre-appointed day and time, I'll be sure to send them over some rubbery fish.

This past week, Otis and I have also been working hard on our plans for The Crafty Monster. We've decided we'll do it as a pop-up at first to cut down on costs, and Hannah has already offered to host us at Big Catch Brewing. And although I'm making moves to start my own business, Dylan said his door is always open to me, no matter what I decide to do with my life.

Life is big. Life is good. Life is *happy*.

Thankfully, Dottie was as good as her word. Her friend Ann's daughter is a foster mom, and Emil's going to live with her for his last two years of high school. She's already promised to let him practice as much as he wants.

But while Emil will be fine, it's not the outcome he and Rob wanted. Jonah took something precious from them. Jonah has taken and taken and taken, with no care for what it costs other people. So I want him to have a reckoning.

Which is hopefully what's happening tonight.

I run my fingers over my necklace. With Rob's permission, I had his guitar pick made into a pendant, which I wear around my neck. And he, of course, reciprocated by having my "unlucky penny" made into a pendant for him.

I suppose this brings us back to Hannah's "sickening" comment, but I'm glad to be sickening.

"Sophie," Hannah says in her mock-threatening voice. "Say you're as happy as you should be."

"You're such a sweet bully." I roll my eyes, but I do as she says anyway. "I'm as happy as I should be."

Then the limo rolls to a stop.

"You ready for this?" Hannah asks, her eyes sparkling, her hair huge.

"Yes," I say at the same time Briar says, "No."

We all laugh as we get out of the limo, drawing attention from the dozens of people milling about in front of the Orange Peel, smoking or talking or waiting to get in. Some of them are blatantly staring at us. Normally it would make my skin itch, but my self-consciousness has faded so much I barely notice.

Liam, Hannah's brother, was recruited to be one of the bouncers tonight, and he waves us over to the back entrance.

I've only met him briefly, in passing, but he is, in a word, terrifying. Tall and thickly muscled with hair somewhere between chestnut and red. But he's undeniably a good person to have on our side.

"They're waiting for you," he says brusquely, nodding.

Hannah gives him a pissed-off look—suggesting things between them are far from great, despite the fact that he's here to support us—and we walk into the rear of the building. The band that goes on prior to Garbage Fire is playing a song I recognize from one of my favorite childhood movies, but Liam leads us backstage, to where Rob and the band are waiting, along with Otis, Emil, and Dottie.

I walk into Rob's arms, feeling that familiar warmth radiate through me as he bends down to kiss me.

"Happy birthday," I say, pulling him a few steps away from the others. I reach into the pocket of my dress and pull out the new boutonniere I made, pinning it to his lapel.

He grins at me. "This one looks less rushed."

"I didn't have some jerk keeping me on a tight schedule."

"Something was certainly *tight*."

I run my fingers over his cheek. "Behave. I have a present for you at home."

"Is it a rainbow of condoms?"

"We don't need those anymore."

"You made me something, didn't you?"

"I did," I say with a smile.

I made him a quilted Garbage Fire pillow that was *not* easy given all the different parts of the logo. Also, just as an inside joke for the two of us, I framed a rainbow of condoms.

"You look like Cyndi Lauper, by the way," he says.

I laugh, not sure he means it as a compliment, but he nestles his head into my neck, near my ear, and adds, "You know, I used to have fantasies about Cyndi Lauper."

"Guys, we need you to focus," Hannah says, gesturing toward Otis and Emil. "The young people are leaving us."

"We're going to go guard the exits with Liam," Otis says with a gratified smile. He feels important and useful, something he needs.

Emil grins. "What he means is that we're going to watch what exit Jonah goes for so we can tell Liam. Because we can't do shit to keep him from leaving."

Otis lifts a shoulder in a half-shrug. "It's an important job."

"Yep, it sure is," Liam says, then surprises me by looking back and forth between Otis and Emil. "You ready, champs?"

They walk off together, and Hannah gives him the middle finger after he turns.

I shoot her a piercing look. "What's wrong with you? He's helping."

"I'll explain later," she says with a sigh.

"You know, it's not too late to douse your brother with pig's blood, Rob," Bixby says with a smirk. "Travis can source anything."

He shrugs. "Sure can."

"So they're here?" Hannah asks.

"Oh, yes," Dottie says. "But there will be no need for any unpleasantness. There should be nothing unpleasant about the truth."

Hannah responds with one of her snort-laughs. "Is that why we recruited my brother to block Jonah from leaving?"

"Some people need the truth presented to them on a silver platter. Others need to be tied into a chair. We'll see what kind this young man is."

"Damn, Dottie," Rob says with a chuckle as he wraps his arm around my waist, his grip firm.

"Now, after I present you wonderful young people, I'm

going to join my man to listen to the story. Afterward, I look forward to a long, joyous celebration."

"How'd you convince Jonah to come, anyway?" Briar asks. "He must know Rob and his friends are playing tonight."

What he wouldn't know is that we're going to tell our story. We even brought a slideshow, and at Rob's insistence, the band is going to softly play the melody to ABBA's "I Have a Dream" in the background.

We've practiced a couple of times after hours at The Missing Beat. It made me cry both times, so I don't have high hopes for staying tear-free tonight.

"Well, dear, I told the truth," Dottie says pointedly, glancing at the three of us in turn. "I paid a little visit to Nora and explained what her young man had done. It became clear to me that she didn't know the truth about him. He'd woven a tapestry of lies, but every tapestry of lies has a loose thread. I spoke with her about you three girls and told her about everything I'd witnessed with my own two eyes."

"She's the one who brought him here?" I ask in disbelief. I figured GingerBeerBabe was lost for sure. She ignored my texts and obviously forgave Jonah for whatever bullshit he'd pulled that had gotten him temporarily banned from The Ginger Station.

Then again, I almost married him, and he'd been lying to me steadily for months. Lies can be subtle, convincing despite feeling wrong in a way you can't put your finger on.

"Indeed," Dottie says. "And there's more good news. She says The Ginger Station may be interested in carrying some of our nonalcoholic drink blends once we have them canned and start distributing them. Of course, we'll need to find a new distributor, but I don't imagine that will be a problem. It seems they'll hire just about anyone to do that job."

"What?" I squawk. "We're canning them?"

"Oh, goodness," Dottie says, raising a hand to her dyed hair. "My memory isn't what it once was. I've been meaning to talk to you about that. We have to set up a meeting with my dear Buchanans to discuss a financial offer and terms, but I'm certain they'll love the idea. I'm not sure if you know this, but my dear Beau, the lovely man who started Buchanan Brewery, originally sold soda. So it's perfect, you see. A return to their roots."

I gape at her. "They're...I'm going to get paid for that?"

She gives me an admonishing look. "Of course you are, dear girl. Do you honestly think we wouldn't compensate you for your hard work?"

"Yes?"

She laughs as if it's a merry joke, and Rob tightens his hold on me. "Know your worth, Soph," he whispers. "Tonight we're gonna show them all that you do."

I glance up at him, feeling a surge of love so strong it nearly buckles my knees.

"Are you sure I should do this?" I ask, glancing toward the stage, imagining what it'll feel like to have all those eyes on me.

"Yeah, baby. I think you should. I think you should own yourself. All of you."

I hear Hannah and Briar speaking. Dottie too. But right this moment, my whole world is Rob.

"What if they hate me for it?" I ask.

"Then we'll move to Canada and take up ice fishing. But I really hope it doesn't come to that. I'm a terrible fisherman."

He leans down and kisses me, then slips something into the pocket of my dress.

I reach in and feel the soft, sleek stone Dottie gave him.

"Stroke it well," he says with a wink, then dips down and kisses me again.

Dottie grins at us, blows me a kiss, and heads out to the stage to make her opening remarks.

"Are you ready?" Briar asks, holding her hand out to me. Hannah reaches for me too.

I take both of their hands. "No. But let's do it anyway."

Dottie's speech passes in a blur...*special storytelling...not to be missed...just like that Moth place in New York...my dear, brave neighbor...the girlfriend of the lead singer of the band!*

And then I'm on stage, and it's me and the crowd and the microphone, and I can see him.

Jonah's standing by one of the exits, a fixed smile on his face, with Liam looming next to him.

Nora is nowhere to be seen, so I assume she, at least, was allowed to leave. She's clearly not a woman who likes to be in the spotlight, which is something I understand. Neither do I. But my friends are right. I need to tell my truth so no one else can tell it for me. I need to stop hiding.

I clear my throat.

I touch the stone in my pocket, but I can't speak, even though I sense my friends next to me. They're waiting for their turns. This is our story, but it starts with my past, the incident Jonah used against Rob. It needs to, because I'm determined to finally move beyond it.

Murmuring starts in the crowd. Then Rob steps out of the back and stands behind me, his hand on my shoulder, and suddenly the words come out in a gush.

"When I was sixteen, I accidentally started a fire..."

EPILOGUE
ROB

It was Dottie's idea to celebrate the launch of the NA canned drink line at Buchanan Brewery on what would have been Sophie's wedding day. I've got to hand it to her. For a sweet old lady who likes to see the good in everyone, she's got a good handle on dramatic timing.

She gave a pretty memorable speech at the start of the launch party, too, saying life doesn't always work out the way we expect, but it always works out the way it's supposed to.

I don't agree with that, but I can't find much to complain about these days. Work is good. Emil is happy and healthy with Ann's daughter—and "Grandma Ann," as she calls herself, gives him scratcher tickets every time they see each other, even though he's technically not old enough to redeem them. And, most of all, I've got Sophie.

I'm in love with her. Deeply, madly in love with her. She's been the muse for more songs already. The music has been flowing out of me like a river, and even though the songs are more sweet than sad, more protective than angry, the other guys like them.

We're supposed to play a couple of them tonight at the party, but neither Bixby nor I have heard from Travis all day. We've got less than half an hour before we're supposed to play. I'm in the thick of the party, with Sophie and our other friends, but my gaze keeps straying to the clock as the minutes pass by without any word from him.

This isn't something I tell people much, but I can be a worrier. When my mom wasn't doing well, she'd drop off the face of the earth, and that would be the first sign she was drinking again. The worry is worse now because Travis is the sort of guy who always answers his phone, sometimes even when he shouldn't.

Sophie squeezes my hand, and I lower my gaze to her. She's wearing a white dress as a final *screw you* to Jonah, who isn't here for obvious reasons.

Word travels fast in a small community, and even though Asheville is a hell of a lot bigger than it used to be, parts of it still feel and act small. Everyone in the brewery world knows exactly what Jonah tried to pull, not just by dating four women at the same time, but also by trying to blackmail Sophie and me about her past.

Nora Leigh, GingerBeerBabe, played her role in taking him down, just like Sophie and her friends did. She hasn't reached out to them, though. It's obvious she'd like to move past the whole thing.

From what I've heard, Jonah's no longer in the beer distribution game. He's gone to work for our father, something he'd sworn he would never do.

Doesn't matter. Sophie and her friends got what they needed: this town knows Jonah for who he is.

My girl frowns at me. "You're worried. Let's go check on Travis."

"I'm not taking you away from this," I say, waving a hand at the gathering. The place is packed, and ironically enough, given it's an NA launch, half the people here are tanked.

Hannah, who rolled in half an hour late, is in rare form, her spirits too high, if anything. At least five different people have asked her what's wrong, but she's responded to everyone in pretty much the same way: "I'd rather focus on what's right."

I can tell Sophie's not buying it, but she's still very much a person who lets other people have what they need, especially if she loves them. Which must be why she grabs my hand and starts guiding me toward the exit.

"You going to check on Travis?" Bixby asks from his seat at the bar. No point in setting up when we don't have one-third of the band with us, let alone a new rhythm guitarist.

"Apparently," I say as Sophie pauses, her hand still firmly grasping mine. She's so damn beautiful. Like an avenging angel, as likely to bop you on the head as bless you.

"I'm coming." Hannah stumbles as she tries to get out of her high-top chair, and Briar has to give her an assist.

"Should I come too?" Briar asks uncertainly. "I told Dottie I'd help pass out samples, but it definitely seems like people have already been drinking something."

"We'll be back soon," Sophie insists, then gives me a pointed look. "*With Travis.*"

"I'll stay," says Otis, getting up from his nearby stool so abruptly it nearly turns over. He was mid-conversation with a girl his own age and has clearly left her hanging. "Anything you need, Briar."

Briar shrugs. "Okay, thanks."

"I'm still coming," Hannah says, pushing forward. "I need some fresh air."

Sophie and I exchange a look, because a party like this—

loud and fun and completely unconcerned about noise ordinances—is usually her scene.

"Sure," I say. "Come with us."

A few minutes later, we pile into my car. As I prepare to drive, Sophie puts her guitar pick pendant into my hand and urges me to squeeze it. "He's okay, Rob. I know it."

Hannah's poring over her phone and not paying attention, but five minutes into the drive, she says, "So, let's not make a big deal of this, but I quit my job today."

Sophie gasps and turns to look at her. "Because of Liam?"

"Forget Liam. This is a good thing. It's like you said. My brother has to take care of himself, and I have to take care of myself. I'm going to get a dumb, mindless job so I can figure out what I actually want to do with my life."

"Do you want to work at Buchanan?" Sophie says. "I can definitely get you—"

"No. Thank you, but no. I think I'm done with the brewery scene for now."

I pull up to Travis's house, my heart beating faster when I see his car in the driveway. It seems like good news—he obviously didn't get into a car accident—but why would he be here but unresponsive?

Sophie squeezes my thigh, which would normally be giving me thoughts, but right now...

"Let's go," I say.

I get out of the car, my adrenaline spiking. Sophie falls in next to me as we make our way to the door.

I knock, steeling myself for—

Christ, I don't even know.

And then a little dark-haired boy answers the door. He's six or seven maybe—I honestly don't know what kids look like at that age, because by the time they reach us they're preteens. His eyes look too big for his solemn face, and he has a pointed chin and dark, slanted eyebrows that look familiar.

"Who are you?" he asks, as if he belongs here.

"Uh, is Travis home?"

But even as I ask the question, Travis comes around the corner from the kitchen, to the right of the front door. He looks completely miserable, and when he sees me, he swears under his breath.

"I forgot. I totally—"

Sophie turns and kisses me on the cheek. "Go talk to your friend. Hannah and I will sit with *our* new friend."

I hadn't even realized Hannah had followed us in, but sure enough, she's next to Sophie, staring at the kid.

"That's your kid," Hannah says, looking from the boy to Travis.

"No," I say, "he doesn't..."

But I trail off, both because Travis looks even more miserable and because that's obviously why the kid is familiar to me. He resembles his father.

"This is Ollie," Travis says thickly. "He's going to be staying here for a while."

Sophie gives Hannah a pointed look, then asks the kid, "Will you show us where the fun stuff is?"

The little boy looks as unhappy as Travis. "There isn't any. My mom just dropped me off an hour and a half ago, and the only thing to do is watch TV."

"Are you serious, my man?" Hannah says, suddenly more animated. "You've got a TV, and you're saying there's nothing good to do? Let's go find some cartoons. Maybe something your mom doesn't like you watching. We won't tell."

He brightens. "Are you going to be my friend?"

"Absolutely," Hannah says, giving Travis a wink.

Then Sophie squeezes my hand and releases it, and she

follows Hannah and Ollie into the living room, to the left of the front foyer.

Travis tilts his head toward the kitchen, and I join him in there. He grips the edge of the kitchen island, leaning on it, his jaw tense.

"This is what that Lilah business was about," I say, putting the pieces together. "The kid she had...he was yours."

"I swear to God, I didn't know," he tells me. "She just...she fucking left him at my doorstep, Rob. Said it was my turn, as if I'd been avoiding my duty. She's going to Australia for three months to follow her new boyfriend's band while they're on tour. She said it was my fault her marriage failed, so this was the least I could do for her. I don't know what to do with a kid. I..." He runs his hands through his hair. "We play shows at night. The program is in the afternoon, and he's too young, and school's already started for the semester—"

"You'll get a nanny," I say. "You can afford a nanny. You'll work it out."

I'm still in shock. The situation also burns a little, to be honest. I was a kid who got left behind, passed from one parent to the other. Used as fuel for arguments. That kid in there has got to feel worse than Travis does. But I know my buddy is nothing if not capable. He's a stand-up guy who's saved my life more than once. If he's really this kid's father, he'll be a good one.

I say as much, and Travis clenches the island even harder, his entire body tensing. And then he lets go, relaxing his posture. He turns to me and claps me on the back. "I'm sorry about the show. I know this is a big day for Sophie."

"It is. Which is why I've got to get back there."

He looks a little panicked but nods. "Yeah, of course."

"This'll work itself out," I promise, trying not to sound shell-shocked. "It'll be good."

"I don't know how to be a father," he mutters.

"You'll do fine," I say, because I want to believe it as much as he needs to. Maybe fatherhood is not the kind of thing anyone knows how to do, until they're called upon to do it. Even then, some people don't figure it out. My father was never much of one, and I know Travis's dad wasn't either.

"Thank you, brother."

We walk out to the living room together, but Travis stops me just before we step into view. From our position in the foyer, we can see them, but they can't see us. Something's playing on the TV, and Hannah's talking animatedly to the little boy, who's grinning, while Sophie smiles at them.

"Holy shit, he's smiling," Travis mutters.

"From what Sophie said, Hannah raised her little brother," I say. "She must be good with kids."

"You think she'd stick around for an hour or two? Maybe help him get settled in?"

"No harm in asking."

He does, and Hannah winks conspiratorially at the little boy. "Heck, yeah, I want to watch some toons with Ollie. You got any mac and cheese?"

"No," Travis says, frowning slightly, possibly overcome by all the things he's not prepared for.

"Well, they invented Instacart for a reason."

"We should go," I say, wrapping an arm around Sophie's waist. "This is a big day for Sophie."

"Yes, leave. We're great here," Hannah says, shooing us away.

Travis looks concerned that Sophie and I are leaving, but I give him a hug goodbye, pat him on the back, and then we're on our way. Sophie leans into me, and I hug her tightly as we walk out to the car. Neither of us says anything until we're inside.

I turn to her. "Ollie's his kid. He didn't know about him until a couple of hours ago."

She shakes her head in disbelief. "I can't believe it. You're an *uncle*, Rob."

A smile stretches across my face. "You think?"

"*Yes*," she says, placing her hand on my thigh. "Travis is more your brother than Jonah ever was. And we're going to be there for him. For both of them."

"God, I really fucking love you." I lean in and kiss her good —hoping the kid isn't peeking through the curtains at us.

Her lips are soft and inviting, and they already feel like home. She's exactly the person I want to be with after hearing big news. The safe place I want to go to when I feel weighed down by the heaviness of the world and my own memories.

I pull back to look at her, soaking in the fact that she's here in my car, and not walking down the aisle toward my brother.

"If everything had gone the way it was supposed to, and you'd married him today," I say, my voice ragged, because even the thought sets me off, "it would have been the worst day of my life, and I wouldn't have even known it. That's really awful to think about. It's kind of messing with my head, to be honest."

She smiles at me. "It would definitely have been the worst day of my life. Maybe Dottie had a point, and it all happened exactly the way it was supposed to."

I run my fingers over her lips and then her jaw. "She usually does."

I want to ask her to run off with me, to marry me today, the day when she was supposed to marry my brother. But that would be a selfish request. So I ask for less than I want, because I want her to have everything she needs, including the time to process everything that's happened. "Will you move in with me?"

I know she'll be worried about Otis being alone. But

they're deep into planning The Crafty Monster now that Sophie has funds from the NA drink line, so they'll be spending plenty of time together. And while her aunt extended her vacation, she'll be returning in another couple of weeks.

Sophie's eyes widen, and for a second I'm terrified she'll say no and I'll have fucked up this day for her. But then she leans in and kisses me hard. She pulls back and says, "Yes. *Yes.* But please tell me we don't have to go back to the party."

"You don't want to go back?" I say, surprised. "I heard there'd be cupcakes and a really kick-ass band with no drums."

She laughs. "Otis played the drums in marching band."

"There you go. Perfect."

"But I'm going to have to beg you to cancel your performance, just this once."

"Oh yeah?"

"Yeah." She leans in to kiss me again, her lips soft but insistent. "Because I'm going to need you to take me home, right away."

"Say that again." I grin at her. "Possibly three to five more times."

"Take me home, Rob."

"Gladly," I say. "And if the mood strikes, feel free to tell me what you'd like me to do to you when we get there."

She smiles at me, and God, I'm so happy I can barely understand it—or stand my sappy self.

As I pull away from the curb, I catch a glimpse of Sophie glancing back at Travis's house. I can practically see what she's thinking.

"You think Hannah'll be okay?"

"Yeah," she says thoughtfully. "I think this is good for her."

"I hope so, because I'm definitely not going back."

She gives me a wicked grin. Then she puts her hand on my

thigh and starts to detail what's going to happen as soon as we close the apartment door behind us. And if I speed a little?

Well, I'm only human.

You know what? I stole my brother's girl, and I'm not the least bit sorry about it.

***

Don't miss Travis and Hannah's story next in *The Worst Nanny Ever*! She's a tornado of chaos, and also exactly what he and his son need.

ABOUT THE AUTHOR

ANGELA CASELLA is a romcom fanatic. Writing them, reading them, watching them—she's greedy, and she does it all. In addition to her solo releases, she was lucky enough to collaborate with Denise Grover Swank on three complete series, with more co-written projects to come.

She lives in Asheville, NC. Her hobbies include herding her daughter toward less dangerous activities, the aforementioned romcom addiction, and dreaming of having someone else clean her house.

Visit her website at www.angelacasella.com or Angela and Denise's shared website at www.arcdgs.com.